A Study In Vengeance
The Trilogy - Book I

Hades' Heart

*

Nicolaus Vagelle, Criminal Psychologist; a selfless act, a ghost from his past, and a job he never wanted.

Alya Korikova, protégée turned partner; forged by darkness, carrying the internal scars of a tragic past, finds a strength of will to turn her life around and stand shoulder-to-shoulder with her greatest love in a battle for survival.

Thriller / Mystery / Suspense

The Casebooks of

Nicolaus Vagelle & Alya Korikova

"If you see it coming, and you give it time, trouble always finds a way to get worse."

"The boy. Medea's curse. I've seen you handle multiple cases simultaneously. I know your aptitude."

"But?"

"This time, I worry about your emotional connection to both. You will fool yourself, feeling in control of these disparate threads, as you usually do…until they control you.

*"Consideration of a **Dark Tetrad**. A possible fourth personality trait. Sadist. Defined as a tangible thrill in the suffering of others."*

"At twelve Papa put me to work. I was tough at twelve. At thirteen the horror changed me."

Five-Star Reviews for:
"HADES' KISS"
*

"Book Hangover Alert…a deft blend of story gumbo. It's this author's love letter to all of the crime fiction writers who came before him, starting with Poe and Doyle…few books I have read have given me such an unrelenting book hangover, embedding me into other worlds so credibly. Hades' Kiss is a book to be savored.

—Denise Dorman
Publicist, *Writebrain Media*

"Thoughtfully crafted and elegant: One might reference Peter Straub or Edgar Allen Poe, the commonality is meticulously-crafted prose to the purpose of inexorable disquiet."

—Terry Rossio
Screenwriter, Producer. *Shrek, Pirates of the Caribbean*

"The book is remarkably and meticulously well researched, which enhances the reader's ability to be steeped in the story unfolding. I suspect this may be one of my fastest reads this year (and I read a LOT) because I don't want to put it down. Great, great book."

—Damon Walsh
LTC, USA (Ret)

"G.J. Bingham's tale of Criminal Psychologist Nicolaus Vagelle is spellbinding from start to finish. The story pacing is excellent while excelling at character development, keeping the reader on their toes with twists and turns along the way."

—Kurtis Fujita
Founder/Creator, *Fifth Ring Studios, Shadow Ghost*

"Jerry (G.J.) Bingham deals in intellectual eccentric mysteries, like Arthur Conan Doyle and Agatha Christie."

—Michael A. Baron
Writer/Creator, *Nexus, Badger, Florida Man, Biker...*

"In his debut novel, Hades' Kiss, G.J. Bingham leaves us with no doubt that he is a creative force to be reckoned with. Full of mystery, imagery, and intrigue, this book is one for the ages. Leaves you on the edge of your seat."

—Murphy J. Alderman
President/Publisher, at *Patriot Comics LLC*

"This book is a literary gem that deserves every one of its five stars. From the first page to the last, it captivates with its rich prose, well-developed characters, and a plot that seamlessly blends suspense, emotion, and thought-provoking themes. The author's storytelling prowess is evident in every carefully chosen word, creating an immersive experience that stays with you long after you've finished reading. It's a rare find that effortlessly balances heart-wrenching moments and spine-tingling suspense."

—Nathaniel
Amazon Reviewer

A STUDY IN VENGEANCE

A TRILOGY - BOOK 1

HADES' HEART

G.J. BINGHAM

THE CASEBOOKS OF
NICOLAUS VAGELLE
&
ALYA KORIKOVA

A Study In Vengeance: Hades' Heart
Copyright © 2025 by G. J. Bingham

All rights reserved. Printed in the United States of America. Thank you for buying an authorized edition of this book and for complying with copyright laws by not reproducing, scanning, or distributing any part of it in any form without permission, or as permitted by U.S. copyright law.

This book is a work of fiction. Names, characters, businesses, organizations, places, events and incidents either are the product of the author's imagination or are used fictitiously. Any resemblance to actual persons, living or dead, events, or locales is entirely coincidental.

For additional information contact:

Drawingfire Publications https://www.GJBinghamwriter.com

The publisher is not responsible for websites (or their content) that are not owned by the publisher.

Special thanks to:
Damon Walsh, LTC, USA (Ret) - for technical expertise and advise.
&
Denise Dorman, Publicist, Writebrain Media - for editorial support.

Library of Congress Control Number

ISBN:

979-8-9891235-3-7 (e-book)

979-8-9891235-2-0 (paperback)

Author's Warning Revisited:

A popular screenwriter has said of the genre:
Thriller is a cross between Detective and Horror.

Edgar Allen Poe, in the origins of the classical detective, had encompassed his world in darkness, at times in the extreme. In the following pages, I have chosen to follow the master's traditions.

I dream for those same thrills passed down by all my brilliant predecessors, but not before advising, respectfully:

This book is not for children, nor is it for the overly-sensitive reader. I venture into black waters, and sometimes difficult subject matter, but in the end summation, perhaps you will find a patch of light under the door.

It's called hope.

—GJB

For Betty

*

Her common sense psychology

and knowing exactly when to nudge a child's interest

in all things essential for growth.

Her art, her music, her literature,

and telling me to change into sneakers before going out to a fight.

She gave only the best parts of who I became.

I am solely responsible for the rest.

HADES' HEART

G.J. BINGHAM

"*A man does not become a hero until he can see the root of his own downfall.*"

—*Aristotle*

"*No tree, it is said, can grow to Heaven unless its roots reach down to Hell.*"

—*Carl Jung*

A Storm's Embrace

The Shooter

…had been to this open field in the past. Had walked the previous crime scene here at its edge. A crime now forgotten by all, save those touched by the blood of it. A property now owned by no one.

The expanse of the former sugar plantation bore no remaining evidence of that ancient cane, only the abrupt absence of towering trees beyond its forest brink to indicate the original owner's saws and plows and intentions for planting. Near the edge of that crumbling antebellum estate, the demarcation between oak giants and vacant expanse, formed a hillock of blown gray lumber. Ancient boards one might assume to be the remains of a workman's barn flattened by hurricanes or the artillery of an advancing army from another century.

The shooter would not expose herself to the openness of the fields but, beginning at the woodpile, she paced away along the tree line a precise one-hundred meters, where she looked back, dropped the knapsack, unslung the rifle, and lowered to one knee. A soft spring breeze pushed the tall grass from the southeast. She laid the rifle across the pack and tied back her shoulder-length blond hair with a black scrunchie.

When the time comes, remember your coloring.

Her light canvas jacket was enough for the climate. She considered removing it, but counter-argued that conditions might prove different on the given day. The memory of *Papa* whispered in her ear:

No one ever dies from too much preparation.

"Hush," she whispered to the breeze.

The shooter found a granola bar in the pocket of the backpack to settle her stomach and followed it with water she had purchased at the Gas 'N Go before leaving the city limits. Seated on the tranquil cushion of grass behind the knapsack, she laid the Kalashnikov across her thighs, then located the thirty-round magazine. She checked its load.

Step by step, Papa whispered in her ear. *If routine is important, never vary routine.*

She smirked, dropped the rifle's safety lever, pulled the charging handle and released. She slapped the magazine into place. As she steadied her breathing, she studied the distant woodpile and found the nearly vertical plank, marked upon her arrival, standing amidst its fallen comrades. Unzipping the pouch at her belt, she extracted the hand-sized bean bag. Then the small monocular and the AKFST—front sight adjustment tool.

The most important element to this exercise, child.

Squeezing the beanbag to limber her fingers, she thought out her process. It had been many years and she doubted her muscle memory until she chased that doubt away. Today was not about her. Today was about her weapon, the old AK, and she had come here to eliminate concerns for its accuracy.

Eyes on the upright plank, three-quarters the width of a human torso and a football field away, she set the beanbag crosswise atop the knapsack, shifted her knees beneath her, and moved her belly to the grass. With the lower handguard nestled center on the beanbag cushion, confidence returning by the moment, one more pull on the charging handle chambered the first round. She noted again the easy push of the tall grasses left-to-right, and tested the weight of the rifle stock for familiarity. The sights were old-school "iron sights," the kind she had grown up with. The rear-sight stood at "P," effective up to 350 meters.

Nudge that to 300, Papa would say. *It's all the same. Now take three breaths, long and slow, out through the mouth.*

Her pulse felt fine. Steady. She snugged the butt of the AK tight to her shoulder, not too tight to jitter the hands, and she focused on the rear-sight first. She traveled through the front sight to the distant gray plank. She pulled the front sight back into focus, and the rest of the world blurred as she released the third breath, then held it while tightening on the trigger.

Do not anticipate, Papa said. *Let the bang surprise you…*

It did.

…every time.

Lifting the monocular to her eye, she could see the plank had moved but had not fallen. All that mattered was she could see the splintered hole where the bullet struck, bottom-right. With the AKFST, she adjusted the front post to the right, she used a pencil to mark the post for reference and then, because her shot hit low, she turned the top screw clockwise. The following five rounds placed within thirteen centimeters of each other.

"Hush, Papa," she whispered to the breeze.

Vagelle

"You say you believe you know why I have involved myself in Alya's life again after so many years," Papa Elin had said. "I say you do not know as much as you believe. She is not everything that you believe."

I stood alone, walking stick in hand, gym bag resting at my heels. July's heat animated the otherwise empty highway, stretching it fore and aft, with the Atchafalaya Basin bracketing hot asphalt to either side. Thick brackish air filled my head with water hyacinth and hydrilla and tupelo and Summer's rotting catfish. The sun had crawled past its apex two hours ago, but even darkness would not diminish these temperatures by much. Not in July. Not until the rains. I stood there long enough to give up hoping for a cloud, while the unmoving cypress giants remained fixed against a wretched pale-blue canopy.

Thoughts drifted until they landed on Alya again, but I reigned them in hard. A painful distraction.

Change focus. Remain in the present. Feel the heartbeat but taste the acrid air. A new mantra for more treacherous times.

Avian sounds became less frequent with the day's oppressive temperatures. A million *morning cicadas* lowered their chatter as the shadows inched on. Nearby, a heavy slap of water reminded me of a gator adjusting its hunt, while the tormenting sun scorched the back of my neck—this penance freely self-inflicted.

I would not move yet.

Muffled by great distance, a gentle growl replaced nature's soundtrack and I squinted against the day to make sure it was not imagined. The dark speck hovered over the highway's refraction with the heat-mirage converting asphalt into something molten. The speck hung motionless, a flea imprisoned in crystal resin. Then growing incrementally, it split to be joined by a second speck.

I shifted my feet by inches to verify I still could. The double growl grew with the shapes as my internal anchor held to the present.

The gap between cars widened. The front sedan took form and grew steadily into a new black Escalade that roared and accelerated like a predator lunging. I marked two occupants behind the windshield. The second car, a drab gray Marquis with three distinct passengers, trailed behind cutting its speed.

My standing ground remained the center highway line.

As my fist tightened on the walking stick, the Escalade blew past by inches. I did not turn to watch, but rather listened as brakes locked and squealed into the turn. The older Marquis braked more efficiently. Both transmissions slammed into park. Only one door opened behind me. One voice followed.

"René, keep motor running."

Before me, the Marquis driver remained behind his wheel. His two passengers climbed out and floated past either fender to converge between the headlights. Handguns carried in a casual display of bravado, I assumed the one at my back held the same. He would be the *Important Man,* the big black Escalade man, in charge of the conversation.

"Señor Vagelle!" a voice I recognized. A hint of South American, possibly Brazilian. "Somebody glue your choos to the road?"

I said nothing, keeping my back to him in my not-so-subtle display of primacy.

"My friends are of such worth? Or you are afraid to face me?"

His friends smiled. The large one raised his Ruger, pretended to fire.

"You have a right to fear me," Important Man said. "So, I will talk at your back. Then I will get tired of talking and my friends will leave you without a face."

"I think not," I said.

"Ha! He finds his voice." He racked a round into the chamber of his weapon, the waste of ejecting a bullet just so I might hear his intent. "So, Meester Vagelle, tough *hombre* Vagelle, I see no cavalry. Maybe they hide in *o lago* listening?"

Large Man eye-flicked to the lake.

Maybe.

"But I think no. I think you pretend you have good poker hand in your shirt, I think."

"I like the poker," Large Man said. Small Man remained silent, eyes too wide. He would be the first to act, but not until Important Man swaggered a bit.

BANG! Important Man fired into the hot asphalt alongside my shoe. I had prepared and failed to flinch for him.

"So, you knew I would not kill you," Important Man said.

"Not before you see the money." I took all weight off the walking stick.

"You think I am *estúpido?* You think to fool me with *bolsa pequeña—*bag not big enough to buy me lunch?"

My head lowered as a likely depiction of easy prey.

"I do not believe you have money," he said. "I think you are about to tell me bullshit. Some bullshit deal I should make with you."

"No deal."

"Okay, Mr. Poker. Show me the money, or die now."

"Proof of *life.*"

"Money first."

I shook my head. I had my answer. Lifting the stick inchmeal, I pointed past the highway's berm to the water's edge and a cluster of dead foliage.

"Money first." He clicked his tongue like a hammer cock. "Manny!"

Small Man came forward as the large man aimed at my head. *Manny* kicked the cane free of my fist, and *Large Man* snorted. Another kick between the legs dropped me hard to my knees. I folded and grabbed my stomach. A kick to the kidney followed, and then he slapped the barrel of his pistol across my ear. The slow ichor ran my jawline until I tasted it.

"Okay. Okay." Important Man needed me awake. "She say you no like guns. It is almost too easy. Last chance, hero. Money. *Onde!*"

She? "There." I nodded to where I had pointed—dead bushes at the water's edge. I coughed. "I...tied it there."

"Go look," he said, and Large Man lowered his Ruger and crossed to the berm. He craned, searching the murk of water and dying foliage.

"It ain't on top!" Important Man said. "Get your hands wet, *bichano.* Find it."

Four days ago I had gotten his call. I would not let him choose the spot for the exchange, but I chose this mile marker, a place I knew, a place he might be assured of our privacy. A place where he could get away with murder. After he agreed I drove out here. I cut cypress branches and oak and scrub and I created this nest, then I tied it off to keep it from drifting. Over the next three days, I returned. That first day I dropped forty pounds of raw chicken. The second day, seeing the results, I dropped thirty pounds more. And again on day three.

Today, I arrived early for our meeting, tied a large canvas sack stuffed with paper, and tied two whole chickens beside that.

Now I held my stomach simulating pain.

Large Man must have spotted the submerged bag and understood he needed to get wet to reach the money. He removed his shoes and danced a bit on the hot asphalt. He rolled his pant legs. He stepped into the foliage.

His scream broke to a frantic splashing, as I reached beneath my shirt. A surprised Manny turned to the scream, so I spun and shot the man behind me, Important Man, through the breastbone. I twisted back and killed Manny and the person behind the windshield to his rear.

Another blast—from behind! I felt fire as the shot tore my left shoulder and threw blood across my vision. My legs vanished, and the tarmac hit me like a bus.

The driver's door opened. Hard shoes approached, slowed, stopped. *René* considered, or so I imagined with my sight painted over. He did not take long to think, but pivoted, and his hard-soled shoes clicked away to his car. I waited for the Escalade to crush me, but he sped past the way he had come, leaving me to wonder why.

Large Man continued screaming, until he could not.

In time, I pushed to my knees. Pain stopped me there. But it could not keep me there. I had priorities. Like survival. Not just mine.

Suffering, the arm lifted, the sleeve wiped my eyes. Then I saw sufficiently through the blur. I unwrapped my belly-holster and rewrapped to secure my left arm to my chest. The crawl to my walking stick ticked by with the seconds. I pushed to my feet in stages. Then, as I could, I shuffled back to Important Man to be sure I had found my mark.

"I am no hero, *Señor.*" I glanced to see that Large Man had disappeared beneath my nest. *I am now the antithesis.*

Not always so. Once upon a time, I strove to change my story. Whoever *she* was, she knew I disliked guns. But I am far from *estúpido, Señor.* And darkness overwhelms righteousness, and survival begets necessity. Yes, I disliked guns. It does not mean they were foreign to me.

Limping faster now, I covered the distance to the drab gray Marquis with the hole in the windshield. The hole continued through the driver's cheek and headrest. I reached in and across with my working arm and removed the key from the ignition. I continued to the rear of the Marquis and popped the oven—the trunk. My stick dropped, though I had always known what I would find.

Bracing against the bumper, blood running from my shoulder to my shoe, I caught a breath and held, weakening fast. I would not have the strength to drag the heavy driver from behind his steering column, but I could not rationalize further.

I managed to wrap four-year-old Danny's naked, lifeless body in the tarp from the Marquis trunk. I do not know how I managed to carry him two miles with that sun baking my brain. I do recall turning as I fell, so he would land atop me.

Foggy, recalling the scream of sirens, but it might have been a dream.

*"See now, **how** men lay blame upon us gods for what is, after all, nothing but their own folly."*

The Odyssey—Homer

Two

Shrink

(recording)

"Where are you calling from?"

"I call too late."

"Do you need help, Alya?"

"I call—*Da*. I mean, *Nyet*—No. I have friend helping."

"You know they give me regular updates. Especially when you present them with problems."

"*Da*. You have said in past. I remember. I—It is bad. I cannot stay. *(traffic sounds, voices)* It hurts me inside there. You know what I say?"

"Yes."

"No one talks. People with rabbit-eyes watching. People growl or scream at nothing. You know."

"You will have ups and downs, Alya. You understand this. You have always fought your way out of these down cycles."

"But you say you know. If you get up date, you know. It is bad. They give to me drugs."

"Yes. Prescribed to relax you. To calm your thoughts."

"*Nyet*. I know what is prescribe. This—I have—It is worse. My thoughts. It is always clouds in there. I do not know me in there. Can you understand, please?"

"Yes, I do. Of course, I do. And I know you always trusted me."

(silence, hard breathing) "*Da.* Yes. But they tell to me I cannot see you. I cannot talk to you."

"And they are right, dear. You know I would never do anything to hurt you. How many years have I been seeing you? We have had this conversation before, have we not?"

(distant shouts, a car horn)

"So, I would like to ask you to believe me when I say, the hospital is not your enemy. The doctors are doing their best for you. When they say I cannot act as your doctor anymore, it is not them saying this. It is the court."

"Court does not understand."

"No, I suspect they do not. But you know me, Alya. I worry for you. Always. I have been ordered to give you into their care."

"Rabbit-eyes. They cannot understand."

"When the court heard how many years I have been treating you, and your situation has not improved…"

"They think it is your fault I am this way. I tell to them no. I believe you are helping—*(breathing ragged, tearful)*.

"Alya, I would like you to come in. Could you, please?"

(silence)

"Alya? Are you there?"

"I know. You will give me to hospital again. The court makes you to give me to them."

"I will not. This will be our secret. What time is it?"

"It is late. I am sorry."

"No worries. Come. Or we can meet someplace."

"You will not tell *him?*"

"No. I never tell him about your visits. How far are you from my office?"

"I am at Congo Square. Tremé."

"Alya. You know it is not safe for you this time of night. Do you have a car? Money? How did you get so far from the hospital?"

"*Nyet.*"

"So, you are not with a friend, like you said. Why did you feel the need to lie to me?"

"I do not know. I am afraid."

"I will leave now. It'll take me twenty-five minutes. Is there someplace you can wait inside? Maybe an all-night diner?"

"I know where is church. Chartres Street."

"St. Louis Cathedral? That's five blocks from you. But this late—No. Just past Rampart, one block, is the Hotel St. Georges. Say my name and they will let you wait in the lobby. Can you do that?"

(click)

"Thank you for waiting, doctor. We should go up. I cannot talk here."

"I show you the pocket recorder, like always, so you can trust me. I think my troubles would be just beginning if my wife learns I spent the early morning in a nice hotel room with an attractive young Russian woman."

"It is too fancy hotel here, I think. I cannot stay."

"The room is already paid for. You might as well take advantage of it tonight.

(distant voices, restaurant sounds of plates and silver)

"You will not tell to *him?*"

"Looks like the shower did you some good. And the change of clothes? I was guessing on the size."

"I will pay back."

"I can afford it. The manager here opened the gift shop for me, so I was limited on my choices."

"*Ja ochen blagodarna*—Sorry. I appreciate. *Spasiba*—I mean, thank you."

"Take a look at the menu. You need to eat."

"I need…to go."

"I know things look dark for you, dear. They have for a long time."

"Since my thirteenth birthday."

"C-PTSD. Do you remember?"

"*Complicated* PSTD."

"Close enough. But don't worry about doctor jargon. What you need to keep in mind is your problem is not merely yours. You are not alone. We see this often when children…"

"You have said to me before. But this is not same as my…fear with touching? Other doctor jargon. Why do I not remember clear?"

"Ha-phe-phobia. We will keep you away from the drugs. It will get better, I promise. For tonight—I hear your English slipping. That happens too sometimes with severe trauma."

"I remember this."

"But I sense you are already improving since our earlier conversation."

"Those drugs…"

"Please, do something for me, Alya, if you can. For yourself."

"If I can."

"I would like you to remain mindful of what you have lost. I need you to get back some of yourself. Your old self. Remember where you were when we first met? When Nicolaus first brought you to me—I'm sorry. The name is still painful for you. But remember, you had so much to learn, and both he and I gave you…and you worked so hard to improve."

"My *Angliski* lessons. And university."

"It is still the greatest gift he could have given you. So, as difficult as this is, please remember who you had worked so hard to become. Don't let this illness take all that away."

(silence, restaurant sounds)

"Do you understand what I am telling you?"

"At hospital…"

"Let's rest the uncomfortable subjects for tonight."

"I went into Group…"

"Dear, if you don't order food, I will order for you and maybe the waiter can take it home to his dog."

"I meet young man there. Part of *Group*. He was in Marines, he said. A vet. I called him *Vetty*, and it made him laugh. He had the PTSD too. And a steel leg."

"Prosthesis."

"He played happy…until left alone for too long. Thinking too much is not good for some, I believe. Then he would…*act-out*, as Nurse Dunn liked to say. Many orderlies need to hold him down. Then I would not see him at Group for long time."

"I'm happy you could find someone there to relate with."

"*Da*. We talked sometimes after Group. Vetty had seen terrible things, but he did not talk much about them."

"As you have seen terrible things."

"But…I think he liked me. He watched me, maybe too much. But he stayed apart, mostly. I do not know if he saw I could not be close— my haph-e-phobia—or if he feared for himself. *Vetty was…*"

"Are you feeling okay? Maybe we can pick it up again in the afternoon. Alya? Alya, can you hear me…?"

(click)

"Darla. I'm so sorry I woke you."

"You know I could never sleep with your late-night emergencies. You said she collapsed?"

"Not exactly."

"Trauma. She should have been taken away from the detective."

"No. That might have made it worse for her. He had been stability in her life for too long.

"As you have said. Even with all he put her through?"

"Doctor? Could you—Is that you, Darla?"

"Yes, love. Here. Let me get the sun out of your face."

(the rattle of window blinds)

THREE

Patty P.I.

"So, you still got nothing to say?"

Again, no response from the far edge of the bed. Hardly a breath as Vagelle continued his marathon study of the closed blinds. I assumed he knew the patient gown had split down the back enough to keep my eyes averted. Nah, he knew me too well.

For spite, I stole his juice box and leaned into the visitor's chair. As I sipped, my heels found the foot of his mattress hoping to annoy him a bit more. Nah, I knew *him* too well for that.

I brushed at the wrinkles in my slacks to no avail, merely a distraction. I really needed to get home and change, maybe sleep for a month. At least give my mouth a good scrubbing.

The young nurse entered with a battle-hardened smile and asked if I would like her to bring an extra dinner tray. *No thanks.* She checked Vagelle's IV and the machine dispensing his meds. She took his temperature, blood pressure, checked his stitches, shoulder wrap, and sling, then asked him if he'd like a second gown. I sniggered. She shrugged for me on her way out.

"This might just be the most blissful room in the whole hospital," she said over her shoulder. "Nobody wants for nothing."

The black sky, starless, a rift between crooked blinds, said time to go. My phone echoed the sentiment and buzzed. A text from one of my agents. *Brown.*

"Coroner report: The boy died two days before going into that trunk."

"The dad?" I texted back.

"Disappeared."

"Naturally," I mumbled and typed, "Frwd names from scene when you get em. Pressure my cop friend if you dont hear back in 24hrs."

Vagelle angled his profile for me. Angular jaw, angular nose, an architect's composition with hard eyes. I mentioned about the boy, but *Mr. Angles* had returned to his scrutiny of the slats. The coroner's report on the boy's death would do little to diminish his guilt. It would, at most, adjust the timeline of it.

"Nothing you coulda done," I said.

No head shake. Nothing.

"Ya know, I once had this friend, I used to call him Gen'ral behind his back. He hated that." I sucked noisily at the dregs of the juice box, hoping for a huff, or a grunt, or maybe a thrown tissue box. "But he could strategize an egg breakfast, that guy."

He lifted from the side of the bed with effort, wincing with the movement. He shot a glance at all his connecting tubes as if he had forgotten them, then he sank back into the sheets.

"Your change of clothes is in a duffle bag in the locker," I said. *Thank you so much, Patty. That was nice of you, Patty.* "Not a complicated wardrobe." Maybe if I prattled on about the color of hogwash, he would at least tell me to shut up.

Instead, with his free hand, he pulled the sheet to his chest and took up his bedside urine jug. He apparently expected me to leave the room.

"This Gen'ral, former friend, Mr. Strategy…" I lobbed the juice box at the wastebasket to prolong his torment. "The guy took care of his troops. I remember this one day—" I missed. "Oh, you heard this one, haven't you? I'll tell it again anyway." By now, I'd be disappointed in myself if I couldn't get a rise out of him. "So, his Corporal goes down in battle…and Gen'ral runs through hellfire and brimstone to carry her out."

To postpone pissing with me in the room, as I knew he would, he further reclined the mattress and closed his eyes.

"Never leave a man or woman behind. That's the kinda guy he was. My *former friend.*"

"You need to go home," he said.

"You think I never heard pissin in a plastic jug?" I got up and grabbed my jacket off the chair-back. "Okay, you win. But tomorrow I'm bringing her for a visit. She has permission to leave the grounds for short periods, with supervision, and—"

"No."

"For her sake. It's been three months, and she needs a trace of normalcy in her life. People she recognizes."

"Go home, Ms. Gunston."

"She needs to know people still care about her. By the way, it's Patty, if I am permitted to jog your memory."

"Go home, Patty."

"Can I at least tell her what's happened to you? That you haven't abandoned her?"

"Goodbye, Patty."

"You are a *Major League sonofabitch.*" I pulled the door behind me.

"I've heard that before too."

A shaved yeti passed me in the corridor. Seven-foot, if an inch. A fit mulatto in work clothes with a scarred throat. His taloned hands strangled a small, limp bouquet. He grinned revealing a double row of sparking silver teeth. Alya had described him to me, Pip, Mr. Vagelle's "sometimes employee." I glanced back as he stopped at Vagelle's door and sparkled for me again. *Mr. Charm.*

Our cop buddy, Pedersen, looked up past his desk lamp as I entered. His door closed on its own, and I crossed the short space and dropped onto the cracked leather couch. The man-smells within the office confines were not quite as bad as a locker room at the Y. Don't ask me how I know.

"Might be nice if you got a pillow for this thing." I stretched out anyway.

"Might be nice if you called ahead once in awhile. The Desk Sergeant is spreading rumors about our clandestine affair."

"I'm too tall to be your dancing partner."

He riffled through file folders on his desk, then changed his mind, slapped them shut. He checked his coffee cup before realizing it was empty. "Shit."

"Grab me a cup while you're out. Large."

"As I'm still out of Jameson's?"

My eyelids could not stay shut. They navigated the black stars cut into dirty-white ceiling tiles. *Second star to the left—or was it right?* No matter. Morning was a long way off.

His return snapped me awake. With the chair pivoting away from the lamp's direct glow, his heavy look roamed the desktop without purpose. The only other light source filtered through the door glass from the formless gray pattern on the TV monitor beyond. He set a second cup at the corner of his desk, but exhaustion had crippled me to indifference.

"You look like hell, Patty. Have you slept this week?"

"And you're a vision of loveliness, thank you. Two days, five hours ago, to be exact."

"I guess I could use a haircut." He checked his reflection on the sleeping computer glass and scratched at his days' worth of stubble. "You just come from the hospital?"

I grunted.

On a bookshelf past his shoulder, fireflies winked in rapid succession from a police band radio. The volume had been turned to a dull, baffled crackling.

"Guess I don't need to ask how he's doing." He stared down the blinking lights.

I grunted again. "The fucker. I'd give up on him if I hadn't already wasted over decade dragged in his wake."

"Yeah, sure."

"What have you heard on our Russian?" I said.

"I stopped in yesterday afternoon but never got to see her." He took up the folders, hesitated like he didn't know what to do with them, then yanked a lower desk drawer and flung them in with the mess. He followed it with a closing kick. I guessed he was not as tired as I felt. "The doctor said she'd had one of her *episodes*. That my face might trigger a negative response, or some bullshit."

"Something ain't right in Denmark." Leaning on an elbow before the struggle of sitting up, I mussed my hair back into place, then stopped caring. "I hear that too often over there. I'm thinking of going to visit her old shrink." I straightened my ankle holster.

"You know he can't talk about her."

"You want to go see Whitcomb with me tomorrow?"

"Vagelle's over-priced suit. What for?" His radio chatter picked up speed.

"Over-priced? When was the last week your buddy didn't get into trouble? But maybe we can gang up on lawyer-boy to force a writ or some-such."

"I've been to see him twice this month. Always the same. That judge has preempted his every motion to appeal. It's like she gets wind of him making an appointment, and her staff greets him at the door with a twenty-page *F-U Order*."

Wall shadows cast up by the desk lamp had a life of their own, at least to my sleep-deprived brain. "The red light on your phone," I said.

A confused glance, followed by another to the wall clock. 12:40— he nearly knocked over his cup reaching for the phone.

"Yo!" He listened for a beat. "The call came in when?" He pitched the receiver at the cradle, surprisingly on target, and nearly upended his chair struggling to stand. "Damn it!" He turned away to tuck his shirtfront behind his belt buckle. "You coming?"

"If you're wanting me for a ride-along, it must be good."

"Dr. Maiwand."

"Aw, hell."

I jogged at his heels through the parking lot to his unmarked Durango where he wedged behind the wheel then backed his seat a notch.

"You ate a donut since the last time you drove?"

"Wise-ass." He shoved the switch for his blue flashers as I buckled in. Then he sped us like lunatics along the riverfront.

"How 'bout giving me a clue?" I braced my elbow against the armrest going into a hard turn. "Tell me Vagelle didn't release himself from the hospital bent on revenge."

"Against who? No, it's his landlord. Seems he surprised a couple punks breaking in through the boiler room. Maiwand heard Hemmings's alarm from his open door. Found the man at the foot of the stairs clutching a head wound, then he called nine-eleven."

"How bad is he?"

"Don't know yet."

"This ain't no coincidence, Frank."

"'Course not."

We met EMS at the curb as they loaded Hemmings strapped to a gurney. The bony warrior fought against his restraints while swatting at the hands of two paramedics like they were buzzards.

"I tell ya, I'm alright," he squawked. "Stop this! It's just a bump. This is my building. You have no legal right if I don't want to leave it."

"Let me take a look at him," Pedersen said.

"Has he been conscious long?" My P.I. license failed to impress the cute medic with connecting eyebrows.

"He's got more than a bump." The medic scowled like we were delaying his smoke break. I figured we would not be besties.

The landlord's head bump had been fast-wrapped in gauze. A bright-red cut across the bridge of his nose resulted in both eyes racooning. Blood had dried in a line from throat to collar, where the medic had failed to mop up.

Dr. Maiwand finished speaking with a patrolman when he spotted us, and they both approached.

"He should be on his way," Maiwand said. "He is at least concussed, with a possible fractured maxilla and zygomatic arch."

Pedersen waved the responders to hurry off. "I heard of maxilla. How the hell's he talking so much?"

Hemmings could be heard after the door to the ambulance slammed.

We followed Dr. Maiwand back into the building. The stairway resonated with the rabble of uniforms and investigators. Pedersen squeezed past and up the stairs to the third floor, while the doc invited me into his second-floor apartment.

"Step in, out of the way. I think I'll hang around a bit, being the sole surviving tenant here."

"Good thought," I said.

"Once they tell me the place is secure enough, I'll lock up and head to hospital and check on our *dervish* landlord. He'll be sedated for several hours, at least. So, do you think I will be the Hemmings House hat-trick?"

"Not unless you know of a curse I'm unaware of."

"Like a curse that skips every other person in a house?"

"I take it you didn't get a good look at the intruders." I paused to study a gray stone tablet behind framed glass. A cracked and broken corner, and a timeworn carving of a seated woman-creature playing a lute, or something like it. "This looks old."

"That would be Saraswati. The Hindu goddess of learning."

"Ah, appropriate here."

"Um, like I told the others, I did not see much. They were by me and down the hall to the boiler room as I came out."

"Then count yourself among the un-cursed, for now. You might have been on the casualty list otherwise."

"I need a cup of tea. Join me? Mother sends my favorite from Kashmir. Hibiscus Rose tea. It is very excellent."

"I'll give it a taste." I trailed him to the kitchenette. "Our Lieutenant friend called them punks."

"Not young, I think. They wore gloves, naturally, but I managed to see the one forearm." He lit a burner for the teakettle. "His sleeves were pushed back, and he had brown skin, weathered. And I got sight of a partial tattoo. The ink was not new, I think."

Surveying his apartment I could appreciate his nostalgia for family tradition, particularly the two Oriental rugs hanging as wall decoration, one dulled and thread-worn with age. The hypnotic designs tempted my weary brain with sleep. "Do you have a guess what the…?"

"The tattoo? Nah. Crude letters like gangs make. Maybe the end part of a word. Something—o-a-t, boat, throat—might it be throat? I honestly don't know."

"Best not to guess. But something's always better than nothing."

He caught me examining the rug and steered the conversation onto his family, his upbringing. Maybe the distraction was as much for himself. With my cup about empty, Pedersen poked his head in the door.

"Seems Hemmings interrupted 'em. They never got through Vagelle's door. I'm gonna check with the boys going over the alley. You wanna come?"

"This must be love."

A crime scene tech, Judy—*one of the boys*—we had met two years ago collecting brass casings at a drive-by in the Gardens. She called my name while lifting a short-handled crowbar.

"Looks to be the culprit," I said with a clipped wave.

"Made a mess of the back door." She lowered the crowbar into a plastic sack. "Not that we'll get much off of it. Maybe we'll get lucky and one of them used it for a backscratcher."

"Or maybe he dropped a Mensa card."

"Shoe prints?" Pedersen said.

"Some. Walker's working that." The other officer lifted his head and nodded before bending back to the task. "Street's still damp from the earlier sprinkling, but if they came by car there's no trace yet."

"Tell your Sarge to keep a man on this door until we get it sealed. For now, we'll take a stroll up the alley. Who knows?"

"I'll take to the right," I said. He turned left. I unleashed the Colt from my ankle. This *was* New Orleans, after all.

The line of parked cars glistened from an earlier sprinkling. Windshields not quite cleaned of dirt from the previous week, they had not been moved in some time. I checked over my shoulder.

Pedersen rattled the links of a chain fence, then waited for movement. The alley ahead cut a zigzag behind uneven buildings, forcing me to pause while passing a four-story parking structure. Then I got careless.

From the shadows a blurred movement startled me. He slammed me against a dumpster, and I didn't mean to pull the trigger, but there you are. The noise from my pistol shocked me, and probably the perp— I heard him yipe—and dogs up and down the canyon of buildings joined in.

Pedersen bellowed my name. My attacker never hesitated but kept his legs churning. Up again and pursuing shadows, I followed the sound of rubber soles slapping wet pavement beneath too many broken and dark alley lights.

Locked onto the runner ahead, I failed to see the second man erupt from the shadows. He bowled me back down.

"Bitch! I'm gonna shoot somebody in the ass tonight!"

Rising came harder for me the second time. Me with fresh bruises, watching them skip off to the light of a silvery moon. Someone grabbed my arm, and I almost killed my escort. "Shit!"

"You okay?" Pedersen hoisted me to my feet. Other cops joined us, and I was glad for the shadows hiding my embarrassment.

"Sorry. I should've had him."

"No. My fault. I knew you were tired and I never should have split us up. That was stupid."

"Okay, I'll agree."

Dr. Maiwand scrutinized us from the back door before shaking his head and turning back to the labyrinth of his accursed building.

Ninety minutes later Pedersen steered us into the police parking lot, bounced us off a curb, and cut the engine. Neither of us moved. He watched my hands shake. So did I.

"I'll need to come in and make out a report," I said. "Firearm discharged within city limits, or some bullshit. What's the heading these days? I should probably…"

"Worry about it *mañana.*" He always pronounced it *man-yona*— probably on purpose. He popped his seatbelt then tucked his shirt into his pants. Rattled his keys. "I'll start the paperwork, run it up the chain. You can come in tomorrow and sign your life away."

I rubbed the sweat from my palms.

"They'll most likely ask you to hand over the gun, at least until everything else crawls in from the alley report."

"I get it. Thanks."

"It'd be a personal favor to me if you didn't kill anyone in the meantime."

"I missed him, didn't I? I think I'll take a run by the hospital, see how the landlord is holding up."

"Forget it." His scowl was enough to convince me. "You need a shower and a pillow, or I'll take the damned firearm tonight. I'll get news from our doctor, and you'll be the first call I make. And I doubt I'll make it over to the lawyer with you tomorrow, if that's still the plan."

"Maybe I'll try to see the Russian first. If they give me any shit over there, I promise I'll never touch my Colt. I won't promise not to hurt anyone."

"Do your best. I'll start the paperwork on that too."

FOUR

Shrink

(click)

"You still need help, my friend. Yes, I keep saying it. I know it's the last thing you care to hear. I also know you will not follow my advice and readmit yourself to St. Michael's."

"There are no saints there."

"It's simply a name on the side of a building. But there are doctors inside."

"Did I sleep long?"

(Darla) "It is evening. We should all go down to dinner soon."

"I am sorry, Doctor. They are not good shrinks in there. I was— There was a priest working in hospital."

"Was he able to help ease your frustrations any?"

"He would sit in with Group sometimes. Sometimes he would visit the rooms. His *rounds,* he called it. A nice man. He listened mostly and looked concerned, so…"

"Go ahead."

"But I did not talk much. He was there for calm. Father Matthew. Do you know him?"

"I'm afraid not."

"He ask me to visit his chapel in hospital, but I do not like icons in churches. My Papa…"

"But of course he would ask. It would be his place of comfort, and he probably hoped it would help you as well."

"I understand."

"If you will not go back to the hospital, you cannot continue with this present path you are on, emotionally."

"Unstable. *Da,* I have heard this word too."

"I'm more afraid for you now, after all this. I don't know of an easier way to drill this in. You will not, cannot fix this on your own."

"I do my best."

"Yes, you are very smart, and you have learned much with Mr. Vagelle's books."

"And my time at university."

"But learning is not experiencing. It would be like me diagnosing a broke-down Mercedes from a YouTube video."

"You are not a mechanic. I understand this drill."

"Even the healthiest of us, if put through what you had to endure…"

"Doctor, if you do not mind—I think I am starving."

"Of course you are. Come, dear. Let's give Alya time to powder her nose. We can all meet in the hotel restaurant."

(Darla) "Good idea. We'll get us a table. Take your time, darlin.'"

(movement, a door opens)

"Alya?"

Pedersen

Exercising. Of course. When I walked in, the patient had perched on the edge of the bed away from the door. His head bowed, his prematurely snowy crewcut caught the sun, while he flexed the arm they'd stitched together only a week before. Slowly, he tilted his face up to embrace the warmth. Seldom seen without shirtsleeves, the corded arms reminded me he was not simply a *thin man*.

"Rest it. Don't test it. You never heard of that?" I shot a glance at the food tray, then at the wall clock. "These scrambled eggs are gonna walk out the door if you don't eat 'em soon."

"Help yourself."

"Guess I'll pass." I poked the eggs with the plastic fork anyway. I only ate half of them. "You want this tea?" I didn't wait for an answer. I sprinkled in the sugar packet and gave it a stir. "They never found that round you took. Through-and-through, you're damned lucky. The doc says a large caliber."

No answer.

"If he was as close as you said, they should have found the shell on the highway. If the car was behind you…that high caliber should have travelled down the road some."

"Enough, Frank."

"Sure, it didn't touch the bone, but doc says—"

A nurse entered interrupting me. She lifted the clipboard hooked to the end of his bed. She checked her watch, then scowled for me.

"Twenty minutes, we'll be back with meds, and I'll have a look beneath that bandage." She left as abruptly as she had blown in.

"Or maybe it kicked off the asphalt and into the water." I watched the door for her return. "You heard about the boy?"

Silence.

"Do you want to know?" I added a second sugar packet to give him time. No, I would've added it anyway. "He didn't die in the trunk. He didn't die from the heat."

"As if that changes anything."

"He did not suffocate."

"People keep telling me what I knew last week."

"I think we're all just looking for a response, pal. Maybe a nod to show you're interested." I paused waiting for the nod. "Okay, you would have seen the blood on the boy—"

"His name was Danny."

"Yeah, Danny. And you could tell he'd been gone for—"

"The word is dead."

"You could tell he'd been *dead* for a couple days. I get it."

"Rigor..." Lifting carefully from the sheets, he moved far enough to reach the string for the window blinds. "Rigor had passed long before he went in." He shut out the sunlight then returned to his seat. "*Blue lividity* was staring up at me when I opened the trunk. It should have been beneath him, settling after autolysis. Putrefaction and bloating had turned to dry decomp, and if the trunk had been shut prior to death, I'd have smelled it."

"You going back to teaching?"

"Are you going to keep asking me questions you already know the answers to? Danny had been dead for more than two days. Probably closer to four."

"You know I'm not insulting your intelligence." I wished for warmer coffee.

"What's news, as of this morning?"

"Daddy Howse is still missing."

"How long?" He turned an eye to me for the first time.

"We started searching soon as we identified the bo—Danny. And we haven't stopped looking. Which means, whatever happened out on that highway, he hasn't bothered to check-in and find out."

"That doesn't tell much. He's either in hiding after hearing the ten-o'clock news, or he's on the run from the same kidnappers."

"Who would be less than happy after the carnage you brought down on the exchange."

"Or he was dead before the exchange. Or he took his own life in remorse, either on purpose or by accidental O.D. Or some Brazilian is still beating him into a mindless gelatin as I sit here."

"If alive, he wouldn't be curious about his ransom money?"

"No."

I realized I still held the teacup and dropped it in the trash bucket before noticing it was not my usual paper cup. I scooped it out.

"There was never any ransom money." *You couldn't have guessed that?* in his tone.

"Sometimes you really piss me off."

"Something else I already knew."

"And you know what else pisses me off? You couldn't warn me about the ransom exchange? You're lucky we found you out there."

Back to silence again.

"Yeah, okay. Not luck." *He wouldn't know luck if a spider bit him and he got super-powers.* "You knew Patty would eventually spill the beans. But not too soon, or us dumb cops might interrupt your dramatic death scene."

"Your entire department had been investigating Roderick Howse's missing son. If I'd confided in you, this would have to go up the chain. I don't blame you, Frank. If anything went wrong, you and the department would be up on charges. Instead, Patty was my fail-safe."

"Thanks for *looking out* for me."

"I was." He poured water from the pitcher into his cup without looking. I'll never figure how he does that.

"Yeah, okay. I know." Pushing my hands into my pockets, I rattled my keys some.

"There's another shoe coming," he said.

"Sure, you also read body language, I remember? Have you spoken to Alya? Lately?"

His stare carried his answer.

"How 'bout Patty?" I said.

"Two nights ago. Get on with it."

"I know Maiwand called you about the break-in. Any idea what they hoped to find in your rooms?"

Barely a head shake.

"Patty rode with me to the scene. Afterwards, when I dropped her off, she talked about checking in with St. Mike's."

"What's wrong with Alya? Another setback?"

"I called the shrink-ward last night. Patty never showed up. No one's heard from her going on two days."

He clung to the stainless-steel IV stand, one wheel clattering on a loose screw. I couldn't tell if he directed the stand, or if the stand kept the stubborn son-of-a-bitch from breaking a hospital tile with his nose.

"You should've let me stop for a wheelchair," I said.

No answer.

"Yeah, I know. You need your exercise. Well, if you trip and land on your IV bag, I'm not throwing my back out trying to pick you up."

"I need to think. Please be quiet."

Somehow, we made it all the way to Hemmings's room without me clobbering him with his IV stand. I flashed my badge to the uniformed officer seated beside the door. Vagelle went in first.

"Are you okay, Mr. Hemmings?"

"Mister—?" His landlord squirmed upright in bed, fear-faced and stammering, dropping his pen, and turning over the newspaper crossword page like he'd been decoding for MI6. "You are here? How did you (cough)?" He fumbled the sippy cup from the nightstand, missed his mouth with the straw, and tried again. "Of course I'm okay. I told those mindless medics last night I was okay. I don't need to be here. I belong in my apartment."

"I'm told you took a few nasty lumps."

"I got a bump on my noggin. Wasn't the first. Won't be the last."

"And stitches?" I said. "And what about the rest of your face?" Which boasted a motley spectrum.

Vagelle trundled to the corner by the window and lowered into the visitor's chair. Hemmings rummaged through the battlefield of sheets searching for his dropped pen.

"Dang-it! Now I have ink on the sheets."

A nurse came in looking like a Saints middle-linebacker wearing a paper facemask, green scrubs with torpedo breasts, and a necklace stethoscope. "We okay in here?" Her voice had all the depth of a canary's, making me glance twice more. She crossed to loom over Vagelle. "Do I need to check your vitals too?"

"I will be fine," he said. "I just needed to catch my breath."

She checked his pulse.

"I'll keep an eye on him," I said.

She worked through Hemmings's vitals. "Doctor said you'll be going home this afternoon. Eat lunch first. Then one more check from the doc on-call, we'll get your meds—"

"I don't take meds. I don't like meds," Hemmings said.

"You won't leave here without them."

"You can bring 'em, but I won't take 'em."

"Keep talking and you'll be in here for another week," I said, and it shut his face.

"And don't you worry about the ink. We seen plenty worse in here." The linebacker winked for me on her way out. I tried not to blush.

"Alright." Vagelle turned to Hemmings. "Tell me about it, then we can leave you to your lunch.

"What's to tell? Maiwand saw as much as I did. I was about dozed off in front of Alex Trebek—yeah, I know he left the show, but I recorded all the old seasons."

"Hemmings."

"That's when I hear sounds like cracking wood, then the motion alarm. So I grab my flashlight and the hammer."

"A hammer?" I said.

"The one I keep next to my door for repairs and for hammering bad guys. So, I run out to the foyer just as these two big goons are tiptoeing up the stairs. They see me coming after them, and they start to run, and I start to run until one of them realizes I'm not big enough to worry about. And he turns on me."

"And?"

"And what? And here I am. He got my hammer."

"And you can tell us nothing about your attackers?" Vagelle said.

"I just did. I said they were big."

"And they wore masks and gloves. What kind of masks?"

"Black masks."

"What kind of gloves?"

"How the hell do I know what kind of gloves? Black gloves. Rubber gloves. Black rubber gloves."

"Hell, Patty got more than that from Maiwand, and all he saw was running down the dark hall." I paced off a circle in frustration.

"So she said." He motored his mattress down to almost flat.

"So who said?" Vagelle read my mind. "Patty? When did she tell you that?"

"Last night."

"She spoke to you last night?" I stopped pacing.

"I just said that. You don't listen very well."

I threatened to rip off the foot of his bed frame and beat him with it. I lowered my voice in case nurse linebacker overheard and twisted that footboard round me like a straitjacket.

"Hemmings." Vagelle rose from the chair. "Focus. The detective is concerned. We are all concerned. No one has heard from Patty in two days. She is missing."

He stammered.

"Bad things are happening, which we have no explanation for, and I need you to *think*. Details about your attackers. But mostly, at this moment, tell me about your conversation with Patty. What time did she call you?"

"She—She didn't call. She was here." Hemmings wiped sweat from his brow. "I was mostly sedated. It was dark. I was blurry. Then I hear a sound and look at the clock. Two-something. Two-twenty-two, I think. And she sits in that chair you just sat in. The blinds are cracked and streetlight comes in, which is why I could see anything at all. So, she talks, but I can't understand at first. But she's asking if I am okay. She gets up and brings me my water cup."

"And you ask what she's doing here in the dark," I said.

"It's after hours, so I am perplexed when she says she only wanted to hang out some. Recuperate, she says. Make sure nobody disturbs me."

"She thought someone might come here? Someone from your break-in?"

"I was too confused to ask. And I fade in and out. Once, when I woke up, she…"

"Think," Vagelle said.

"It almost sounded like her crying. I know, I don't believe it either. Not her. But I'd swear she was. Then she's talking about someone in her apartment. She's in the bathtub. Her lights go out. So…" He rattled the newspaper like he had finished talking.

"Wrap it up!" *Vagelle preparing to murder the small man?*

"I'm remembering. A large man, she says. She maybe knew him."

"She obviously got away to come here," I said. Vagelle's glance said I should shut up.

"I tried listening more, but I faded. And she got quiet. I thought maybe she fell asleep."

Vagelle had finished listening. He nearly rode his IV stand into the hallway. "I'm checking out."

"Then what?" I chased after. "What do you think you're going to do in your condition?"

"Kill somebody."

"I didn't just hear that. You know I'm a cop, right?"

Hemmings whimpered behind us.

Five

Pedersen

The building had been cordoned off, street traffic pinched down to one lane, that lane frozen as in tribute to the other. Dark uniforms stepped aside as we worked the stairway to the seventh floor. The work involved my patience and Vagelle's faltering speed every moment of the climb to Patty's apartment. I stayed two steps behind, convinced that he would collapse somewhere mid-journey.

"How 'bout we sit on a stair and strategize a way to keep my breakfast down?"

Of course, her apartment was the obvious one with the human logjam into the hallway. I had phoned ahead the moment we left Hemmings's bedside, but someone had beat me to it. NOPD had responded like the mayor had a personal stake in Patty's disappearance.

We entered, patrolmen standing to the wings, CSI rummaging and well in command of the modest rooms.

Police Captain Beaudry and Nicolaus Vagelle had a mixed history. Beaudry stepped into our path for this afternoon's proclamation.

"Shouldn't he be in a hospital?" He said it to me but glared at Vagelle. "Or haven't you heard he's a civilian? This joker's still under investigation for the botched child ransom, and his direct connection to the child's missing father, to say nothing of his long association with Miss Gunston and the reason we're all congregating today."

Tempting me into saying, *There's a lot packed into one sentence right there.*

"Whatever we turn up here, he might be involved with it. Get him to the hallway. Better yet, the alley."

"I will turn around," Vagelle said, before I could speak. "But I'm the only one in the room who has been here before."

"Captain—?" I started.

"I know her habits, and I'm the only reason we believe she may be in trouble. I'm guessing your investigators have yet to find evidence of a crime?"

The captain squinted, quirked his cheek, crooked a finger, and led through the living area to the bedroom. He turned and pointed past my shoulder to the blood spatter high on the wall.

"I stand corrected," Vagelle said.

"No, you don't. That's just your duplicitous way, son. Belittling my investigators to get into my crime scene."

His attention on the wall, Vagelle appeared to be plotting the map of thrown blood. His head turned, deliberate, and he pivoted as if studying a ghost reenactment of the attack.

"Just stay clear of everyone and touch nothing." Beaudry emptied his expression while moving to the cop on the door. "Keep close to him. He touches anything, cuff him and throw him out the window."

Vagelle inched closer to the wall designs. Eyes on the carpet, he walked in a small arc. He read the furniture.

"Nothing's been moved yet?" he said.

"No sir." The young tech cradled the print kit as if awaiting approval.

Vagelle drew an invisible line through the air from the bathroom doorway to a delicate pattern of red specks between the bed and dresser. Carpet fibers hinted at a violent compression.

"We got that, sir," the tech said.

"Of course. What lights were on when you got here?" Vagelle stepped wide of the compression and edged himself close to the doorframe. "May I?"

"We haven't been in there yet. The only light on in the apartment was the closet behind me."

Vagelle nodded. He examined the bath from where he stood. "Anyone find a wet towel in the apartment? And what about the gun?"

"We got one Colt, still in an ankle holster. Found it in the living room beside the recliner. A Ruger in a kitchen drawer behind silverware. And a .12 gauge in a broom closet behind the vacuum."

"If you don't mind, shine a light under the dresser. Behind the left-front leg." Then to the tech's raised eyebrows, "She always kept a spare Mauser there."

"I think I'm falling in love," the tech said.

The cop on the bedroom door clicked the flashlight app on his phone and passed it to the tech, already on his knees.

"Nothing," he said.

"Thank you. Does that look like a fresh nick in the wood skirting?"

"So. What do you know?" Beaudry muscled in again.

"She said she was in the bath when all the lights went out. A big man, someone she may have known, grabbed her, dragged her from the tub to the bedroom. She fought. The crushed carpet shows the struggle, but your CSI already knows that. It's most likely her blood beside the bed. She would not have been easy."

"Not easy? She was naked," Beaudry said.

"I repeat, *Patty* would not have been easy. One of them dragged the sheets aside there. The nightstand is crooked where the lamp hit the floor. But the tussle ended over here, between the bed and dresser…right beside where she kept the Mauser. She kicked him off long enough to make the grab. The wall spray is high and trailing upward, so the shot came from down here."

"Is 'at it?"

"As she showed up in Hemmings's hospital room fully clothed, it means her attacker took the bullet, but he got away."

"We found blood trace and large fingerprints near the front door," a second tech called from the living room. "Most likely a man. As well as scattered drippings. Not arterial, sadly."

Beaudry had turned his back, pretending to follow the logic. "You'll be staying close to him, I take it?"

"That's the plan, Capt'n," I said. "Unless you've got something else for me."

He waved us away.

Vagelle opened his street-side windows and leaned onto the sill, single-handed of course, with his left arm slung tight to his chest. No air moved in, but temperature and humidity rose immediately along with the boulevard's familiar language of motor and foot traffic.

"You want I should shut off the air conditioning for you?" I said.

"Give it two minutes. I need to exorcise the haunting police sweat and cheap cologne."

"Should I shower?" Yeah, the police squad funk had been locked in overnight. I dropped the wad of yellow crime scene tape into his kitchen trash basket and took a chair at the dining table. After all my years of stopping by, Alya's absence left the apartment weighted and colorless.

As he walked an invisible course around the angles of his rooms, his thoughts swept the baseboards. Surveying each bookshelf, he continued into the kitchenette where he opened and shut cupboards. He paused to run water into a teapot. He pulled the drawer and cabinet on the dining room sideboard.

"That's okay. Don't offer me a drink," I said.

"You never needed an invitation before."

He turned his attention to the bedrooms. When he returned, his final stop was the swivel chair at the black L-desk by the window. *Alya's desk.* I had not seen him near it since before her court case. It made me recall our first meeting.

A child of the hurricane, I called her. Nineteen-years-old, living at the storm-wrecked boat docks, and our super sleuth had recently started his *consultancy* by searching for an expensive Shih Tzu related to the wife of a cocaine smuggler.

He opened desk drawers and the tandem file cabinets.

"Everything in its right place?" I said.

"There's really nothing too important kept here anymore."

"Meaning, whatever Heckle and Jeckle came to find was never here in the first place. But then, Maiwand did say they never got in here."

"Investigators did, however."

"Sure. Any idea what they were looking for?"

"No." He might have been studying fingerprints on the desktop for all I knew. "Maybe."

"Which means, like usual, you got nothing to share." The kettle whistled at me, so I lumbered to the kitchen where I poured a cup. "You want one?" When he didn't answer, I opened the skinny pantry.

"Nearly out." He ran a finger along the window blinds for dust. "You'll find a small cup in the refrigerator."

I found it. Not enough sugar to satisfy a hummingbird. "I guess I'm the only one uses it."

Eventually, he left the chair, returning it to within inches of its previous position in the desk notch. He posed at the window again.

"So," I said, "I know your motto is *confide nothing*, but step outside your own head for half a minute, will ya? You get shot up in a ransom exchange, your landlord gets beat with a hammer, our P.I. friend gets dragged out of the bathtub, punched around, and now she's missing for two days. You might conclude I'd be a wee bit concerned too."

He studied the mostly dark landscape above the fake fireplace. His eyes trailed to the mantel.

"This has been moved." He touched, then nudged the small golden bell trophy to one side, and lifted the dusty, black book—R.L. Stevenson. It had always been there. Turning it to the window's light, he blew on the dust. He opened the cover. A playing card fell free, and he stared after it before bending.

My phone hummed the first bars of Dean Martin's, "Ain't That a Kick in the Head?" so I wrestled it free of my pocket. "And? What's the card say?"

"Patty's handwriting." He tossed Stevenson onto the settee and shoved the card into a shirt pocket. "Same thing she said to Hemmings. Steer clear of Gunston."

"Her offices. Why?" The phone chittered before I could raise it to my ear. "Well?"

"What about the call? Another problem?"

"Your Alya." I anticipated his reaction. "Escaped from St. Mike's five nights ago."

He dropped what little expression he had.

"Our judge *friend* has issued a new warrant."

A shuffling outside the door. A slap to the woodframe startled me, but Vagelle's raised hand kept me in place.

"It's unlocked, Mr. Hemmings," he said. The door opened.

"Mr. Vagelle," the landlord said, "this is unacceptable. My house has descended into violence. Again! I cannot live like this. Look at my face. I look like Picasso—My nose is crooked! I wheeze when I breathe. You can frown all you like. My mind is made up and—"

"Mister Hemmings." Vagelle glided in on him like a spider studying a cricket. The landlord cocked his neck but could not meet his eyes. "Your nose was bent when I met you. No doubt your attitude had something to do with it. At present, I am considering withholding the next two months' rent. Plus the rent for the fourth-floor apartment that I pay you to keep vacant."

Hemmings worked his jaw with a turbulent silence.

"I may withhold this as a punishment for you failing to maintain a secure building."

"But you can't—"

"You have known my profession for over a decade. I paid cash for you to have security measures upgraded on this building.

More silent sputtering.

"I paid more than it would have cost you to have iron doors and NORAD-quality locks installed on that boiler room. And I bought you the .12 gauge so you would not need a hammer propped behind your apartment door. Maybe I should buy the paper on this building, so you can find more *suitable* employment elsewhere."

Hemmings spun on his slipper, grabbed the banister to steady himself before plodding back down the stairs. Vagelle slammed the door in an unusual display of bother.

"Excuse me." A breath before taking two reflexive steps toward the fireplace niche where he used to prop the cane. He halted again. Cursed. "There's a screwdriver in that file cabinet. Do you think you could remove the air vent over your head?"

From the vent I retrieved his belly-holster and the Sig Sauer I had stored there after finding him on the highway.

"I seem to remember a time you hated *carrying.*"

As he entered his bedroom and shut the door, I double-checked to ensure the burner under the kettle had been turned off. When he came out, I assumed he wore the belly-holster under his shirt but could not figure how he managed it one-handed. "Your cane?"

"I lost it in that highway hoedown."

"Sorry." I knew its sentimental value.

Opening the sideboard, he drew a spare magazine for the Sig Sauer and pocketed that.

"Well, I know some of what's ricocheting around in that crowded skull, but do you want to explain a bit for me? Off the record? I figure you're going to ditch me first opportunity."

"You figured that, have you?"

"Yeah. You with a police escort is like having a sidekick dragging a fork along a chalkboard."

Hauling a heavy Psych textbook from its crowded shelf, he flipped the cover and removed the concealed burner phone from its cutout pages.

"Only call me on this," he said, and I caught it on the fly. "And we've roamed New Orleans gutters long enough for you not to suppose it's only when I need your badge."

"Okay. My apologies, but…"

"But we have things to do, and you need to accept the importance of the world that's been thrown at us. Stay on the boy's kidnappers, oversee the break-in here, and you need to work on finding Ms. Gunston."

"She's not a priority for you because…?"

"We need to assume, yes, there is a ticking clock on her disappearance. But we both know Patty. She's missing, but it is because she does not wish to be found. The lady has many resources and can take care of herself, to an extent. The urgency is that someone else is searching for her as well. The man who dragged her from the bath, or someone he works for, will try again."

"You're right, of course." The door stuck. I gave it a tug. "And it's easy to figure why you ain't coming with me."

"I've left her alone for a few weeks…"

"Or a month and a half."

"She needed to forget things here."

"And you figured she needed to forget you too, right?"

"Don't lecture me, Frank." He followed me onto the landing and locked the door.

"How many friends you got left?"

"Before you go, remember two things. Patty said stay away from her offices. It was important enough to say it twice. So next time you go in, should be after you know why she said it. Second, before you learn differently, assume nothing these past months is coincidence."

"Do you know where to look for Alya? Is she just a runaway, or how much urgency do you see there?"

"In years past," his thoughts gripped him in the moment, "I would trust in her ability to take care of herself."

"But not in her present frame of mind."

SIX

Alya

Move at night. Sleep by day. If I can ghost myself in a crowded city where so many are homeless, looking for the same thing…

Rikki-Tikki-Tavi. Kipling, memories returned. A favorite early gift from Nicolaus to young Alya. The mongoose. Could I become a burrowing animal, to make shelter in the heart of them while surrounded by so many larger threats? Would I only draw out the snakes…?

The denizens. *Denizens?* In the day's heat, they crowded the shade of doorways and under bridges and parking garages. Within stolen tents or makeshift lean-tos of cardboard and blankets, chickenwire and graffitied plywood ripped from shuttered windows. They huddled together.

Broken people. Or those about to break coupling with their own species of illness.

Words, my lost English, returning to me. Not fast enough.

Empty buildings, once thought of as shelters, now more dangerous because *empty* was only a word. Those places of crimes mostly unnoticed by police. Mindless crimes. Physical. Fueled by drugs, alcohol, creature lust, or simply for the sight of newer shoes. Of course, teen gangs loved hunting in those darker places.

Denizens? A word half-remembered from…where? Stevenson? Memory struggled to dig for lost things. RLS, the first book *he* asked me to read so many years ago. Ten, almost ten years.

I was nineteen when he found me. My *Angliski* (English) not so good. He told me life would be easier here if I learned. I knew this before he told me, so I played along. And he became *teacher of many things.*

"…*multifarious…denizens.*" Stevenson, not the best place to learn a language. I once looked up multifarious, but now the word looked alien in my brain. I used to love poetry…now, every struggle remembering the old lessons angered me, frustrated me. It became a stolen thing of value.

Vagelle

Queen of Hearts.

I slid Patty's playing card warning back into my pocket. The scribbled message, *"Steer clear of Gunston—Alice."*

Why a playing card? She disliked gambling.

She had run to my apartment immediately after her attack. This had to do with her disappearance, and based on her note, likely someone from her company. Where did she get the card, if not from her attacker? Why this card? A lover? Former lover? What else did it tell me? Deep pen gouges. She wrote in a hurry afraid someone else would find it, or she would have written more. Perhaps the return of those who had attacked Hemmings. Or maybe afraid of another police search.

She knew enough cops through her P.I. business. She should have gone to them for protection. She did not.

Still, why a playing card? Because, cryptic enough, Patty knew I might be the only one to decipher its meaning.

Why Alice? Alice was not a fan of the Queen of Hearts.

Bobby J. cleared the doorway to his club only by dipping his head. His thick fingers encircled Lenny's neck, a neck like a young mule, an analogy befitting the rest of Lenny as well. The larger man, Bobby J., threw him to the curb as if pitching a softball. Lenny crashed into the fireplug and turned fetal. Considering the stricken man, Bobby wiped his hands across his wide apron, stooped beside him, and apologized. Then he spotted me crossing beneath the streetlights.

"Mr. V! It's been a long year without a visit."

Only three weeks. He clamped my outstretched hand like I was a toddler. I might stand as tall as an Arkansas grave, but my head tipped back for Goliath. "Is he going to be okay?"

"Oh, him? Sure. Used to play Center for the Angola road team. He just needs to get his wind back."

Lenny groaned.

"And he needs to remember this is my club, my rules, and not to line powder on my bar top. Come on in." With a leaden paw on my shoulder, he ushered me into his Bobby J.'s Black & Blues Club. His paw changed shoulders with, "Sorry, Mr. V. I didn't realize."

"I imagine you heard the news. Are all your white shirts in the laundry again?" A reference to the uncustomary and faded blue T-shirt with the Navy emblem peeking over his bib apron.

"I'll change before dinner hour. But hey! Still fits!"

Amateur sax filled the room with Stardust as my sight corrected to the low-light. A Bobby J. regular, whom he only referred to as Ol' Jamaican, had one foot up on his wicker chair in the far corner, as I had last seen him. Alya once described him as a nut-brown Karl Marx in tropical-print shorts and docksiders, so I could never see him as otherwise. He skipped a few beats to wave at me, then resumed playing. For years, Ol' Jamaican wrangled a meager wage out of Bobby to keep the customers warm and satisfied before the headliners took the stage.

Dinner hour, and the club had already packed to capacity. Bobby J.'s had become a landmark here in the *Skillet*—the neighborhood so-named for its jambalaya temperatures in the dead of Summer. The crowd maintained a respectful buzz below the soft saxophone.

Bobby nodded to the station waitress, took up a towel and sidestepped to take his post behind the bar. Charlie Parker, the black and white version, played his silent note from behind the poster glass over Bobby's heavy shoulders. Unlike the rest of the room, with its kaleidoscope of signed headshots, LP covers, glints of brass from old band instruments mounted like hunting trophies, Charlie was the only portrait of privilege back there.

"Looks like you ain't stayin for the floor show," Bobby said. "Your private booth is lookin mighty lonesome lately."

"Soon, Bobby. Tonight I'm on the move." I leaned across the bar to keep from shouting. "I'm looking for someone. More than one someone. Have you ever heard of a South American gunsel named René? He may be running without a crew lately."

"Lately?"

"Yes. He's the sole survivor of the ambush. The one who nearly took my arm. René chauffeured an Escalade, new, black. I never saw him, but his boss sounded like a bad *bossa nova.*"

"And there's a good chance they stick to their own, from the same region at least. Bangers tend to have trust issues."

"My thoughts."

"That's a job ahead of you. You know there's plenty of Renés in this county." He raised a paw, waved for his sax player.

Ol' Jamaican wobbled through the room, grinning large, always anxious to be of service. Bobby relayed my request.

"Common name, here'bouts. Mostly da Français, some Spaniel. I even knowed one from de Chitimacha tribe. Depends how it spelled, you."

"He only heard it spoken," Bobby said.

"Mr. Vagelle might have better luck going with the 'ficial gang check. Quite a few from de Cent'r Mex, and more south-er. More dese days den we's used to seein, I tink. Dat name…she might be a new handle for him. Don't sound like a usual slang most invent for demselves, I tink. Sound like someting, a alias made to sound like a real name. Or mighta been a slur his boss give t'im."

"Good thinking, friend," I said. "I'll keep roaming. Maybe the two of you could keep your ears to the ground for me. René is a dangerous guy. There's one other. A big guy, not young, he has a tattoo on his arm—something-O-A-T. GOAT?"

Ol' Jamaican levered his bushy brows and smirked to Bobby.

"Even I know that one," Bobby said. "So rough he wears the *Greatest Of All Time* on his arm as a challenge to his fellow punks. So far, those hanging with him believe it, and give him space. He used to come in here. Liked to order my guests to give up their tables to him."

"But you handled him."

"Me and *Stanley.*"

He laid it on the bar. Stanley, the manufacturer of Bobby's "dead-blow" mallet. The head of the mechanics' dead-blow resembled a bright orange sledgehammer, a thick hollow rubber filled with loose steel shot, designed to re-distribute the weight upon impact. I had seen him pull Stanley from under the bar only twice. He never needed to use it, that I was aware of.

"Either of you know where I might start looking?"

Ol' Jamaican's brows climbed further.

"I'd warn you against digging for him." Bobby busied himself with bar glasses. "But I know you too well."

"Him and his crew are *hobby sellers,*" Ol' Jamaican said. "Dey sell anyting. Meth, ladies, boys, stole cars, guns. Dey sell to deir own kind, a'course. Most nights, dey's de ones makin N'awlins City Park a uncomf'terble place for tourists."

"I've never seen his face," I said.

"He's a easy one to reco'nize, with the top o' his ear bit off."

"Good enough." I stripped two twenties off what I had in my pocket, and he pretended not to need it. Customarily, I forced it on him. "And next time I'm in, I'll buy the drinks all night."

Bobby shook his head. Ol' Jamaican strutted back to his chair and his sax like he had just scored a gig at the Orpheum Theater.

"Now, Bobby, for the main reason I came. Tell me, have you seen Alya recently?" It stopped him cold.

"What happened? Is she not—? Please tell me she is okay, my little Ruskie."

"I'm looking for her. I don't know her condition, but I am concerned. Somehow, she got out of St. Michaels."

"And?"

"And now there's a warrant out."

"What can I do?" He stripped his apron with a savage flourish. "Can I go somewhere? What do we know? Is this GOAT involved?"

"Slow down, big guy. Right now, there's nothing anyone can do. All I know is she ran and is likely in hiding. Yours was my first stop. I came here thinking she might turn to her *Big Bear* for protection."

He propped his elbows on the bartop for sincerity, and said, "If she gets hurt, I'll twist the head off that judge like a crawdad."

"Easy. God knows we all left the courtroom in a rage, but I've spoken to the judge since, and she promised me hospital was her best option. My lawyer agreed."

"Judgie sat through the hearing like a block of wax from Madam Trussaud's window."

"She calls it *impartiality*. But according to her, Alya broke a man's collarbone and four of his fingers, putting him out of work."

"*Work!* His work—pimping and fentanyl. You know it. And if not for Alya—"

"Yeah. But he was also smart enough to grab emergency room pics, and an ambulance chaser on standby."

"I'd like to grab something. Pop his head like a grape."

"Judge said her only options for Alya were hard jail time, or full-time psychiatric care."

"If you say so."

"Not agreeing, my friend. But right now my number one job is to find her. You stay here, take care of business, keep your ears open for me. If, by chance, she contacts you…"

He re-tied the apron round his barrel waist and began washing glasses with fervor and a worrisome grip.

"C'mon, man!" A red-eyed patron in a wrinkled suit and crooked lavender tie slapped the bar top. "I been waiting on my whiskey sour and pink martini since President Jackson."

"You might give the man a few moments." I backed off.

Then, with Bobby's scowl clearing his vision, red eyes flicked to the dead-blow resting on the bartop. He retreated with a wider stare.

"I need to go, Bobby. Don't break anything."

They were right, of course. All of them. The mistaken judgement was mine, and by keeping my distance from her, I now had no idea of Alya's present emotional state. She might be running scared, avoiding *everyone* due to her phobia, or in an over-medicated fugue. My imaginings stoked the heat within my chest.

I had never accepted the court's presumption that she posed a danger to others. She's more likely a danger to herself?

It took a degree of awareness for her to break out of the hospital, so I determined her to be at least somewhat lucid and motivated. Being locked inside, close to others, could only feed her anxiety, and if nurses needed to physically restrain her for any reason…

…but the doctors were all aware of this. They would need to keep her in protected status.

I crisscrossed the city searching her customary haunts.

Passing her apartment—if she rationalized her situation, she would avoid it, but to me, this was eliminating the obvious first. The undercover stakeout in a drab Chrysler had parked at the end of her block. The occupant slumped behind the wheel blowing smoke through a window slit.

One block over, I checked Alya's parking bay for her Impala, and I got out long enough to survey the car's interior. Layers of dust told me it had remained untouched since she entered St. Michael's. A quick call to Petersen's burner confirmed the stake-out had been authorized. That his Desk Sergeant had called every emergency room in lower Louisiana, probably an exaggeration, and the APB went statewide.

She would avoid crowds, of course. That would include mass transit.

Cruising the parking lots of West End Marina, a place she had escaped to in the past, I could not justify breaking into every boat in the harbor without some indication of her. It brought to mind the question, how was she getting around? Or had she found shelter and sequestered herself? Had her fears kept her frozen in place? Was she still somewhere near St. Michael's?

She had few other friends to turn to. Patty. But of course, Patty had fallen off the map as well. My final words to Pedersen resurfaced. *Before you learn differently, assume that nothing these past weeks is coincidence.*

How long have I been living in this emotional fog? Since the attack at Hades' farm? After Alya's crime and conviction, what had been my strategy then? I knew the truth, and felt ugly by it.

Avoidance. Not hers, mine.

"So many wrong moves," he said. "Too many wrong moves for the *celebrated detective*, you are thinking." I could recall minimal physical change in *the Shrink* over our fifteen-year association. Salt-n-pepper mustache to match a full head of hair that always looked wind-blown on a still day. A Clint Eastwood squint, though I doubt he had ever seen the southwest desert.

"You're off your game, doc." Staring at his familiar doormat, *Abandon Trouble All Ye Who Enter Here*. "You know me too well. I don't think of myself as a *detective* of any kind. I specifically stamped *Consultant* on my business cards to avoid misrepresentation."

"And you are too proud to ever read the headlines after your successes, am I right? But rhetorical minutiae is side-stepping, isn't it? The problem that recently walked in out of your past. That boy who grew up and had a boy of his own."

The empty sidewalk past my shoulder beckoned.

"You now tell me he was *the boy?* Your old ghost?"

"The *ghost* would be his mother," I muttered.

"Danny's grandmother. Convenient, certainly. She was your *Medea*, if I remember correctly."

"You remember everything." Medea's claws traced the length of my spine.

A car door slammed behind me as a young couple ended their date. They walked away without noticing the *celebrated detective* leaning on the shrink's doorframe.

"You're tired," he said. "So, when his own child is taken, this son of Medea comes to you for help after all these years. Have you questioned the coincidence, or his logic?"

"He was scared. It was a simple ransom exchange."

"Simple? Wave at me with your left hand and remind me again how it ended *simply?*"

Simply standing flat-footed on the highway center line, now flat-footed on this doorstep, wishing for what? For my aging professor to shred all my arguments and however much self-esteem remained?

"Your *death wish* is a banality, Nicolaus."

Fight me, doc. Prove me right.

"So, now you have more killers to add to your ghost-list."

I understood them, I anticipated them, I manipulated and set them up—then I finished them. "Yes, they have been added."

"Enough with this nonsense, Nicky," Darla said from the foyer. "You come inside now. Have a nice glass of Pinot while I heat up leftover lamb and asparagus spears. And don't argue."

"We know what defines a sociopath, doc," I lowered my voice.

"That's the one question they never ask themselves. Are you writing for a quiz show now?"

"Because they've spent a lifetime carving their excuses into their gray matter, they believe they are justified in all things. Do they not?"

"So." He crossed his arms, a *tell* that he had not anticipated my change in direction. "You keep asking that of yourself, maybe to assure your conscience that you are not one of them."

"*Reasons* complicate themselves, doc."

"Unacceptable. I don't believe I have ever seen *this* man on my doorstep. Even at your lowest, you retained a modicum of stoicism. Even amid all the personal struggles, you withstood the storms with grace. Now this—?"

"Nicky," Darla said.

"Psychopathy? Really?" He tried masking the anger in his words. "You know better. And the very question is an embarrassment. But that's why you came here, isn't it? The whips of doubt. Self-flagellation with an audience. You would rather believe that you are *not* the paladin. That would be too easy, no? Well, I would rather not be a part of your self-destruction. How's that? Physician, go psychoanalyze thyself. You should get that tattooed.

"Ha! *Medice, cura te ipsum.*"

"Like the amateur doctor fallen ill, you surrender and can't discover by which treatments to cure your own disease."

"You're translating Greek to me?"

"Paraphrasing Aeschylus. You wanted the word-game. Are you sure you won't continue this inside?"

"It's too late. I didn't even know where I was going until I turned into your neighborhood."

"Look at who you are kidding, *Consultant.* How much should I charge for this Threshold Therapy? My shin splints are killing me. Come." He turned to his wife.

"I need to go." I adjusted my sling as an overly dramatic excuse.

"Nicky!" Darla called.

I followed them into their designer-appointed living room and took the offered easy chair. I accepted Darla's glass of Pinot Noir but begged off the meal my stomach would not digest. She brought a plate anyway. I sipped thoughtlessly at the bitter glass, wishing its transformation into my standard, Widow Jane Bourbon.

They took the floral sofa as I caught a hurried glance between them.

"So, you have spoken with her," I said.

The shrink did not reply, which was reply enough.

"Darling—" Darla started, only to be cut off.

"I can say nothing," the doctor said.

"Not even with her missing—? Yes. I understand, even if I don't want to." I set the glass on a coaster beside the chair's arm.

"She is very confused." Darla held up a hand to stop her husband from interrupting. "I am not saying what he doesn't already know. We tried to comfort her, Nicky. But she would not trust even us, and she ran away."

"So, you *both* met with her."

"She met with us. She appeared well, physically. A bit thin—"

"Enough!" the doctor faced her with more annoyance than I had seen in him. "If you betray a patient's trust, dear…"

"Please." I lifted from the chair. "You needn't say more. I know you care for her. I can guess at your conversation."

They remained seated. He took his wife's hand as I turned.

"Nicolaus."

"We're still good, doc." My fork pierced a lamb tip, a courtesy to Darla. I chased it with a final sip of the Pinot and winked. In the doorway, I paused and straightened. "You gave me the thrashing I suppose I'd come for. We're good. Always. Love you, Darla."

"About the other thing," *the shrink* said. "The boy. Medea's curse. I've seen you handle multiple cases simultaneously. I know your aptitude."

"But?"

"This time I worry about your emotional connection to both. You will fool yourself, feeling in control of these disparate threads, as you usually do…until they control you. Promise me, if you begin to sense an earthquake, you will come see me."

By the time I reached the Mercedes, Rorschach-like concepts took form. What I had once referred to as "cognitive triage" began with it. As battlefield surgeons needed to prioritize which emergency took precedence, so this stress naturally pulled that trigger within me. My brain automatically sought order in the chaos.

There could be only one first-response. Alya's safety.

Seven

Alya

After sunset I turned away from the neon and holiday-colored lights, and followed below white-light balconies to sidewalks less tortured by drunks, the stoned, the mad *refuse—another word that snuck in. Refuse.*

I hugged familiar neighborhoods with more upscale tourists, or at least those who had discovered soap. The tourist assortment in New Orleans might be the most varied species on the planet. A peacock might disappear in this horde if he kept his beak shut.

But that word *familiar* came with the sneaky attack on my nerves. I studied approaching faces for signs. A face I knew, or a knowing look, people to avoid. An Alya sighting could send me back to the police. Could send me back to…St. Michael's.

Something else—I sensed it like a renegade scent. Maybe a sound out of place. Maybe footsteps that never changed direction, never drew closer, never fell back. A thing blocked from my side-vision stalking me. Or a thing imagined.

Hurrying as I could, I distracted less trustworthy senses with lessons from my previous life. Lessons from my criminal *Papa.* Or from my more recent employer—but I skirted that deeper relationship as quickly as emotions elbowed in.

Hospital—I shoved that away too. Its nearness a sour vinegar to my stomach. *"Der'mo!* (shit!)

"With C-PTSD, any excitement, no matter how small, may trigger a shut-down." Shrink said about *forgetting my second language.* I will work again on it. I must.

I needed to steady me or…

…or I become no better…than…

…*that dying addict curled beside the dumpster in his own urine.*

A black corridor screamed. *Baba Yaga?*

A glance past my other shoulder. A man followed. Large man. Dark man. Large hands flexing the air. A *familiar,* scary-familiar shape with a glittering smile. When I spun, he vanished between buildings.

A shout. A door slam. A young man, maybe a teen, with bright standing hair and a neck held in place by many strings of colorful plastic beads.

Bulging eyes threatened from a bistro doorway, then backed into the swarm.

I walked into the street to avoid the touch of passersby. A car rolled along the curb, its passenger stretching his neck to follow me. A horn rattled my insides. A doorway woman in rags with a cardboard sign opened her toothless mouth wide and threw her plastic cup at me. Empty, *spaciba* (thank you).

I avoided them each as I could.

Then the return to my apartment nearly destroyed me.

Re-entering my beloved space, eight years my home, crushed me now with its grip on my heart. Every corner whispered its dreams to me. If I stalled, relaxed on my sofa, that demon would enfold me in its leather wings and drain my soul, and I would never rise. Only desperation could silence the tempter, and push me forward across the room.

I needed to shower again. The hotel bath left me somehow unclean. Or it was all the walking last night and trying to sleep on a bench in the Tremé. Or the closeness of others. Or the trolley I tried for less than a minute before leaping off to be away from *them*, the gawkers, the groping tentacled strangers.

Even Shrink's new clothes itched like some ant's nest against my flesh when I knew they should not. My scalp would never be clean again, or so the brainworms believed.

Standing too long in the dark tub, beneath sharp, scalding pellets, a steaming rain ripped the invisible dirt from my pores. My own soap, its spice carried a loving kiss to my senses, and I stayed hugging my towel for long minutes. When I unwrapped to the scented bathroom, my world pushed further awake. Or it began to.

For many months, they had kept me hopeless. The nurses and doctors with their drugs, with fake promises. Now, a few days' exercise, my escape through the city, even my physical torments, aching feet, legs, back, told me I was *waking*.

My old fears still shivered me when I thought too long on them.

New fears crawled round the edges of logic, but I ordered them away—they would not win.

I silently raged.

Below the window, the false radiator tugged at my ghost-leash. Another lesson from Papa—*I was small and watched him create hollow appliances to hide his contraband from militsiya* (police). Tonight, I needed the comfort from inside that hollow radiator front. My *security*. My old Kalashnikov rifle, stolen from a crime scene when I was young and afraid. Its promise of safety had bullied me for years. Now, in my weakness, it drew me again.

Such a fool's comfort. What would I do with it? Carry it over my shoulder while I marched through the Garden District looking for something to kill?

Push away the durak (fool). I could not rest here. I needed to move.

With the thought I shrugged quickly into baggier clothing, two layers worth, and comfortable sneakers to blend in with *everyone I hoped to avoid.*

Thoughts came unasked for, fractured thinking. I knew their origins. As long as I knew it, I could stay sane, or so I told myself.

I wrapped my hair in a dark babushka. Slopped on greasy makeup. Noticing the clean white of my sneakers, I bent and rubbed mascara across them. Camouflage for a journey.

Footsteps. Voices outside my door froze me until they passed.

Before moving, I remembered my hidey-hole of emergency cash behind a wall sconce. There! Still undiscovered by investigators. A third of my money and the burner phone went into my pocket. The remainder went back. And with a deep breath to stiffen my nerve, I flew from my sanctuary for the bedlam of night on St. Charles Avenue.

Where to go with this battle, walking aimless? Confused by memories. Accusations from within. *What am I?*

At twelve *Papa* put me to work. I was tough at twelve. At thirteen the *horror* changed me. The dark garage with young monsters attacking, changing me into a monster. After this...*Papa* found other jobs for me. Ugly jobs I never spoke of to anyone. Not even—

Wandering hand-in-hand with the corrupted memories, I grew smaller in a large city.

Loneliness. That returned too. I had nobody back then. The occasional impermanent friendships. Some I trusted, then learned the lessons why not to trust. But I would try again. And again. Some losses hurt worse than others. Eventually, one comes to expect betrayal. But once the sting dulls and drifts on, only a memory murmurs softly enough to try again.

As now. Again. It had been so long ago, that sting, I forgot myself. I gave in to the temptation, the hope for a different outcome. Those moments returned me there. Running, without direction. Small, alone and surrounded. Fear of being touched in a sea of hands.

"Think. You have been here before. And worse. Use the frightful memories to remind yourself of what you have conquered."

With time, I became more aware. I shivered in a doorway across the street from *his* apartment. Hemmings's skinny four-story with the special tenant on floor three. *Him. Nicolaus.*

His windows dark, his rooms more familiar even than my own, the breath of those rooms called to me a seduction, and fear fought me like a reflex. Pulling my babushka forward to conceal my blondness, again I walked away.

Moving beneath the lights again, another crowd, a hand touched my arm—and my vision went white.

I flailed sightless at the sky. Another hand, and I exploded from the walking pack and ran. I crashed into others.

By the time the nightmare exhausted itself enough to look back, a crowd of the frightened or furious faces had parted for me like a biblical sea.

Vagelle

I parked one block over from her building and retrieved the leather shoulder bag from my trunk. Easy enough to bypass the sleepy sentry in his car across the street, then up the side stairway to her fourth floor. This time of morning, those I approached in the halls suffered from their own self-induced fog, so I would vanish spirit-like from their thoughts the moment I passed from sight. Alya's duplicate key in hand, I cleared the door as quickly as the police tape could fly with me.

I plugged the deadbolt at my back. My senses delayed me. Her scent, all these months later, with her rooms locked tight against the outside world, it surprised me.

Patty had suggested maintaining the apartment for as long as Alya stayed *away*. She would check in, set a mild thermostat to hold New Orleans humidity at bay. Another aroma, this time of fading disinfectant. But Alya had been here recently too. I recognized her soap.

Hustling through her rooms, aided by outside lights slanting through window blinds, I halted before the bathroom door. A towel, still damp, hung over the shower glass. The tub and sink glistened.

Damn-it! My arteries cooled with the thought that she may have taken the thing I'd come for.

With the pipe wrench, where she'd always kept it beneath the bathroom sink, I raced back to the bedroom, directing my penlight across the walls to the radiator beneath the bedroom window, her false radiator front. Systematically, I seated wrench to nut and turned. The bolts fell away, but not willingly, then I flipped the radiator front over onto her bed. By its weight, I already knew *it* was safe. The Kalashnikov lay strapped within.

Hell, girl. You scared me.

I removed the braces, then disassembled the Russian's rifle, dropping the parts into a pillowcase. I loaded that into her old satchel found at the back of the closet amid a small collection of shoes. Her sneakers were missing. I re-secured the faux radiator beneath the window.

One more task. Naked and forsaken in the corner of the main room, her small desk had been stripped by investigators before her trial and, until today, she had not returned to it. I knew the drawers would be empty, but I pulled them anyway.

Standing on a chair to reach the acoustic ceiling tiles, I nudged one. If she had the laptop before police arrived, she would have hidden it here, so I unslung my leather shoulder bag, folded the straps, and slid it up into the opening. Then I replaced the tile.

Confident I had removed traces of myself from her rooms, I retrieved to her cloth satchel with the pillowcase that smelled of her and her AK-radiator accessory.

That's when the old-world gods threw me another curve. Pedersen called to say they had found what they believed to be the 6.2L, V8 horse, formerly black Escalade, now disguised as a 6,300lb charcoal briquette.

Alya

"Ma'am?" The man in the gray jumpsuit hovered above. Embroidery over his heart spelled *"Jesus,"* and the sun framed him, not with a halo, and I appreciated that.

Traffic sounds. A trolley's clatter and clang. Mingling voices. Distant riverboat sounds. His closeness toggled my nerves and I scooted back. His nametag read "Jesse" now. My brain flexed, still fighting off the nap.

He saw my fear. With a raised palm, he retreated a step to assure me. I felt the grass under me and tried to stand, wavering.

"*Señora,* you are not—?"

"No. I am okay. I am." I backed to a low wall and steadied against the bricks, my surroundings business-like, tall buildings, people in suits, designer glasses, briefcases, or having conversations with cell phones. The grass underfoot became a mere strip of the *otherworldly* between cement walkways. I held my face to stop the spinning. "I will be okay. Thank you."

"You need doctor? Too much party?" Behind him awaited a wheelbarrow and tree-trimming equipment.

"Where is this?" But the street signs told me. This corner, the crosswalk, and a building number. That building of the Gunston Detective Agency, Patty's P.I.'s offices. Jesse continued talking while I said to myself, "Apparently, I find my way better when I am half-conscious."

EIGHT

Vagelle

The Lower Ninth Ward. The muddy banks of the Industrial Canal beneath the old Clairborne Avenue Bridge, a dramatic structure of mirroring towers, gray iron crossbeams, with a vertical lift bridge that could raise its span in a single length to allow for ships' passage to the River. The word "Lower" referred to the neighborhood's location downriver from the city, stretching toward the Delta and the mouth of Ol' Miss. Throughout the years, the bridge had been the scene of countless dramas of its own, from tugboat collisions or a barge mishap, to crossing gate malfunctions, cars plunging over its sides and, of course, Hurricane Katrina.

I rumbled across, turned south and looped to N. Clairborne Ave., then onto the soggy path recently cut by emergency trucks and others. All the flashing lights made it easy to follow.

A baby-faced patrolman halted me. I said Pedersen's name and he directed me to park. The Lieutenant waved for me to join him at the wreck, the black Escalade. I would accept a professional guess as to the car's original color. At this moment the black referenced its similarity to an enormous pork roast forgotten on a bonfire overnight.

"No body, I presume," I said.

"And cool to the touch." Pedersen shifted his attention. "Don't know yet when it landed here."

Distant voices laughing, young teens calling from the bridge, calling "Fuck off!" to police. Two policemen yelled profanities of their own, and the teens ran off cackling louder. And the policemen laughed.

"Let's pretend René parked it," I said.

"The desperado who got away." Pedersen scowled for the police jokers already moving away.

"The one who didn't kill me when he could have, and I'm still confused."

"Ya think maybe he saw the mess he'd made of your shoulder and figured you for dead? I often ask how many of the nine lives you've got left."

"So, why destroy a good car no one else could identify? The techies are finished here, I suppose? Do you have an extra pair of gloves?"

"Barnett!" He nodded for a young woman with light strawberry hair, plain clothes, a tan windbreaker with a Sgt. pin on her lapel, chocolate slacks sharply creased. She pulled blue rubber gloves from her hip pocket, and with a glance at my left arm sling, returned one glove and helped pull the other onto my free hand.

I nodded thanks.

"You're not thinking of climbing in this thing dressed like that?" she said.

The driver's door hung open, its window shattered. I motioned to Barnett.

"When you got here, the doors were locked, which is why you needed to break in. I assume you had reason not to wait for the crime lab."

"Yeah, kids screaming someone was in there."

"And windows too smoked to see. Find anything of interest?"

"One set of shoe prints around the car, pointy toes with deep heels in the damp soil. Not unlike cowboy boots. Size nine-ish? Other shoe prints, mostly sneakers, but not so close to the car. Maybe curiosity seekers who realized they'd find nothing here worth taking after the cookout. No one got out the passenger side."

"Small boots." I propped my gloved hand against the upper doorframe to lean my head inside.

"Small man, I'm thinking," she said, "from the position of the seat and steering wheel."

"Maybe five-seven, at most. Good observation."

"We found a cell phone cooked into the passenger seat."

"Which is why we found none on the boss-man out at your crime scene," Pedersen said. "We got one off the other car's driver. We're still digging for data there, but his out-calls haven't given up much. Yet."

"These guys were too meticulous." I checked the gutted rear seat as well. On the floor, the flaky black remains of an empty file folder. "Nothing salvageable there, I suppose. Except for intent. Random South American gangbangers don't generally carry paperwork with them."

"Some rushed delivery? Something a boss didn't want on their phones?"

"Like a photo of me, maybe?"

"You're right popular with the socio-types."

"There is something else." Barnett brushed my arm as she pointed over my shoulder to the driver's seat. "Not sure what to make of it. One of the labs caught it and dusted a patch of the charring there. Looks to be knife cuts in the seat leather. Like I said, not sure what it means."

"Razor cuts between the driver's thighs. Our short chauffeur friend got bored. He didn't expect to be on this job for long, and he knew his expensive car was scheduled for a fiery finish. His banker wouldn't care about defacing the fine upholstery."

"So, he planned to cook this wagon from the git-go?" Pedersen said. "Or maybe a driver with a grudge? Maybe he left you alive to get back at his boss for back-seat driving."

"No. Not simply acting out," I said, and gently cleared a touch of surrounding leather ash. "Graffiti resembling a gang member marking his territory. Remove these odd branches from the S-line, those are initials. F-S. I've seen similar."

"Not anything I recognize from Planet Ninth Ward." He then checked Barnett for her reaction.

"Remember I mentioned the leader's language and accent, possibly Brazillian?" I said. "If I am not reaching too much…I'd think *Família Sangue.*"

"Blood Family?" Barnett said.

"They had taken root in south Texas until the Feds stifled border traffic. After that they took up water sports, and New Orleans became their Disneyland. You speak the language?"

"A little."

"And you've made a ground search for the gas cans or other accelerant and found none, or you'd have mentioned them. And the trunk was shut when you got here."

After a stroll to take in the wider patch of ground with too much foot traffic in the soft earth, Pedersen accompanied me back to my car. "How you holding up?"

"What are your thoughts on our cop-friend back there."

"If I was twenty years younger…" He glanced to make sure she had not followed, while my look shifted to his belt-line. "I saw that. Okay. Besides, her boyfriend plays hoops for the Pelicans. His hand could palm my head."

I stopped without opening my door and waited. I said, "Ask her what she thinks of an arsonist who locks the car doors before cooking. Her reply may be telling."

"You're holding back, friend."

"Ruminating."

"Too much staging? I already figured that out."

"Keep going."

"It wasn't some random bangers picking any kid off the street."

"*Família Sangue?*" I prompted.

"Is that a false clue? They had marching orders from somewhere local. An expensive ass car to pick up a ransom. A file in the backseat with photos…to recognize you? And why the dump and burn way the hell out here, the other side of the city?"

"So we would find the car and leap to all the wrong conclusions." I held back knowledge that I had a personal connection to the victim. "Okay, what?"

"How you doing on the Alya front?"

"You're stalling. What's really on your mind?"

"Okay. I finally got a full autopsy on the boy."

"Danny."

"Yeah, Danny. A detail overlooked in the prelim, then our Chief Pathologist had questions and went back in."

I waited.

"The reason they'd missed it earlier is because of the—Danny's age. He was only four, right? Well, he was missing a tooth, a molar. Young boys don't start losing baby teeth until about age six. That's what the doc says. So, he looked closer thinking maybe it was trauma related."

"And it was."

"When he found abrasions on nearby teeth, he went in with a scope and came out saying it appeared to be pliers at work. Needle-nose pliers. Like electrical. A sloppy job."

Distracting myself with sounds, I turned to regard the approach of the flatbed coming for our Escalade.

"Christ, who tortures a kid like that?" he said.

I had answers for him, but kept them in. "Danny wasn't the first."

"Shit. Yeah, I know."

Burnside. An hour's drive northeast of New Orleans center, set on the river's north bank across from Donaldsonville, just a blot on the map. A loosely incorporated township, primarily Ascension Parish, surrounded by back-breaking farms with a port terminal to support them. With a Regional Airport, Post Office, Dollar General, and a Subway. The area boasted more churches than restaurants, a major chemical plant downriver, and more than a few cemeteries. But the standout landmark for Burnside would always be the old plantation house. The community hereabouts took its name from John Burnside, a prominent businessman, owner of more than eight hundred slaves, according to 1860's census. Useless trivia, a century and a half, naught but mind-clutter interfering with my purpose.

This was now, as I navigated the bend of The Great River Road. I had come for St. Michael's Medical and Mental Health Facility. For eight months the home of my friend.

The long drive helped move thoughts of Danny to a mind cabinet somewhere in the shadows, but that drawer would not shut. Electric-like flashes of the four-year-old in a car's trunk intruded on my concerns for Alya.

St. Michael's resembled many late twentieth-century hospitals with its clean gray lines, hard angled corners, and descriptive blue signs posted at every bend. A gate guard at the head of the driveway checked my credentials. He then checked his logbook to verify I had called ahead and directed me to short-term parking. Inside, a directory across from the elevators told me the ward, the patients' rooms, rec center, meeting rooms, even the cafeteria, were all discretely positioned far from visitor traffic.

"What can I do for you, Mr. Vagelle? Or is it Doctor Vagelle?" *Standt Administrator* had been printed on the brass desk plate. Chestnut hair trimmed well above dust-gray lapels, and a white shirt buttoned to the stiff collar, all framed a face constructed for pleasant diplomacy. A certificate on the paneled wall to her left said, "Elizabeth Standt." She gestured to a red leather chair aimed at her desk like an open mouth.

"It's just *Mister* these days. Call me Nicolaus."

"Don't look surprised, Mr. Vagelle. Many of our doctors here know your name and are familiar with your *work*." Deliberate emphasis. Apparently, I had been a topic of discussion around these halls before today.

"But you are not a psychologist, Ms. Standt?"

"Strictly hospital executive, slash board member, slash trouble-maker for the county." Self-deprecating and performative. "As you know, we have more than one court psychologist we do business with here at St. Michael's. You had spoken with our Director several times after your—after Ms. Korikova had been admitted to our care. Could I get you a coffee? Water?"

"And of course, I've sent you more than one patient over the years. My name should be familiar."

"Hmm." Her focus drifted across the desktop to my lap, to my sling. She moved a folder, clearing space for I knew not what, then she apparently remembered me in the chair. "Well, it's easy to guess why you've come. I'm afraid there isn't much more I can tell you, other than the Day Nurse went in to wake her for breakfast, and found she had disappeared in the night. The court issued a Retrieval, and Ms. Korikova has not been reported since." She opened the folder scarcely enough to produce the court document, stamped and signed by Judge Tresor, as if I needed official proof.

"Courts are quick to correspond these days."

"The judge takes a personal interest in all the patients she sends our way."

"There are a few things I would like to understand, from a less-than-official point of view. Such as the patient's absence going unreported for four days."

"She had been reported missing that afternoon, after we had established she was nowhere on the grounds."

"The report went to whom first?"

"The nearest responders. Officer Gander, Ascension County Sheriff. I have no idea where her reports go from there."

"And you called no one else?"

"The officer said her office would handle notifications and begin a search. She has worked with us in the past, being the nearest reliable authority. She knew of the patient's background and had been called in on more than one occasion. We concluded there was little more St. Michael's could do until the patient surfaced."

An expected defensiveness in her tone. Perhaps fear of legal troubles for a lack of security in this prominent state-sponsored facility. Perhaps simply an animus for psychologists outside her hospital's control.

"You've had problems with her before this?"

"You are aware that she is prone to violent outbursts. Hence the court's original determination for confinement."

"I know why she was sent here, Ms. Standt."

"I only tell you this because the reported incident is a matter of official record, and you will be informed shortly. It will most likely affect the length of her stay."

"Specifically?"

"She attacked one of our orderlies, and injuries were such that a police report became necessary." She must have caught my skepticism. "The victim suffered abrasions, scratches to his face, a bite on his wrist, and he needed a chest X-ray and blood tests."

"If his ribs were broken, you'd have phrased it as such."

"Regardless—"

"Did you get a statement from Ms. Korikova on her reasons for the attack?"

"She is a violent offender, Mr. Vagelle. But the deputy did take her statement, and only a judge can release those details to the public."

"Are you legally permitted to tell me when this incident occurred?"

"Two nights prior to her leaving."

"I appreciate how busy you must be." *Cut this short. Emotions will only get in my way.* "And I thank you for being so forthcoming."

"Of course, we are aware of your connection to the patient, and any need for clarification."

"Would it be possible to speak with a few of the staff she may have had regular contact with? Not necessarily your doctors. I understand confidentiality. But it might help if I could get a feeling for any changes in her situation, extreme behavioral swings."

"I am aware of your history with—"

"More important to me, Ms. Standt, I'm also her court appointed guardian. I believe I can find her and get her back here for help."

"I'm afraid that would be impossible." She centered the folder on her desk and opened the cover page with precision. "I understand your past legal responsibilities. But it says here, you may have also facilitated her change of identity years ago, and not quite lawfully. New birth certificate, medical records, a driver's license. You even helped her gain admittance to university." The folder closed, almost on its own.

"Ancient history, irrelevant today."

"After you phoned, I put in a quick call to our lawyers and they were emphatic as to the limitations of this interview." Her authority leveled like a railroad crossing gate.

"I understand." Producing a business card from my wallet, *N. Vagelle, Consultant,* I waited for her lip movement, then interrupted any sour comeback. "One more thing, if you could. I would also like to know how Ms. Korikova managed her escape. To my knowledge, aside from staff access, yours is a fully secure building at night."

"We believe she had help."

"One of the employees?"

"Hardly, Mr. Vagelle. We believe it may have been another patient. I'm told they had developed a close relationship in recent months."

That caught me off guard. I was thankful her eyes lingered on the folder.

"Could I not have a word with him? Supervised, of course."

"Certainly not." She had shut down.

"Do you know his name?"

"We need to end this interview, Mr. Vagelle."

So, why the obvious lie, Ms. Standt?

I needed more than ever to interview the people in this building, but I would not get that today.

As I boarded the elevator, a thick man hurried to catch the closing doors. A soldier's crew-cut and a white jumpsuit. Buddy Holly spectacles, a wide *howdy* smile, and three recent claw wounds trailing from ear to jaw. His nametag read "Colin." He slapped the Stop elevator button and his movements spread a scent of sweat and lavatory soap.

"Yes, Colin?" I said.

"I hoped to catch a few words before y'all left."

"Of course, Colin. How's the cheek?"

Slow to process a response. "I recognized you from your earlier visits. Y'all ain't been back for quite a while."

"The circus interferes. I'm sure you understand."

"She missed ya, ya know. Quite a bit in the beginning. But, as y'all can imagine, prison life changes attitudes over time. 'Specially in solitary with no visitors. Only the eyeballs of other inmates, untrusting, too curious, sometimes a bit wacky like her. Loneliness would almost surely evolve into self-preservation, or some-such."

"And is that why she did that to you? Self-preservation?"

"I can see how y'all might think that. But everyone else knows she's just a violent criminal with a psychotic history and a hatred of men."

"A hatred of men. And you just wanted to show her how she should be more appreciative of your *manliness.*"

"I believe y'all are trying to provoke me, Mr. Vagelle." He closed the gap to prove his size advantage.

"Funny. I thought that's what you were attempting." I adjusted my arm in the sling to signal a posture of helplessness.

"M'kay." His mocking grin spread.

"I usually charge for my advice, but this one's for free."

"Yeah?"

"If you have difficulty assaulting a frightened woman, think twice before you take on someone closer to your size."

There was the spark. Then the telegraph as his thick right shoulder twitched half-a-second before the throw. I turned easily, and his fist crashed into the elevator wall. He grunted, bent, and grabbed his wrist. I pushed the button continuing our descent.

"And a game of wits," I stepped on his spectacles as the doors shooshed opened, "is better waged on someone closer to your own grade-point average."

"'Tain't over." His teeth got in the way of his threat. "And if you ever find her, I hope to God y'all bring her back here for a nice siesta."

I watched until the elevator doors shut him in. An ounce of payback for what he had put Alya through, but I knew when he boarded the elevator, this would not end here. Exiting the building I pulled his wallet from my pocket and read Colin's driver's license. "Charles Fend." A name also repeated elsewhere in the billfold. I left the credit cards untouched and returned it to my pocket. Maybe an interested cop-friend could grab a thumb print. Then he can return here with me for a legally sanctioned questioning.

A thought took my foot off the gas as I drove past the gate guard. I braked, convinced Colin would follow, knowing if he lost sight of my Mercedes he would expect my turn for the Sheriff's office in Gonzales, or for the Interstate and home. Both meant I'd be headed east.

I passed a low-growth farm of tomatoes and soy, then the taller stalks of a cornfield with harvest a few months away. The road bent right. I could see behind, through to the crossroad. My wheels coasted off the pavement onto stiff gravel, and I slammed into park. If he tried catching up, the corn would block his view until he was well past. I gave him five minutes to make his decision.

I imagined Alya cornered, maybe in her room. He said she was isolated. Frightened of her own reactions, she would have been avoiding any close personal contact—so, he had to come to her.

I lifted the Sig Sauer from its holster beneath the center console. He would not approach me unarmed a second time.

Two nights after his attack, she made her escape. A friend helped? Someone who understood her fears. Someone she confided in. A self-admitting patient? He came and left during daylight hours. He could have blocked a door lock. Maybe he lifted an employee's swipe card. I needed to check hospital security measures. I doubted I could get a court order to view the camera footage.

A burgundy '68 Camaro flew the turn with Colin-Charles at the wheel. He missed me completely. Rage does that. I was almost sorry.

Nine

Alya

Not burrowing, Rikki-Tikki-Tavi…

I spent half the day roaming, wondering what to do, never straying too far from Patty P.I.'s offices. Once every hour or two, I returned to the parking garage attached to her building and checked her slot. Number 52, Level B—my memory working better, okay.

All day with no callback, I worried for her. The one person, or one of two, guaranteed to answer my calls no matter how busy.

Every ping of the elevator tempted me to go up to her office to assure myself. But that would be foolish. She would call if she could. I also thought on my appearance, the calculated mess I made of myself so the New Orleans nightcrawlers would leave me alone. Building Security would drop on me the moment I entered her lobby.

Near sundown I strolled past Patty's favorite places. A beignet pastry shop, a favorite lunch spot, The Clam Bucket—always on the lookout for her Lexus. I did my best not to linger at the windows fearing a mutual friend, or enemy, might recognize me. Catching my own window reflection startled me, then as I continued, I used as many reflective surfaces as I could without being obvious. Car mirrors and shiny bumpers, door windows, storefronts. I even looked too long at a cowboy's silver sunglasses as he approached before turning sharply away.

"Paranoia, right on track and full-steam ahead," Vetty once said in Group.

Finally, all that hiking had me daydreaming on food. To avoid the eyes in any sit-down restaurant, I stopped for carryout, a slice of pizza and bottled sweet tea. I carried it to the parking garage, where I ate seated on a striped sawhorse in a shadowy corner of Level B. The corner might be a viable spot to spend the night free of curious hobos like myself. The pizza taste made me sad, reminding me how many months I had been locked away from everything I loved.

Quitting time, garage elevators opened and closed with regularity. I merged with a deeper corner, away from the headlights, as the car herd thinned. Noise, mostly mindless chatter from office workers escaping the day's drudgery with opinions on food or alcohol or sex.

Much later I alerted to sounds of the garage gate lifting before a gleaming chocolate Lexus sped too quickly up the ramp and slid with a jolt into bay 56. The driver's door opened and the dome light revealed handsome Agent Brown, Patty's right-hand man. He pushed out slow, and hurried with a limp to the elevators. I ran to catch him.

"Devon!"

Startled, one hand flew up to halt me as the other drew a pistol from his belt.

"Devon, it's me."

"Alya?" Relaxing, still uncertain, then more so as I stepped beneath the harsh lights, he straightened and lowered his HK to his thigh.

"*Izvineniye*—Sorry, I mean. I did not want to startle. I—" I wiped my hands on my slacks. Pushed back the babushka. Smoothed my hair. "I am a mess. I know."

"You're out of the hospital." Concerned, he scanned the garage. "I know you've been having a rough time. We all heard. Would you like to come up to the office?" He replaced the HK at his belt but continued checking for garage movement.

"Oh, no. No. Um…I should not be here. I know. I just came for— I need to see Patty." Now, I looked around. He felt wrong to me. "Is she not working today? She does not answer her phone."

"You haven't heard? Patty's been missing." *Uncertain?* "It's…It's been a few days. We can't get ahold of her either."

"No. Has she been—?"

"Everyone's searching. Police, even…our office has dropped all other cases to focus on finding her." *Something not genuine.* His stare, the wavering, the way he turned them slowly back to me. He held my stare as if trying too hard for *sincerity.* I knew that look.

"Her car—" I backed a step. "Did she—?"

"They found her car a couple nights back. Up in Ol' Metairie."

"Why would she—?"

"We don't know anything else, Alya. She might've been heading for the Causeway, or Louis Armstrong."

"The airport?"

"Or someone stole her car and dumped it up there. Or she might have been going to your old place in the French Quarter."

"I am sure the cops checked my apartment." I took another back-step. "Though it is nowhere close to Met-ai-rie."

"C'mon upstairs. If you're with me, security won't bother you, and the office is empty by now anyway. If you like, I can check before you go in." He came forward, reaching for my hand.

He knows I do not shake hands.

I spun and raced for the broken geometry of shadows.

"Wait!" He continued for me. "Alya—!"

I threw the sawhorse behind me and kept racing, zigzagging between cars toward the exit ramp. He ran after, but with that limp. I skirted the bumper of a new Porsche, slammed both hands onto the fender, and the alarm bleated and echoed throughout the concrete cave. That slowed him, scanning for witnesses. He was in good shape, but I was always a fast runner. His new injury sealed the outcome.

When I glanced behind, he had the HK back in hand. That answered my every doubt.

"Damn you!" I yelled, and tears surprised me. *Betrayal. Did he do something to Patty?*

He failed to keep up, and I lost him in the bump and squeeze of sidewalk traffic. Crowds unavoidable now. Self-preservation overruled my lesser fears. I slowed to a speed-walk.

But last night's tentacles reappeared everywhere. Tentacle-fingers. The hands of the crowd. Eyes that followed. Laughter from the shadows meant only for me.

I changed direction, side-streets or well-lit alleys when I could. Any light became my ally. Even bright windows hinted of sanctuary from the dark. North, then northwest, then north again, until I realized I headed toward Old Metairie. *Was he telling the truth?*

Through Middle-City, not yet morning, I suffered short trolley rides to get there. Uptown Canal St. on the Red Line. I blinked for a second, and when I could see again, we had arrived at this trolley's *final destination.* The Cemeteries Hub Station.

Either ride back the way you came, Alya, or get off and find another way forward. I got off at the Cemeteries.

Perfect irony. I knew this place too well. Canal St. meets Canal Blvd. to be surrounded by a neighborhood of graveyards sometime before dawn. Cypress Grove Cemetery, Greenwood Cemetery, Holt Cemetery, Masonic Cemetery No.1.

My intended target, Old Metairie, lay farther west, but I mired myself here in these haunts.

East of me spread City Park, with terrifying memories. Our last case. *Hades.* This place began with meeting a beautiful and suffering young Posey who had been raped and abducted and tortured...

An overture leading to my own *lifelong horror* reintroducing itself. Memories tore through me. Again.

Soft dirt puffed with my toe-kick beneath a sign for the Canal Boulevard bus line. That would eventually U-turn at the Lakeview Loop, Pontchartrain Blvd, outside the West End Marina. The thought scared me almost as much as standing in the dark, amid all these cemeteries, while remembering evil men.

The night gave way to a sharp, rhythmic clapping on the stones. High heels. And like an apparition, a stick insect woman came running under LED streetlights. A blue-white face framed in elbow length, blood-red hair that shimmered too much. *A cheap wig. Did I see her on the trolley?* Maybe not. I had avoided passengers leering. Also, she came from the wrong direction, from Greenwood Cemetery.

"Wait!" she called.

I waited, nerves quivering.

C-PTSD, child trauma, made me fearful of so much. Too suspicious of everyone, every little thing. So, to prove myself normal, I refused to move.

The wraith-woman slowed to a trot, growing taller as she neared. She wore skinny jeans with intentional slashes. Stripes of white flesh exposed. A short white feather vest with bare arms and midriff. Her shoes, flecked with dried mud, might match the shiny redness of her hair.

"Thank you so much. You're sweet." She twisted her neck like a jittery heron. "I—There were two men. They chased me, but maybe they were drunk. They couldn't keep up." Blood red nails to match the wig. A colorless black-line butterfly tattoo filled the back of one hand. A gentle web line turned to script and traveled up the arm to her shoulder. She touched my elbow, and I pulled away too fast. "Sorry if I scared you."

"I do not see anyone now. You are okay."

"Your accent—are you Russian?"

"Lithuanian." My lie reflex.

She lowered a hand to her purse, flashed large teeth, and drew out a cigarette. She offered, and I shook my head.

"I should buy my ticket. The bus driver looks to be leaving soon."

"Here. Let me buy your ticket," she said around the cigarette in her teeth. I'm going up too."

I protested, but she touched my hand again and handed the fare to the attendant. "Two, please."

The bus readied for leaving. We might make the loop by sunrise. I took the first seat to avoid the congregation behind me. She sat beside me, *of course,* regardless of the empty seats. Headlights glared back at me through the bus windshield.

The driver frowned at my escort and asked once if I was okay. Butterfly lady never stopped talking. Her breath on my ear kept me from hearing most, or responding. I shivered.

"You okay, darlin?" *That smile. Those teeth.* I nodded my response. A question I could not hear, then something about me wanting to make "good money." The shreds of my thinking narrowed and fixed on my harbor destination.

Leaving my seat at the top of the loop, with my brain sapped and thick with whatever remained, my companion called out.

"Sorry if I talked your ear off, luv." Her smile bent. The words followed me past the driver's seat, and he pursed his lips for me. "I had me a scare back there, and I always talk too much when I'm scared. You have a blessed day, now."

I believe I said, *You too,* as I stepped free of the final stair.

With early traffic sparse enough that I did not die crossing the streets, I managed a wide patch of grass. A few parking lots. Finally, draining the last of my strength, I reached the water's edge. The forest of sailboat spears thrust up through the wicked orange sunrise. The low, gray harbor wall held me upright.

Once upon a time, this began my life here. This New Orleans safe harbor. At nineteen—*stowed away* on a cargo ship. We docked days before a hurricane destroyed this West End. Among Poseidon's yacht wrecks, I lived here for my first weeks, stealing what I needed, survival, until *he* found me.

Mr. Vagelle, early in his "consulting" business, searching for a rich woman's Shih Tzu, but finding trouble. I managed to help, *chut'-chut'* (in small ways), and he answered with a reward that made me question his sanity.

His kindness, a stranger, it reshaped me. For nine years he was my school. My life guide. *Until the horror of that last case.*

But this was where he first found me.

With sunrise revealing the docks, the slap and clang of boat rigging, gulls crying, water licking at the curved hulls, early morning sailors calling to their comrades. The bitter smells of Algae blooms, saltwater, and fish…

…all…all stabbing at my heart. I trembled against the railing. Everything I had gained since my arrival here…my decade's struggle was a past now lost to me. Even *him*, lost to me.

I plopped down with my back to the wall, my face in my arms.

I woke beneath a high summer sun, my layers of clothing baking against my flesh. My head felt cooked. I rose stiff-legged, teetered. When I could, I fled for the shadows.

Before ducking into the alcove of a ladies' room, I glanced back. A big man, an olive coat too heavy for the season, swiveled his face like he'd been caught shoplifting. He pretended moving fish crates.

Under a missing restroom mirror, replaced with graffiti, I splashed my face and neck and imagined a reflection more hideous as a result.

I am okay with it.

TEN

Vagelle

Opening my apartment the sensation hit me that I had made a wrong turn somewhere and wandered into unfamiliar territory. The feeling scattered like microbats the moment I glimpsed the uniform by my window. A plain clothes sergeant named Breize occupied the swivel chair with his back to the black L-desk—Alya's desk—cleaning his fingernails with a toothpick. A shard of resentment stuck. Across the room, Pedersen leaned his elbows on the dining table. Captain Beaudry lounged in my wingback chair by the fireplace, legs outstretched, crossed at the ankles, the only one who did not look up as I entered. His shoe polish of primary importance, no doubt.

"How's the arm?" he said to the shoes. Breize moved the toothpick from his nails to his teeth.

"I don't recall handing out keys at the Policeman's Ball." I further opened the door at my back and moved clear of the frame, indicating they could exit.

"We don't need keys." Beaudry finally lifted his head. "This apartment is still a crime scene, and you are only allowed in here by my permission."

"My apartment was never broken into, so crime scene would be an exaggeration. You didn't find what you were looking for with the last search?" I connected with Pedersen. He would play mute in the presence of his superior.

"And you have made a habit out of tearing down crime scene tape, haven't you, Mr. Consultant? So what were you looking for over at *Miss* Korikova's place?" He hissed on the Miss. "Did you manage to find her? Maybe you instructed her on how to avoid the new arrest warrant?"

"She could teach you."

"'Scuze me?"

"It took four of you to break into my home. If you had a warrant for me, I'd be making paper airplanes by now. So tell me why you are denting my favorite chair cushion, then you can go."

"Gettin uppity, civilian." Breize sneered. "Y'all mind that now."

"You were seen leaving her apartment carrying a large shoulder bag." Beaudry did not smirk. "I want it."

I looked at Sgt. Breize. "That was your stakeout?"

He shrugged.

"Okay," Beaudry said. "You're not under arrest, yet. But I need a few answers."

"If it's about *Ms.* Korikova, you know I wouldn't say anything, even if I knew where she was."

"Which is why I won't ask about her. Or about an incident out at the Crazy Palace. I'll let the Sheriffs harass you on that. It's not my jurisdiction. I'm here to look you in the eye while you lie about the dead boy."

"Danny," I said.

"Yes, Daniel Howse. *That* Danny. I need you to tell me about your relationship to him. And to his old man. And before you get all creative with your memory, I'll let you know that I read about the family curse and your early involvement. Not your finest hour, eh?"

"If you've read the case, and the trial notes, then there's nothing more to tell. The father, Roderick Howse, was the eight-year-old son of a killer. He was present when his mother died. I had not seen him since that trial, then, all of a sudden, he showed up at my door saying he has a son that's been kidnapped."

"And he thought you were the perfect man to handle a ransom exchange. After all your *commendable* history with his family. That's it? I'm expected to swallow that drivel?"

"Unless you want me to get more *creative.*"

"So, you know nothing." He continued his glare, hoping I'd blink, or maybe confess to new atrocities I was yet unaware of. He emptied his lungs in an effort to push his weight off my cushion. "But you still managed to shoot and kill four men on a deserted highway, with nothing to show except a Band-Aid on your shoulder."

"A crackerjack police Captain like yourself could use a lesson in public relations."

"You're pushing, *consultant.*" Spittle gathered in the corners of his mouth. He flicked one of my business cards at the fake fireplace.

"And you're the one who broke in here with all this police back-up to tell me your case is floundering with a dead-fish investigation, and gang members I helped take off your street. I already have a court date for that. Come on, Beaudry. They weren't even taxpayers, and I doubt you could drag them to a voting booth when you run for Mayor."

"Vagelle?" Pedersen warned. Brieze lifted off Alya's swivel chair and flicked his toothpick at the fireplace, falling short.

I wanted to follow up with an ugly impulse. Instead, "I apologize, Captain. We've both had a lousy week."

The bomb temporarily defused, sort of, they all made it past me, and down the stairs, and I heard the first-floor door close before I shut mine.

I put on a pot of tea with my burner dialed low. Five minutes later the kettle whistled and the street door buzzed. Shoe leather slapped the stairs to my landing as I filled a cup. "It's open, Frank."

"What did he forget to tell me?" I said.

"You got a beer in there?"

"No."

"I guess tea is okay." Pedersen took the cup hand-off and the spoon. He knew where I kept the sugar bowl. "Well, there was something else."

Having anticipated, I had already crossed the dining area to stand beside the black desk, studying headlights and foot traffic three stories below. He returned to his place at the dining table, stirring his cup far longer than necessary. I gave him time.

"It was something I found. With Beaudry out of the way, I should tell you about it. I did the research. Do you remember the name Jamie Anders?"

I set my cup on the windowsill.

"An active investigation two years ago," he said. "Not my case, but I knew about it."

"A six-year-old went missing." Heavy falling mist blurred the streetlights almost on cue. A pigeon touched the sill before noticing me and fluttering off.

"Eight months later a tour boat pilot found partial remains out near Segnette Park." His spoon ticked again, while I waited again. "Ever hear of Victor Delcour?"

"The Delcour family. Big money in trading. A family said to have had ties to the Sicilians back in the 1940s. More recent generations seemed to have cleaned up the family business, then, 2013…three-year-old Victor vanishes."

"Big money is thrown at the investigation," he said. "Private detectives. A large reward offered for information. For the longest time the Guatemalan *au pair* was everyone's chief suspect. She'd run off, they thought, until the day they found her weed-choked body floating out near Jesuit Bend."

"Eventually, the boy's parents got the ransom note." I forgot my cup on the sill and found myself standing at the head of the dining table, staring down at him, while he stared into his cup. "How many?"

"Six possibles. 2013 is my oldest, *maybe,* so far. I've been assigned a small team."

"How small?"

"Two, not counting me. They have such confidence."

"Well, I hand it to you on this one. A lot of kids go missing in this state every year. It was a good catch, with the teeth."

"I'm still not sure of them all. The Anders boy was only partial remains. After what a gator can do out there…but the coroner report said the skull was mostly intact."

"Except for the missing tooth. And Victor Delcour was never found, but the ransom note came with two eyeteeth wrapped in plastic."

"Yep. There is that."

Into the kitchen, I took a small baggie from the cupboard, crossed back to fireplace, and used the baggie to pick up the discarded toothpick. I zipped it, and for lack of a quicker option, dropped it into a desk drawer. Pedersen watched in silence. With a thought I pulled my laptop from a file cabinet and opened it at Pedersen's elbow. I tapped a desktop folder then turned to stare across the room at nothing.

After a time he said, "I still can't imagine your bo—Danny is connected to those others."

"Open the page marked Manteau, Jules," I said.

"That crew you had it out with…" he paused and I waited, "…we got proof three of 'em were in this country less than two years—

"Aw, shit. I missed this one."

"You connect at least four of your six, and this *child project* is larger than two carloads of Brazilian gangsters and Danny."

"Five years ago…" He read more. "You circled this? M.E.'s notes. 'A ragged tooth extraction proved to be pointed pliers, crenulated—' *Monsters!* He was *seven*. It says the body was found—" A longer pause. "Okay, this is different. *St. Louis Number One.* A stray dog led a cemetery attendant to the body."

"Dramatic, no?"

"At the back of Laveau's tomb? Yeah, I'd say. Is the stray dog a coincidence too?"

"It would be hard not to jump to conclusions." I kept my back to him to discourage his following that *White Rabbit.* He hopped anyway.

"Nicolaus Vagelle's first blockbuster headline? The case that put *you* on the map. The Ripper killings, the cemetery, a boy with a dog…"

"By the way, Delcour's eyeteeth, you should find out if they're still in an evidence box somewhere."

"I already have someone on it." He tapped gently at the monitor as if hoping for a PC spirit to open a door with answers.

"Someone good, I hope."

"You're avoiding, but I know you understand what I'm getting at." Tap-Tap. "Your Shrovetide Ripper was almost nine years ago. This Manteau, four years later. Different M.O., the Ripper dead, but the coincidences—"

"They don't appear until today, and only if we do somehow connect that boy with Daniel Howse."

"Did you get the right Ripper—? Yeah, okay, never mind. Sorry. I don't like stating the obvious, chief, or believing in happenstance, but seeing this connection coming to you in the form of Danny. Or his ol' man? You were twenty-five at the time? Roderick Howse was what?"

"Eight. Let's not get over our skis, as you like to say. We know what appears to be the obvious answer, but we need to find the father before we make our conclusions fit our assumptions."

"Learn to walk before we ice skate? But…" He stood away from the table, glowering at my laptop. "As the psychology guru in the room, you're assuming that boy, Roddy, raised with crazy—his mom killed right in front of him—he probably grew up to be pretty bent, right?" He took a stick of chewing gum from his pocket, unwrapped, and pushed it between his teeth.

"He is damaged."

"No shit."

"The connections are still tenuous," I said. "Check your math. Today Roderick Howse is still just twenty-two years old."

"Which means they can't all be connected. Or someone else is the *dentist.*"

"Or we've got a copycat. Let's rethink."

"Yeah. You're gonna say don't replace old assumptions with new ones. Still, if we're connecting this many dots, we've got a serial *collector.*"

"Or someone who wants you to believe the profile."

"You always gotta have the last word."

ELEVEN

Alya

Just one more of the shuffling-dead homeless drifting along the lakefront. Marina security ushered me to a safe distance from all the expensive floating toys, so I caught a fish taco from a mobile food cart. For my own reasons, I kept my distance from the dock worker's lunch-hour line. The string of dockside restaurants tempted me with outdoor patios and well-dressed customers cracking buckets of crawfish, cob corn, and washing down raw oysters with pink margaritas. I avoided the risk.

I stopped at a gift shop where a skeptical cashier probed me with a look. I laid dollars on the counter with my selections. A floppy rain-proof hat and movie-star sunglasses alongside one chilled bottle of lemon-almost-juice and one of sparkling water.

"Dobre utro (Good morning)." I smiled at her confusion.

Back to Breakwater Park, beneath bent palm trees throwing shadows on a strip of grass. Here I could spend the day far from crowds. Hypnotize myself with hobby fishermen casting their long poles at the water. Pretend I belonged somewhere with someone.

I moved with the changing light. An hour before sunset, I strolled west then south along Breakwater Drive. Keeping my study to the inside of the loop, I checked tight alleys between garages and warehouse shacks fronting the inner harbor. The boat docks.

This part was unfamiliar. Many years past I was forced to find shelter here—ten years exactly. Today, my after-hurricane memories resembled a bomb blast. Now, local money and insurances had rebuilt this into a delicate, but manicured, shelter for yachts. Still, I recalled my process for survival here.

Look for signs of disuse, improper care, *a thing abandoned*. Rare in this prime place of elite docking fees, and Yacht Club fees, and taxes higher than my apartment's rent.

Could there be a shabby boat here? Ignore clean yachts. They would have caretakers. Look small, but with a secure cabin below deck, a bit of rust along the outer edges. Green along the waterline or dripping moss on a bow rope. An ugly duck. I am not here to fall in love.

A bit of luck.

A rift between storage lockers had become a rat's nest of marine debris with one small, disastrous pedalo. Cheap, filthy, cracked fiberglass, blown leaves and gull droppings, spotted with algae and lichen, but this just might float. It might carry me sixty metres across open water to the first line of parked boats. The last line from the Harbor Club's point of view.

The sky lost its color and harbor lights brightened. The first two yachts stayed dark, so I gambled. Keeping low in the pedal boat, I crossed open water undetected.

Light-protected walkways with, I assumed, well-hidden security cameras, but I had time to be cautious. Avoiding curious eyes was the priority. I steered between the shadows of darker yachts, then let it drift forward.

Oh, look at this ugly beast. I pedaled alongside her.

Green mold, more gull leavings, and brass fittings pitted with rust. Cabin windows clouded with grime. Yacht would be too strong a word. *Yacht-lette,* maybe. With large, dark sailboats parked to either side, she could be perfect.

Leaving my beloved pedalo, I pulled myself over the side rail and lay motionless against peeling varnish, listening for cries of alarm.

Could I manage two crumbs of luck in one day?

Snapping the cabin's door lock proved easy enough. Down the steps carefully. Outside dock lights filtered through the window grit. Rodent droppings throughout—

A horrifying high-pitched scream two yachts away. My nerves frosted instantly. Then another, lesser scream, then…the sounds of *udovolstvija* (pleasure). I collapsed onto a covered bench—

I jumped to my feet. Stripped the dirty bench cover. Threw it to the floor as baby spiders skittered happily. Flurrying hands over my hair and clothes, back to front, I then collapsed, this time onto cleaner cushions.

I do not know how long I slept.

A small sound. *A rat?* I tried to let it pass. Almost fell back asleep. Another sound, *like breathing.* I jerked full-awake and strained my vision against the dark. A darker shape in the claustrophobic room. A fearful shape.

"You are okay," Patty whispered.

Choking, I struggled up. I threw myself at her, and she caught me. "So are you." I shook with the contact.

"How are you here?" My thoughts scrambled and I scooted back along the narrow bench for breathing space. "How did you know? Who is with you?"

"I'm alone, sweetie. Give me a little credit. First, I run a successful company of investigators. Second—"

My heart relaxed. "I wish I could see you."

Second, I've known you how many years? If you take a drink, I burp." The shadow of her hand dropped to the bench while holding a pinpoint of light.

"But, I did not know I would be here."

"You've been more than a little confused, don't you think?" She clicked, and the point of light became a phone's flashlight, which she kept aimed at the floor, but which reflected faintly to her smile. Her tired smile.

"How long were you following?"

"I wasn't the only one. But you have used this harbor more than once over the years, so I waited for you."

"There is someone else?" My throat tightening, I rose.

"I didn't have your lucky pedal boat. I had to wait for another way in here without swimming." She flinched as I touched her cheek below two dry red scratches.

"You are injured?"

"I've been worse." She clicked off the light. "We're better with this off. But you're okay, obviously."

"Was it…Mr. Brown?"

She snorted. "Shit, you do continue to surprise me, don't you?"

"I went to your building. The garage." I described my scary encounter.

"The bastard."

"You said someone else was watching me?"

"Not him." She caught my look. "And no, it wasn't Nicolaus."

"But it means we cannot stay here. I hoped…"

"I promise he didn't see you board this luxury cruise ship, but let's assume he's still canvasing the marina. If we try to run, he will see us."

Careful moving near the windows, we limited ourselves to the shadow portions of our narrow cabin. Upon standing, we hunched, but for the most part, sat across from each other and talked. The lemon drink from earlier was gone, but I had saved the bottle of sparkling water in a deep jacket pocket. I offered Patty first swallow.

"Good thinking. You go first," she said. "Any onboard water would put us in a coma."

I unscrewed the bottle cap, sipped enough to rinse my mouth, then removed my babushka and touched it with water. "You should try to clean your wound."

"Save it. We may be in here awhile. Besides, I cleaned shortly after the fight. Use that there to clean some of the mud from your face."

"Have you heard from him?" I did not want to ask, but it slipped. "Does he know I am out?"

"If you mean Nicolaus, he didn't know five nights ago. But he probably does by now."

"It is not face dirt. I used makeup so strangers would leave me alone." Wiping some of my face with the damp rag-end, I needed to explain my week. "I could not stay in that place, that St. Mike's."

"Yeah, I figured. It would've driven me batty."

"Do not worry. I understand I am crazy."

"Horseshit! I don't believe that for a second."

"My whole life…"

"Listen, girl. Ninety-nine percent of this city has problems, and ninety-eight percent of them are crazier than you. That's talk from too many shrinks picking at your brain like crows on a roadkill."

"Like Mr. Vagelle. He is a shrink too."

"He may be the craziest of the lot." She moved to the darker rear of the cabin and squinted over the window's frame. "No, I didn't mean that. But like you, most of his problems are self-inflicted."

I stopped to think. Not meaning to, my eyelids lowered. A fear dream and a touch on my shoulder snapped me awake.

"Are we still okay?" she said. "I would never belittle your *problems*, or his. That was my exhaustion speaking out of turn. Sweetheart, your issues are anything but self-inflicted. I know what you have lived through."

"It is more than scratches on your cheek," I said, lifting to my feet, stepping back. "Why do you keep your right hand in your pocket? You waited for me to open the water bottle and drink first."

"You see everything. Always have."

"When you drink, I burp." Another back-step toward the door. "You always have a gun. You know I know this. There is no reason to hide it from me."

"Alya, stop! You've been away too long, and you are thinking way too much. If you think I could hurt you—" She revealed her right hand with a plaster cast from her thumb to forearm.

"What?"

"Just a crack. It'll heal. I didn't want to upset you, but since you already know about Devon, there's no point."

"Sorry." I let her guide me to the bench.

"They did a number on you in there, Russkie." Softness padded her tone. "You've been free a few days now, I can't wait 'til you get your old-self back."

"I have, a little. *Chut'-chut'.* I have moments—confused. I—I do not like this new self."

"Yeah, like this." She tapped a knuckle on the plaster cast. "A gun, seriously?"

"Bang." Then I pressed her about the attack.

She talked about Devon Brown and the terrifying bathtub assault. She did not cry, but I heard a shake to her voice.

"You were so close for so many years," I said. "You have no idea why?"

"A shadow, a storm building, I think. Nicolaus said as much."

"He said—?"

"He feels under siege. He is usually right about these things."

"About these things."

Trying to reach a finger into the top of her cast, she said, "Damn thing itches like baby ants."

"You said he has self-inflicted problems?"

"Oh. I was talking about the impulses that keep biting him in the ass. Mostly his guilt. But you know that. He feels responsible if a plane crashes in the Himalayas, while he's napping on a Mississippi flatboat."

'Da.' So many things I had not thought on for a long time, now swirling back. "Did he feel…guilt about me?"

"Oh, please. He was afraid to visit, darlin. Afraid he was responsible for your breakdown. That last case, *the farm…*"

I pushed up and paced the cabin, pretending to see the stars through filthy windows.

"More than that. Your whole history together. But I also know he went in to argue with that judge many times. He brought his lawyer, he brought other doctors…"

"She hated me so much at the trial."

"One cop used to say, she thinks she is the Justice statue carved in a block of ice."

"That hospital—"

"He imagined your seeing him would keep reminding you of your tortures. So, his work became…too much of everything else. He took jobs he shouldn't have."

"What? What happened to him?"

"He is getting better. He was shot. Yes, again. But he is getting better."

"How—?" I turned to hide my face. "How bad?"

"Shhh!" She rose.

I corrected my sight around window grime. Inside the front gate, Pier No.1, they fanned out, moving to different sections of the docks. Five or six men, from what I could see, wearing black and shouldering backpacks. They took to the yachts in order. With most empty this time of night, they boarded, broke locks, and forced their way inside.

Interior lights flashed. The invaders held forward what I assumed were credentials. Short conversations turned brutal.

"They will get here eventually," Patty whispered.

TWELVE

Vagelle

"Our only witness identified a photo, said the boy came walking along with the parade, with one of them fancy costumed dancers, and that he looked confused. She asked where his parents were. When she looked away for a few seconds, he must've been swept off in the Mardi Gras chaos. This was sometime after ten." Pedersen held the file print-out on his lap as he drove. "Morpheus Friday, along St. Charles. But the family lived in Holy Cross, over from Bywater. A full zip code away from the parade route."

"Forstall Street, old single-family housing," I said. "I already know what's in the file."

"Naturally. It says notes from the investigating officer say she admitted to drinking that day. On top of it, the page naming the witness has been conveniently redacted."

"You mean torn out of the report. I can drive if you want to keep reading."

"Not making you nervous, am I?"

"If you drive us into a lamppost and tear my shoulder open, I might be a tad bothered." The sling pinched and needed adjusting as we approached the Clairborne Bridge. We drove beneath busted street lights. Considering the neighborhood I moved the spare .9mm magazine to a more convenient pocket.

"Morpheus Friday." He dropped the papers over his shoulder to the back seat. "Sounds about right. Little Jules had a load of drugs in his system."

"There are upsides to this report. It tells us we have a possible preplanned event, not an impulse kidnapping."

"If that is an upside. How do you figure?"

"I never believed a seven-year-old could wander on his own, on foot, from Forstall Street to a St. Charles Avenue parade. Then, what is the motive for tearing pages out of a police report by an unreliable witness? And who had access to that report other than…?"

"Hold on there, pal."

"Now, five years later, and the killer has not sought attention for his, or her, *ingenuity*. The day, the means of murder, the cemetery body dump. The messaging is still ambiguous but it's in there. Timing is the anomaly. For a run-of-the-mill serial killer, something like this is generally a compulsion. But this one leaves too much time between kills."

"I still have a sick feeling about all this."

After dark, the Lower Ninth carried an otherworldly charge. Block after block of fragmented cityscape. New construction, or properties of stalled renovations, side-by-side with remaining debris or Katrina ravages, even twenty years on. Shadows crawled amid shadows.

"Get your ME's confirmation on Danny's bloodwork," I said. "Opioids would be one more checked box linking him to Jules."

"The *timing* thing…you think we have other bodies yet to find, right?" Pedersen tried for the indifference of a cop's expression.

"I hope you're keeping track of all the *coincidences* we keep stumbling over."

"Like how close the Manteau family lived to a certain Escalade barbecue? Yep."

"It may be staged to mislead us, but the chauffeur, René, gains importance."

"What's the common denominator?" He spun the wheel like punctuation.

"Like I said, if Roderick was somehow involved in his own son's kidnapping, I can't see him as a seventeen-year-old and a part of this Jules Manteau case."

"Even so, the other *dentist killings* go back a lot of years."

"Too far back. The timing. Manteau's Mardi Gras killing, then years pass by before the Danny Howse murder in mid-Summer."

"I'm talking about another common denominator. Your reputation-maker a decade ago. *The Shrovetide* killer? Shrove Tuesday is the final day of that clown-show, Mardi Gras."

"You don't need to instruct me on my own investigation."

"I know you're seeing it." He gnashed and popped the gum between his molars. "I'm letting you know that I see it too. The parallels. Then and now."

"Why? Why you come here all these years late? Can't you not understan a Momma's pain? Please!" She fell against the open door, clutching her face in one hand, holding the other to her breast. "My life ended wit his. I don live now. How can you not to understan?" Her knees weakened and Pedersen grabbed her, crossing the threshold quicker than he had moved in years.

"I'm so sorry, Ma'am. It is late. I know." He supported her into the house.

I hurried to the small kitchen, then returned with a glass of water.

"I wish we had other options, Mrs. Manteau." He knelt beside the couch, holding the glass for her. "I know this is inexcusable, coming to you years after."

She hid her face in the cushions and pushed his hands away. "Just go! I can't…can't."

I knew it would be easier on her to avoid adding my voice to her confusion, but Pedersen had run out of words.

"Take small sips," I whispered. "It will steady your breathing."

She swallowed until the shake of her hands upset the glass, and Pedersen pulled back.

"Is there someone else in the house?" I scanned the unkempt room—chipped wood furniture, old dropped food scraps, carpet stains, cigarette ends cluttering dirty dishes, empty bottles and dropped beer cans. For so many, the grieving never lessens. "Can we call someone for you?

"There is no one," she said. "He—He moved out four year ago, and a half."

"Have you had someone you can talk with?" I avoided the crooked crucifix nailed to a dented wall. "I am—"

"I know, you are sorry. Everybody sorry. 'Cept my *bastard ol' man.* He sorry for hisself."

"We will leave you in peace, ma'am." My voice as temperate as I could manage. "We came—"

"You came to tell me my boy is still dead."

"We came because we need to find this person," Pedersen said. "This *animal* that took your boy from you."

"All of a sudden? You jump into action? Some comic book movie you seen? You, all of a sudden, to find my baby's killer? Git out!"

"We have new information. We believe he has taken another boy. We know you would not wish that on any other mother."

"How you know what I wish?" She coughed and fresh tears fell behind her fingers. She wiped her nose on the back of a hand.

We waited. Pedersen extended the glass once more, and she eventually accepted.

"We read the reports and your statement, many times," I said. "We think we understand some of it. The how, the where—I cannot possibly know what a mother feels after a tragedy like you have suffered. Truly. But I too have recently lost a young one, four-years-old. His name is Danny. It hurts me every day."

Pedersen glanced to me then quickly away.

She searched me for empathy.

"I think I know how you must have relived this—you must still relive this every day—which is why we hated to come back into your life after all this time. I know the pain, however I, too, search for meaning in my own way. I needed to ask you…for the sake of the others, other children."

"I tol it all. I got no more to tell."

"Maybe you could say…did you take him to see the parade? Or maybe you knew somebody else had taken him?"

"I would not take my boy to see them devils celebratin. You know what it is. Drunk, wild crowds, and prostitutin. A blasphemy before the Lord's holiday. What kinda mother—?"

"Yes. Of course. I could tell you were not that sort of mother. Only, we couldn't figure how your young boy could get that far from home, down St. Charles, on his own. Maybe his father?"

"That worthless baggage. He couldn' drag his drunk ass off the chair long enough to make a peanut butter on bread."

I signaled Pedersen toward the doorway. "We should leave you in peace, Mrs. Manteau. I am so sorry we had to visit you with this."

"Sorry, ma'am." Pedersen joined me moving toward the door.

"Do you—?" She rubbed her nose and sniffed hard. "Do you really think he did this again? That monster?"

"I am afraid so." He stopped.

"It's—I mean—Juli…They was watchin the parade on the TV for days. And Juli kep axing—for days he kep on axing us to take him to see the floats and parties and butterfly dancers. *Prostitutin*, all face-painted like skel'tons, and them black leotards stickin to 'em like they's nekkid-black with dancin bones, twirlin 'em butterfly wings. *God-Jesus help me!* He'd sit bangin on a empty coffee can like it were a drum…so much, he banged, it liked to make his Daddy throw a beer can at him."

"I'm sorry—"

"Then my Juli ran out the house. And I ran out yellin for him, but he were gone. Just gone. I'll never forgive that…"

"I'm am sorry, Ma'am. Are you sure we can't call someone for you tonight?" I revisited the coffee table, laid a business card beside her cigarette pack, drew a pen, and wrote a phone number while she watched. "Maybe you will remember something in the morning."

"I won't."

"The number on this card is a good friend, a doctor that I know. He can help you talk about your trouble. Trust me. And don't worry, it'll all be paid for. I would like to help you if I can."

She did not answer. Her reaction said I had surprised her, but that she understood.

Outside, Pedersen said, "I didn't know you and Danny…"

"I never met him, alive." We crossed the street to his Durango. A quiet street, but for the distant boulevard traffic and an open window next door announcing tonight's television drama. "The witness statement in the report, the one with the pages missing, I wonder if the officer asked what costume the dancer was wearing."

"You lost me."

"Mother Manteau specifically said Jules was fascinated with the butterfly dancers."

We let the street fall quiet until the boys came from the shadows.

Six that I could see, ages ten to seventeen, maybe. Two carried small automatics, one a pistol-grip shotgun. We halted in the street, my functioning hand beneath my shirt. Pedersen had already drawn his Glock and held it against his back.

"Wha' we got, mo'?" shotgun boy said.

"Lookin like a cherry ride," the tallest said.

"We gonna take 'er-a nice test drive, mo'. I be wantin to visit my rich mo-fo uncle in Lost Angeles. He gonna put me in a movie."

First, youse drop the gun, chubs." Tall boy bent his wrist in three directions like he planned to shoot Pedersen from around a corner. "The one at your back. I'll take dat as my ride-along piece."

Shotgun boy swung hard and shattered the Durango passenger window. The car alarm cried, and the gang circled the SUV.

"Eee-asy," Pedersen bent to lay his handgun between his feet. "Nobody wants to die tonight. I'll give you the keys. Drive it for a few days. You get tired of it, call and tell me where I can pick it up."

"Funny-man." Shotgun boy narrowed the distance until he held the barrel inches from my chest. "And what you got to trade, bro? What you got under the shirt? Another gun, I'm hopin."

I drew my empty hand free and pointed to my sling. "Just an old war wound."

"'Nother joker. We got us some clubhouse comedians, nig—"

Sirens and flashing lights broke the scene, screaming around the corner. Two squad cars. Shotgun boy jerked his head. I grabbed the shotgun barrel and pulled to the side. It threw him off balance, so I swung and connected the pistol grip with his eye, hoping to change his lifestyle. The rest of the gang had already begun to sprint.

I dropped the shotgun and held my good hand in the air as police climbed from their cars. Pedersen held his shield aloft until they passed the headlights. We recognized one, Sgt. Barnett, then he stooped to retrieve his pistol.

"No longer plainclothes?" I said.

"Filling in on patrol. It's easier this way." Her expression flat. Humorless.

"In the nick of time. You're everywhere, apparently. When did you get in the rescuing business?"

"I texted her when we got here," Pedersen said. "I knew they'd be in the neighborhood."

"And you spotted the kids as we pulled in."

"Figured they'd be here, more like."

Barnett pulled him aside for a lot of conversation I couldn't hear. When he turned back to me, he made his excuses. The sergeant offered to drive me home or wherever I needed to go.

"I can take the trolley," I said. "Or you can drop me at my garage, if you don't mind a couple more miles."

"Not going home?" Barnett swiveled her spotlight as we passed moving shadows in a doorway. Just a couple energetic preteens practicing tough poses.

"*Available units!*" Radio chatter never rested in the city. "*Report of a disturbance, four-two-five Basin. Code twenty-four, and thirty-five…*"

"Four- twenty-five Basin Street. That's St. Louis Number One," I said. "Disturbance, Suspicious Activity?"

"That would be the popular cemetery for *suspicious,*" Barnett said. "Especially late-night with all the kids and weirdos and dopey tourists making memories, thinking they need to drop a scare onto their pals. But they never tuned-in for the gangland shooting competitions on the Ten O'clock News."

"It's not far out of our way. How about we swing by?"

"Ghost hunting?" Her profile tipped as if spotting a thing of interest out her side window, but it may have been to mask her expression. "Or maybe the connection with Manteau? You expect to find what up there, after all these years?" She had studied the old crime reports well, but I had to wonder how she made that connection. Pedersen had only learned of the Jules Manteau killing that afternoon, when I let him read my folder.

"Let's say, it's the old bloodhound in me."

We crossed the bridge. I surveyed the street herds as we passed.

"The Lieutenant said to drive you where you wanted to go."

I shifted my thoughts to our destination, as she skillfully maneuvered the cracked and crumbling pavement. New Orleans road crews had become a thing of mythology over the past twenty years, regardless of the neighborhood or city taxes.

I evaded her too frequent side glances, intrigued by the smart policewoman with a professional manicure, a uniform she was not required to wear, but that fit her like she had married a tailor. Her streaked, strawberry hair had been strangled into a knot at the nape of her neck. The ambitious young cop who took fill-in duty. It was easy to understand Pedersen's fascination. Her practiced way with speaking, enunciating with a cool pleasantry that did not quite fit her manner.

I once knew an actress this good. *That's my focus slipping again.*

"So, what are your thoughts about our oldest surviving cemetery?" she said. "Or more precisely, our most famous tomb being the place of deposit for the murdered boy?"

"Which boy?"

"Manteau, of course."

"I think too many in this town love their occult heritage. As to those without conscience, I have yet to attach an opinion."

"Interesting." She looked bemused rather than interested.

"Interesting that my opinion is no opinion?"

"That, and that you might believe this spot has no bearing on the inner workings of the killer."

"Or killers."

Again, she could not disguise the spark. There was that mouth twitch as she returned her attention to the road and said, "That's interesting as well."

I waited.

"I'm glad to have met you, Mr. Vagelle. Your reputation in this city, especially in the Department, has been a curiosity to me. Frank gives you deference in most areas of police work, yet you spent so little time actually on the force."

Uh-huh.

"Sorry. Sorry if I touched a nerve. It was unintentional, I promise. Having read a number of your cases, I can't imagine you quitting because you were squeamish."

I returned to sidewalk watch. Having learned enough about her, I let her believe I had grown bored.

Two a.m. We parked with a corner view of the walls, Tremé and Conti Streets, the two least trafficked streets bordering St. Louis Cemetery Number One. A neighborhood well-illuminated, security monitored within the walls—or so the sign read. Of course, this was the most popular cemetery in the city, especially with the tomb of the Voodoo Priestess, Marie Laveau, at its heart. Possibly the most obvious place to dump the body of a murdered child, if one wanted to blame an easily maligned subset of New Orleans culture.

"You're seriously expecting to climb the wall with one arm in a sling?" she said as we approached the gate.

I responded by reaching beneath my shirt for the packet on my belt and removing a set of lock picks. Stooping to oblige my sling-arm, I held the tension tool to the keyhole with my less-than mobile hand, while the other maneuvered the pick. Awkward enough, but I managed the pins with time and opened the old iron gate as quietly as I could.

Barnett began to speak until I motioned her to silence.

Naturally, having lived most of my adult life in the city, I knew these alleys of the dead. The city within the city. Miniature house shapes, crowded sepulchers and tomb walls of crumbling brick and stone. Some had been white-washed over time, most beaten by the ages, discolored by flood, fire, or graffiti for well over two centuries.

The policewoman knew where she was going. I let her lead. We strayed from the open Center Alley, weaving through the upright mausoleums. Light from the outside made flashlights unnecessary and I skillfully avoided stepping into ubiquitous trash tossed by the disrespectful. We halted simultaneously, alerting to hushed voices and the sounds of shoes less cautious than our own.

She rested a hand on her holster. I pointed to a rift between crypts where a moving light passed more than once. Sounds of a whispered debate.

"Kids screwing around where they shouldn't?" She gestured that I should circle from another direction.

As their movements grew louder and their shadows played across the walls, they became much more than "kids." They moved on a line that should take them to Barnett, but their movements shifted to a more erratic dance.

Two of them argued. The clang of a kicked beer can immobilized the others for a breath. Then they scattered. Hearing their sounds of retreat, I rushed to the tomb.

My pulse quickened at the sight of a small shape in the tomb's shadow amid old offerings of candles, beads, and dead flowers. An obscene collection of red graffiti slathered above. Then, in the loose dirt, a familiar playing card looked up at me.

I knelt for the child first. I felt for a pulse. Cold. I turned the child face-up and stared into the face of the deceased Danny Howse.

A crack, sickening, and electric sparks flew across the night sky with a sense of falling into *Lethe*.

> *"…arriving at a barren waste called the plain of Lethe, through which the Careless River runs."*
>
> *Plato's Republic*

Thirteen

Alya

"That man with the limp, the end of the pier," I said. "He directs others?"

"Looks like him." Patty leaned across my shoulder. "Good eye, girl."

Voices raised. One sailor objected. Limping man pushed him until they moved behind a schooner and out of view. But we heard the splash. Next we saw of him, the man I believed to be Devon Brown opened a box on the Yacht Club wall.

"Years ago," Patty said, "our security company installed all the electronics out here. Right now, that ass is cutting cameras and alarms."

Commandos in black stormed a princely-priced sailboat. Lights flared inside. As Vagelle would call it, *a prelude to chaos.*

"Fuckin maniacs," Patty said.

"Are they here for you or me?" I said. She did not answer. "We cannot stay." I re-looped the babushka round my hair.

With one hand, Patty freed her pistol from its ankle holster. Outside, the violence accelerated. "Stay." She then crawled out of the hatch. I watched as she kept the plaster cast free of the water and lowered the rest of herself into it.

Stay? I do not take orders well.

Aways too impatient with trouble. Papa would say, *"If you see it coming, and you give it time, trouble always finds a way to get worse."* Patty knew this without knowing my Papa. But she had the gun and momentum.

Away from the windows, I removed the extra layers of clothing down to my T-shirt and jeans. My fists clenched wishing for my Kalashnikov. No success, of course.

I cleared the hatch and snaked to the rear of my filthy yacht-lette. The pedalo had not drifted far, but I needed to get wet to reach it. Marina water held onto the day's warmth. I hoisted myself into the bucket and directed its easy drift far enough to see clear of the boat's prow. The other docks and the far-off Yacht Club crawled with the invaders keeping to their mission. A near comic performance, like a movie plot without meaning.

This harbor inlet came with two main walkways, each with four branches. Each branch housed twenty-five boats at capacity. Not all boats were in dock. What there were proved too many for a five-man team to cover in detail in a short time. They needed to spread themselves thin. Patty had guessed they would.

She climbed from the water near the middle of the upcoming branch, then flattened in the shadows to wait. I wished she had waited for me.

As each two-man team moved onto the neighboring craft, I nudged my bucket's pedals gently enough to clear the space between boats. Once there, I waited for the next opportunity. Impatience tugged at my leash as the intruders never stopped moving.

What would you do, Papa?

Papa would charge them with a knife in his teeth and an Uzi blasting. You are still no help, Papa.

I had a destination in mind, if I could reach it. *Metre-by-metre,* one turn of the pedals at a time, I aimed, weaving strategically for the Yacht Club.

The hour dragged pitifully, with the dark teams speeding their operation. The more commercial-minded boat crews would be here prepping long before sunup, so the hunters needed to find me before then.

Or are they here for Patty?

They would not reach me, but they would find her, and I could not let that happen. Not with her alone.

The distance between us widened. I stayed my course, boat by boat, as did the hunters, boat by boat. They grew anxious. And angrier. And sloppy.

They kicked on a hull, or beat windows to rouse sleepy tenants. They broke doors. If they met with angry captains, they no longer asked questions but immediately knocked them down or kicked them into the harbor. They split up. Separate branches of the pier and docks. And all of them too busy to look for my little pedalo drifting among the shadows.

I nearly passed her position when Patty moved again. Her quarry appeared. A solitary hunter in black made the turn onto her branch. He cracked a yacht window. Shined his light through. Then to the next window, the same. Then, almost running, he hurried for another parking bay, jumped onto the cruiser there, hammered the door. Again, no response. He broke in, and back out, like an angry bear.

He skirted another prow and never saw Patty flying from the dark. She landed on his back and hammered him with her pistol-butt repeatedly until he lay motionless. She sat scanning for the others, as did I. They seemed not to hear. Grimacing, she cradled her plaster cast and kick-rolled the body into the water. With a pivot, she spotted me.

I waved her back and pedaled away as the other four hurried along their respective runways.

One hesitated and nearly turned in her direction.

Remembering his missing comrade?

That was when I decided to make noise. I pushed my pedals hard. Water churned. Racing for the end of the docks and the Yacht Club. That got his attention, and he charged after me. The others, more distant, also heard and came running for my noise. But I had almost reached the end.

I slammed the right pedal and spun my water-bug sideways, sliding across the final ten metres of water, crashing into the low wall. I kicked free of the pedals and threw myself onto the boards.

Behind me, the first shot cracked loud and split the corner of a Bait & Tackle sign. A second shot—! A man screamed.

Patty taking advantage of the chaos?

No time to look back. I beat my palms against the Yacht Club door, not expecting it to open, but I had to try. I sprinted round picnic tables and the concrete benches outside, past dining room windows, enemy reflections closing the distance behind me.

Another missed shot blew out the window.

Ducking from reflex, deciding in the moment, I dove through the gaping, jagged hole in the glass. I landed, and the stinging shards cut through my jeans. No real pain yet. Not enough to stop me. Stopping would be to accept death.

I rolled to my feet and pressed on. Pushing through chairs. Pushing past tables, and in through the kitchen doors.

A single fluorescent tube glowed from a corner above the ovens, where I moved more carefully along steel islands that could easily echo my movements. I plucked a glass sliver from my palm.

More shots from outside. If I had time, I would cry for Patty.

Someone had entered the dining room behind me, shoes slow-crunching over glass. I reached the pots and pans. The racks of cutlery—and I drew a long chef's knife and a broad cleaver that some called a bone knife.

Kneeling between the center cooking cabinet and the cold-preparation island, I located the exit. *Someone* pushed a door behind me. I sprinted and came out behind the bar. A man yelled my name. It was Devon.

Course correcting, another corner, a short, dark corridor, and I barely avoided running the chef's knife through Patty's breast, and we fell in a heap. We both levered our backs to the wall as *he* stepped into view.

He nodded. "Sorry about everything, Ms. Gunston." He raised the pistol.

"No, you are not." I slid my knees beneath me.

"I'm sure you made quite a haul on this contract," Patty said.

His eyes flicked to her. I screamed and threw the cleaver, and it sailed past him into the far room. Caught by surprise, he laughed.

"And I will miss you, Lady Moscow."

He grunted as something large collided with him from behind. Something very large. *Someone!*

The two men fell toward us, wheeling like planets through the dark. The next shot deafened me. They continued to roll, and we backed quickly to the corner until, finally, inches away, the frenzy slumped dead.

Patty fought to hold me back, but I struggled madly and freed myself. Then I dove at the mound of men with my chef's knife high and needing payback.

I plowed into Brown to roll him, to show him my warrior face—but satisfaction had deserted me. The cleaver stood wedged between his unmoving ribs. I kicked the handle out of spite.

The man beneath moved, and Patty helped drag Brown off of him. I did not recognize him in the dark corridor, but he coughed and his raspy voice said my name.

"Vetty?" I said. He tried to laugh.

"You know him?" Patty said.

Vetty coughed again, flecking his chin with blood. He struggled to sit up. He grabbed the messy hole in his upper thigh and fell back.

"Little Russian," he said, examining his damage. "I knew you would help me find trouble."

"How came you? You followed me." Pulling my babushka, I tied it tight above his wound.

"Go," he said. "I'll wait for…whoever comes first."

Patty frowned with questions.

I shook my head. "No. We can take you."

"You'll bounce me along the docks? I'll stay, thanks."

"Whatever we do, it should be soon," Patty said. "They will arrest us all before we can explain that the sky is blue, and they will lock you back inside."

That fear sparked me, and between her and me and the wall, we pulled Vetty to his feet. Fear overruled *haphephobia*. With each of us under an arm, with Vetty hopping on one leg, we worked through the restaurant wreckage. The other two commandos lay lifeless, and we re-emerged to the harbor boardwalk.

"Back to the boat." Patty said. "We won't get him much farther."

We did not make it in one go. Stepping around one lifeless baddie, Vetty turned to see his trail of blood on the dock. We hurried him out of his old fatigue coat, and I tied that by the arms like a sack beneath his knee. I could feel where his prosthesis began. We struggled on.

With immediate danger passed, others left the shelter of their boats and fled to the exits, ignoring, or not seeing, us. Sirens came with the morning's glow, pushing our limits to return and re-board my *ugly beast*. *Pipe Dreams* had been painted in flowery script across her stern, the letter edges chewed with age.

We laid Vetty on one of the benches. I broke away from the physical contact and hugged myself and allowed for my shivers. *I do not shake hands* was the mantra taught by my shrink nearly a decade ago to aid recovery from my curse.

"You're okay?" Patty fumbled for my jacket I had forgotten on the floor. She wrapped my shoulders while I nodded too much. I then took the offered water bottle.

"Imagine my surprise," Vetty forced a breath, "to find my *fragile* friend facing monsters in the dark with kitchen utensils in each hand. Group therapy, my ass."

"I guess you haven't known her long," Patty said. "What about you? You ready to pass out yet?"

"Maybe soon." He glanced to each of us. "Who was…? There was another following."

"Another?"

"A large black, bigger than me. One of the badguys had a bead on your back. I couldn't get to him in time, but this black Gulliver, out of nowhere. He looked like he held an orange sledgehammer, for cryin out loud. He fell on him like a building. I was too busy to check back with him."

"I need to make a call," Patty said.

"In that pile of clothes." I continued shaking. "The sweatpants pocket. I brought a burner."

"I would expect no less of you."

Vetty tried to object, but Patty shut him down.

"Doctor. I'm sorry to wake you, but it's about Alya—" He interrupted her. She told him where to find us, and to be careful about our location. By the time she hung up, Vetty had closed his eyes.

"He followed me from St. Michael's." I passed the water bottle back to her. "He helped me escape, and I—I said not to follow."

"No need to explain. It's why you call him *Vetty*. A veteran. I saw the metal shin when I tied up his pant leg."

"*Da.*"

She knelt to retie Vetty's tourniquet jacket. The bleeding had slowed. "I guess the bad guys cutting security cameras may work to our advantage. For a time, anyway."

"It is my lucky night," I said, and she laughed.

"At least so long as the cops don't bring dogs to our party. They'll assume anyone capable of taking out a small army, won't be stupid enough to stick around."

"Like us."

"You're a comedian tonight. We should beat up scumbags more often." On the floor, she scooted her back against the bench, preparing to let her strength go. "They'll rope off the harbor for a while. Do a boat-by-boat search, but may not break into this wreck of yours. They'll keep busy with those already broken into, and a soon-to-be flood of the furious, wealthy yacht owners demanding public executions of whoever."

"That is a lot of hoping."

"We wait 'em out. If they do otherwise, we'll be among the last. I'll lower you over the side if I'm wrong."

"And I will swim back to Lithuania."

"Easy enough," Dr. Maiwand said, "what with all the emergency crews swarming the docks. I showed my hospital credentials and, as soon as I could, lost myself in the swarm. Good to see you, Alya. It has been a long time."

"I know the court ordered you to stay away from me."

Patty tacked blankets over the windows. I kept lookout for curious investigators, but most had their hands full back at the club for now.

Vetty found consciousness while the doctor turned him and examined his partial leg.

"How's the pain?"

"You got good drugs there, doc. How's it look?"

"Not immediately life-threatening, as far as I can tell. With the amputation, they gave you a femoral bypass, which is why you had so little bleeding where the bullet tore through."

"So, an upside to having my leg blown to smithereens?"

"Something like that.

"Thanks for turning your heads 'til I get my pants back up, ladies."

"Think you can give me some of those drugs, doc?" Patty said.

"I hate to say this," Dr. Maiwand said, "but you cannot stay here forever. I have stitched what I could. I can leave you with pain meds and antibiotics, but if you don't get to a hospital, things will get much worse."

"I've been on borrowed time for years, doc."

"That is an unacceptable cliché. I am here because of what you did for my friend. You may be a decent person, but I am not driving away without getting you to real help."

"He will never get through all those police," I said.

"What if…?" Patty rubbed her neck where I assumed she had taken a fall. "Okay, here's the plan. It may not be foolproof…"

"Should I keep being comedian?" I said.

In the end we decided, after a bit of recovery time, we could get Vetty out onto the dock. Dr. Maiwand would enlist a couple of the remaining EMTs with a gurney, telling them, and the police, about this one-legged homeless veteran who had been caught in the crossfire. Then our "attending doctor" will demand to accompany him to the hospital.

"There goes my license if this turns sideways. Heck with it! Vetty, you will lose consciousness, and the authorities won't I.D. you until you're out of surgery. Would you like me to hold your dog tags until then?"

"I guess there's no way I can talk y'all into letting me crawl away."

"I need someone to tell me a story," Dr. Maiwand said. "You owe me that, at least."

Vetty had floated back to sleep, so between Patty and me, we told him what had happened, and what we thought we knew.

"And he planned your escape for you?" The doctor pulled a fat pill bottle from his valise. "Listen, Alya. I understand your fear of medications, but these are only herb supplements. Ashwagandha, tumeric, and a few others in there. My mother uses them to help her relax at night. No drugs, I promise."

I stared at the label.

"This is a nightmare." Motionless, except for the shivering hands, Patty's ordeal looked to be catching up. She stared at Vetty's exposed steel ankle. "Devon…" She massaged her arm above the cast. "We worked together so many years. A friend."

"I am sure it took a lot of money for him to betray you," I said. "And how much more to bring all his comrades? Papa would tell me, *Friends are friends, until the money passes the what-you-need point.*"

"Professional killers bought by the bushel? Who has that kind of money?" Dr. Maiwand said. "Do you have that kind of enemy in your past?"

"It's more than about tonight, doctor. It's more than about me." Patty kept her eyes from me. "It's about something that connects me to our friends."

Fourteen

Vagelle

The night lasted an hour or a week. *The black waters of Lethe* meant forgetfulness, especially of time. I willed myself to look to a midmorning light sparking a puddle of filth in the alley behind my building.

I waited for strong arms to lift me onto a gurney. When they refused to emerge from the cloudless blue, I finally sat up. My initial thought—check shoulder stitches—no new blood. A second thought grabbed the new pain at the rear of my skull. I moved taking more deliberate care. The alley door loomed. A whisper reminded me that slow was better than falling my face to the pavement. It took dexterity to find and ring the buzzer, and I congratulated myself.

Six long rings. Wait. Four more.

I heard the keys on the other side, and a furious-faced Hemmings threw open the door, and it almost bounced back at him. To his benefit, the anger drained from his face the moment he recognized me beneath the muck.

"Mr. Vagelle! Holy darn! What happened to you?" He nearly lost a slipper shuffling over the threshold, and he wrapped me with an arm, despite my filth. Checking the alley behind us, he then directed me through the dusky boiler room to the foyer. "Are you okay with stairs? You come into my place and lie down a bit."

"Thank you, no. Just help me to my rooms, please."

"Are you…"

"And don't argue. Please." I grabbed the handrail.

"Yes. Of course. It would be better. Should I call—?"

"My head hurts, Mr. Hemmings. I believe quiet is what I need."

"Of course. I under—" He assisted me to the third floor. "Um, do you not have your keys? Of course not. You rang out back."

He helped me to perch on the landing, then scurried back downstairs. He returned in record time. Once inside, he struggled to remove the key from his ring, then he placed it on the end table.

"Can I help in some way? Dr. Maiwand has not been in since last night."

My head shook and I gestured to the door. "Thank you, Mister…" In the bathroom, I ran a cold tub while stripping judiciously with the tile wall lending support at my back.

Cocooned in colder bathwater, I shuddered awake to a hammering on my apartment door. Once I understood it would not go away, I lifted from the tub one-handed, slipped and nearly injured myself again. I yelled, "You're gonna have to wait." The hammering stopped.

Needing the support of one hand atop the dresser, I glanced across my old copy of Odysseus's epic, remembering it was the last book I had given Alya to read.

I shambled forward, dripping across the hardwood. I opened the door wearing a towel for a skirt. Frank Pedersen frowned.

"Where the hell you been? Do you know that sling round your arm is soaked?"

Returning to the bathroom while he continued to blather, I toweled off. The mirror reflected defeat. Eyes bruised, lips swollen, I checked my inner mouth. Fortunately, the teeth appeared unbroken.

"I been calling a day-and-a-half. We got more than one problem case, and you're involved in most. Sgt. Barnett—"

"You may want to keep her away from me for a while." I scrubbed my head with a cleaner towel, testing, forcing the pain, hoping for his eventual silence.

"What the hell you talking about?"

"I'm talking about getting cracked on the head and left for dead while she was supposed to be my backup."

"That's horseshit."

"Did she make it home alive?" I walked naked out of the bathroom and let him see my damages up close.

"She told me—"

"Why are you here? Because I didn't check in this morning? You want to charge me with offending your girlfriend, while I'm too pissed to give a shit?"

He spun quickly, but hesitated at the door. "In case you're wondering why I got called away back on Forstall Street? We had a reported theft at the Morgue."

No kidding. It lay in the muck of St. Louis Number One, but I kept that to myself.

"The body of the boy, *Danny Howse.*" He used that as his dramatic exit line, and the door slammed.

Pacing my own rooms like a crime scene, I tried remembering things that should have come easy.

I sat at the black "L" desk, Alya's black "L" desk, and glowered at an empty notepad. The header that read: "N. Vagelle, Consultant." *Inveigle.* I almost forgot why it mattered. Then I did forget. The pounding of my skull made me forget. Danny's dead face in the darkness beside the tomb of a 19th-century witch made me forget.

My brooding curdled my gut. I attempted to rise, but only made it halfway. I did manage to crawl to the bedroom and fall into unconsciousness again. Concussions are like that. I've had too many to count.

He had walked out of a dark past, a past I spent half my adult life trying to forget, and knocked on my door.

My *daimōn,* as the ancient Greeks had coined. A disembodied lesser spirit. A spirit-guide, according to Plato, individual to each of us. A follower haunting our decisions throughout life, sometimes beneficial, often the opposite. Our so-called "conscience," and now my exclusive *daimōn* had been made manifest. At least as metaphor.

He was that *opposite*—a malevolent spirit. A shapeshifter, at first taking the form of a child, eight-year-old Roddy, now becoming the adult Roderick Howse at my door.

Kakodaimōn. Again, it was Plato who took the concept of soul and believed it to be the source of life we were, each of us, born into. Reason, Emotion, Desire, three parts of the psyche. All of which we could not exist without. Plato's Soul became the thing within that steers us, the thing that thinks for us, and when the spirit becomes unhealthy, it was usually Reason that had abandoned its place in line.

Kakodaimōn, my particularly twisted inner-self, arrived in the form of this lure, this original cut. A knife through my heart that forced my life's descent toward that pre-Christian Purgatory, or Plato's *Underworld.*

Because of the child-Roddy, I had changed my name, run off to finish my graduate studies, returned anonymously to this city to set up a new business for myself. Just me. No employees. No associates. One or two outside friends who knew my past and let me forget.

Then came the friend I had found along the way. The girl. The unique bond.

Deceiving oneself is the easiest form of deception.

I could not know how *he* found me, but Roderick Howse stood on my threshold these fourteen years after his mother's killing. He had grown from child to man, and he beheld me with an aching carved into his features. When he told me his name, and begged for my help, a lesser part of me thought to turn coward and run.

Why he searched me out so long after that earlier failure, how he found me, I did not stop to question. That memory of an eight-year-old's eyes questioning my soul as he endured that living room, and his mother's fresh corpse, it stripped me of any conflicting decisions. Reason and Desire were now beyond reach. Only Emotion remained.

My Kakodaimōn took control.

On my doorstep, I did not ask him in. I did not ask about his life, or question his well-being after the courts took him to foster.

But his son was dead before I opened the trunk. Everyone said I could have done nothing to prevent this. Still, that old self-contempt resurfaced.

The child-Roddy was only eight.

A high-pitched scream woke me. So high, it could not have been human. *The Sirens from Odysseus.* It pierced my cortex like a jeweler's needle from Hell's Watchmaker. I grabbed my head with my free hand, the other hand strapped tight to my chest once more, and I threw my legs over the edge of the bed.

The scream dissolved, with remnants of the needle more reluctant to leave. I realized the origin of the scream was, in fact, my inconsiderate teapot in the kitchen.

Then I understood someone had replaced my shoulder sling and covered me with a bedsheet. A melted icepack lay on the floor beside my slippers.

"Doctor?" I said through a ragged throat. A ghostly Maiwand materialized in the bedroom doorway. "Hemmings called you?"

"Correct. He was concerned."

"How long…?"

"Eighteen hours, off and on."

"Hell." I fell into my pillow.

"You'll find pain killers and water on the nightstand. Your tea is on the dining table with soft-boiled eggs and toast. Don't neglect food with those pain pills. Now that you're up, I have another patient to check in on."

"Wait. Nearly a full day? What happened in the meantime?"

"The world still turns." He left.

I wasted the ensuing fifteen hours between my wingback chair by the fireplace and my bed, while I avoided the bathroom mirror because it reminded me to shave. Important considerations for the make-believe hero. Someone had removed the bourbon from my sideboard. My guess was Maiwand. I imagined calling for a delivery, but I didn't care enough. I almost thought to feel sorry for myself, but I didn't care enough about that either.

Zeus dazzled the windows, followed by a cracking thunder. Fat rain pellets beat the glass and I decided to take a walk.

"The Thunderbolt directs all things."—Heraclitus

FIFTEEN

Vagelle

I had followed Roddy for a short time, from a distance. *How short? A year?*

I investigated his third family, until they proved to be decent enough, then I moved on. My *due diligence*, as I had recognized it from my rearview. But University studies beckoned. My next obsession became *forgetting*, turning my back on my life. The failure cop, Lt. Terisi.

Never a thought to ask about his life, or it was my subconscious turning a deaf ear. Alya's *Shrink*, my psychiatrist friend, wanted to see a paladin. Alya had wanted me as a savior. Others needed a hero. But self-inflicted purgatory had colored my world for too long.

With *the adult* Roderick on the landing, with my memories of the boy, any pretense within me cracked like dropped china. He hovered like a prison sentence in my doorway. I feared his answers, feared to learn what I had created.

I walked without much thought to my direction, or the assaulting rain. I rode the trolley as a distraction from the monotony of sidewalks until I found myself on the back of a horse-drawn buggy, like so many tourists. Unlike the tourists, I lost sight of the streets. My mind lumbering in the aftermath of concussion, I barely took note of the hunched man at the reins, and he never turned to speak. The rains lessened and I started again on foot.

A neighborhood I recognized. *Near the edge of civilization,* I used to joke. Far enough outside the main city, but prosperous enough to boast old families who had inherited older antebellum homes. Trees grand enough to wish they could return to the swamps, their roots pushed paving stones in an effort to do so.

In my other lifetime, I knew an actress here.

We had touched each other's hearts for an intense two years, but I was the younger, too young for her kind of love. As a memento she gifted me with a symbol of that first night we met in front of her theater. Standing in the rain. I had been examining the play's poster, a design encompassing a fancy, wolf's-head walking stick with its extended blade. She laughed when I pointed out the problem poster revealing the mystery's finale before entering the theater.

Tonight, I stood across the street from her father's home. I missed that walking stick.

A wretched two-story without lights, with shattered or boarded windows, hanging shutters askew, a portion of roof sagged and pitted by a multitude of storms. Another family I had lost track of, intentionally forgotten by a young Terisi with too much heartache, and an emotional cowardice that burned away memories of them. After her father moved away, with the death of mother and daughter, I let go. I dug a hole and shoveled my work in after me. Work became a comfort, or at least another form of feeling.

An unsteady veranda, I tore down the planks nailed to the doorframe as storm clouds assembled again. I crossed into the dream mouth.

Moonlight came and went beyond the hole in the roof, revealing enough interior to keep me from tripping on loose floorboards or plunging into another hole. A wretched collection of furniture had been pushed or overturned close to the walls. Fetid upholstery ripped, cushions housing any number of small species, repulsive to anyone but the senseless. Transient debris. Trash. Years of food scraps long past fungi, bent spoons, crushed syringes and other drug paraphernalia, the reek of urine and feces, rat carcasses skeletal or half-chewed by larger predators.

Along the walls, graffiti overlapped graffiti.

A delicate and glimmering water spilled from the overhead opening to where the sofa used to stand.

She was a beauty beneath the rain. Glistening in blue-white light, she smiled gently for me, and I stepped forward. A harsh cry, a slapping noise, and thrown rain jarred me. I reeled, wide-awake now, still standing, as the beauty of a great blue heron launched toward the ceiling, then the sky. *A phantom.*

Moving toward a heavily shadowed corner, I followed lines of more recent graffiti. Five languages sprayed, slapped, or carved amid scrawlings of nonsense. Spanish vagaries, bad English, broken French-Acadian, along with two similar West African dialects.

Other designs surrounded the intersection of walls above a minor accumulation of rotted blankets, towels, clothing, and *the impromptu placement of a single sofa cushion?* On closer examination, the African morphed and created words familiar with Hoodoo, with some lines of competing *Voudon*—? To some, an actual religion.

I strained to read into the deeper shadows with older, more faded drawings, until I pulled my phone for its flashlight and began snapping photos. Among the visual turmoil I found a drawn monarch butterfly, with an older butterfly emerging from the spine of a poorly drawn human-thing.

My examination followed to the floor, the exact corner, and dozens of real, dead, monarch butterflies. Most had deteriorated. Some remained whole, I guessed them to be less than weeks old.

This lepidopteran funeral held significance to someone.

Then I wondered why I had been brought here, and who my carriage cabby was.

Patty P.I.

Alya woke briefly. She'd had a fitful downtime, and I knew she needed recovery.

Throughout the afternoon we steered clear of her sanctuary "yacht-lette," and watched from afar until the crime scene kids lost interest in the ugly sailboat, and busied themselves elsewhere. Still, we made comings and goings a clandestine achievement. Once comfortably aboard we whispered, or laughed, of our adventures until nodding off.

I had also slept rough because of the adrenalin hammering in my head. Old memories, old cases, fear for my friends had driven me into a new combat. This should never have happened.

I woke to the sounds of war, heavy gunfire, that turned out to be last night's thunderstorm.

And now, Devon—that dead bastard will keep me from sleeping for the next decade.

Alya needed sleep. I needed to move and occupy my brain. I left a note and made a grocery run. I picked up a Saints baseball cap to tuck my hair into. In the marina parking lot, I found the old Chevy II I had hot-wired to get here. It used to be white many years before the dirt and sea salt picked at the paint. And its condition told me the owner wouldn't miss it for awhile. It still cranked up, so I filled the tank and "borrowed" it for another day.

I returned to her with a Denny's takeout container of bacon, eggs, pancakes, and coffee. I made soft, but intentional, noises to ease her awake.

"Sorry. I didn't want your eggs getting cold, but I'm afraid it's too late for that."

"Oh, *spasiba!* Thank you!" She attacked the breakfast. "They cannot be as bad as psych-hospital cafeteria eggs, where no one answers when I ask what kind of bird lays square egg patties."

We talked as she ate, and I got the new phone working. I sent her a quick "testing" text to give her my number. Before long she confessed to needing more of what I called "decompression time," so I motored off again.

Lunch hour traffic slowed for the Business District, but even back in my own territory, a DMZ felt safer than lurking in broad daylight around the previous night's West End massacre. Still, I avoided close contact with my condo and office building.

I called Vagelle, but he wasn't answering. Anyone else in my life could imagine me dead, and I was fine with that. As a matter of fact, I was thinking to make it a permanent condition, complete with legal name change. Maybe Lucille, Lucille Ball, so I might laugh at what my life had become.

A mid-afternoon snack at a coffeehouse I knew to be safe-eating, and afterwards, needing the anonymity of crowds, I wandered more. Over to the park and Congo Square, where I sat with my coffee on a bench, listening to street performers on bongos, staring at the large statue of antebellum slaves playing music and having a frolicking good time. Irony felt like familiarity today.

"Patty?"

I spilled my coffee, happy that it missed my leg.

"I'm sorry, Ms. Gunston. I didn't mean to startle you."

Senator Holcroft's blush spread his already ruddy cheeks and brow like he had been jogging in this ninety-degree heat. Since his early campaign days, and habitual lapsing into whatever food frenzy put him in this condition, I could not imagine him at a quick walk.

He had known me from my work, of course. Calling for help whenever he feared his official security detail might discover the latest sexual harassment victim.

The last, over a year ago, proved to be a prostitute hired by his wife to secure a more than healthy stipend.

Today, he shared his stroll with an attractive, very young woman, light toffee flesh-tones, wearing a blue sundress shot with a pattern of tiny flowers. She stared at her scuffed pink sneakers with new-ish yellow laces as if they held a rare importance to her afternoon.

"No worries, Senator. My fault. I was daydreaming." I touched the coffeehouse napkin to the drip-spill on my shoe. "How have you been?" Not that I cared.

"I was thinking about you just the other day." He did not glance to his awkward companion. "I should say you look dazzling, Patricia."

Dazzling? Who says that?

"I've not seen you out and about, outside your office walls, in some time."

"Nice to meet you, miss." I extended a smile of greeting for the girl to verify my guess that English was not her chosen language. She scanned the crowd as if deaf to me.

"And so..." he said, "I believe...did I hear your name on the local news? They said something about a possible incident in your apartment, and your subsequent disappearance. I am so relieved to see you back in circulation, as it were."

"Thank you, Senator. I heard about that too. Shocked, actually, as I was out of town when my apartment was broken into."

"Oh, you just got back?"

"Yes. The newscast forced me to cut my trip short."

"Oh, the time!" He had been staring at his phone as I talked. He touched the girl's arm. "We should get together some evening, dinner and drinks. Informal." He'd already begun walking away. "You do look wonderful, dear."

I swore under my breath. *Damned careless*. I had not intended to return to the land of the living this soon.

Maybe I'll get lucky and he'll forget, with all his "official duties," and that personal baggage in tow. It's not like we traveled in the same circles.

Stopping at a public fountain, I wet my napkin to blot the coffee spill. Another stain that wouldn't go away, oh well. When I looked up, Holcroft had disappeared with his "friend" through the bazaar. I spotted the black suit with dark glasses and military-haircut following with his head on a swivel.

I returned to my stolen car.

Still avoiding my offices, I headed toward the river with the intention of circling through the Lower Garden District, then over to Vagelle's building, and back north to spend the evening on the boat with Alya. Without much brainwork, I traveled on a direct path into the nest of New Orleans office buildings and courthouses.

At a red light, I stopped short of parallel to the black limo with the Senator in back. His head tipped onto the headrest. He might have been asleep. I wondered about his, now-invisible, companion. Then my thoughts went muddy. His driver turned, but I moved quicker.

The limo swung left, then right, and maybe I was bored or curious, but I fell back into traffic and followed. Zigzagging turns—Had the driver made me? But I nixed the thought when we merged onto the I-10 at a relaxed cruising speed. Twenty minutes later, onto Chef Menteur Highway, and the *scenic* route through the marshlands of Michoud. Thunderheads expanded on the horizon.

"What the hell's out here, Senator?"

Not much was the answer. Waterside suburbs. Lagoons and things the map called Lakes. Incorporated stretches, mostly scattered, due to an earth too waterlogged to support the foundation of a doghouse. Thin, snaking roads with rough fishing villages. Structures clinging to land's edge, hoping on the next hurricane to release them from insurance bondage.

Avoiding detection, I opened the gap between us and wondered if I should follow him into Alligator Bend and Lake Borgne. But I decided an old Chevy II did not come equipped with life vests.

Brake lights, and I pulled over as far as possible without sinking. He angled between sheds of clapboard and ribbed-aluminum siding, held together with containers and chicken-wire.

This felt eerily like the nightmare barns of *Hades' Farm*. I inched along the berm.

Some eighty yards and across the road from where I suspected the limo had turned in, I nosed the Chevy II behind the rusted hull of a former shrimp boat. Another glimmer of taillights muted by drizzle— on, then off.

Movement, as the tall man, dark suit, walked around the limo's tail and to the far side.

I left the Chevy II to better see past the boat wreck. But the limo reversed back onto the blacktop, spun round, and came at me.

My Colt had found my hand. I ducked behind my fender. The limo sped forward approaching dangerous speeds, and as it passed, I moved to the far side and waited for it to slow. The driver never touched his brakes. He disappeared.

Colt on the seat beside me, I rolled forward and stopped off the road. The limo had occupied a tight space in a short string of weathered boxes, maybe a baker's dozen in all, mostly shoulder-to-shoulder, or leaning into one another. As I got out, the gun went into the belt at my back with my right hand wedded to it.

I halted to listen. Naught but cicadas, crickets, and the clatter of crows. A distant heron flapped into an increasingly stiff breeze.

"Yo!" I called. A dead town never answers. "Yo!" Louder, no response. "Anybody?"

I continued into a stunted plywood alley. The soil turned to sponge, with deep shoe prints beyond the tire tracks. I scanned for stray planks to avoid the joy of rusty nails stabbing through my shoes. When one step resulted in the muck halfway to my knee, and with a darkening sky, I decided whatever had happened here should remain a mystery.

At this point, no reason to chase, I continued driving straight. No motivation other than finishing the drive I had begun. Menteur Highway peninsula. I could turn back before the Rigolets Bridge.

Highway 90 snaked north. The bridge loomed beyond the few low trees, and the sky over Pontchartrain surrendered its heat to the encroaching night clouds. I angled onto an access road before the bridge, then into the empty parking lot of Fort Pike.

It had been several years since I visited the place. And even beneath darkening skies, the structure, like a crumbling nineteenth-century castle grown to seed, impressed my romantic imagination. The landmark struck a nostalgic note, a time machine to my high school days. I angled into a parking spot with my headlights casting blue-white against dark bricks.

The picture of the young lady, too young, with the pink sneakers, kept me staring forward. I poked 911 into my phone and, once an actual human answered, I told her about witnessing a girl being assaulted at that location. I worked sufficient emotion into my voice, begged, then hung up before answering the switchboard questions. Maybe that would relieve a bit of the guilt for not searching those sheds for whatever, whoever, might have been dropped there.

I opened the side window to inhale the briny breeze and shut my eyes. I nearly slept. Then that breeze grew to a heated wind blowing its mist across my face. A devil's breath.

Sixteen

Vagelle

Dawn.

The ache at the back of my skull might have been a permanent gift. I found myself in my own bed, staring at the glow between shadow-blinds as they inched across my ceiling. Then I rolled out. As I splashed my face, I reminded myself not to search for too much meaning in the mundane.

The internet would have the information I sought, but it would be smothered in a riot of samples and additional website links. I knew what to look for specifically, and which of my books to consult.

Everyone who had ever attended the parade knew about the tangential relationship between the butterflies and Mardi Gras. "Morpheus Friday," the Greek god of dreams, a family living in Holy

Cross, and the Jules Manteau killing, and I determined to prove to myself the connection was too obscure. I bent over the black desk and flipped the pages. My memory told me where to land.

"The Dead Monarch:

Interpretation, Spirituality, and Traditions"

Many dissimilar cultures regard the monarch butterfly as emblematic of the soul. Witnessing a monarch's death, just as significantly, denotes metamorphosis, a transmutation…or as a connection to the spirit world.

For some it can be a form of blessing. Perhaps a deceased family member come to assist the passing of a loved one. Or more simply, a great and imminent change in one's life. Good fortune, or not…

In Mexico…a symbol to represent the Day of the Dead in celebrations. For Christians it may come to represent hope: Christ's Eternal Life. For the Irish…valor…and adversity over death…

Alchemy in Folklore:

…and superstitions may come to interpret a monarch butterfly's death as a foretold glorious conversion—nigh on phoenix-like—akin to a firey and spiritual rebirth.

Finding a dead monarch is a warning from those who had previously "crossed over," to be mindful of future tokens…

Finding a monarch violently torn, prepare yourself for similar…

Finding a monarch remains in decay is a pronouncement to prepare for your own passage to the afterlife.

I turned my back on the open pages. Not much here I couldn't have pieced together from memory, but it helped solidify a delicate picture of madness that might draw the attention of a curious child.

Alya

It happened. As if a slow return of clear skies.

It could have been my being away from their influence. Or a week away from the influence of their sedatives, and whatever else they forced into me. Maybe it came from the night attack at the marina. Both fear and adrenalin, survival bringing the world around me into blade-sharp and immediate focus, even for that short time.

Not saying all my internal problems could vanish overnight. A lifetime of psych-torturing phobias, unseen scars across my thoughts, and a repeated opening of old wounds would never find a cure. I knew enough about who I was not to create those sorts of lies for myself. But for this moment…

During the marina attack, I forgot how to cower. I still had that strength buried in me somewhere.

My dear friend, Patty P.I., had rushed out to meet the threat. I had thrown off my own fears to defend her. An instinct. *A readying for war,* my Papa might have said.

The fears not gone forever, *never forever*—and those words in my head caused a tremor of sadness. But for the first time since the trial, I had the suspicion I might be able to survive it, as I had for so many years working with the Shrink and…Nicolaus.

"Pipe Dreams" remained our undiscovered sanctuary.

The following day, investigators moved off while I slept. Patty went out to check with Dr. Maiwand. She returned with groceries and a case of bottled water, and reported that Vetty had improved and was already on his feet.

That night I drove with her into Old Metairie to retrieve her Lexus. Untouched since she had parked it, she imagined Brown had been the only one still looking for her, until he stopped breathing.

"Have you thought about your plans?" The Lexus slipped back into night traffic, and she blew a kiss to her "borrowed" Chevy II.

"I worry my feet are not under me yet. Not completely. I still want to avoid familiar places."

"I get it. Just remember, you have a lot of friends."

"Da."

"Normally, I might say, start your return with the most obvious."

"Sure. Mister Barrel-of-Laughs."

"Look-it you! Cracking jokes like you were normal."

"When I get to normal, I will turn back. I think…" Normal and me were not even distant cousins this week. "I think, if you believe he is the real reason for all this, you need to go talk to him. It was his case, right? The Hemmings building broken into. Can we figure he has more answers tonight than last week?"

"Of course, Vagelle being Vagelle."

"You know him as well as I do."

"Not quite, darlin."

"Okay, almost. But you know how to get close to him without alerting *your* enemies."

"Our enemies." She slowed. A P.D. cruiser screamed past in pursuit of a thing invisible to me. "Speaking of *shit we don't know…* how well do you know our one-legged friend who's been following you all over town?"

"But he sacrificed to help us—"

"Keep your mind and your eyes open. One month ago, I had full trust in Devon. Tonight, the only person I trust completely is sitting in my passenger seat."

"The crazy person. Good job." Distracted with pedestrians moving in and out of the lights, I quieted. *Stop being pleased with yourself just because your brain started working again.*

Against her arguments, and my better judgement, I asked her to drop me a block from my building. She should wake Vagelle, if he actually slept these days. I could get into my building unseen, and if I encountered a serious problem, I would break the light bulb on the first-floor landing, and she could pick me up at Bobby J's club.

She shook her head and popped the glove box. "Take it." A short-barreled revolver, Taurus .38.

"You sure?"

"It's unregistered. If you kill someone for fun, you're on your own. Now shut up and go before I think better of it."

I spied the stake-out through the rear window of a dark Camaro. Anyway, I assumed he watched for me. Parked alone in his car at two-thirty a.m., at the corner across the street from my fourth-floor apartment. Not police I knew, or a car I recognized.

Before reaching that corner, I turned and cut through the pinched corridor between buildings, a path I had used many times. The alley snaked some, lit by a single yellow bulb near the bend, and it let me out on the side of my building. In times of emotional stress, I avoided elevators, preferring the sour odors of a stairway to the tight company of strangers. I held my breath and checked for drug addicts before jogging to the fourth floor.

The crime tape from my earlier stop home had been torn away. I entered on alert, my hand resting on Patty's pistol-butt in my waistband.

Closing the door at my back, I tested for peculiar smells. Sounds. Shadows. With light filtering through the mini blinds, I checked room by room.

Facing the bedroom window, the corner of my mattress felt like home and I allowed for a moment's comfort. Seated, feet flat on the floor, promising I would not rest long, I stared without seeing beyond the windows.

I turned to my pillow, then it struck. I jumped to my feet. The corner of my blanket had been turned back. A small triangle unnoticed before this moment. I spun, fearful, examining the dark room's corners then—*My important thing!* I dropped to my knees and studied the radiator's face. The mismatch leapt at me. One hex nut had been turned.

Habits that stuck with me for my lifetime. Borne of my teenage phobias, they were more than mere habits. They were cries for survival. They never varied. One habit for almost a full decade here, was the exact position of the bolts and nuts holding my false radiator face to the wall. The facade hiding my ultimate defense. My Kalashnikov. Each night, at a glance, these nuts told me all was well.

I reached out. The nut turned loose in my fingers. Another broken habit. Those nuts required the pipe wrench beneath my bathroom sink. The radiator face fell to the floor and I was on my feet again with Patty's pistol in my shaking hands.

"Finger outside the trigger guard," Papa, from somewhere.

I backed into the angle behind my nightstand. Trembling, tears threatened. My logic hung on the edge of a cliff. My whisper, "Neuro-logi-cal Dys-Dysregulation." Of all the many struggles to remember—Shrink had told me to memorize this.

I ran to the living room. Collapsed onto the sofa, then bolted upright with the handgun still in both hands. I said the words again.

Say it. The long name. Over and over, focus on the syllables. Aloud if you have to. Neurological Dysregulation. Challenging brain-works will distract the fear. If you can't say it, breathe it. Until the heart steadies and regulates itself.

After a time, a long time, the tremors steadied. My brain sought recovery. Reason slinked in and out. My hand slid the Taurus behind the sofa cushions.

I was not yet ready for this.

My Kalashnikov—Patty—but she would have said something. My vision bounced. Furniture, tables, corners, kitchenette, my desk. No. My security ran off. The desk chair hovered out-of-place. But the desk had been stripped previously by investigators. I rose by seconds, noticing the ceiling tile not quite square between its braces.

Nicolaus. Yes, you bastard! He would have taken it to protect from anyone else finding it. Or from myself, my uncontrollable self. My *self* like now. I maneuvered, then stepped up onto the chair and reached beyond the ceiling.

I forgive you. I will always forgive you.

Seventeen

Vagelle

Roderick Howse was the key.

That key had fallen into someone's pocket a dozen years ago, and today the police could not find so much as a fingerprint.

No bank records. No tax or employment records. State offices had lost all record of him, or they never existed. No property tax records, no vehicle registration, no driver's license, even his birth certificate had disappeared. Not like the old days of policing, where a suspicious fire in a courthouse could wipe away a criminal's identity. They had all been linked with computer age record keeping. If Roderick had married Danny's mother, that paper had fallen into the magician's hat as well.

I had personally witnessed Roderick's Birth Records during my original investigation into Madeline Howse. Lawyers had needed them for the inquest and during my trial, so he could not be written off as my own personal hallucination.

That he could be so completely erased from the world, not only spun a thicker web of questions, but also confirmed he had not merely stumbled onto my threshold. Roderick had been a plant, part of a more complicated agenda. Some creature without pity knew of my emotional attachment to Roddy and decided his child should die a pawn. Four-year-old Danny, nothing more than an innocent cricket on a hook at the end of a fishing line, lowered to entice me to bite.

Waves of remorse rocked me. *"But that's why you came here, isn't it?"* Of course, the professor had known me better then I knew myself. *"The whips of doubt. Self-flagellation with an audience…Physician, go psychoanalyze thyself."*

"Yeah, doc, maybe I will get the tattoo."

No, Roderick could not have done all this on his own. *Remember, this is no isolated attack.* Patty. Hemmings. If Alya was the first, tortured with her months of trial and incarceration—her greatest phobias set aflame, confined—

Was her hospital assailant a part of this?

Awareness that she would be my greatest torment. The creature knew me that much, understood that violence to myself, even death, would be as nothing compared to watching Alya suffer over time.

Remain mindful. Anger will also keep your thoughts jumping and unfocused. I desperately needed another set of eyes—

But they knew that too. So clever, to eliminate those closest to me first. Even Patty was in the wind. I kept realizing I missed her steadiness.

I phoned a tech expert I knew, a distant friend who ran her own company of animation wizards in the Los Angeles Valley. She thrived with an assortment of skills I could appreciate, one being an ability to listen to details and comprehend three-dimensional logic.

Surprised to hear from me, yet gracious after many years apart, we exchanged banter, a few brief anecdotes, to loosen up. I explained my predicament, the child's death. Without a breath's hesitation, she offered to rip up databases across the country in her search.

As last resort, I called my occasionally antagonist *pals* at the Bureau. They told me they had a few investigators working the whole "child thing" in New Orleans. They had more missing kids here than anyone cared to dwell on, but they would "run it up the flagpole." All of which meant any request from a private troublemaker like myself would be thrown onto the pile and, by week's end, filed at the bottom of a landfill outside Natchitoches.

Exhausted. My world veiled in fog. My own research kept slamming into firewalls. I needed computer retraining myself, but—no time. The clock nagged at me. *Never enough time.* After years of relying on Alya's skills, now my right arm had been severed. The murder clock ticked forward, and *I did not have the time.*

More children like Danny would happen. Not a guess, or an assumption, a certainty.

I toweled my face and neck as the windows brightened. Sitting on the edge of the bed, I closed, then opened my eyes in a half dream-state with a sound I failed to place. I caught a scent that was not mine and lowered my feet to the floor. I touched the pistol butt beneath my pillow.

Before I made the bedroom doorway, his profile adjusted a half-turn as he occupied my wingback chair. He must have heard me. With my left arm still strapped to my chest, I racked the slide on the Sig Sauer, so he could hear that too.

"No concern necessary, Mr. Vagelle."

"I will decide that."

"I am unarmed. Sorry, I thought this was a business address, not your home. Your door was unlocked."

"A common mistake." *But you turned the knob.* "Should I know you?"

"You will eventually, so I figured to make the introduction. I can leave and come back at a better time, but it is important."

Moving cautiously into the room, I rounded the chair until I had a better view of him. A strong man, early-thirties, wild hair to his fatigue jacket epaulets. An old scar in front of his left ear. Another scar had replaced three inches of hair from his scalp. His knuckles told a history of damage as well. Clothes and jacket well-worn, low-cut Army Chukka boots, despite whatever else he had lived through, he continued to spit-shine. Above that, an ankle had been replaced with steel, and the odd shape to his knee told me it went for most of his leg.

"I think you're too young for Desert Storm." I lowered into Alya's desk chair to face him. "IED?"

"This came from Afghanistan." His hand went subconsciously to the prosthesis, then he tried to mask the move by pushing it into a jacket pocket. "I made it out better than some. Let's leave it there."

"Understood." I studied the pulse in his neck. The hand returned with a black coat button in his fingers. The button matched nothing on his person. "Before you get into why you're sitting in my favorite chair, I'd like a name. And maybe how you broke into the building. That's a bit too frequent these days."

"Friends call me Vetty. The real name is Jergens." He glanced down when he said his name. I took the opportunity to tip a thick book off the corner of the desk. When it slapped the floor, he snapped forward again. I guessed PTSD. The button turned between thumb and fingers like a poker chip.

"Should I assume you were a Sergeant Jergens?"

"Once upon a time. Got in a bit of a to-do, and they busted me to private before I *Discharged* myself."

"War will do that to a guy. You did a little time in rehab?"

He nodded.

"Meet anyone interesting there?"

"Boy, you are quick. She said you'd be quick."

"An assumption. You were a Vet. Vetty sounds like a name she might come up with. Were you there for her escape? If you're searching for her here, I haven't seen her for some time."

"No, you got that one wrong, Mr. Vagelle. I left her a couple nights back."

I tried concealing my surprise by lifting from the chair and crossing to the kitchen. "My mouth feels like the bottom of a cat-box. Can I get you a cup of tea?"

"That sounds like a line I heard recently." His calm said he knew I tested him with Patty's line, and he was testing me right back without saying. The turning button started up again. "A water would go down good about now."

I stopped in the kitchen doorway to look back. Was I off my game? Or was he that good? "Your *matter of importance* does not feel desperate. I guess the ladies found each other. Is it too much to hope both are unharmed?"

"Like a two-woman army. I have seen things."

"But they are not completely safe, correct?"

"Ready to *wrastle* alligators when I left 'em. I got past your building security here with the help of your neighbor, Dr. Maiwand. He convinced me to take his couch for a couple nights."

"How bad were you injured?" I continued with the teakettle. "He would not have brought you in otherwise. You had taken part in the *things you had seen*. Somehow they brought Dr. Maiwand to administer medical aid?" I brought his water.

"You sure make two-way conversations unnecessary, sir."

"Habit. Especially when I feel an urgency to get to the point."

"Fair enough. I took a bullet. Nothing dire. The doc snuck me into the ER, and brought me back here before the cops could question me."

"I'm assuming other casualties. And the police are involved. Do they know who they're looking for?"

"Doubt it, unless forensics has come up with trace. It was a big crime scene."

"Evidence is always a probability in the aftermath of chaos. Both ladies have files, prints, and DNA recorded from past work."

"Like I said, I've seen them at work. They do know to lay low."

"But we'll need to move them soon."

"Well, it's been a couple days, and they've probably moved themselves."

"What don't you want to say, Jergens?"

"As I'm sure you imagine, if I followed her all the way from St. Michael's, then into the firefight and all, we had gotten close over those months at the clinic. After a bit, she opened up about herself. And the two of you."

"You believe she would rather not see me."

"I don't care to speak for her, but…"

"I think you just did."

When I called, the doctor hastened upstairs like he had been waiting for me. I let the two of them fill in the details of the past week, and their suspicions on all the connecting threads leading to myself. Denial kept pulling me away. I told myself more than once to rein in my ego. I was not that important to anyone.

Getting Patty's closest operative to attempt her murder, hiring a platoon of killers, ludicrously over-the-top expenses.

Where was the intricate planning in that harbor raid? That was all hurry-up-and-get-it-done.

What had she done to precipitate this extreme response? Something connected back to me? Obviously.

Roddy Howse, the key, I could not shake it. But this raid felt disconnected. A haphazard effort by Devon Brown, after failing to take Patty at her apartment. That suggested no time to plan. He had been on a schedule.

I asked Dr. Maiwand his appraisal of Alya's condition.

"I had not mentioned it to you because of my promise to her." He took a circuitous explanation before finishing with, "I believe you should give her distance for a time."

Vetty fell silent then, pushed the black button back to its pocket and, without a full backward glance, followed the doctor downstairs. I heard the street door soon after, prompting me to wonder if he would return to her.

"Steer clear of Gunston—Alice." I turned the playing card in my fingers, like Pvt. Jergens turning his black button. That would be his coping mechanism for post-traumatic stress. His version of Alya's, "I do not shake hands."

Why the Queen of Hearts, Devon? Patty had used it as her messenger, I guessed, believing I might deduce the card's importance where she could not. So, I had the Gunston reference, but not the Queen's purpose…*person, relation, or action?*

Brown was not stupid. Unless he had a deep-twisted desire to be caught, he knew leaving personal objects, like calling cards, dramatically increased the odds of our fancy crime lab finding trace evidence at the scene. Still, a professional killer's statement.

Bounty hunters, snipers in theaters of war, gained infamy with their playing cards marking a kill. Like a gunslinger notching the pistol grip. This was their ego, building a reputation, or creating fear within their "community." *Or proof of mission to the employer.*

Body count could also increase an assassin's price tag.

"Ace of Spades" was common. Or the "Suicide King," title taken from the King of Hearts who appeared to be stabbing himself in the head. But never the Queen of Hearts, unless Brown was gay, which I doubted after all the years I had worked near him. I'd also have known if he was a professional killer. A thought that vanished, considering his sloppy work with Patty.

Two sloppy jobs, counting the West Side Marina fiasco.

So, by my guess, either he needed a pile of money, or someone blackmailed him to do the job—someone with a lot of hate, and a burning impulse to keep me broken and demoralized. Patty was in the dark, or she would have said what she had been working on. For all of our years, she stood as one I counted on to never be caught by surprise in a bathtub. Patty with her guard down was like a Doberman with capped teeth.

And she was one of the few longtime friends who knew of my relationship to the victim, Danny Howse.

Roderick Howse's record of existence has been professionally cleaned. Before Danny's kidnapping? That's a heck of a lead-time.

So much money thrown into this. So nonchalant. Just for me?

"She say you no like guns. It is almost too easy." Escalade Man said, before I killed him in front of his car. *She. The Queen?*

Eighteen

Pedersen

Headlights seen through a windshield waterslide, alternately blinding, then toying with the wipers. Streets bleeding beneath crimson taillights. Side gutters filled, moving faster than the traffic. My driving sloppier than normal down sloppy streets, I played a fun game of showering the pedestrians with every flare of brake lights begging for a collision. I hated being wet in a hot car on a hot night.

Chatter, never-ending from big city police radios, cheesed me off on the best of nights. Worse on the bnights following a mass killing at the marina. Most of us get used to it with time but—I had turned down the volume to little more than a beehive in a tin box. The drone kept me from thinking too much. Sometimes thinking too much about the wrong shit develops a Maalox addiction.

My phone sang from my pocket. I checked the caller. *Kan-Do (a code name she invented)—speaking of upset stomach.*

"Miss Kandy. I thought we had an agreement about you calling this number only in an emergency."

"So, one in your sack is a crystal ball telling you this idn't the emergency, right Shug?"

"And don't call me Shug."

"Ooh. You are in a mood, ain'cha Shug? So, how 'bout I run my tongue over another po-leece man who appreciates a gal with slippery gossip to share?"

"Okay, Kan. Despite never having your tongue anywhere near me, you want me to apologize. What do you got for me?"

"Ah, 'tain't that a easy thing? A gal's got to eat, ya know."

"You'll get your usual, provided it's a thing I can use."

"Nah, you ain't list'nin. I gotta eat. I'm faah-mished. And this is worth more'n your usual greasy biscuit and egg. I'm all dressed up and need a cloth table-cover to eat off."

"Oh, for Chrisssakes, Kan. What do you got in mind? And it better be the stuff that gets headlines and promotions."

A Cut Below, sure, the sort of restaurant I couldn't afford if I had a chance at proposing to Salma Hayek. And Kandy was a different species. Not quite ugly. As a matter of fact, on nights with the bar lights low, and if she piled on the makeup evenly enough…nah. Unlike some in my job, I get the heebie-jeebies just thinking about a *"professional cuddle."*

The A.C.B. ran a thin crowd of neighborhood royalty, exclusives, except on weekends and holidays. Tonight was no different. The maître d' looked me over like he wanted to take my coat, that I was not wearing. Instead, he waved for a busboy, who scurried over with a bar towel to brush the rain from my shoulders. He almost asked if I had a reservation, but I beat him to it.

"I see her at the bar."

Kandy on a barstool looked better from behind. Especially in a clingy, wet, red something with the back cut out. She must have seen my reflection in the bar mirror. She said my name without turning.

"I'm hoping you called ahead," I said. "The joker at the front sounds like he's expecting a run on escargot within the half hour."

"You're such a class-act, Shu—sorry. Frank." She tilted her cheek with a smirk she thought was sexy. I guess it was, in theory. Her fake lashes could confuse a moth, and mascara drawn as only a stripper could get away with. Lipstick the color of a bad bruise, she tilted a martini glass and drained it.

"Sir?" maître d' said from behind. He led us to a table in the corner, beside the kitchen doors, where the better dressed customers wouldn't be put off their food.

As he walked away, Kandy said, "You look to be in pain, lover. Don't worry, I'll order off the kids' menu."

"Nah, it ain't that. I got—I just got a lot of crap on my plate…sorry. Poor choice of dinner table language—with cloth tablecloths and everything. So, what you got for me? Hope it's a terrorist plot or something easy, compared to the rest of my life these days."

"Hmmm. Let me get started on a appetizer anyway." She ordered another martini. "You said nothing about my git-up. Not bad, huh?"

"It is a new look for you Kan. And those—um…did you go in for another augmentation? I don't recognize those bumpers."

"You're not supposed to talk about a gal's enhancements. Pretty good, though, huh?"

I doubt I'd mention them if you were a gal, I thought, but kept it to myself. "I've been trying not to stare."

"Well, that's the best complement you ever gave me, Frank."

"You're welcome."

"So, I can't tempt you into a bit of—"

"No. You know I don't bend that way."

She quirked the bruised lips as if to say, *Well, a gal's gotta try.*

"I can't afford you on my salary, anyway."

"True, dat." She adjusted the V at her chest. "You ain't seen me since my newest *benefactor,* have you? He paid for these here." She had to underline them.

"I suppose not." Trying not to search for the five-o'clock shadow.

"Nothing but high-rollers for *Kandy-Crushes* from now on. Johns with a capital J. Lawyers, poly-ticians, a TV star or two. I had me a gal last month, a famous Congress-lady who got rich runnin her own charity. Believe that shit? You know, I still don't mind throwin one for a buddy on New Orleans' Finest."

"No, Kandy. I'm good."

"There's such a thing as—"

Dinner arrived on the arm of a waiter who must have been told to speed things along. Kandy had not ordered from the child's menu, but it was a small steak. She devoured half before breathing and continuing her conversation. Her *benefactor* must not spring for food stamps.

"So, Kan…"

"Yeah, okay. As I was sayin this—is damn-fine meat." She talked around the next bite. "This new politician friend, you'd be surprised how talky some johns get after having their bell rung. Mostly while waiting to see if they're still young enough for a round two."

"TMI, Kandy."

"Yeah, I forget. Mister Sensitive."

"You don't forget after all these years. You keep trying to get a rise out of me."

"Okay, *Father*, I'll stop, for now." She tried her flirtiest smile. Another slice of bloody meat entered the unknown. And another martini. "Well, I cleaned up some, started pulling up the garters, when he pulled me back down. He began talking 'bout hisself. Telling me shit, almost like he was thinking marriage on our first date. Like he wanted to introduce me to the President. Then he got talking about our mutual acquaintances. Maybe because of me looking a bit like my momma from Havana—" (a bit?) "He's goin on about some bad guys from South America…"

She had me awake now.

"…he's talking about shit I wouldn't go near. You know me that well. Right, Shug—?"

"I know you, Kan. You have your *scruples.*"

"Damn straight, I do."

"So, about these banditos of his?"

"So…okay, the reason I called you. I know you have this friend. This private-eye guy. And the minute he says the name *Vasquel*—? And he says about some shoot-out out in the swamp, and maybe the bad guys killed a kid—you know how I feel about kids?"

"I do," because she was expecting a response. "You are the motherly type."

"Damn straight, I am."

"So, I'm kinda waiting on a punchline, Kan. What do you have for sale here, besides the obvious?"

"He's talkin 'bout how this trigger-happy South American-type must be pretty well connected to somebody. 'Cause some days after the shoot-out, he's got this high-roller lawyer comin to his office for a sit-down. He's trying to head-off any legal bullshit. Like trying to strategize for any pre-hearing, long before the news hits the fan. And why come to a politician with this, right?"

And why spill any of this to a hooker, I thought. "Kan. This is important—"

"You know I can't be giving out names of clients, Shug—"

"I need something, Kan. These guys killed a kid. Maybe tortured him. I know how you look after kids." Now, I needed a stronger drink, but good sense won out. "And this may not be the first, or the last."

"I don't know 'bout these kid-killers. And my Senator is not a part of the—" She picked up on my squint. "But maybe if I had the lawyer's name. He's not a client. Yet."

"Any name, Kandy. I need *something.*"

"And you never say where you got this? My name goes in no report, *ever.* Right? I have a new life going on."

I gave an excuse to rush off, leaving Kandy with more than the price of dinner, and telling her to buy a nice desert, a week's worth of deserts. The rain had stopped, but I nearly ran to my car. Then, step-by-step, my brain-wheels clicked. I slowed. By the time I buckled in, I scanned the near-empty section of the parking lot with signs for: A Cut Below Parking Only. Instinct told me to wait for Kandy to leave.

She must have skipped desert. I wondered if she had time to repaint her bruised lipstick.

At the driveway entrance, straightening her clingy dress beneath the see-through raincoat, she lifted her head with a "happiest time of my life" face. She hugged a friend I assumed to be another starving hooker, based on my decades of practical street experience. The six-inch spike heels, mesh stockings strategically ripped, and a leather skirt short enough to see her favorite brand name G-string. A white woman with a '70s 'fro the color of a *Go* traffic light.

Their hurried hug might have been prelude to their "gal's night in." Kandy grabbed her hand and they strutted off to someone's party.

I had seen enough. I had things to do. Places to kick over.

Back to the offices, I nodded to the Desk Sergeant's, "Hey, Pedersen!" I avoided chit-chat with other officers during the shift-change. Many still buzzed about the more macabre elements of the marina crime scene, and the expected new humor invented for the occasion: "Don't tell my heart, my achy, breaky, stabby heart..." and other inventions of lyrical artistry. I ignored crime scene humor as a necessity for a first responders' mental health, but I preferred not to engage most nights. Tonight I needed my thoughts uninterrupted.

At my office I normally started with pen and yellow pad. It's easier to get things down quick and not distract myself with which key my thick fingers hit accidentally. I worked to recall as many micro-details of our chat as I could. If she glanced over her shoulder or stopped chewing, like poker "tells," one never knows what's important until they become important.

Maybe none of it. But my gut told me this was more than just an informant looking for a free meal. A real suspect possibly. *Vagelle's shooter?* With a lawyer involved. A Senator, for fuck's sake. And a murdered four-year-old. Maybe more kids in the ugly tapestry. Maybe. This was the makings of something.

What? More than your average gang shootout on a deserted highway in the swamp. But Vagelle and "average" fit together as often as—*the moon, your eye, and a pizza pie.*

I decided not to involve him until I had some sort of confirmation. Especially as we were not on speaking terms.

As per routine, I laid down my pen and moved to the computer. I tried to reorganize and label, and I dragged the accumulation into my Active Cases Folder for delivery.

I hesitated sending the email to Sgt. Barnett. Why? Because Vagelle was pissed after the incident in the cemetery? Not just that, but because whenever I ignored his advice over the past decade, I lived to regret it.

Hell. I can't live with his ghosts too. She's an integral member of this investigation.

I hit *Send.*

I got the official call early the next morning. Not in my District, but closer to where I had dinner the previous night.

Marco Pascal, a.k.a. Kandy-Crushes, lived on the fourth-floor in the Bywater neighborhood with an enviable view of the river. Nice furniture. The sofa and loveseat appeared new. Lamps still had sale tags on them. By the look of the living room, she had company the night before. Well-behaved company who cleaned fingerprints from wine glasses, doorknobs, even emptied ashtrays and took the trash bags when they left.

The bedroom told another story. A story of destructive fury.

A knife had slashed every element of clothing in the closet and dresser drawers, gouged new-ish oak furniture, destroyed window blinds, sheets, and pillows, sliced the walls…and Kandy.

The naked *woman* who had asked me to treat her to a fancy dinner with cloth table-covers, lay handcuffed to the brass headboard and footboard, spread like a human X, with what remained of male genitals less-than artfully removed. Likely by the same knife. Her expression a mix of terror and pain beneath the wild smear of facepaint, a second scream had been cut into her throat, forcibly widened, with her genitals shoved through.

I had been a cop for a lot of years. I had seen bloody horror carnivals up close and personal, and I had walked away and ate breakfast two hours later. At this moment, standing at the foot of this bed had me quaking. Trying not to see her—my long-time snitch, my "strictly professional" relationship for at least seven of those years—made my vision fog.

My stomach caught up with what I saw. Shoving past Detective Arnte, I raced to the bathroom, thinking I would empty into the sink, but kept it down. Seated on the toilet lid, I wrung my fingers and stared at my shoes, cursing aloud.

Not like I'd never seen torn bodies, open wounds, brains, intestines, protruding bones, that dead glare. What did he expect? He chose this lifestyle. She! Most of them wind up in the earth at a young age. I stopped warning them, those like her, back before I sewed on my first stripe.

"Lieutenant," Arnte said. I looked up at the cop cluster leering from the bathroom door. "Lieutenant, you're contaminating a crime scene." Not scolding, simply reminding me of his job.

"Fuck it," I said to myself and pushed to my feet. "Sorry. Not aimed for you."

"Sure. I'm gonna need you to come to my office and talk about this."

"Naturally. You called me down here to watch my reaction. You knew I knew the vic because she had my call logged into her phone.

Yeah, I met her for dinner. She worked for me—I've known her a long time."

"We got Pascal's receipt from the restaurant last night. The manager described you pretty close."

"I'm not denying dinner. But he most likely said I left the restaurant before her."

"Let's continue this back at my office. Do the Miranda thing and all. For your sake.

"Yeah, my sake." I knew the drill.

Nineteen

Vagelle

Hard not to see yourself while shaving, but I gave it a best effort. I showered and located the least wrinkled gray shirt in the closet. I even took the only sport jacket I owned, lightweight khaki, a close enough match to my rumpled slacks. Alya used to say, I still dressed like 1999.

Cory Landers, Esq., Landers Legal, the name had been expunged from the lawyerly ranks all the way to the Louisiana State Bar. Rather than hurt my vision with a *National Records search,* I decided on the quicker path through my personal attorney, Whitcomb.

He picked up without the assistance of his office manager, like he had been waiting for my name to appear on his phone.

"Expecting my call?" I said.

"Your name never misses a news cycle these days. Have I said that you already put my kid through college?"

"You don't have kids."

"Well, if I did, I'd thank you more often. How is Ms. Korikova?"

I asked him to meet for lunch. He had a court appearance at three, so I let him pick the spot and said I would not keep him long.

A narrow cavity between office buildings, the Athens Deli was run by an old-world Greek family, unsurprisingly. Inside hung the aroma of rosemary, olive oil, and southern Mediterranean gardens, a pleasant cliché. An amateur's mural of a fictional *Old-Country* covered the long wall. Late afternoon, the tables interrupted a dark sea of lawyerly suits and briefcases, like no other profession dared eat amongst them. Whitcomb scouted the entrance from behind Olympian-sized plates. He smiled weakly at my approach.

"I figured you had not eaten in a while," he said, as I scanned the surrounding clientele.

"You know a room full of lawyers gives me a rash."

"And who did you expect to see across the street from the courthouse? You only get a rash when you're near the blindfolded lady with your name etched on her sword."

"Be prepared to eat that pricey lunch, my friend."

"You can afford it. Remember, your taxes flow through my office too. Besides, it's cheaper than paying for my pro bono services whenever you need bailing out."

"Touché."

We paused as the bushy-browed proprietor brought espressos, a saucer of *old-country* olive oil, and sweet New Orleans French bread, along with his practiced joy. Whitcomb insisted I take first slice, so he could attack the rest.

"Let's begin again," he said. "How is Ms. Korikova?"

"Yes, I know you'd been informed of her escape, probably before I found out." My fork stabbed at the Horiatiki salad. "I haven't seen her in months."

"Can you at least blame it on your recent hospital stay?"

"That's unkind of you."

"Okay, Nicolaus, I'm done prying. As you like to say, it's always better if I don't know everything." He mopped the oil with bread. "So, the reason for your call?"

"For starters, it's a name you and I both know. From way back. From before I quit the force."

"A name connected to you, your old case. I went back to the files when I saw the name *Howse* tethered to your present problems."

"I knew I paid you the big bucks for a reason. Fancy words like 'tethered.' Yeah. I need to dig back, but deeper. People's records keep disappearing. Roderick Howse no longer exists."

"Gone since the age of fourteen, as my secretary found out. So, he comes to you for help finding his son, Danny. Now that boy is also gone."

"Literally. Danny's body has been stolen from the morgue."

"Guaranteeing…" he laid down his fork. "…your original case, Nick Terisi, is likely the source of your troubles today. Or so you are thinking." A clatter of silver on the table at his back startled him. "So, what can I help you with?"

"I need to find out more. Everything I can.

"You're meandering, Nick."

"Sorry. I'm doing that too much lately. I've started with the names I knew, beginning with that moment in time. I thought to check with my attorney from that case."

"Cory Landers." He folded his napkin, his standard deep-in-thought gesture. "I guess you had no reason to keep up with him. A few years after your acquittal, Landers began having legal troubles of his own. His company took a turn. As did his wife, who took him for most of his assets. And he couldn't win a case after yours. Even his lesser clients seemed to pit him against reps from Tresor's much more high-profile firm. Like he'd become targeted for an official takedown. Eventually, his partners split, then more legal problems of his own…coke dust discovered in his trunk…"

"Discovered?"

"Supposedly a random traffic stop from a K-9 unit with a drug sniffer. His spiral escalated."

"Don't say it."

"He took what he thought to be the easy way out, a belly-flop off the Causeway."

"Jesus. I wish he'd have reached out."

"I doubt you could've done anything for him."

"About *Tresor,*" I said. "So, despite my spoiling her perfect conviction record, still, her ascension accelerated at record pace until she won for herself the youngest judge appointment in Louisiana history."

"Not quite. Nearly."

"Would you happen to know what happened to her old law partners?"

"Not sure I would go there, Nick. I'm afraid they fell off my radar. I recall a bit of bad blood within their ranks. Her getting her very own prominent courtroom seat a few years later may have helped their decisions to relocate out of town."

"All of them? That had to be something more than just a judge's appointment."

"Sorry I wasn't a part of your case at the time. I can't be of much assistance to you now."

"Maybe that's lucky for you. At least you're still on the upside of grass."

I paid the grinning Greek, while Whitcomb waited for me at the curb with his bag of leftovers.

"Speak of the Gorgon…" He nodded across traffic to the courthouse steps where Judge Tresor ascended side-by-side with a familiar figure from my old, much smaller, Parish. A posture and walk I knew well, dating back to my troubled youth. The small-town district judge who facilitated many nights behind bars for my never-ending string of misdemeanors. These days the faded marquee read, "Louisiana Senator Holcroft." He never crossed a television screen without my thinking about term limits flushing some of his corruption to the Gulf.

"I need to get this chapter over with," I said. "So it begins with me climbing the rocky island of *Sarpedon.*"

"Without a shield, Perseus? To what end?"

"Thoughtful deliberation is not working for me these days. Maybe I need to be impulsive."

"I hardly recognize you lately."

Judge Berenice Tresor, once upon a bad time, Prosecuting Attorney Tresor.

Having worked my way through the mental Rolodex of names who might still be familiar with the Howse family curse, Roderick in particular, she would be the most informed. Also, the last one I cared to involve in another of my struggles. Hardly an ally. At odds most recently over her verdict and incarceration of Alya, but she had been with the Howse thing since the beginning.

Back then, a hot young "Superstar" prosecutor whose personal mission became taking down a "killer cop," she knew more of Madeline, her son Roddy, *and my involvement,* than any surviving human. She was always a blade in my side.

Today, I hoped that my unannounced visit might be greeted with less than machine gun fire. I did check her docket before strolling in. Her first case of the afternoon was two hours away, so she made me wait in the lobby for an extra twenty minutes.

Her judge's chambers, as noted on my many previous visits, might have been designed by an uninspired Hollywood architect. Dark cherrywood across the surrounding walls, tall bare windows, two full walls of floor-to-ceiling bookshelves with unimaginative law book titles, case titles, and abbreviations for law-things outside the ken of mere mortals.

No photos of family or loved ones, aside from an old Harvard Law School class photo of a young woman I had discovered in my earlier investigations. Her aunt, Eliza Montrésor. The woman who had apparently inspired Berenice's passion for the profession. Any other wall frames boasted diplomas and awards and a few clipped news headlines to intimidate visitors or bolster her own self-image.

One solitary shelf had been chosen to represent her world. A small collection of imperial jade figurines. A featureless globe of Mandarin garnet squatted atop a gold-wire pedestal. A clay bowl antiquity that might have been unearthed by an archaeological expedition, then pilfered from a London museum simply for the honor of adding to the judge's display. One edge of the bowl had been chipped, the base showed a hairline crack with a tight script painted in rings descending into its pit. *Aramaic?* I still wondered after all these years. *An incantation bowl.* It must have been a forgery, but an excellent reproduction from where I stood. It begged a closer inspection.

Wouldn't it be a joy to send a snake-haired Gorgon up the river for receiving stolen goods? But that was self-serving of me.

Singularly, perched on a corner pedestal, encased in a square of glass, a beautiful urn of crisp porcelain with elaborate indigo designs befitting the Ming Dynasty.

I figured the whole display to be worth the price of a new Ferrari—except for a technical anomaly within the indigo motif eliminating any bloodline to Ming. Nearly indistinguishable from the intricate florals, twisting vines, and mythical Asian creatures, a thin pattern encircled the urn's cap. A pattern of familiar, stylized lilies, heraldic French in design, dating back to Europe's Middle Ages. Fleur-de-lis. One could not walk the length of a shoe in this town without tripping over one.

Berenice Tresor had come to town with her own personal trademark she claimed as ancestral inheritance. A family coat of arms dating back before the Louisiana Purchase, and an ancestor who had served Napoleon's court. Her fleur-de-lis was never overly conspicuous—no flag above the door, nor shield behind the desk—but even in our earliest encounters, she never appeared without the tiny gold "lily" drilled into her earlobe.

I waited in the open doorway until she laid the pen to the blotter and waved me to her visitor's chair. Theatrics.

See, I am busy, but altruistic with my time. French royalty.

Every element atop her cherrywood desk had been laid with Marine Corps parade-ground precision.

As her rooms appeared unchanged, so were her looks over the past fourteen years. Seems Father Time feared her as well. Perhaps several pounds thinner, cheekbones more pronounced with scant webbing at the eye and mouth corners, *but no snakes for hair.* At forty-four, the Judge might still turn younger heads at a political banquet without turning anyone to stone.

An anemic smile served before addressing me.

"Mr. Vagelle. It is still Vagelle, no?"

"Your Honor. I am grateful for your time and promise not to take too much of it. Knowing you as I do, I can assume you have some inkling of why I have come."

"Not Alya this time."

"No, ma'am." Perhaps I expected her to open with *How's the arm?* like everyone else. I appreciated that she didn't.

"Then it would be this Daniel Howse matter. You still keep a vigorous lifestyle, I see."

There's the arm reference. "I don't work at it, but the style seems to have chosen me."

"I do not surprise easily, Nicolaus. I suppose, with so many cases before the courts over so many years, so many violent outcomes, you should be lauded for your *sustainability.* However, I must admit to a raised eyebrow when I read about you working with Roderick Howse after all this time." Much effort and the best finishing schools had nearly eliminated all trace of Cajun parentage from her tongue.

"No more surprised than I at finding him on my doorstep. I am afraid I lost track of him shortly after *the big show.*"

"And so now, he loses his son." A cheek twitched.

Thanks for reminding me.

"That business on the highway. Well, you extracted a bit of vengeance then."

"It was not my intent."

"Naturally." *There's that twitch.* "Your report to the police claims self-defense."

"Yes, it does."

"The child was dead before you opened the trunk, you say. Four abductors, dead. The father is missing, presumed dead."

"The child's death was verified by the Medical Examiner. No presumption on my part, your Honor."

A single sharp nod. "And now we learn the body of tiny Daniel has been spirited out of the morgue in the dead of night. A ghostly apparition returning in St. Louis Cemetery Number One, beside the tomb of Marie Laveau, of all people."

I wondered if she might claim ancestry there as well. It reminded me of the incantation bowl. She followed my eyes to the artifact.

"If I had not followed your career so closely, I might suppose you had grown accustomed to all the melodrama of your profession. Perhaps reminiscent of a much earlier case, the entrapment of a serial killer in your very apartment, and the killing of your former partner."

My temperate mask held firm.

"And what of your other associate, Ms. Gunston, from the Detective Agency? Another friend of yours now MIA? Her business partner killed? I will not ask if you aided in your Alya's escape from the hospital. Or if you have given her refuge?

"You are, as ever, well-informed."

"Reports have been filed by an orderly assaulted on the hospital premises. You are getting sloppy, Nicolaus. Or should I say sloppier? Is the violence coming easier to you after so much of it? Do you have nothing else to offer?"

"Regretfully, no. I apologize for taking your time. Honestly, I had come in hopes of putting aside any long-standing feud. There are few people as close to the old Howse family as yourself, and I have reached a dead-end in my search for Roderick. He came to me for help. I failed him, yes. But my hope is to find him, and do what I can for him."

She stared in silence while I waited for the *royal dismissal*. Her chair moved to face the window, and I rose.

"I will see what I can find on Roddy," she said. "Are your contact numbers the same?"

"Yes, thank you."

"Nicolaus." She halted me at the door. "The boy-Roddy had been in and out of trouble for years. I last saw him in my courtroom eight years ago. I felt sympathetic at first. We both came to know him as a child, didn't we? The mother's wrongful death case."

Of which I was exonerated.

"We tried fostering him several times. He ended up in juvi-lockup."

St. Martinville. The ugliest place for a kid this side of The Divine Comedy.

"I ordered mental health visits. At sixteen, first came deferred adjudication, then probation. Two years later, when he continued to violate, he received twelve months in real jail. I gave him every possible opportunity." She turned her chair to face me once more, sunlight touching her features as if directed for film. "I hope you find him too."

TWENTY

Vagelle

One sees a strange assortment of humans on any courthouse steps.

After my meeting with the Gorgon, back out beneath the cleansing afternoon rays, with lawyers toing and froing among the rough boys, I barely considered any of them individually. My internal camera clicking, not just snapshots of recent events, but steadily returning focus to Alya. Her expression. My final look back, as I walked beyond the hospital doors.

I descended several stairs behind a gazelle of a woman in painted-on leather slacks, a satin blouse colored to match her glistening shaved head with a centipede tattoo crawling down her neck. An idiosyncratic choice. She stroked the centipede like it itched, and I marked the black lines of a tattoo butterfly engulfing the back of her hand.

Another butterfly.

My opinion on coincidences nearly shouted itself, but was stifled by the sight of the man ascending. He also caught her gesture. Approximately my height, but with shoulders that threatened the seams of a crisp yellow shirt, probably a first meeting with a Public Defender. Too tall to be René, though possibly from the same part of the world. Dark-weathered, with gray eyes that turned sharply when he spotted me. I recognized the half-ear with telltale teeth-marks.

A dirty white cargo van, with workman's lettering scraped and poorly painted over, idled at the curb with two occupants watching yellow shirt walk away.

GOAT caught me looking, whirled, and raced ahead of me down the remaining stairs. The passenger jumped from the van, threw wide the sliding side door, and flew back in. GOAT dove into the back. The slider slammed after him.

My strapped arm made running awkward. The cargo van wove away through traffic before I reached the sidewalk, and I had parked too far to do anything but spit.

Ms. Gazelle had vanished. I speed-dialed Pedersen's "mailbox is full," then Patty. Out of frustration I dialed nine-eleven and lied about a fictional hit-and-run by a white cargo van, with the last four of the plate that I grabbed before traffic intervened. I hung up without listening to questions.

Calling my FBI pals, I asked about GOAT, and they were precisely as helpful as the last time I called.

I called Pip. He knew as much on the NOLA bangers as just about anyone. He picked up sounding distressed, and promised to meet me in the morning across from the Trinity Episcopal Church, in the Lower Garden.

Pedersen

By now, thanks to television, most of the world was familiar with police interrogation scenes.

A gray room with flickering fluorescent lights. The suspect alone, seated on a hard chair, at a hard table, a mirror on one wall, or a camera in the corner with a blinking red light. Maybe someone brought him a Dixie cup of water or, if lucky, bad police station coffee. He had already been read his Miranda Rights, so he sat staring at his hands as cops in another room crack jokes and waited to see if he squirmed. Then they came in, either together, or one at a time, good cop, bad cop.

But this wasn't that. Though we had never "socialized," Detective Lieutenant Arnte knew my history, knew my familiarity with police routine. I adjusted my fanny on a padded guest chair in his office. The blinds had been pulled for privacy and he studied me from across a desk exactly like mine. He laid the small card on the desktop, the Miranda card, and tipped his weary smile.

"You've done this too many times, Frank, so I won't insult you. Let me see you look at the card, so I can write down that you've been read your rights."

I did. I used my handkerchief to wipe some of the residual ink from my fingers. As all cops have their fingerprints on file, this was their less-than-subtle way of telling me where I stood. A uniformed cop set a coffee on the corner of the desk, and I thanked him. As much as I wanted it right now, I didn't ask for sugar.

"I guess it's up to me to decide where to start this, huh?" Arnte said.

I watched the cup.

"So, we got all the preliminaries over and done, now I'm gonna say up front, in my mind, you are not my suspect. Before I called you to that scene, even knowing you by reputation, I did my research. And from what I read about your history on the force, my thoughts are, to do a thing like we saw in that room, you'd probably have shown signs along the way."

"Thanks for saying."

"Yeah, you're thinking, here's the *good* cop. Maybe so. So let's start with the vic, Marco Pascal. You said he'd worked with you for a long time."

"Six-seven years. He had a bull pimping him out fairly regular, and the bull liked to pound on him fairly regular. I stopped a beating one night. A week or so later, Marco called to tell me about another hooker who choked to death on a fistful of crack, and this bull drove it into her throat with a fist. We got him off the streets."

"And over time, ya-da ya-da…"

"Over a long time. I went a full year without hearing a thing, then I needed information on his beat. When I pressed him, he came through. And it became an off and on thing."

"And, all these years, no *special benefits?*"

"C'mon, Lieutenant. The only DNA of mine you will find anywhere near him, might be on a cop business card."

"It says here, you never been married. Maybe a girlfriend years ago?" He kept his eyes averted.

"Cops and relationships. I think you might have heard about that somewhere. It doesn't mean it turned me from a pitcher to a catcher."

"Don't get all adversarial on me. You know I have to ask."

"Yeah, I know."

"How 'bout we fast-forward to more recent events? You working on anything that might lead to that boudoir disaster today? What was that fancy dinner about?"

"It's nothing I've got going." I took my first sip of the bad police coffee. At least that cliché held up. I needed to keep portions of Kandy's experiences to myself for now. She hinted at too many big players in that one dinner meeting. "She—Pascal called me."

"Yeah, we got the log."

"She picked the restaurant, saying that what she had to tell me was worth the price of a decent meal. Real decent. So, I took her at her word."

"Well? Was it?"

"Not sure. Nah, I don't know. Fantasies about things I have no corroboration on, and she left too many *possibilities* dangling for some future meeting. It might've been some b.s. she got from pillow talk with a john. She suggested as much."

"Did she name the john? Why do I think you're not in a sharing mood? I've been straight-up with you, Frank."

"I know you have. And I appreciate it. Really. If I had squat to share, I'd give it up. I want you, or me, or anybody, to find the psycho who did her like that. All I know is, I saw her leave the restaurant and she met with a half-starved thing who looked like just another hooker to me. At least that's how she dressed. But they were too far away. I can say she looked white, tall, with a large, bright green afro. I'm guessing a wig. They were all huggy-kissy and I didn't follow them home."

"You wish you had?"

"Before your wake-up call, the first thing on my day's schedule was to find out who Kandy's best friends were."

"You know your schedule has been changed, right?"

As per official procedure, I turned over my badge and gun until my story cleared.

Back home I tried sleeping on the couch. I stripped to my boxers. When that didn't work, I showered and tried sleeping again. A daddy long-legs in the ceiling corner may have been as tired as me. I decided to let him live. For now.

I tried to distract my inner spiders with anything but pictures of Kandy's death, then decided I wouldn't be sleeping for a few days. I nearly tripped pulling into my pants and wondered at my fitness behind the wheel, so I got back behind the wheel. I felt for the holster screwed beneath my driver's seat with my backup piece, a Diamondback 9mm. I almost felt whole again.

Bywater. I drove past Kandy's building and around the block, maybe just to torture myself. But I remembered that apart from colloquialisms, murderers don't usually return to the scene of the crime.

I cruised at a crawl, checking early morning streetwalkers and gutter life, or lack thereof. Too many, too filthy, barely able to stand, and leaning against hydrants or in doorways, or leaning on each other in a drug-induced sense of camaraderie.

The better neighborhoods tended to have a better class of hooker. Some dressed almost normal. "Boys" were usually the most flamboyant or aggressive, with exposed midriffs or bare- chested, and jeans cut well above their ass-cheeks. Not that the "girls" were too much more restrained. With my curb-crawl, I drew them like a worm in a traveling bucket of catfish.

My search became more Kandy-specific. She had grown to a higher status of client, based on the new boobs. She would be judged by the company she kept, and she knew it, and likely shuffled her *friendship* deck accordingly.

A red light and a trio of interested ladies.

One young lady, who had dressed this morning for a bank teller job, surprised me. Wearing a tan, cleaned and pressed, pantsuit, she even appeared to have showered recently. When she knocked on my rear passenger-side window, I rolled it down. As she leaned forward, beneath the face-paste, she looked all of sixteen. I reached for my shield until I remembered I'd given it up this morning.

"You a cop?" she said.

"What gave me away?"

"The black SUV and the sidewalk-stare." She turned away. "'Course the broken window under plastic gave me doubts."

"Quick question from a curious good-guy who ain't on the job."

"What's a nice girl like me?"

"I'm looking for someone."

"Now there's a new line I ain't heard for five minutes."

"Look, I'm serious. I need to find someone, anyone who knows Kandy."

It froze her. "You too? You think you're the only cop who's brought up her name since breakfast? Everybody who works this neighborhood knows her, and not just 'cause she's been at it too long. We all heard what happened."

"And that doesn't inspire you to get off the street for a few days?"

She waved goodbye.

"Listen. I knew her for a long time. Like before she was a she."

"Sure thing, lover."

"And I've got a special dislike for the monster who did that to her."

"Ain't nobody out here gonna talk nothin about nobody." She yelled it loud enough for spectators down the block. "What got done to her is a message. Like a six-foot telegram."

"How do you know what got done to her? The info isn't even in the papers yet."

"Never heard of social media, grandpa? We all seen pictures."

I must have left my mouth open too long.

"I'm done talkin without suckin." Others on the sidewalk watched her flip the bird as she strutted away.

I wanted to yell, *You're too young for this shit!* but figured she already knew it. There's no such thing as caring in *the profession.*

Others moved away, or grabbed their crotches and thrust fingers at me. I drove on. Another turned her back. Something in her shape or her walk reminded me of Sgt. Barnett, except for the straight black hair and the tramp stamp above her low-rider jeans. Of course, I'd never gotten a peek that low on Barnett.

Maybe all these early morning good-timers had me horny and daydreaming about the impossible. I desperately needed a change of scenery.

I decided on scenery inside a not-so-greasy diner, and staring at a plate of runny eggs.

"Looking a bit rough today, Frank." Rosa waited for my nod before tipping the coffeepot. "You might use a razor."

"Gracias. And here I showered and put on my best shirt just for you." I waved the menu away. "The usual."

"Three eggs, lookin at ya, bacon and sausage, hash browns, white toast, a side of Tabasco. You want the usual pie with that?"

"Not today, lover. I'm watching my girlish figure." Then I said, "You'll need to bring more sugar for the coffee though." It made her laugh. I think Rosa's laugh, genuine and generous, is the reason I kept eating here. She stepped away with a slap to her *double-wide backside,* as she called it.

Two uniform officers I did not know got up from the counter checking me like I had smeared crap on my forehead. They paid at the register, and checked again before rattling out the door. The counter waitress looked my way often enough to know I had been the topic of conversation.

Rosa startled me out of coffee-gazing when she laid the plates out.

"Just so you know, Frank. I don't believe a word of it."

I tried smiling.

"Not one word. More coffee?"

"Please. I am wondering what they're saying, of course."

She squeezed into my booth. "Yesterday, your Captain comes in here. Him and two others. Stella, at the counter, overheard 'em talking about you being out of a job. Captain says you'll be lucky if you ain't vacationing to Angola by the end of the month. I don't want you sent to Angola, dear."

"They didn't happen to say what I'm guilty of, did they?"

"I should get back to working." She scooted from behind the table and leaned backwards. "I like you, Frank. Since day one you come in here, I say, if this man likes to flirt with big Rosa, he must be good people. Please tell me you didn't do what they're saying."

I touched her hand when I said, "I didn't do it."

TWENTY-ONE

Patty P.I.

"Nicolaus. It's me."

Silence from the other end.

"Breathe or something, so I know it's you."

"It's good to know you're still alive."

Bobby J's Black & Blues Club, dinner hour. Vagelle said he had just left his building. He asked my location and suggested meeting here.

I called to check on Alya, but she said she had fallen asleep and would call back once she put herself together. She talked rough, and I thought about driving to her anyway, but Vagelle sounded like he had plans and I didn't want to put off our reuniting.

The "Closed" sign hung on Bobby's window, house lights turned low. Dinner hour? Never. As I tapped on the glass I could see the Hulk pushing a mop like a grudge. He lifted his head, predatory, until he recognized me. Then came the big smile, he set the mop aside and opened up. Not being the hugging type, I touched his arm.

Bobby's club had been a fixture in all our lives for many years. He and Vagelle had a special history that went back so far even I did not know its origins.

Setting a bottle of Parish Beer in front of me, he dragged over a chair to keep me company until our friend arrived. He couldn't fit into his own booth.

"Ms. Patty, Alya is…?"

"She's fine." Considering where I left her, I hoped she was. "Still the toughest woman I know, on the inside. What's up with the closed sign this time of day?"

"I created an emergency when he said he needed a place to talk."

"That's an expensive emergency."

"Hmmm. I mighta got my temper up these past weeks, with him keeping me in the dark, and thinking about Ms. K wanderin the streets alone. She shoulda called. I got rooms upstairs…"

"We've all been in lockdown, big man. I found our wayward Ruskie a few nights back. And with Nicolaus, I'm sure you understand where his head's been these past months."

"I do. Yes. I understand. Guess I let my frustrations boil the pot over—"

The door squawked. The lean man entered and walked directly to the booth without looking up.

"You didn't have to close the place," he said.

"I did." Bobby hoisted from the chair. "You want your usual?"

With a hand on his shoulder, Vagelle urged our giant back down. "No. Stay. I'm sure you want to hear about Alya as well."

I emptied half my beer, realizing how long I had gone without, then told them about what we had been through. Vagelle let me tell it before admitting he'd gotten most of the story from our steel-legged soldier. He agreed that he was still uncertain as to Vetty's intentions.

He asked me about Devon, and if I knew why I had been targeted. I considered a few cash-heavy clients from my past. I even considered a few my brother had embezzled from, back before his federal maximum-security vacation. But I had no clue who would pay that kind of dough to drop me in a box.

"He knew I had hired you to investigate my own brother, way back when," I said. "So, there was no chance he could talk me out of siccing the cops on him after his bathroom scare. But that night at the marina was different."

"Something told you his team was not after you."

"Not entirely, anyway. I didn't share this with Alya. Yeah, I survived the tub, but he knew if he waited, he'd eventually get a second chance at catching me alone. In a garage, or running me down in the street, there are too many easier ways to croak a person. Cheaper ways, without bringing an army."

"Then you learned Alya had surprised him in your parking garage. He was able to track her." His fist tightened once, then relaxed.

"The same way I knew where she would go. But that's just it. If he ran with that kind of crew, I would've known it before now. We worked too close for too many years. And unless he had a trip to Vegas I knew nothing about..."

"You're right. I'm just trying to see if we've both reached the same conclusions."

"Did you ever find out what those clowns were looking for when they broke into your apartment?" Bobby said.

No answer.

"You suspect something," I said.

"I am sure of nothing yet."

"This is where I check out." Frustration pushed me from the table. "As usual, you let me spill all the details and give nothing in return. I'm about tired of your close to the vest shit, Prince Vagelle. Withholding information gets your friends killed, and not just me, and that seems fine with you."

"Sit," Vagelle said. I continued for the door. He said softer, "Sit, please."

It stopped me.

"I apologize. No, Patty, I am not certain of anything, except that I have too many *details*. Too many crimes, simultaneously. Crimes of a personal bent. It's a nest of wasps, and when they swarm it splinters my focus from any single threat. I try to follow them all at once. I used to be good at that…" He stiffened his back into the cushions, head forward, angrily reading table rings.

"But, since Alya…"

"I don't want you charging off in a wrong direction. I need your mind open. I rely on you."

It drew me back to the table. "You know I've been doing this long enough to parse assumptions from facts. I understand your concerns for Alya. We all share them."

"'Scuse me buttin in," Bobby said, "about your wasps you can't focus on…?"

"Yeah, friend?" Vagelle fought to smile.

"Well, I know it smells faintly like a *campaign.*"

"You're reading my mind," I said.

"Y'all know, if I had me a grudge against some smart son-of-a-buck like Mr. V, I might think back on ol' Bobby Lee. He knew all them West Point boys liked to sit around plannin and figurin every inch of a campaign. Meanwhile, Gen'ral Lee would charge in, flip the table before they were ready to saddle-up. He'd send his cavalry circling one way, while Stonewall's entire corps charged in whoopin and hollerin with Lincoln's generals still dug in trying to figure out what Lee was up to."

"Bobby Lee never let them breathe," Vagelle said. "He kept pounding."

"Sound familiar?" I said.

"Whoever this new general is has done a great job of pounding."

"So, when did the battle actually begin? I think it was before your Roderick Howse visit. You've floundered through this head-swamp since—"

"Since Alya's trial. I am aware." His index finger motioned as if writing invisible cursive instructions to himself on the tabletop. "Whoever this is, they know me too well. Every bloody inch of me. They were aware that hurting her first would be their easiest shot at knocking me off my feet."

"At least onto the ropes."

"And keeping you there," Bobby J. said. "And her escape from the hospital, had to be dealt with quick and permanent. Keep on pounding. Keep you *hunkerin down.*"

"Patty, hearing your account of the marina, this threat to my friend escalating as it is—"

"Sure," Bobby J. said. "She is still *just your friend.* And this dumb bull should sit here and let you pull my nose ring."

"If you had a nose ring." I winked.

"Maybe I'm the one who should go." Vagelle needed to calculate some before rising to his feet.

"This is important," I said. "And you should listen to someone else for a change, psychologist. She has lived all these years under a traumatic weight, and you know how she—" I saw the silhouette back-lit by the door glass, and any strength in my voice disintegrated.

The others turned to look. Bobby rose up. "My little Ruskie—!"

Alya spun. She threw the door and fled, and I ran after her.

Vagelle

I could not chase. She would be gone before I left the booth.

They had all said, even Dr. Maiwand advised me, to give her space. It tore at my every instinct, until I convinced myself that instinct was nothing more than injured ego. I forced myself to drive away, the opposite direction, out of the city, and keep driving. I found a highway, or it found me, and I tried to wring blood from the steering wheel.

Eventually, I propped against the Mercedes fender on a dark street I used to know. A steady breeze kicked and spread sand over the asphalt, and kept it sliding with purpose until it tinted the dark neighborhood with its drab grit. Not sand, but a fine grain dust, barley dust mostly, carried these many miles from the farms and silos and railroad conveyors where recent southern rains had yet to dampen.

The familiarity of these streets chilled me despite the heat. A sickness squirmed within, residual acidity left in Alya's wake, but now crawling on its own. This street, a street without working lights, without sound, but a street etched in time.

Many years ago I had parked at this curb. I had monitored the front of that house across the street. There had been a light in the window then. Not now. The entire block hung in darkness as if some powerful entity had thrown a switch anticipating my arrival.

I recalled the neighbor who had suffered simply by existing next door to the crimes. A never-ending horror show for her. Tonight, I only thought of the victims.

Standing in silence I grew my own brand of heat. Like a first chug of whiskey scalding the throat on its way to light a fire in my belly.

Those same dark windows I had focused on long ago, they did not stare back at me tonight. In that earlier time, they held a dull blue glow from another room. I waited for a change, a movement, a shadow, but now I wished for that quivering, soft blue light. It might turn back the dial. Might erase all the intervening years.

My imagination heard the scream again. My feet moved with leaden boots pulling me across to the other side—*back then, I ran.*

I had anticipated what was coming. I had staked out this house for weeks. I had been threatened by lawyers, other cops, my direct supervisors. My partner, Murphy, had warned me. He worked late at the office that night, but he predicted this as well. I dropped the restraining order back at my desk, beneath my desk into the wastebasket.

With the screams, I called Murphy for back-up. He ordered me to wait for him, but he was too far. I ran, flashlight in hand, gun in hand, through the side yard to the back of the house. I broke into the kitchen—as I did tonight.

But tonight, the kitchen held only emptiness. Empty counters, empty floors, except for the softening dust of years. Footprints, some recent, many older and holding onto their own dust.

A sound from behind, and I spun. But the yard held onto its emptiness too. Imagination filled the void to that other time—she had followed me, the neighbor. Dallas was her name.

I turned back to the kitchen, and I crossed that space to the dining room door. A dining room just as empty, just as dusty, cleared of furniture, cleaned of any signs of life. Even cleaned of blood.

Tonight, there were no screams.

Into the living room. Those large windows lacking the old light from without, streetlights now dark, merely a dull moon two-hundred-fifty thousand miles off. Barely a spark off that thing on the floor. The silver blade of the meat cleaver. Madeline's meat cleaver, or a clean imitation left in the thick dust for me to find.

New footprints in the dust among the old. I turned with the new prints, following along the short hall, expecting night demons flying in. The prints turned to the right rear bedroom. The boys' bedroom.

No furniture. Within the doorless closet, a crumpled bed quilt with cartoon designs obscured by dirt and dark stains, stains of blood or feces or both. More footprints, and in the room's center, the dust had been wiped in a deliberate design.

I clicked on the phone's light. I needed a backstep to the hall to get the full picture and understand it. The years of dust had been wiped by a human shape. I moved the light, and kept looking until the form made sense. The sense of a child's snow angel, but adult-sized, where the arms and legs had wiped away like wings.

And I continued to look until the wings were not angel's wings. *Butterfly wings.*

I dream-walked back to the living room and the meat cleaver. The eight-year-old no longer stood in the corner with wide, accusing eyes. A corner, now nothing but a darker shadow-wedge, beckoned me to step inside.

The Mercedes recrossed the bridge into old town Donaldsonville, mostly dark this time of night, save for the familiar Sheriff's office. Nothing much changed poor Southern towns from one decade to the next, as if a can of paint might cost too much. Well, to them it just might.

I pulled in with a thought to the mock murder weapon, the cleaver, in my trunk. How long it had lain beneath that window was of little consequence. Whoever *they* were, they had known I would return once this game stomped me long and hard enough.

Another stab for my memory worm, like Danny's body left for me in the dirt of Marie Laveau's tomb, intended to rattle my nightmares. However, this one had the opposite effect. This was one gambit too far. It merely helped solidify my conviction that the monster believed they could toy with dinner before devouring me.

Had René been under orders to leave me alive on that highway? To prolong my pain?

The sturdy woman behind the desk, behind the badge, informed me the Sheriff I once knew, Tantillo, had left the job before she moved into it.

"Near-on eight years now," she said. "Have a seat, Mr. Vagelle." She poured me a coffee. "You like a drop of something else in your cup?"

"Not tonight. Thanks. I have a drive ahead of me."

"I'm 'bout starved for conversation with any new face in these parts. But y'all showing up here after midnight without calling ahead, inquiring after the old Sheriff, says there might be a story in the making."

I did not give her as much story as she wished for. I had come in search of information, and decided early in the talk that she might not be the person to confess my transgressions to.

Tantillo, as she told it, had come under scrutiny from state magistrates not long after my case. His personal connection to a witness in that case, Dallas Verde, began to "haunt his objectivity," or so she said. Then Dallas disappeared and, rumor had it, he hung up his star in order to chase her trail. This Sheriff pronounced it, "…chase her tail," a Freudian slip or maybe intentional, so I chose not to tread too far.

I left her with a false portrayal of an old war buddy, just passing through town. As I cleared the door, it occurred to her she might ask for a name or business card. I pretended not to hear.

From the edge of the parking lot, I glimpsed the man hunched at my passenger door. Naked from the waist up, except for the crowded roadmap of tattoos or scars, from his scalp and extending the length of his torso. Sodium lights winked off the blade in his hand.

I reached beneath the arm sling for the belly-holster, grabbed the butt of the Sig Sauer, and jogged forward.

He heard me coming and moved in a curious animal gesture, beneath the lot's lights. I paused. His glare flickered, then he turned and vanished into the shadows, through the trees, between the buildings, and gone.

My gunhand hung limp at my thigh. "…*the monster believed it could toy with dinner before devouring me.*" I nodded. The implied hubris in the words told me more about them than they knew about me.

Even at this distance, staring into the shadows that had swallowed him, even beneath his patchwork body art, I knew I had been close to Roderick Howse once more.

TWENTY-TWO

Alya

Dawn. The same crew cut seen through the rear window of the same Camaro. Whoever he was, spying on my empty apartment, had a lot of time on his hands. Temptation pressed me like the feel of Patty's Taurus under my belt. A fantasy of pushing the gun barrel to the driver's ear had me shivering. My fears fought me for control.

I took the same side alley to my building and up the stairwell. I had not planned on returning tonight, but *angry* does things to me.

"Angry has a way of replacing common sense," Nicolaus said more than once.

"Angry replaces everything," I said.

The shoulder bag with my laptop dropped into the laundry hamper. I followed it with a towel, a feeble camouflage, then returned to the bedroom window.

His car had not moved.

A big part of me wanted to be afraid again. The angry part hated being afraid. I could not live with *afraid.* I tossed the Taurus onto my bed, fearful of its touch and the impulses it planted in me.

Returning to the bathroom, I grabbed the pipe wrench from under the sink. I wrapped the handle with duct tape, and continued wrapping my hand and wrist with blind or absent reasoning. Yes, that angry. I was aware enough to wrap tight with the sticky side up, so the glue clung to the back of more tape rather than my flesh.

Papa left me with so many useful lessons.

Slow descent to street level, dragged forward by the heavy iron, cleared my head a bit. *Chut'-Chut'.* Not enough to stop me. I reached the curb, thinking the ugly weapon would be enough to frighten off any would-be attacker. I had yet to see my stalker's face.

Standing behind his driver-side bumper I sang to him. "Do you have an appointment?"

He squirmed, shook himself awake, checked his side mirror round-eyed, until the eyes smiled. His door groaned. His shoes touched the pavement. He pushed himself up, turning that full-face grin on me, until I recognized him.

Colin. St. Michael's orderly, or whatever the hell they called him. And he knew me, *the old me, the heavily medicated me,* well enough to believe his Cheshire cat leer would drop me to my knees, gasping.

He remembered when he had me alone, dizzy and helpless. He wanted to touch the scars I had raked into his face, but his right hand stopped short. His grin wobbled a touch. I saw the hand's bandages, then I smiled. And I let him come to me.

Like a scene from a movie, he slowed his steps and shuffled a little dance. I waited with my heavy right hand, ten pounds of iron shielded by the Camaro's rear fender.

"You know what I plan to do with you," he said through clamped teeth. "And it don't resemble a square-dance, hon." Another step forward. "So nice of you to save me from chasin." He glanced at the morning-quiet buildings on either side. "Y'all are too scared to even run. Or maybe y'all want what I got for you."

Close enough, he reached out for me.

Every particle of strength went into my swing. With his hand wrapped in bandages as white as a baseball, my wrench connected. His arm flew back. His scream shook my bones and echoed down the thin street. He hopped back once, clutched at his new injury, and continued to scream and fall into a curl. His hands pressed between his thighs as the screams lengthened.

"Not fair!" gagging on tears.

In a battle rage, feet astride his head, ten pounds of iron death a single breath away…I raised the weight with both hands.

"You never learned." I sounded like Papa when I said, *"Fair* is a fantasy."

He whimpered.

I held and grew numb. The iron and my arm stopped shaking, then lowered to rest at my side.

"Papa is disappointed today. I am not Papa."

A procession of one, I climbed the stairs. The stairwell door to the third-floor popped open. A partier from the previous night examined me like he should know me, until he scanned down to the appliance at the end of my arm. He vanished behind the slam of the door. I continued the march one more floor to my room.

Pulse relaxing, my mission ended, I laid my forearm and pipe wrench along the counter's edge. Long-bladed scissors from the kitchen drawer snipped at the edges of the duct tape. I took my time. If police knocked, I would accept the arrest, though I doubted that criminal would make such a call, even if he could push the buttons of his phone.

Once free, I searched the cabinets for my can of WD-40 and scrubbed any remaining glue residue from my forearm. Then paint thinner. Then I showered for twenty minutes.

Not wanting to stay, I stepped into baggy jeans and even baggier cotton shirt as mid-morning split the mini blinds. Then I recalled the laptop.

Tea kettle on simmer, hunger announced itself, so I discovered Patty had stocked the cupboards with non-perishables and other things. A tin of sardines, crackers, a cheese wheel. I took the lot to the sofa and raised the laptop cover.

A square of paper drifted to my feet. I opened the fold to a child-like drawing in ball point pen. A strange combination of lines, two parallel arching lines, a large house with a stick-figure animal on the roof—maybe a deer, or *antelopa*, or maybe a greyhound wearing antenna. It might have been a cave drawing beneath a single arching word where his rough pen tore the paper. *"GRYAZNYY"* (filthy)? *Seriously?* I turned it over. He had scratched, *"N-P-M."*

More mysteries. Thank you, Nicolaus.

While the computer booted, I wolfed crackers and cheese, and sipped tea. Once connected, I scrolled along file catalogues hoping for a sign. Nothing appeared unusual or out of place until I landed on an unremarkable folder. "NPM."

Well, maybe that was too easy. I forgot about my hunger, and I would never finish the cheese.

(Line one in red marker.)

Dark Triad / Machiavellianism

Lecture Notes: Clinical Psych. 9/20—

Prof. Terisi (Vagelle's forgotten name)

Dark Empath:

Exhibits understanding in order to gain trust.

Exhibits affection in order to manipulate.

Employs Cognitive Empathy to gain control.

Psychopath:

Predator—Parasitic—Impulsive.

Sensation Starved—Cannot resist temptation.

Narcissist:

Self-Dominant - Impatient when challenged.

Dismissive of other's Emotions.

Ruthless when confronted.

Both project Charm & Confidence. Both without Empathy. Both seek to control.

But as the Narcissist is impatient, demands the world's respect, Dark Empath uses his patience, planning, subtle or emotional arm-twisting.

DE studies others' reactions, learns to simulate normal emotions - which they do not possess - expert at changing the masks used to manipulate and convey normalcy.

All DEs are Narcissists. Not all Narcissists are DEs.

Dark Empath knows and can recognize a Narcissist's "subconscious desire to be controlled." Narcissist — fooled by their own god-complex, will never admit to a chink in their armor, or another's preeminence. Thus, the Narcissist may see the Dark Empath coming. But they will believe he is one of them. They will not truly know him. Not fully.

A knock at my door shocked me like a live wire. I scooped the pistol from behind the cushions while quickly scanning a paragraph in red type:

*Consideration of a **"Dark Tetrad."** A fourth personality trait.*

Sadist: defined as, "A tangible thrill in the suffering of others."

 I leaped to the far side of the couch, a thick enough barrier to make my last stand. A stand I was ready to accept.

Vagelle

When he spotted my car, Pip hurried across the intersection. Always easy to spot from a distance, six-foot-six, light-skinned enough to resemble his half-Dutch father on a cloudy day. He flexed his hands as he neared, a nervous habit whenever I called. His silver-capped smile flashed with uncertainty in the daylight.

"How we doin, Mr. Vagelle?" We met under a small oak several feet from the car. "Heard about the arm. Wish you'd called me."

"Be glad I didn't. You're a bigger target and might not have gotten off this light. You still attending group meetings across the street?"

"I'd like to lie. Been busy with work, I'm afraid." He faced the high church front with a touch of guilt. "I stop by some Sundays. When I can. Past couple weeks, I been renovatin a business close by. Work's pretty steady. I can't thank you enough for, you know."

"You proved worth the effort a long time ago." I watched the flexing hands. He watched the street, left then right. "You sure you're good? You look *uneasy.*"

"Ah, no, Mr. Vagelle. I'm clean. Just wonderin, with your callin, needin a hurry-up meet-up, and with your recent troubles, should I be expectin gunfire?"

"Nothing like that, friend. I'm looking for information, is all. My usual sources are playing hooky."

"It's about my old life? I ain't been near that shi—it's been years. Ya gotta believe me."

"Oh, I do. Nothing but good words when I hear from your clients. I'm trying to get a line on somebody. A real bad guy, I'm told. Strong. With half his ear bitten off."

"You don't wanna be near that Harlen." Head tipped, studying the pavement cracks. "Don't even like you bringin his name up."

"The GOAT?"

"That's him." He nodded too much, for a guy who does not worry easily. "Harlen's the only other name I ever heard used."

"He likes to hurt people, I hear."

"Him and his crew. Thing 'bout these brothers with the worse reps, every mo-fo runs with 'em is out to prove they's just as bad. They got to."

"A dog pack. When the others sense you're the weak one, they'll cut you out."

"Like that. So, they keep a low profile in the day. They got to take care of the money-side. But if you cross 'em..."

"I get it."

"But you plan to cross 'em." Not a question, a statement.

"It's what I do." I wrinkled my lip.

The hand-flex. Another head shake.

"I didn't call to get you involved, Pip. 'I'm looking for leads, that's all. I know about his late nights and City Park. I thought you might know where he likes to do business at other times."

"Trying to catch him when the crew ain't hiding behind the next tree?"

"Something like that."

"He won't talk with you, ya know. Once his boys realize who you are, they'll spray you. I don't like this. I surely don't."

"I'm touched."

"Yeah, in the head. Sorry, Mr. Vagelle."

TWENTY-THREE

Alya

Another hard knock, "Alya! Alya? I know you're in there. Alya?" Frank Pedersen's voice.

I opened the door and his eyes widened.

"You gonna shoot me with that thing?" he said.

I lowered the Taurus. He crossed into the room.

"Put it on the sink so I can relax."

"Are you going to arrest me?"

"If you plan to shoot me." He opened the refrigerator, twisted the cap off a bottle of water and threw it at the sink. He swallowed half. "You realize, half of *Orleans' Finest* knows you're home after the radio call this morning. I'd ask about it, but if you want to remain a free woman for a while, I suggest coming with me." He pushed Patty's gun into his waistband.

I stuffed the laptop, with a couple clean shirts, clean shorts, and an extra water bottle into Vagelle's leather shoulder bag. Pedersen led me to the garage. Duct tape held a plastic sheet in place over the Durango's missing passenger window.

"Your last ride-along escaped?"

"Have you seen Vagelle?" He steered out onto the boulevard. The flapping plastic too raucous close to my ear.

"For a few seconds this morning, I saw the back of his head. Do you have earmuffs?"

His glance turned skeptical until I explained where I had seen him.

"I'm not gonna ask if you were involved in that massacre up at the marina."

"Good."

"Were you involved in that massacre up at the marina?"

My side-eye. "I killed no one, copper."

"But you were there. You know what happened."

"I am too tired for interrogations."

"Okay, but I need to know about the man lying in the street. Some early riser called it in. Said it sounded like someone being tortured."

"Can I ask where you are taking me?"

He insisted I tell about my victim, so I did. I told him about my terrors at St. Michael's hospital. The drugs. And I told him about Colin. His constant threats, his cornering and attacking me. I explained I had no idea the orderly from the clinic was my stalker this morning, parked across from my building, until I faced him. Then I got scared and angry.

"Like my Papa always taught me, it is better to meet your fears than wait for them to catch up with you."

He nodded like he believed me, and we remained silent on the drive turning down Galvez Street, then taking the driveway onto the property, the brick and glass behemoth adorned with the logo for New Orleans VA Medical Center. He edged the Durango to the front doors and parked at the "No Parking" curb. Before cutting the engine, he tapped his phone.

"Yeah, it's me. What's the scoop?" He listened to the lengthy reply. Once disconnected, he popped free of his seat belt. "Looks like our friend may be in for a few sleep-overs."

"Which friend?"

"The one who slipped in a puddle this morning and broke his hand. Quite a few bones, so the doc says. Some fairly crushed. It'll be a complicated surgery resetting as much as they can."

"Colin? He's in there?" My stomach caught fire.

"You're usually quicker than this, lady. Or maybe you are tired. When I heard about the incident in front of your building, I sent a man to sit outside his room." Pointing to the phone, "That was him."

"You should have told me."

"Listen, I don't want you in there. It would only complicate things. I need you to wait in the car while I go in and talk to a few people. Can you do that for me? When I come back, I'll tell you what I find, then we'll figure out where you would like to go."

"I don't want to see him, ever."

"As I figured. You won't have to. From what you told me, I guarantee he won't press charges for this morning. I know who he is. I want to know how he got a job at St. Mike's."

The first sprinklings of rain fell as he rushed through the front doors. Then turned back for one last finger-point, unnecessary, for me to stay in the car.

Retrieving the laptop from the shoulder bag between my feet, I remembered the pen drawing in my pocket. Lines, house, deer—maybe—and *griaznaja* (dirty). Nicolaus loved his coded messages. As brilliant as he was, today I wished he had taken a few art lessons.

Cracking back into the laptop, I found the open Wi-Fi network for VA Hospital-Guest and logged on. I avoided the NPM folder, planning to revisit when I had more time—*or stability*. It had reminded me of our early years together, when Nicolaus taught me tidbits from his old Psychology lectures, so I might better understand how he worked. Looking back, he may also have been trying to make me understand how *I* worked.

Standard searches pulled up local NOLA news articles on the "massacre at the marina," as Pedersen had called it. Too much fantasy speculation from reporters who had few facts to write about. Names of the dead had been "leaked to the press," and released, all but one of them unfamiliar to me. Some guessed a drug cartel raid, others called it a botched military-style attack, one even invented a possible CIA Black Ops move against terrorists moored in the West End harbor. No proofs were offered. They seldom were.

I followed news articles back in time, until I glimpsed the name Vagelle. I read articles about a "shootout in the swamp." He had been injured, bad, and I needed to pause, but my tears held off this time. The young kidnap victim, Danny Howse, had been dead for days prior, making the entire incident unnecessary. To me, after what I knew so far, the shootout seemed more about killing Vagelle. The boy was a means to an end.

Howse. I knew that name. Roderick Howse. Of course, living so close for ten years, I had learned much of Nick's history, professional and personal, well before I sailed into it. At one time I had been obsessed with finding truth about him. What made him do these things. His black moods. His often suicidal—*no, not that*—*his careless life.*

I had covered what was available on young Roddy, and his mother, Madeline. "Mad Madeline." And my friend's reasons for quitting police work.

Roderick's reappearance now screamed set-up to me. Is it possible he failed to see it? Was he so wedded to the guilt from all those years ago that he somehow needed to trust whatever some *Domovoy* (house ghost) told him?

Again, it saddened me. And it angered me that someone would inflict these tortures on my *friend.*

Difficult to comprehend, the man had been the stalwart for so much of our life together, to see him now so reduced…

I barely turned my head when the motor rumbled past. A Camaro, dark burgundy, I caught part of the plate through the dripping window. This morning, standing at his bumper, I had looked down past the weapon taped to my arm, and I saw that plate.

I nearly lunged from the Durango to run after the Camaro, but it had already turned the corner to park legally. I lifted in my seat trying to follow the burgundy roof as it crossed between parked cars.

A man got out—Not Colin, of course. A small man, shaggy black hair, Latino, grim. Maybe, bringing Colin's Camaro for him? I heard wooden heels clop toward the entrance. I slumped in my seat, peering through passenger window-plastic as he jogged by.

Then, against any sensible whisperings, and Detective Pedersen's insistence, urged by my inability to see more through the rumpled plastic, I left the car.

"Can I help you?" the woman at the desk said.

"I'm with—do you know which way he went?"

"Fifth floor." She pointed to the elevator sign.

I thanked her over my shoulder.

I got off the elevator on four, and took the emergency stairs to five. I cracked the door by inches. Half a hallway away, shy of his destination with Pedersen talking to a policewoman, he turned abruptly into the nearest room. His head reappeared, clearing the doorframe, as a child spying on the ice cream man.

The elevator beside the stairway door pinged, opened, and I eased my door shut. The rattle of wheels passed, and I looked. A tall nurse pushing an IV pole. I questioned the cheap blond wig needed for her job, but my mind was on Colin's friend. As the nurse passed, he grinned like she was a stripper serving cocktails in that IV bag. She ignored him and continued toward the police.

Whatever he had planned, our Latin Lothario changed his mind and returned to the elevator. I let my door slip shut again and listened. The elevator chimed. Thirty seconds later I left my spy hole and hurried to Pedersen's side. When he noticed me, he chewed his cheek.

I intercepted his scolding and whispered about the man I had followed in.

"So, who we got here?" Policewoman said.

Pedersen's thoughts traveled elsewhere.

"Hello, I am Cherry," I said, scanning Colin's room and the food tray with red Jello. Disco nurse moved the tray to the window chair. She replaced Colin's IV stand with the one she had wheeled in.

The cop held out her hand. I had anticipated and pretended interest in something else.

"Gotta run," Pedersen said to her. He touched my elbow, and we hurried to the elevators.

The exit doors shooshed open. Pedersen threw wide his passenger door and sped round his bumper to the driver's side.

"I see the Camaro leaving the lot." I buckled in. "Left."

"Got him. He ain't running. He has no need to feel anyone's following."

Palm trees bent to the breeze. At the Galvin St. intersection, the burgundy car remained visible. Pedersen backed off the gas and fell in line with regular traffic crawling beneath a growing rain.

"Do you have a plan?" I said.

"Why start now? You said you got the plate?" He pulled his phone. "Wait!"

This neighborhood might have consisted of nothing but hospitals. The University Medical Center, clinics, and across the street, New Orleans VA Medical Center, all appearing as if the city had given birth to an aircraft carrier. It took the Camaro two turns before we realized he circled the properties. He obeyed traffic laws, speed limits, traffic lights, even used his turn signals, so Pedersen let out his leash.

"Do you think he saw us?" I said.

"No."

"You need to speak up. I can't hear with your window drumming."

"No. He's waiting for something.

At the rear of the campus, across from the cafeteria entrance, the Camaro slowed into the bike lane with emergency flashers keeping a beat to our windshield wipers. Pedersen locked on him, which is why I saw the woman first. Tall woman, red hair flattened by rain, with a bag over her shoulder. She trotted between parked cars. At first, I thought she ran to get out of the damp, but she tossed a white jacket over her shoulder, and the wind caught and spread it onto the hood of a car. Red continued running into the street.

"That's her!" I yelled.

Pedersen jerked. "Who?" Then we both saw her throw the bag at the gutter while rounding the Camaro fender and sliding into the passenger seat.

The Camaro shot forward and slid the first turn, cutting off a city bus, and forcing already perturbed pedestrians to jump from the crosswalk.

Pedersen swore and tried to keep up.

"It's her," I said.

He flashed at me.

"The nurse. I know it is."

"From the hospital?"

"You are usually quicker than this, Frank. Yes. The one from Colin's room. I saw a blond wig in that bag. And—"

His phone sang the Dean Martin song. "Yeah!" he yelled at it. "Tell me—Tell me." He listened. "Shit."

"—that nurse strolled right past the police, smooth. She replaced the patient's IV stand. And I watched it happened. Now I can see it. Replacing the IV bag that was more than half-full."

"You won't have to worry about Colin coming after you."

"He's dead," I said.

"Right in front of us." To the phone, "Seal the room—Yes! Even hospital personnel. Allow one doctor to check for signs of life. Touch nothing. Keep a man on the door. We need Forensics down there ASAP."

A stream of cars through the pounding storm, with a professional driver willing to injure pedestrians, they lost us. The Camaro drove like my Papa taught me at fourteen when running from *militsiya* (police).

Ruthless always wins.

When we returned to the hospital's "No Parking" curb, beneath the door overhang, Patty P.I. waited with her backside to the Lexus trunk.

"Should I ask how you knew we would be here?" I said, as we climbed from the SUV. "Your police radio, never mind."

"I'd heard the initial call-out in front of your building, but you were already gone before I got there. Inside, with open food wrappers and extra water bottle, I figured someone you knew dragged you away. Probably this jamoke here. Then the report of your victim at the hospital. I figured you'd return."

"I can't stand here tongue-wagging," Pedersen said. "I gotta get inside. Can this jamoke suggest you take Alya somewhere she ain't under police scrutiny?"

"Are we good?" Patty said.

"Yeah," I said. "We're good."

Twenty-Four

Alya

Much like Nicolaus, or the way I used to see him, the *safe house* never changed. And like every time before, walking through the front double-doors hit me like a wet towel across the butt. I must have hesitated, as Patty had already charged past me to the alarm panel on the foyer wall. I called out the security code.

"I remember," she said.

"I have been away so long—I forget things."

A foyer like a mini-cathedral with a staircase, "Like Gone with the Wind," I said. "When I was younger, much younger, Nicolaus gave me that book to read. He said it held many lessons. I could only read less than half, but this is what it felt like. Tara."

Marble tiles shimmering like a watery chess table beneath the blazing chandelier, the foyer smelled as pristine as it looked. Those stairs begged me to climb for the princess bedroom I knew to be up there. Memories of unimagined warmth, comfort, especially after my many recent months of St. Michael's, with its prison-like smells of disinfectant, cold floors, cold walls, and cold stares of other inmates.

Even the chittering of Louisiana cicadas failed to penetrate the inner sanctum once its doors shut. Only the barely audible hum of air conditioning found my ears.

"Hardly a plantation house." Patty finished the alarm sequence. I followed slowly down the short, curved hall, past the living room, family room, and den, to the kitchen. "You've seen a few of those, as I recall. This is nothing more than a modest millionaire's taste of sun-burbia." Then, with her clap, the kitchen burst to a blinding glory of light, that bounced off stainless steel and polished marble, and hanging rows of artful kitchenware.

"Did you ever meet the owner?" I said.

She chuckled. "There are still some secrets Nicolaus keeps to himself, even with us."

"I used to hate those secrets before I learned better. He usually has a reason for keeping them."

"Pull up a chair while I see if anyone's stocked these cupboards. I haven't had a thing all day and I could eat a gator."

"If you find gator in there, I will pass."

A six-pack of bottled water made its way to the center island and I carried it to the breakfast nook. I had also forgotten that view over the Mandeville rooftops to a glittering sunset at the edge of Lake Pontchartrain. A lake so vast, and with the evening fog drift, the far New Orleans skyline might have disappeared into space.

After my many months of confinement, emotions were peaking again. Meanwhile, Patty checked the packages for expiration dates.

"Nicolaus once told me he hired a woman to make weekly deliveries and clear away the old." I could not break away from the stars in the darkening lake. "He comes out here so seldom, I guess it is worth it to him."

"Here." She popped bottle caps and set two cold beers on the table. She returned to the refrigerator, and next thing I heard was the slap and sizzle of meat dropped onto a hot skillet. She chopped at the board. Sizzling peppers and onions attacked my memories. "I figured you haven't eaten anything but cafeteria food since—"

"Oh…that smell."

"Don't worry. You'll love my gator meat."

My smile faltered with a drifting sadness. After some minutes, I felt her arm encircle me, and I did not cringe.

Patty and I survived much through the years, yet we talked so little about the bad things, as if speaking about them would shrink their importance. It was an intuition we both shared. She had been a sister, closer than anyone in my real family.

She returned to her dinner, and I heard the plates and silver and more. I focused on the grandness of the lake. A bloody sun had long cleared the horizon, and the remaining clouds of dull fire turned to a more merciful amethyst.

She talked on. I heard "Vagelle," and a child-like laugh. A story about her early days with her detective agency that I had heard before, from *him*. But I let her tell it. She needed to share. Her words trailed off when she talked of some she had worked with. And I shivered with her memories of the one who had dragged her from the bath.

Afterwards, she forbade me washing dishes, and she cracked a second beer for herself. I declined.

I opened the leather shoulder bag with the laptop. Again, I was reminded of the cave drawing, as the paper unfolded where my plate had been.

"That's why you wanted to come here." Patty rested a hand on the back of my chair.

"And not just the fancy upstairs bedroom?"

"Don't kid, wise ass. You figured it out. Those two curved lines."

"The double bridge, Pontchartrain Causeway. And here, the Safe House."

"What about that animal?"

I almost knocked myself out of the chair and sprinted for the garage, with Patty tripping on my heels. I reached and found the light switch. My breath caught in my throat.

"Getting all weepy?" she said.

"Almost."

"Forgive yourself a pinch of emotion for once, okay? You've had a real shitty year."

"This is all…too unexpected." I stepped forward and down onto naked concrete, beneath the hanging fluorescent lights, to caress the old *griaznaja*. My *filthy* sky-blue Chevy.

"Your animal. Fuck." Patty lifted her beer and swallowed hard, and followed with a burp.

"I don't know how you figured that drawing was an impala," Patty said. "I thought it was a skinny rat with horns."
"He draws like a six-year-old."

We opened the Impala's doors and windows. The key still in the ignition, I slid behind the wheel, and it turned over without fussing.

"Of course it would." Patty had leaned in over my shoulder. "He ran it out here only last week."

"He filled the tank too." I cut the engine keeping the doors open to air it out. And while I slumped into the lumpy driver's cushions, and savored my familiar cockpit, the garage door lifted, and she drove her Lexus into the second parking bay. The large door growled shut.

I flicked off the garage lights in case neighbors got curious about the habitually abandoned millionaire's *taste of sun-burbia*. She ruffled my hair like I was a teenager who just found his lost puppy.

I carried the laptop to the den. "We are spending the night. Right?"

She snorted. "At least. Hey, I know Vagelle has something more than beer out here."

After two hours of unconsciousness, I shook myself awake, slid out of the chair, and touched her arm as she slept on the loveseat.

"First door to the right of the stairs is mine," I said. "You get the master on the left."

But with steam on the window and the mirror, the golden swan faucet and pretty carved flower soaps, I fell asleep seconds after lowering into the tub's hot water.

It might have been my last best night.

Twenty-Five

Vagelle

Jesus had grown to a lean nineteen under my distant eye, ever since the night he killed his father on the rooftop of the Hemmings building.

His mother, Sophie, now managed two coffeeshops in the neighborhood. Whenever I stopped in, she grilled me regarding the mysterious envelope of cash deposited in her purse at random intervals. Despite my unconvincing denials, I knew she was clever enough to figure me out. What she did not figure was my spare key to her cupboard where she kept the purse during work hours, along with my alternating couriers.

On Jesus's sixteenth birthday, I all but begged Sophie to accept tuition for her son to attend LSU. It may have shamed her. The anger in her gaze had been enough for me to stop pressing. My envelopes maybe grew a touch heavier, but I decided she could not fight what she could not prove, and she only had so many locking cupboards to move her purse to.

Jesus maintained a friend's demeanor whenever I came by, but as he grew, he became more affected by his proximity to the Hemmings building. An unease, no doubt, with the ghost of his father and the night of his greatest childhood trauma, the night his father went off the roof.

Recently, Jesus started his own handyman business, and I passed his name to friends I trusted. I kept him far from anyone I did *my business* with.

Stopping home for a clean raincoat, I met Dr. Maiwand on the second floor, and he waved me inside.

"I put the kettle on. You have visitors."

"Serious?"

"I believe so."

Seated around his dining table, Hemmings, Vetty, and Jesus, all wore similar expressions of uncertainty. Glaring at Vetty, Jesus squirmed like he had rats gnawing his ankles. Vetty appeared unintimidated, despite a recently bruised cheek.

"He did this?" I said, pointing to the boy. Vetty said nothing.

"He did." Hemmings said.

"You know I don't like it here, Mr. Vagelle." Jesus eyed my sling and my injured wing. "He grabbed me out front and wouldn't let go. He forced me in here. I don't know him, and I didn't know the doctor knows him."

"Seems reasonable," I said. "But we haven't seen you here in a long while, and someone might ask why you were hanging around out front."

"That's for me and you. Not for these others."

"Unacceptable," I said.

"What? Why, unacceptable?"

"Jesus, ours is a long association. Sometimes it gets rocky. I have tried to be your friend. Now you are caught spying—"

"No, Mr. Vagelle. Not spying. I would never!"

"And now, when you are caught, you physically assault another acquaintance of mine. There is a loss of trust here. You can see that, I know."

He swung his young anger toward me.

"You can go," I said.

He rose. "But…"

"If you have any respect for me, you can tell me what this is about and allow me to make up my mind whether I want to share with the room. If not, I have had a tiring afternoon. I won't detain you."

He scrutinized the faces at the table, faces as perplexed as his own. I moved for the door.

"No. Mr. Vagelle, it's about…about something I seen."

"I need more than that."

"A friend of yours."

"Someone at this table?"

"Remember when you got me that job? Working for the painter after the last hurricane? Mr. Pippen. Lucien."

"Doctor?" I said. "Would you and the others allow us to have the room for a few minutes? Thank you."

No one balked. They simultaneously pushed away from the table, and Maiwand led them out and closed the door. I heard Hemmings invite them down to his apartment.

I waited until Jesus spoke. He studied the Oriental rugs on the wall and began by insisting again he would never spy on me.

"I believe you. I needed to let our big military-type friend believe that you can be made to understand the repercussions of punching people you don't know."

"You mean besides you telling him to punch me back?"

"Sort of. Now, what about Lucien?"

"First, I wanted to come here right off, but Momma was telling me about how you've been having your own problems. You and Miss Alya. Then, knowing you the way I do, I figured you'd want to know anyway."

I filled the space with a nod.

"Well, I guess you know Mr. Pippen still calls me once in a while when he's got extra work. He pays pretty okay. So, this week I'm working for him, doin clean-up after he finishes the heavy stuff. It's a remodel on a first-floor shop—not a storefront type shop. It looks to be a regular house, back of the Quarter, off the main—"

"Jesus. I can tell this sounds important to you, but maybe hold off on all the details until you tell me what this is about."

"Mr. Vagelle, I hate to just come out and say a thing like this if I ain't sure I seen what I seen. But I think I seen a murderer."

"And you suspect this because?"

"He ain't a *suspect* that I know of. But he was wearing more blood that any man I ever seen who was *not* a murderer. And no, it wasn't Mr. Pippen. He's been good—"

"Okay. Let's get you a glass of water, you can catch your breath, and we can go back into all those details. I'm sorry I interrupted your flow."

"It's a old house, back of the Quarter. But they's all old, ain't they? But it's got one of them historic plaques beside the front door to let visitors know it's officially old.

"Anyways, Mr. Pippen gave 'er a new coat of paint on the outside, a dull minty color, you might call it. Then him and his boys moved inside and spruced up the first-floor. When they moved upstairs, that's when he called me to clean away the leavins—I mean work debris.

"Now, I seen the owner come by a few times, and he always treats Mr. Pippen like they's best friends, but then most folks do. I seen how Mr. Pippen gets when folks try to get all up in his biz-ness, and that tends to change their temper right-quick.

"You prob'ly seen this owner on the streets at times, wanderin close to the tourists. Too close, if you know what I'm sayin. Calls himself a *priest*. Priest Theo. But he's easy to spot. Tall. Taller than you. Wears a long black coat on the hottest days. A red pirate bandana and dark round glasses.

"But he's got this shop, see—not quite *his* shop. He's got a gal runs the place. Tall, skinny gal. She looks like Mardi Gras all year round, that one. Peacock feathers stickin out of her head.

"When she comes round, she plays like she likes me and all, but I can tell it's part of her act, smilin with only half her face. I learned the hard way when she comes by with a plate of her beignets for lunch, and suddenly I'm nappin in the side yard half the day. 'Twas the first time Mr. Pippin ever cussed me, but he sent me home with half-a-day's pay and said to sleep it off and come back tomorrow.

"Anyways, they don't come round much after that. Maybe once in a while to check see if the work's progressin.

"I ain't really stupid. I know what goes on. Their historic house brings in the tourists. When the workers finish, it'll go back to regular business. They'll put up their shelves of gris-gris and jars of powder and straw dolls and devil T-shirts, for when the tour groups stop by.

"At night the side yard opens up, and Ma'dam Peacock brings in the johns what need servicin. She's got two other gals help her out with that. But for now, we're just fixin the place.

"To get where I'm goin…three nights back, I'm in the yard fillin trash barrels, when I hear 'em conversin inside. Priest Theo and Ma'dam Pea. And he's yellin at her, and he's saying 'bout how some other lady is throwin the wrong johns her way, and she'll spread for a monkey if this other lady says. Them's his words.

"Ms. Pea talks back, maybe too loud. Like how this other lady is makin him rich with her especial clients. And she says a name she maybe shouldn't have, so I hear a hard slap. And I'm lookin through the window sheers to see Ms. Pea flashes a shiv and holds it up to his eye, and his eyes get big knowin she don't bluff.

"The next night, I'm workin 'til after dark, cleanin out the second floor where Mr. Pippen finished up. He's helpin. We get all the junk to the backyard. We're done loadin barrels. He hands me a Yuengling and a joint while he goes out to his truck to get my day's pay.

"That's when I seen what I seen.

"Ms. Pea gettin out of her ragtop with one of her gals, and the two of 'em draggin some guy by the arms up her porch. This guy, I can't even tell the color of his shirt, for all the blood. Mr. Pippen wants none of this. Says how she should take that shit somewheres he ain't. But she tells him fuck-off home. Pardon my French."

I asked Jesus the name Ms. Peacock should not have said.

"Not sure. Sounded to me kinda like a tree. A bow tree, whatever that is."

When we reached the door, I paused with my hand on the knob. "Two things. First, it takes a big man to apologize." I studied him anew. "I am sorry. I shouldn't have scolded you in front of the others. That was wrong of me."

I opened the door and led him to the ground floor. Hemmings heard us on the stairs, and he and the others joined us in the entryway. When I opened the street door, Jesus hesitated.

"You said, two things."

"The second is, I want you to know I am proud of you for coming to me with this. It took guts."

He nearly blushed.

"And that worries me too. I know you're too experienced for this old man to tell you what to do, but for your mother's sake, I need you to stay away from those people. Stay clear of their secrets, bury your curiosity far away. You do your work for Mr. Pippen, collect your wages, and go home at the end of the day. They are more than pickpockets and prostitutes, as you now know. They are dangerous and they will pull a trigger even if they suspect you've seen the wrong thing. Do you understand me?"

He studied me back and nodded.

"Tell me you understand."

"Yes sir." He then turned to Vetty. He pointed to his own cheek. "I am sorry."

Vetty winked.

"Jesus," Dr. Maiwand said, "you know us now. We are all friends here. If you need to talk to anyone, about anything, don't stand out in the rain. Ring the bell."

Bobby J. asked Pedersen if he wanted a drink, or if he was on duty.

"I won't be on duty 'til Hell sells ice skates," he said.

"Just beers," I said. "I'm going to ask the detective to take a drive tonight." To his surprised look, "I thought we might meet here first, neutral ground, so to speak."

Bobby nodded, then to me, "Had us a curious visitor last night. Large Acadian in a tailored suit, silk tie. He sits across the room, that table there, like he needs a sightline to your booth here."

"Did you happen to get fancy man's name?"

"He said William, but he didn't look like no William. When I asked if he'd like a menu, he said, I'm waiting on someone. And he sits there for two hours, not eatin, not drinking, but staring at the door. He left this." Bobby dropped a business card in front of me. "Says, in case someone's asking after him." The business card logo stood for the Court Clerk's Office. I dropped the card in my pocket.

"More government intrigue," Pedersen said. "By the way, if you called me here to accuse another cop of being crooked, I won't have time for that beer."

With the house band about to wrap the last set for the night, we waited for their break. The singer tossed her hair and tossed the microphone to the bass player who caught it on the fly. Bobby set two beers on the table, and I thanked him. He handed me a folded napkin, which I read and stuffed in my pocket.

"I called you here to ask if you'd like a hand lifting this boulder off your neck. No matter who it involves?"

"Why am I not surprised you know more about my execution than I do?"

"No magic, Frank. I've known about Marco Pascal working with you for years. You were spotted cruising for *ladies* the day after his murder.

And then a friend on the force drops in with the news that you're off the job."

"And now you're gonna tell me another cop is setting me up."

"I'm not here to tell you. I'm here to ask if you would like my assistance."

He had his back to the door, so his jaw opened when he looked up at Sgt. Barnett, out of uniform, standing beside the table.

"I don't take up much room." She waved for him to scoot over.

"What the hell's this?" He scowled but scooted into the booth's curve anyway.

"Somebody had to tell him. So, when he called me and said he'd heard about your Kandy—"

"She wasn't *my* Kandy." His sightline fixed on me.

"I went, knocked on his door. He didn't shoot me, so I went in."

"If brass finds you sharing police business with this civilian…"

"She explained some things that needed explaining," I said. "I told her about rumors of a new I.A. target for Pascal's killer, and she confirmed. She didn't tell me anything I hadn't already figured out."

"Apparently, I'm the last to find out. Doesn't say much for my Dick Tracy Handbook lessons. Today, I learned that my own Captain is talking shit about me in public. I had to learn it from a waitress."

"From what Mr. Vagelle says," Barnett flagged Bobby's barmaid, "there may be a reason for that too." She ordered a Shirley Temple.

"So, he's got you believing department conspiracies now?"

"Would you just listen?"

"Or don't," I said. "I don't have everything I need to convince anyone the sky is blue. I need both of you to do me a favor though."

"You need my help?" He finished his beer and picked up the bottle I had yet to touch.

"I need to take a road trip. It's necessary."

"And you need a chauffeur?"

"No. I need you on stake-out. We have too many spinning plates and I can't be everywhere at once. I have friends in trouble, or they will be. I know you have time on your hands."

"Gee, thanks."

"I have a young friend who may be unaware of the danger he's in. He's been a witness to some bad people. So bad that I need you out there. I asked the sergeant to back you up if the scene turns sour."

Then I told them about my conversation with Jesus and asked them to keep an eye on the mint house. On my way to the door, I pulled the napkin from my pocket. "@ (and a pictogram house)."

I reached the Causeway after midnight.

TWENTY-SIX

Patty P.I.

The sound woke me. The softest metallic tick, but it had me wide awake and wondering where I had fallen asleep. The breath of confusion vanished the moment I recognized the dull spark on the glass bottle, Vagelle's Widow Jane Bourbon. Alya must have left a light on in the kitchen so I could find my way up the stairs without breaking my neck.

I listened for a follow-up tick and scanned the room's shadows. Once I determined tiny men from Mars had not crawled in from my dreams, I released my Colt from its ankle harness and pushed quietly from the loveseat cushions. Two steps. I halted, soundless, listening.

How long you gonna wait?

There it was. More than a tick. A far-off tinny something coming from the garage. Metal on metal, I thought. A careless misstep. My mind sped up. Yes, I had shut the large garage door, but had I locked the windows? No, we wanted to air out the Impala.

Stupid, Patty. Fucking stupid.

Marble floors. They extended from foyer to hallway to kitchen, so I kicked free of my shoes and bare-footed it, not-too-quickly, down the short hall. Options raced through my skull like rats looking for an exit. I came up with too many arguments against phoning 911.

I strained for the follow-up sounds before angling toward the kitchen.

Colt at the ready, I ducked my head round the corner to check garage access. The knob lock—still engaged. Maybe I should barricade the door with a heavy appliance.

No, silly. Whoever it is will find another way inside and will wait until I'm not ready. Right now, I know where the threat is. And the threat does not know that I know.

What about all those damn-big kitchen windows? Should I worry about another platoon like at the marina? Doubt it. More invaders would not need all this pussyfooting around.

Intuition told me to wake Alya, but I could not take my eyes off that door and I feared the slightest beep from my cell phone buttons.

The low kitchen island with its high-sheen granite top separated the distance to the garage, and I moved forward to the more defendable position. My disadvantage was that light above the gleaming stove rebounding off stainless steel, which would frame me perfectly once the intruder breached the door. He would be in shadow.

Where's that next sound, pal?

Had he come in through the garage window, or did he break the lock on the pedestrian door? *And you never reset the alarm before falling asleep. Too much stupid gets you killed.*

Either way, he would pass my car first. But he was not a car thief. And if bold enough to break in knowing people were home, he was smart enough to avoid touching the new Lexus with a factory alarm. He would have no such worries about the Impala. His object was this inner door, and he was here for one of us, or both. I hoped it was a *he*, and not a *they*.

Soft soles on the concrete. Grit on the steps. He took the knob, trying for gently, which meant he had not heard me yet. The agonizingly prolonged quarter-turn halted with an abrupt click of the lock. Next, he either has the skill to pick the lock, or he ceases to care about the noise and bangs his way in.

"Patty?" Alya cleared the corner behind me as the door jamb broke.

I jolted and cursed. "Get back!"

The door crashed inward before I could turn the Colt's muzzle back. The thing entered.

Alya gasped, as did I.

Few things could freeze me like the sight of him. Fully naked, a six-foot walking crime scene. His flesh, from face to crotch, a patchwork of scarring.

"Don't move!" I yelled.

But he did move. One step forward, into the kitchen's full light. His arms, in a Christ's "T," displaying his glory. A grotesque work of art, with himself, the artist, demanding audience approval.

Maddening. Thick, dominant scar-lines presented as a forensic pathologist's autopsy cuts. A "Y" at the top of his torso, and a long vertical drawn down the sternum. Other lesions, like pink or white tattoos without the ink, criss-crossed deep along his biceps and thighs, lighter along the neck, avoiding the arteries. *A purposeful intent.* More X-ing on the face and scalp. One eye had been bled off to a milky white. An upper lip pinched with scar tissue revealing one chipped canine and misshapen gums. Most of the cuts appeared old, some many years old. Several might have been drawn last month. And in his outstretched right fist, he clenched a thirty-inch machete.

My mind clawed its way out of madness as my handgun trembled in both hands.

"Please stop." Alya shouted from my side, and he shifted his glare. When he recognized her, a grin opened his face, and the machete lifted over his head.

"Roddy!" A man's voice roared from the garage. Vagelle's voice.

Roddy almost looked back, but he was committed. He charged forward into the kitchen, and that damaged mouth spread wide without a sound.

Two simultaneous shots. Explosive. One from my Colt, one from the garage. Roddy spun, first one way, then the other, like a raging windmill. The machete struck high in the doorframe and remained there. Roddy slammed into the cupboard's edge. He stopped. Almost surprised. He attempted one more step. Then fell.

Twenty-Seven

Vagelle

I ran toward the light. Through the garage, I rounded both cars and leaped the two steps into the kitchen. The brilliance shocked my vision momentarily, but cleared quickly. I first sighted Alya hanging onto the kitchen island like a life raft. I ran at her. Patty anticipated and stepped clear as I encircled Alya with my free arm. She let me hold her while she shook. I whispered to control her breathing.

Patty then moved on Roderick Howse. She lowered to one knee and felt for a pulse. She drew her phone, called for an ambulance. When I heard her say, "alive," I grabbed a fistful of dish towels and rushed to slow the bleeding and give aid.

"He's so—monstrous." Her breathing hitched. "What happened to him?"

"His childhood," I said. "I'll explain at another time. Neither of these wounds appears life-ending, provided EMS gets here soon. *Alya?*" She needed distracting. "Bring me a wet cloth. Make it two. Then, make sure the ambulance doesn't pass by this address."

"Looks like you need a new *safe house,*" Patty said.

"Before the cops get here, Patty, I need you to check the yard, back to front. I don't know that he could have found the house on his own. Be careful. You see a car leaving, get the plate if you can. Nothing was moving when I got here."

I wished I could get Roddy to talk, but he was out. His breathing ragged and sputtering, but uninterrupted by the sounds of it. My shot had hit him from behind, broke a femur but missed the artery. Patty had fired the more deadly of the two. It passed through-and-through beneath the ribcage and likely ruined his liver and more. I concentrated on controlling that bleed, entrance and exit. Then came the convulsions.

"They have GPS." Alya knelt across from me. "You do not need me standing at the curb." She wrapped the thigh wound and added pressure.

"You're absolutely right."

"And you are concerned for my *condition.* I understand."

I tried but could not read her. We heard sirens and Patty came in on the run.

"Grab a clean cloth for yourself." She directed Alya. "Go out the back before the police pull up."

Alya stared at me, her T-shirt and panties a red mess.

"There's a vacant house two doors to the left," I said. "Lock yourself in and steal what you need. We need to keep you out of lock-up."

She studied her hands as if willing them clean. She nodded then ran.

"If you want, go with her." I said, but Patty just shook her head.

Unlike New Orleans City, Mandeville Emergency Medical was local to the St. Tammany Fire Protection District, which no doubt helped their response times. Two paramedics rushed in with a gurney. One EMT carted his own equipment.

Patty waved them to the kitchen. They took in the scene at a glance, and the EMT waved me aside in time for a flood of police blue, weapons drawn and hoping for a target. Two detectives split the wave. The elder, seeing two handguns on the counter and both Patty and me with our bloody hands on our heads, came to me first. He displayed decorum by lowering his pistol and raising a badge.

"You know the drill?"

"Sadly," I said.

"I'm Captain Mead. You the owner?"

I shook my head.

"You?" He eyed Patty.

"No, sir," she said.

"Is he?" Pointing to the naked man being fitted for the gurney.

"Nope," I said. "My friend lets me use his place. He leaves town for the summer."

"Wait!" He waved for his associate who appeared mesmerized by the Roderick Howse body art. "Read them their rights." He frowned at the victim then signaled for a paramedic to lower the shiny thermal blanket. His instinct, shock, pushed him back a step. "What the fuck!"

"That's what I said," Patty whispered.

He spun on her. "Do you even know him?"

"Never saw him before tonight."

"Officer," I said, "I'm sure you looked up the homeowner while en route. I'm old, but not that old."

"How 'bout you tell me his name?"

"Deacon Pettijohn, Colonel."

"You could have learned that while ransacking his place."

Then why'd you ask. "Sir, I can give you a list of names to call, but if you could have your tech check us for GSR, fingerprints, and whatever else, I'd appreciate being allowed to wash my hands. And I'm sure Ms. Gunston would like to lower her arms. I admit those are our firearms on the counter, and we both shot Mr. Howse there."

"And you'd like to tell us all why?"

Patty pointed to the machete still lodged in the doorframe.

"Shee-it. Wait. Gunston? That's you?"

Twenty minutes of questioning at the scene, Captain Mead had separated Patty and me, then the lieutenant and captain and Chief of Homicide picked up the discussion again at the Mandeville PD Offices.

After permitting me to clean the blood off my hands, they printed me a second time. Two more hours in the gray room, then two more behind steel bars to "…get my head right." I handed them the list of names to call, even a few I considered antagonists.

The lieutenant said my lawyer, Whitcomb, could not be reached, but I knew that was a lie.

Mead stopped by once to look into the cage because he figured I could appreciate a good laugh. "Captain Beaudry said to make you swim home across Lake Pontchartrain with shark bait tied to your ass."

At different times they each stopped by to say I was a suspect in a child abduction and murder. Maybe they hoped for a different reaction.

By seven a.m., a desk sergeant woke me with a rattle of keys. He escorted me to the same gray interrogation room, where the Chief of

Homicide made me retell the story from earlier. I believe I used the exact words, to which he said, "You must have rehearsed that a long time." He sat and drank orange juice and coffee and ate scrambled eggs from a styrofoam box while watching me write the long version of the night, and the break-in, and the shooting. He took my six pages out the door.

Ten o'clock, the lieutenant entered and told me to go home. They had finished with my car. I would find it at impound two blocks east. "You can walk it."

"I guess you finally found Lawyer Whitcomb," I said, as I collected my personal effects.

"No. But you know better than to return to that house. Just get your ass back across the bridge."

"What about Ms. Gunston?"

"We released her a few hours ago."

"Aren't you romantic."

"You want I should extend your vacation here? Maybe you enjoy the cuisine?"

"Can you tell me if Roderick Howse made it through the night?"

He did not answer. We were met by a couple uniforms who escorted me to the police parking lot exit. At the open door, I called, "How about the name of the person who inspired my release?"

"If it'll shut you up, it was a judge. Tresor."

That shut me up.

Judge Tresor?

If one person on my list hated me more than Beaudry, I had counted on her. For her to request my release felt implausible, to say the least.

My apartment landing, the door was unlocked. Seated at her black L-desk by the corner window, *her desk*, Alya arched her back with a stretch. She did not turn immediately, but contemplated the street below her window like she had never left.

My volume of "The Eudemian Ethics" beneath her hand, brought me a smile. I went in carefully, expecting her to pivot and kick me, or at least slap me with the book. I watched the back of her until she swiveled.

"Aristotle?" I whispered, then put a finger to my lips, took a pen from the desk and scribbled on the notepad. *"Bugs. Don't speak."*

I began a serious search in the bedroom, the closet rear corner, my shoebox awaited. In the toe of one shoe, my audio jammer, and in the other, an electronic bug detector. Flipping the switch on the jammer, I laid it on Alya's palm, then began a tedious search with the detector.

Once completed, I grabbed a set of household tools from beneath the kitchen sink, unscrewed a face plate on a living room light switch, and removed the first bug. I pried off a short length of baseboard in the bedroom to find the second recessed in the drywall. The third had been duct-taped in the fake fireplace flue. Grabbing an empty mayonnaise jar from under the sink, I filled it with water and let the bugs drown.

Alya tracked my every move from her desk chair. I crossed the living room and loomed over her. I had been starved of those eyes.

"Can I hold you?" I said.

She began to rise, but I lowered to my knees, and she pulled my head to her breast. We held there just breathing, waiting for time to move backwards. I always let her decide when to let go. She touched my cheek.

"You need a shower."

"I imagine so."

Twenty-Eight

Alya

"I did like he said. I stole what I needed." My response when Patty said she liked my new look. She called it "business casual." A black sleeveless pullover with Mick Jagger's mouth below my breasts, and gray designer-brand "slouchy pants." I never heard of slouchy pants. "You know what pants are in Russia?"

"Yes. You tell me every time you hear the word." Patty carried bags and containers from her favorite Cajun restaurant into the kitchenette.

"I was young when I ran away. In my Papa's house, girls did not talk of underwear."

Mr. Hemmings had entered behind her. He wanted a hug, but I told him hugs were still difficult for me. We said some nice things. I mentioned the fresh scar on the side of his head, and he straightened a touch, prideful.

"Nice shirt," he said as he turned for the landing and his first-floor bunker.

"Well," Patty said, "as I like to say, if you're going to steal clothes, do it in an upper-class neighborhood."

"The other choices were worse. I guess women with money do not wear jeans anymore. And I do not like T-shirts with sparkles."

Nicolaus left his bedroom, showered, but wrinkled like he had slept in his clean clothes. When not wearing the sling, he kept his left hand in his pocket, his arm held tight to his side. Patty handed him a beer. He glanced at the food sacks on the counter.

"I appreciate all this, but I hope you aren't visiting restaurants that know you well. Until this morning, you were still MIA, and the wrong people will want to know you are back."

"You're welcome." She spooned the food onto plates as I set the table. "But I imagine Mandeville will change all that."

We ate, and she updated us on her day. She had called Lawyer Whitcomb, and he would have papers at Mandeville PD by the end of day. She had also called Colonel Pettijohn to give an explanation of his house, the latest Mandeville crime scene, and Whitcomb said he would follow up with him too.

"Pettijohn will get over it," Nicolaus said.

"He said he'd take care of everything there. He said he knew anything was possible when he offered the house to his *troublesome* friend. He said he needed to remodel anyway."

The night returned to shiver me.

She also called the hospital to check on Roderick Howse. Stable condition, was all they would tell her.

"Our cop buddy called me looking for you," she said. "He sounded like he wanted to argue with someone until I described our morning. Then he got all concerned and said for you to call him whenever you surfaced. No emergency, but he said that may change soon. Whatever that means."

Nicolaus gave us a rundown on Pedersen's forced vacation from the department, then his discussion with young Jesus, and that he asked Pedersen to "keep an eye on *the kid*" while he went off to keep an eye on us.

We pushed away our plates when his phone buzzed. I carried dishes to the kitchen sink

"You're on speaker, Frank, with Patty and Alya. I've been catching them up on our circling the wagons.

"You're sharing? That must have been some jail cell catharsis. Hey, Russkie. Word that you are okay may be the one bright spot in my year."

"*Spasiba*, Frank," I said.

"I couldn't wait for your call, Vagelle. We had a development last night. A minor emergency averted, I think, but your young Jesus is caught up in something. I suspect an escalation tonight if I don't show our hand, and my involvement."

"Jesus is okay?" I said, remembering the young boy.

"First," Nicolaus said, "when you and Beaudry and Breize were at my place, did you arrive with them? Or were they here when you arrived?"

"Um, no? Beaudry called to meet him here. I was across town."

"Well, I have a gift for you. Consider everything that was said in my apartment since that day, public knowledge. I found their bugs."

"Aw, shit. Don't tell me that."

"That's a full week. Take stock. Especially searching for the missing kids, our trip to Forstall Street where your friend showed up, her driving me to St. Louis Cemetery, and my cracked bean. They knew about Alya and Patty, and the boat. As well as Private Jergens, Vetty."

"I should be kicking at the end of a rope any day now. But this call is clean today?"

"Yes. Alya told us about your car chase. You both figure he was a professional driver, and his roadside pick-up, the woman, was Colin's killer. And the description of Mario Andretti, right down to the cowboy boots."

"That takes us to your Escalade. You nailed it early. You said, until we got word to the contrary, assume everything is connected."

"And going back further, it's no stretch to assume Colin got his job at St. Michael's to monitor Alya. Or more accurately, to torment her, giving proof to the outside world that she was mentally unstable."

I dropped my cup. His words another slap, a realization slap.

A renewal of the orderly's attack on me from beyond the morgue. For a moment I did not understand, then I did. I just did not understand why. Blood drained from my head with thoughts of a return to the land of "unstable."

"I'm sorry, Alya. I should not have said this right now. I should have prepared you. None of your friends believed that about you, you know."

I glared at the phone beside his plate without seeing it. He rose, but I held an outstretched hand. "No."

"Alya," he whispered.

My back touched the wall. "No. I will be okay." I waved them back. "Why? Tell me why this happened to me? This goes back to that man— that *der'mo* (shit) attacking the woman? The man I hurt. And the judge who sent me to that Hell-hospital?"

"Alya?" Pedersen said from the phone.

"I do not understand." I said from behind my hands.

"Think soft, Alya." Nicolaus wore his teacher voice now. "This is not an attack on you. It is an attack on me through you."

Stop, please.

"Whoever is behind all of this, the killings, even back to that *der'mo*, and what was done to you, to Pedersen, to Patty, even bringing Roderick Howse back to life. Using him to mess with my head—"

"That man last night is not the killer?" Patty said. "This makes less and less sense."

"It started to until the *professional* driver resurfaced. Someone hired him. Someone has been playing this, maybe for years. I won't know why until I find the who."

"Madness."

"Precisely."

"You sure that's not you wanting the guilt for every calamity?" Pedersen's voice.

"It's not ego." Vagelle said, his voice far away. "I am thinking clearly, first time in a very long time. If everything is undeniably connected— even last night, the madman's dance, him knowing my name change and finding my apartment door, then finding my safehouse. No doubts now. I am the link."

"They started with the one person you care most about in this life," Patty said. "Whoever they are, they know you this well."

"They know us, Alya. And until this moment, I thought I might never find them."

"Now you know them?"

"Not yet, Frank. But I will. And I don't want you near this. You will need plausible deniability."

"Vagelle…?

Pedersen talked.

"We got there before dark. Parked in the alley close enough to see two sides of the house. Yeah, a disgusting color, even for NOLA. Barnett checked the database to find the owners. Two of 'em. One we both know pretty well, Priest Theo. His real name, Morrison Beaudry."

Suddenly, I did not want to hear that phone voice.

"Yeah, I couldn't believe it either. The Captain has a brother apparently. But Theo wasn't home last night. The department does have a pretty good sheet on him. I guess we know why he never served time for any of it."

Turning my face to the wall, I leaned my forehead against cool plaster.

A hand on my shoulder. Patty. I shrugged her off.

"Back to the car, before dark," Pedersen continued, "we watched the house lights come on. Workers working late. I didn't see your friend Pippen…tossing the top floor, throwing crap out…the lawn…"

The voice faded in and out like electrical interference on a radio signal. I felt my feet moving.

"One of them fit your description of a lanky seventeen-year-old. The kid…running down steps…chased by…then *she* crossed the window…Miss Peacock-Feathers…" Fading out.

Silence. The room around me felt empty, like it shook off its occupants, and all else, to become the bleak cell in the *Saint Hospital.* Then Colin…

I ran a flight of stairs. Blurred by tears. "Dammit! Damn me!"

Someone called my name. Someone not me. Again, with the bad reception as I fled into a blinding bright sky.

I ran hard. Too hard. Not picking a direction. Other voices calling. Strangers.

But my breath caught, again and again. Not right. I slowed, tiring too quickly. My pump hammering in my ears. Stop. Too quick. The pavement rushed at me. Dark.

Darkness. When I could, I held a hand to my chest to feel my heartbeat.

Darkness softened and became dark angled walls around me. My other hand found a gritty, rough-plank hardwood floor as I pushed my back up against a wall to sit. A smell like dust, like wood from an old coffin—but not that, just grit, dirt and cobwebs.

Still too fogged in from that sudden crash of emotion, I begged my head to clear. I did not yet know where my crash came from.

Eventually words formed and filtered back. And from a greasy photo book in my mind, a shadow loomed. Became a person. A person without a face, like a rubber mask not fully formed. I believed this to be the person who had orchestrated my terrors. The person I could not see.

And he transformed to the other, the person who made me what I was today. The tall skinny boy who raped me on *trinadsat* (my thirteenth birthday). The boy I followed and beat to death with a lead pipe. But then he became another, larger man.

My vision struggled with the dark until I could see the face.

"Vetty?"

"*Kak vy?* (How are you?) Can you hear me?" He sat across from me, not too close, and set a water bottle on the floor within reach.

"You are speaking *Russkiy?* How am I here? Where is here?"

"Your breathing is better. I waited for you to leave the building. I did not expect you to come out this way. I could not run fast enough to catch you." He knocked on his fake leg. His prosthesis. "Another episode?"

"Another." I accepted the water. My heart found its pace.

"You know the drill. Drink. Focus on the drinking. Remember Group? Empty your mind, like you empty the bottle. Little by little. Control your breath."

"You are sounding like my shrink. You have been to a lot of sessions, sure. How long was it for you in there?"

"Mine is different. Just good old-fashioned PTSD."

"Sorry."

"Drink."

I did.

"You are in a place I lived in for a time. This used to be a supply closet in an abandoned office building. Now it has forgotten to be even that. Quite a few of these in N'awlins, even before the Covid. Fortunately, when you fell, this place was close by."

"Why were you waiting for me? It is not a good feeling, someone waiting and I do not know why."

"I am…After you escaped St. Mike's, following was only a curious thing. Like when you were chased from that underground garage and ended up in the boat yard. Seems everything you do…sorry, I am only curious and, well, I have nowhere else to be."

"Is that all? You are uncertain even of that."

"I guess it looks bad, huh?"

"You speak Russian."

"Some. A little."

"You did not speak it to me before."

"I was not sure…" He thought before answering. "Not sure your bad memories would connect you to it. The language is why I was in Afghanistan. Russians were there for fifty years. Many Afghans speak it better than English."

Fear made me question his logic. I drank more water.

"You wonder why I do what I do?" I said. "I run because I cannot stop. Running away is because I need to be alone. Running away to think when my brain is too crowded, or because I cannot think beyond my fears. I run because I know I am hunted. I ran from my Papa in Russia. Then he sent men to find me here, and I ran. Until Mr. Vagelle made him stop."

"He was a good find for you, Mr. Vagelle. A man to help in your darkest times. And ask what from you in return?"

Nothing. "Now, I run from memories. And now from police, and whoever is trying to ruin my life. Fears and more fears. And now I felt you following—"

"And I became one more person hunting you. I—I did not understand."

"I know, but knowing does not help me."

"Finish your water." He rose slow. He turned away and became a guard dog on the supply closet door. "I will stay until I know you feel well again. Well enough. Then I will not follow you."

"That would be best."

Twenty-Nine

Vagelle

A double knock on the door. Hemmings.

"Come!"

The door crept open. "Mr. Vagelle?" He surveyed the room. "Oh my. What happened here?"

"What do you need?"

"I didn't mean to disturb you. I—you are always so organized, I did not expect this." He adjusted his head wrap and inspected the room like a fire marshal after a bomb blast.

"I am extremely busy."

"Evidently. Um—if this can wait for tomorrow, maybe I can assist in some—but it's been a long day and…"

I dove my attention back into the scattering of loose papers, books, and folders across the floor, settee, tables, and every other flat surface in the apartment. As he had not finished the statement, when next I looked, he was clearing dinner plates and detritus from the dining room to the kitchen.

"Don't bother. I'll get that later." I found forms I had been searching for inside a folder color-coded red. Alya's most recent case folder. The court case.

"Maybe you didn't see, it's already later. We're into the a.m." Silverware clattered, and water splashed into the sink. "I know you have a printer. If you'd spend a little time scanning those—I see you are already not listening."

"Quiet, please."

I began organizing folders in chronological order, first by date, then stacking by level of importance and association with each of my primary suspects and threats. Folders with police incident reports and violence, I had given their own discrete floor space of honor.

Partway through the process, I concluded that Alya's difficulties did not begin with the assault and criminal court case. I found an almost regular pattern of minor confrontations. Petty traffic tickets. Her apartment broken into. Police responded, but she could find nothing missing, so she never told me about it—or had she?

Another night, officers were called to a confrontation in a restaurant when a drunken city official threw a drink because she turned down his invitation to the adjacent barstool. Patty held her back, the drunk rushed the table, and Patty broke his tooth with the barrel of her Glock, God bless her.

The incident emptied the restaurant. By the time police arrived, the bartender was ready to blame the two women for interrupting his evening's tip percentage.

There were other such incidents going back nearly a year, a few not long after Alya's nightmare on Atius Russo's farm.

Naturally, I failed to recognize the patterns because I had been too steeped in my own selfish distractions. *Self-flagellation.* As the toll of deaths moved in around me, I had isolated myself for fear of emotional contagion to my friends.

"Her car is gone from your garage." Patty had returned to stand in my doorway.

"As I assumed. Here." I tossed a thick accordion folder at her feet. She decided not to glance down.

"Whatever you're looking for, chief, should I be confused about you not out there looking for her? She's still sick. She needs help."

Water poured into the toilet, then Hemmings emerged from the bathroom, yellow rubber gloves past his wrists, a bucket and sponge in one hand, a mop in the other, sweat rings under each arm.

"You heard her leave, Hemmings. Which way did she run?"

"East." He set the assortment on the landing.

"And the garage is west, so we can assume she ran some distance, until she decided to circle back for her car. That means cognition had returned. She was calming."

"Listen to yourself, Professor Gives-a-Shit." Patty spun a military about-face and went for the refrigerator.

"You could not catch up to her. I wouldn't have been able to. I don't know where she went, especially if she has the car."

"Few people can outrun that woman," Hemmings said.

"Which is why you are here, Pat. What about the leather bag?"

"My guy working crime scene cleanup at the safe house, he found it in the sitting room and pinched it for me. As I chased after our girl, he rang. Said he found her car. Your bag's now in the trunk."

"That was fortunate timing."

"Then I checked her usual places." Patty cracked open a beer. "Bobby's, her apartment, the boat. I covered half of New Orleans, then checked with one of my PIs I could still trust. I asked him to start a search with his contacts." She squatted, set the bottle between her feet, and opened the folder out of curiosity.

"Maybe her one-legged friend followed and is acting as her bodyguard, wherever she is."

"How would you assume that? *Assuming* is not like you."

"He's been across the street on stake-out since she came back."

"He does act a bit like a puppy looking for a new owner. So, what am I supposed to do with this here?"

"I'm hunting for associated names, either connected, or out of place. The red folders in there are Alya's court case or related. The names I'm interested in are Colin, an alias for Charles Fend. Elizabeth Standt. Gander, last name. Or Devon Brown." I caught her unspoken response, then returned to my document search. "Oh, and Roderick Howse and that whole family, of course."

"As I'm not the genius in the room, you can repeat all that once I find a pencil?"

"You can use the dining table now," Hemmings said, then shuffled spiritlessly for the door.

"Nicolaus?" Patty whispered.

"You are right, of course" I said. "This is busywork. I am..."

"You are lost."

"I worry about your emotional connection to both. You will feel to be controlling these disparate threads until you cannot."

"Excuse me?" she said.

"Oh, something an old friend said recently."

"This afternoon you as much as said, whoever is orchestrating all this is messing with your head. Sounds like it's working. You're finally accepting their success? Are you broken yet?"

A growing intensity heated within. "Never." Understanding her verbal manipulation, I permitted it to work.

"So, do we continue with your files?"

"There can be only one course for me." My back straightened. "If the rest of the world is burning, Alya becomes my sole priority. We all keep thinking she is the damaged person the authorities are trying to convince us of. We observe her outbursts, and while she may lose sight of the moment, I know she keeps fighting to come back. She may get lost, but this woman has been through too much. She will refuse to stay lost."

"She's learned to deal with that trauma her entire life," Patty said. "Now, with her back against the wall, Alya will be angry. You've thought of that. Will it be a controlled anger, reasoned, and looking to fix what appears broken?"

"She will not hide," I said. "She will hunt. And we need to find her before she finds those she deems a threat."

Patty would track her instincts, as I trusted. However, I had one last detour. I told her I needed at least seven hours, and gave her a few places I could use her assistance.

I explained that we needed to start thinking like Alya. She would be looking for answers, but she might find the wrong people in the process.

I asked her to check in with Pedersen first. I had sent him to watch after young, Jesus, but now he needed someone watching his back—someone I trusted.

"You don't need someone checking your six?" she said.

"Thinking like Alya, I know a few names she might chase down. First, I need a long drive to see another friend. That's why I need the time. I believe it is important for all of this."

"And you? I would like to at least know your whereabouts, in case I have to call out a mob with pitchforks and torches."

"Charenton."

"Well." Her brows lifted. "That was an unexpected answer. This has nothing to do with—"

"No. That farm is barren ground. Nightmare stuff, but nothing more. Like I said, a visit with a friend. I'll be back by morning. Getting back to Pedersen, you be careful. The people there are dangerous, deceptively so. If our lieutenant has things under control, you can keep checking the harbor. Tomorrow, I could use you on Roderick's hospital room."

"Because that might be an obvious place for our dear Russian to look for answers? Oh, and on your way out, poke your head in at Hemmings. He needs you to say thank you."

"Are you still a night owl?" I texted, fearing a call might wake her.

I spent many years avoiding contact with Daniella Murphy. Perhaps more than avoiding. I simply feared speaking to her. I feared more what a rekindling of the memory might do to her, especially after all this time, a late-night intrusion, and my voice she no doubt despised. I last saw her standing graveside as her husband's box lowered toward the hole. Since then, I could not think of her without those eyes locked onto mine with such legitimate resentment.

I had tried reaching out, maybe once a year, on Christmas, or her birthday, until her automatic response became a simple hang-up. Now, I wondered if a meeting with this ghost from her distant past might be akin to Roddy Howse materializing unexpectedly on my threshold.

"Still working graveyard shift," her typed reply. The last time I checked on her, she worked dispatch for the Tribal Fire Department.

"I hate to ask this…"

"You need to talk." A cop's wife comes with scalpel-sharp instincts.

"I hated to call. To remind you of things."

"Well, you have done that now, haven't you?"

"I am so sorry, Dani."

"You would not have texted unless it was life and death. Should I guess? Are you already driving out here?"

"Thought about it. But decided that would be even less fair to you. Are you able to talk?"

"It's been so long."

I considered my response.

"I would like to see you, Nicolaus."

THIRTY

Alya

My mind felt a loosening of the chaos waves into ripples. Maybe enough for me to understand I could survive this episode.

Vetty left me. Before he did, he again reminded me of Papa by saying, "Fear is a bear. You know you can never outrun him. Running makes him see you as prey and he will chase all the harder."

Then Papa would add, "*You have two choices. You can lie down and die. Or face him, stand as tall as you can, and attack.*"

Then I would say, "*But Papa. I can never scare a bear.*"

And he would say, *"Maybe not. But it is better than offering him a meal.*

I made my way to the street without falling, so I mocked my own weaknesses. I told myself, commanded myself, to stop triggering. I kept losing myself with the internal uproar. But Shrink always came back with…

"Neurological Dysregulation will be a lifetime battle, dear Alya.

Your rational self can fight your way back, but you will not anticipate every trigger." And I was the only person who could decide *fight or flight*.

Outside, my bearings obvious, I soon found my way back to the garage and my Impala. My first turn of the steering wheel dropped a folded note between my shoes.

"Please let me help—V."

I left it on the floor, stopping long enough to open the trunk. His messages were seldom without layers. In the trunk I found the shoulder bag with my laptop. He knew I would latch onto a goal, and he left me the means to achieve it.

"Find your threads." I could hear him say. "Follow the one you choose."

Beginning with the torment I understood, I knew Colin, and I knew he was dead. Nicolaus said the name on his driver's license identified a Charles Fend. He did not mention Fend's address, an alias as well? What else did I have? His last employer.

I left the city on the northbound freeway and turned off at the Gonzales exit. After sunset the poverty-cursed neighborhoods appeared slightly less cursed, with uglier details hidden from the light. I recalled Donaldsonville, across the river, from an earlier time. Also, I knew the Ascension County Sheriff's Office existed only to be avoided.

The city of Gonzales would be much the same, but with more industry, I knew there would be a touch of good along with the bad. That was where I needed to be, but I did not know if I could drive past *St. Michael's Mental Health and human theme park*. For eight months my prison, the closer I got, the sicker I felt. I focused on the blacktop dotted lines.

Pulling into the well-lit parking lot of a late-night diner with all its neon intact—so the neighborhood must be upscale—I felt the need to coat my sour stomach. I took the shoulder bag in with me.

When I ordered chicken-fried steak with no gravy, the waitress tipped her head like I had said Russian caviar. I requested Earl Gray tea.

"We got Lipton or Lipton."

"Do you have Wi-Fi?"

"Girl, you must be new. You're lucky to find a working landline out here." Sarcasm I understood.

A separate rattle when I dragged the laptop from the bag, Nicolaus also left me with a new cell phone and charger. *I am so predictable.* Keying the phone settings, I found "Mobile Hotspot and Tethering."

In years past, he had installed what he called "diving sites" on the laptop. Websites, some private, where he could access less-than-public information pages, some of them government affiliated. I dove into the DMV site. "Charles Fend," no luck. I tried the license number on his Camaro, but it came back registered to a Mildred Sweeny in Lake Charles. More bad luck.

Dinner arrived while I brooded. I Googled St. Michael's, and St. Michael's Medical. I only got into the public pages. Some staff names with photos but no personal information, of course. I tried the diving sites for the name Standt, Elizabeth. I discovered that she drove a 2020 Ford Escape.

Waving to the waitress, I signaled for more tea. When she came with the hot water refill, I asked to borrow her pen. Her look roamed my face like I might try to run out the door with it. She left it and went straight for the counter to grab another. I jotted Standt's license number on a napkin, then found her address.

I left the waitress enough tip to buy a new pen.

Stopping for gas I bought a Louisiana map in case I lost cell connection. Still unaware of my own intentions, I did not know to be anxious or happy that I had no gun in the car. The chicken-fried steak knife I stole from the diner reflected a shiny inadequacy.

What if she had a family? She had money, might she have a gun of her own? Probably. A large house with security cameras? Maybe I'll sleep in my car and wait for her to leave for work tomorrow.

11:15. Traveling past dark businesses, grocery stores, an old hotel, street signs, I checked the map. I turned the intersection alongside a busy lot with glowing signs for "Ladies Night," and "Dance 'til One." It caught my eye long enough for me to spot a new-ish silver Ford Escape. I nosed forward and read the plate.

"Too much coincidence, or luck, or—" Vagelle whispered the warning, *"The gods setting you up for a fall?"*

I waited. A young couple left their parked car, headed for the entrance. I hurried behind, ready to enter with my two-person moving shield.

Head down, my hair just long enough to hang across my eyes, luck delivered again with the first booth unoccupied. I immediately slid into the curve. Pretending to check my phone while keeping my hair forward, I observed the busy room by sections. For once I wished for a more crowded room.

Dance 'til One? Also, "Karaoke Night" apparently. A DJ, two couples shifting their feet, trying to melt as one, and a round-bellied singer in bib overalls and a plumber's cap at the mic. The sounds were indescribable. Another booth cradled lovers with busy hands. Most club patrons swarmed the bar ready to kill for Last Call.

"You here to drink or watch?" A waitress had appeared. At least she smiled.

"Do you have Widow Jane Bourbon?" I smiled back. "How about white Zin?"

"You got it, love. Don't know that I've seen you in here before."

"Escaping…the husband. Just driving through."

"Don't I know the feeling, love. Did he get physical? I ran from three husbands who liked to knock me around. Do you have a place to stay? I might…"

"Oh, no. Thank you." That will teach me. Nicolaus always said, *If you are inventing a story, keep it simple. Others may want to turn it into a conversation.* "I have a sister across the river."

"Well, if you need to escape her—here, let me get you that drink."

As she cleared my line of sight, I saw through a crack in the bar crowd to another table. A man with his back to me, and a woman. Her. *Standt.* And she kept twisting her neck, like she feared being recognized, until he shook a finger at her face.

Too far for me to hear, but she responded, angry. They each leaned forward. His finger turned into a fist, then he pulled away. He had gotten the attention of some at the bar. When he looked around, I recognized the profile. The Camaro's driver. Colin's hospital visitor.

I lowered my head again. My drink lowered in front of me, and the waitress scooted to the other side of the table.

"Are you gonna be okay, love?" She held out a hand to touch mine, but my hands flew to my face as if hiding tears.

"You are very nice. It is…" I felt bad deceiving this kind woman.

"It must be new for you. I remember what that feels like, from those first two *a-holes* I ran from." She continued by telling me, in too much detail, about her relationships, but I had stopped listening. Standt and Camaro Man on their feet, still arguing, now they headed toward me, toward the door.

One more ounce of luck on the night, my compassionate, talkative waitress. I watched through my fingers as they passed and let the night air into the room.

I smiled sadly for my companion. I let the wine touched my lips. "I really should go. It was a bad idea to drink tonight, and I have to drive." I reached for cash.

"Of course, hon." She pushed the bills back to me. "Don't you worry about it, now. I've got you covered. If you ever get back through here—"

"You cannot know how much I needed your voice. I hope we meet again." I left the money on the table and escaped.

As I did, I recognized the Camaro silhouette backing out from between muddy workmen trucks. Having witnessed his driving skills first-hand, I hung back in the club parking lot for as long as was practical. The taillights drifted to become twin embers on the mostly dark boulevard. I pulled out with my headlights off until I knew he could not easily clock my movements in his rear view.

I had driven all this way hoping to find *Administrator* Standt. I had even grown sick with the closeness of St. Michael's, and thoughts of facing her down. Seeing her across the bar, brought me closer to violence than I had come since that night at the harbor. I still clung to grim fantasies of following her home.

And then what?

The Camaro taillights moved around and between other cars.

Maybe he spotted me? But a car turned off and my quarry reappeared. He swung the next corner.

A classier neighborhood, and this late at night, turning behind him would be an obvious mistake. I drove straight through the intersection and accelerated to the next. I sped into that turn.

Killing my headlights, I slowed to a roll and thought back on the map. *Der'mo!* This was Standt's part of town, as I recalled her address. No need to follow Mr. Camaro. I knew where he was headed. I glanced to the map again.

Now, how to interpret this? They left the club fuming. Her car already out of sight when I came out.

I reached the spot one block over from where I knew he would stop. Behind Standt's home. I inched past her front door, a two-story Colonial with manicured lawns and artfully shaped hedges almost encouraging bad guy concealment.

A second-floor light winked off. Either she jumped into bed quickly, or I had spooked her.

U-turning at the cross street, I parked three doors away. I slumped behind the wheel.

Now, my dilemma became do I stay out of it and let him eliminate the target of his anger—and mine? Or do I knock on her door and risk her shooting me? Was I not some crazed escapee from St. Michael's who had tracked her down? But, no decision really.

A car door closed one block over.

He would not dally. I walked the sidewalk until my feet touched the curb across from her house.

*One…two…three…four…*He would have reached the back of her house now. Glancing down at this neighbor's shrubs, decorative river rock lining the base, I heard splintering wood from behind Standt's pretty home.

My smooth, round stone sailed nicely over the street, the sidewalk, and through Standt's bedroom window.

Thirty-One

Vagelle

It took less than two hours of reckless driving through the night, out Route 90—once nominated as the most dangerous highway in the country. Passing Morgan City, crossing the Lower Atchafalaya River, with its many snaking tributaries amid black swampland and old farms, I pumped my brakes at the sight of dark movement on the road. My lights defined the thing in time for me to swerve. I halted twenty-some feet beyond the struggling young, four-point buck.

I moved slowly onto the shoulder, reversed a touch, then pulled the emergency flashers. In the side mirror, the crimson lights pulse saddened the animal's efforts. I left the driver's seat and walked slowly back to him.

Forelegs kicking in a vain attempt to stand, head turning, staring and not comprehending, he fought to drag his crippled hind legs along the hot asphalt. Two feet, three feet, four. He stopped, ribs expanding by harsh gulps. When I got to within five feet of him, he ceased his struggles to stand. He looked up at me. I bent and laid a hand on his neck. He stilled. I apologized before ending his pain.

Difficulty raising my head, words seemed useless and foreign. An emptiness touched me. That other highway. The ghost of a child held in my arms. I pushed it away. With the distant lights approaching, I re-holstered, took a firm one-hand grip on an antler, and threw my weight into the pull. In time for the passing of lights, I dragged the victim to the edge of the asphalt, and off.

I cruised into my destination, St. Mary Parish and the Chitimacha Rez., Charenton.

The oldest tribe in Louisiana, many had moved away with the centuries and the hardships, until those remaining locally had whittled down to little over a thousand. But those who stayed had remained tight, mostly. A community like few others looking out for their own.

With the death of her husband, my partner on the NOPD, Daniella moved back here for her people. Familial comfort.

Thirty minutes out, had I texted my ETA, and she sent back her address. She stood framed in the light of her open doorway as I pulled to the curb in front of the tidy red-brick house. I had spent the entire drive anticipating where this conversation would transport us, without lingering long enough to speculate. With shadowy pictures of Murphy haunting my thoughts, that walkway from my car to her door felt, in my chest, like a gallows' walk.

"Come," she said.

I thanked her.

With many lights aglow, despite the time of night, the living room looked as if a maid service had left an hour ago. Tidy comfortable furniture. Walls hung with family photos, traditional weavings. Corners with a few reed baskets to hold books or knitting. Many keepsakes. One such keepsake perched at the edge of a shelf, a small gold heart holding a delicate, pink glass center, and within this a lock of child's hair. A gift from me nearly fifteen years ago, after the birth of their daughter, Sylvia.

"Before you ask," she said, "no, I did not bring that out after your call. I'm having coffee. Would you like a beer—? Did something happen? You look a mess."

"Oh, sorry." I appraised my dirty sleeves. "Might I use your restroom? Deer trouble on the highway."

"Of course. First on the right. Use any towel in there. Wait!" She disappeared and returned holding a man's white button-down shirt.

"Coffee would be perfect, thank you," I called from the hall.

"You look different," she called back. "Not counting the mud and sweat. But I guess we all do."

I certainly felt different. Stripping to my waist, I scrubbed as I could, unable to wash away the night's highway sins.

"More snow on your roof," she said on my return, then moved back into the kitchen. "And you've lost weight in your face. Are you eating well?"

"You still look good, Dani," I said.

"And you never learned how to lie, Nicky. That hasn't changed. I put on thirty pounds since..." She returned with twin coffee mugs.

We faced each other from opposite sides of the living room. I nearly said something less than profound.

"So, you drove two hours to chat with your shoes stuck to my throw rug? Sit. Go on."

I obeyed.

She held both mugs while gazing down at me, until some whimsy tipped her cheek. She passed me a mug.

"Yes?" I said.

"Oh, just a thing I thought I'd never see. You in my living room, sitting on this couch."

I did not know how to respond, so I said, "Is Sylvie home? I hope I didn't wake her."

"She's home on break, but she knows all about you." Dani headed off my concerns with a head shake and a soft tilt to her eyes. "When you pulled up in front, I looked in on her. She's asleep with her headphones on."

"I hope—"

"Okay, Nicky. After eight years, let's beat around the bush some before you spill why you made this jaunt. Don't know that I've ever seen you this uncomfortable." She squinted up then dimmed the overhead lights before taking the adjacent armchair.

"You didn't see my last court appearance."

"There's a comparison. Okay, I need to say it. Say it right off, to get it out of the way." She blew across the mug, pausing to think without sipping. "Yeah, it's hard seeing you too, especially here in my home. But if time does not heal, sometimes it lends perspective."

"Dani—"

"Let me." Her look avoided me and settled on the gold heart with the pink glass and the feathery curl of hair. "Hate is a monster. It eats folks up. I never hated you, Nicky."

"You sure as shootin wanted to sometimes."

"I blamed you for a long time. Guess you figured that, huh? That psycho in your apartment, she took my Murph from—from my Sylvie."

This was what I feared. That my coming here would be for my own selfish reasons, and could only bring back the pain to her life. "I've always known there was nothing I could say—"

"I wasn't finished. That hasn't changed in you either."

"Dani, my failings never move on. I could write a book on me."

"Drink your coffee so I can talk." Her cup changed hands, then back. "I said I blamed you, past tense. But in time…I know my Murph, Darlin. I know better than anyone how he was on a job. Too damned much forward, and never back. Never taking things easy. Sure, I wasn't there that night, but I have lived that scene in your apartment every night for eight years."

A thought touched her eye, she rose from the couch and crossed to the television stand where she lifted a framed photo.

"You'll get a kick out of this," she said.

I kept my silence as she held the photo out for me. A pretty girl, mid-teens, wearing a track uniform and cradling a golden trophy. Sylvia smiling up at her proud mother with one hand on her arm, and the other holding two fingers poking up behind her head.

"Two beauties," I said. "I seem to recall most photos of you and Murph, and you with that same gesture."

"Her daddy would be so proud." She returned to sit beside me on the couch, rather than the armchair. "Those horrors in your apartment, in my dreams—I've come to accept it was my husband who came to you with that case. That serial killer case."

My finger traced the girl's face in the photo.

"You had been gone from *the life*. You quit the force because you wanted distance from those things. But she had killed too many and would continue the killing. My Murph knew you were one of the few he could trust to bring her to ground. He said as much, and often that last year. He also knew you could never say no to him for long."

There was no comeback worthy of her love for him.

She let the silence become uncomfortable, then, "She is a beautiful girl, isn't she?"

"You just finished telling me I never learned how to lie."

"He loved you, you know. My Murphy."

"I was his *boot.*"

"Bootcamp. He told me. He made himself your drill instructor."

"Pretty much. Not literally, but pretty much."

"And—I know how much you suffered from his loss as well."

Laying the photo on the coffee table seemed a viable distraction from talk of the old days.

"I was a train wreck," she said. "A depression lasting for years. Now, I hurt knowing how much I had affected Sylvie's early life. It took a great grief counselor to point that out to me. Between Sylvie and her—she's the one who convinced me to examine my husband more closely. I believed I knew everything about my man. Then one day I opened his lock box in the garage. His *secret stash of personal life,* I call it. Did you know he kept a journal? How many men do that?"

"I can believe it of him. Always afraid he'd eventually get old and forgetful, like his Pops, and lose all his best memories. Mostly memories of you."

"But not always good memories. He had to remember all of it. *The good and the shit,* he used to call it."

"The good and the shit." Murphy's words lifted me a notch.

Dani let the talk wander, almost as if she needed to tell me about everything I had missed since those early years. *"Lost in the weeds,"* Murphy would say about his conversations with her. I asked her more about Sylvia, and she appeared happy I brought it up.

She carried the storytelling forward. That eventually bled into her mentioning her brother's dislike of me. Chief Deputy Dupré, a sheriff over in Iberville Parish. A nasty case I had pulled out from under him, found a killer he had been protecting, and he lost his position with the state police because of it. She said he moved back here to the Rez after that.

"Tribal Police and Fire have a permanent *Now Hiring* sign. Scarcity of applicants, and all," she said. "If you don't mind, I won't be telling him about your late-night visit."

"That's probably for the best."

"Speaking of which, we should get around to your reason for making the long drive." Then she sat through my full story.

She had met Alya back when I first took the girl in.

"That pretty girl with the accent? She was what, nineteen, twenty? And she stayed around all this time? Murph used to say she'd be trouble for you."

"I guess the only real trouble was…"

"She grew up. Don't tell me. You and her?"

"We grew together, Dani. Friends. Close friends. You might say she has helped get me through quite a bit over the years." And I continued the story of Alya, her difficulties, and how it fed into our present struggles. I told her my reasons for tonight's visit, how they connected to my reason for leaving the force. Murphy's final "official" case with me. The death of Madeline Howse.

She listened, and with appropriate intensity, as she had lived that case, day by day, through him. I worried again about bringing this story of her husband in on her after all this time.

Excusing herself, she left the room. Perhaps I had overstayed her invitation. She returned carrying a heavy box. I started up to help her, but she ignored me until she could set the box on the coffee table.

"Journals. I wore the darn things out with all the page-turning over the years. I think Murph would want you to read these."

"You're sure?" My fingers tightened.

"You are mentioned in here often enough. Maybe it's time you knew more. But I want them back when you finish. I may never read them again—no, that's bullshit. Who am I kidding?"

We wrapped the night with a few good memories. She eventually led me to the door, and I carried her box. "If the sun comes up, and a neighbor sees your fancy car out front, they'll likely call the cops. Then we'll both see my brother."

One step out the door, I turned. Past her shoulder a slender shadow movement within the deeper shadows of the hallway. A soft spark in the eyes. As she did not come forward, I pretended not to see. I said softly, "I have missed you, Dani."

"Oh, Nicky." She wrapped me in her arms, crushing the box between us. "Bring back my box." Her tears touched my cheek.

THIRTY-TWO

Pedersen

The mint house, aka "Peacock's Coven and Curiosities," except this time of night, more the color of dirty swamp moss.

Sgt. Barnett insisted on driving. I argued until she pointed out that my SUV might go unnoticed a second night, but the passenger window's plastic sheet stood out a bit. Besides, she still had the badge. On duty, plain-clothes tonight, she might get called away spur-of-the-moment. She impressed me as one of those women who never lost an argument.

Zero parking nearby, like last night, we left her car two blocks back and hoofed it in.

A half-block over from St. Ann Street, away from the popular parade routes, not all of the French Quarter could boast Mediterranean black iron lace, hanging plant pots, year-round Christmas lights, and balconies draped with drunkards. Here, whole blocks had been beaten into submission by the years and the elements. Pavement had broken away, with cobblestones askew or gone missing. Proper street drains left to the imagination along with the curbs to direct the all-too-frequent storm waters. Here one might even find a street-level business closed before ten p.m.

Last night we had marked one such small, two-story, Cajun bakery with a direct sightline to the mint house. Barnett proved her additional skillset by picking the front door lock.

She walked the inner rooms checking for occupants, while I dragged two hard-backed chairs into the shadows, free of the window's falling streetlight. She eventually joined me with a loaf of day-old bread and two bottles of water.

"Thanks."

"You'd rather I stole a plate of yesterday's beignets?"

"Well, yeah."

Last night, conversations proved awkward—or I should say I proved awkward in conversation. Until I could see her, not as a woman, but as a fellow cop who liked talking shit about herself as much as most guys. She could blather about her shooting scores on the firing range or taking down a perp with a slap to the Adam's apple when no one was looking. She seldom required a verbal response, so I could tune her out and think about Captain Beaudry choking on a chicken wing.

I considered Vagelle's warning. Something dangerously off about this place, but he stayed mum on specifics, as usual.

Years past, I had a couple of run-ins with Priest Theo, Morrison Beaudry. A tough guy in a scrap. Taller than his brother, the Captain, but no excess meat, just lean gristle, and large hands he used to crack walnuts out of habit. The last time I brought him in, he'd been I.D.'d for picking the wallet off a vacationer in a cemetery tour group. A healthy college jock took a swing at him, and Theo grabbed and broke his windpipe. The only thing keeping Theo from serious prison time was high connections, an anonymous benefactor, and a last-minute hand-of-fate in the name of everyone's least favorite judge.

Come to think of it, that arrest was the first time the Captain suspended me. He claimed excessive force, when it was Priest Theo who nearly broke my wrist with both hands.

"I think we got here too late." Barnett looked ready to make another water-bottle run.

"Probably. Vagelle said the work crew stayed late most nights. Pippen's usually a late riser and starts around noon. His clean-up crew comes in toward the end of his shift each day. I caught a movement in the house when we got here, but no one's come or gone since."

"Near the witching hour," she said, "and neither hide nor hair of our palm reader either."

"Funny. Hey, what's today's date?"

She scrunched her face like I had passed wind.

"It ain't close to August yet, right?"

"You lost me, copper."

"August first and second, their Harvest—Never mind. It's that whole Hoodoo and tarot thing I'm staring at for hours in the window over there."

"Cue the spooky music time?"

A crash. A shadow crossed the upstairs window. Seconds later, the shadow flying downstairs bent me forward like my chair was spring-loaded.

"You see that?"

"Huh."

A scrawny man flew from the door, leaped down the front steps into the light. The kid, Jesus, hit the walkway, likely expecting a curb where there was none. His ankle buckled. He limped in pain, and a larger man chased after him into the street.

I hit the bakery door expecting it to open. It didn't. Locked. I glanced at Barnett and, in frustration, kicked the glass out of the door.

Priest Theo, dragging Jesus to his feet, looked up at the crash, with me struggling through the broken pane.

"What's the matter with you?" I yelled over my shoulder.

"Sorry. I—" was all I heard from Barnett.

"Mr. Ex-cop!" Theo braced to meet me. He must have gotten the memo from his brother.

"Freeze, Beaudry!"

"What're you gonna do, Ex-cop? Mr. Soft-In-The-Middle Ex-cop? We gonna *rastle?*"

I slowed my walk. "Call it in, partner." But Barnett must have taken a retroactive sick leave.

Theo started my way, flexing his hands, cracking invisible walnuts.

"Boy! You okay?" I called.

Jesus limped away from the impending shit-fest.

"Of course he's okay." Priest Theo closed the distance, held out his hands in surrender. "I'm just helping my worker to his feet. I'm sure we can find a reliable witness somewhere."

My right hand held at my back. Theo laughed.

"You gonna shoot me in cold blood, Mr. Ex-cop?" Thirty feet apart now. "You got no badge. You can't even pretend you got a gun." His hands dropped, then one lifted his shirt-tail. The other drew a Bowie knife from his belt. The large, fat blade flickered under colored lights. It changed hands and winked at me.

"Barnett?"

No answer.

"Don't do this, Beaudry!"

"Ya scared?" Grinning like a year-old corpse, he picked up his pace. He had not gotten the memo that I still carried Alya's pistol under my shirt. At ten feet, I dropped him. His Bowie landed first.

I closed the distance, my caution marking his tremors. He failed to sit up and witness the blooming stain beneath his sternum. His stare shifted in his head, still looking for the source of his death, afraid to blink. I kicked his Bowie at a watery pothole.

A woman screamed from the house, snapping my attention. Shaken, I raced up the steps. Then a lifetime of cop training held me at the door. More slowly, my gun hand led the way inside. Footsteps from behind turned me. Jesus followed at a limp.

"Sir?" Whispering. "She—"

The backdoor banged, and a lightbulb shattered to death.

"Wait here!" I waved behind me and, with a curse, continued through to the rear of the house.

"She's gone." He pointed to the window and I caught the barest glimpse of a lanky woman galloping through a sliver of light between tight buildings. Jesus sniffed into his hand.

Damning Barnett with every other thought, I called for a meat wagon and back-up. The boy flexed his ankle beside me, and cast a frightened look at the hallway.

"What?" I said.

A clipped headshake.

Down the passage to a storeroom, I halted at a crunching beneath my feet. Broken walnut shells. Piled boxes blocked my path, but I pushed through to the kitchen. Dark, but enough light from outside to make out the grime and refuse. I smelled ancient cooking grease, and other less pleasant things.

"Through there," Jesus whispered.

"What are you taking me into, boy?"

"It's—I found it—"

Beyond the kitchen, to the left, an old-world mudroom. Nineteenth Century rain gear, cloaks, and furs and costumes for festivals I couldn't imagine. Yard tools, in this hood with a scarcity of yards. Twin shovels, a pickax, a barrel of who-knows-what, and against one wall, like a thing I had last seen in a hunter's lodge when I was a kid, a horizontal freezer.

Jesus gripped the doorframe making sounds with his mouth.

I lifted the freezer lid.

Patty P.I.

I got there late. I cruised past the greenish house and circled the four-block area many times searching for his SUV, coming up empty. I phoned repeatedly, but he must have turned off his ringer. Understandable on stakeout, but frustrating for anyone trying to make contact. I left messages. I texted.

The house appeared unoccupied with a single light in an upstairs room, maybe to deter vagrants while the house underwent remodeling. The workers would have finished hours ago, or so I imagined.

I widened my search.

I checked at an all-night diner, knowing Pedersen, then a popular cop-owned bar, only to be greeted by hopeful ogling. I even strolled into a couple of rowdy clubs, trying my "back off" attitude while scanning for faces I might know. Two young SWIs (Standing While Intoxicated), impressed with my stature, tried to convince me I was "enough woman for both of them." One called me a "Hot MILF," but my snarl sent them back to the bar to stare into their drinks.

Phoning a friend at the precinct, I asked him to put the word out for Pedersen, MIA. His colleagues, he said, might throw a party if he was found face-down in Blind Lagoon.

"Tell them Patty said I'm baking dog-shit brownies for their next Thanksgiving soirée."

Driving more circles I grew increasingly frustrated with post-midnight traffic. As experience continued to teach, the later the evening, the more frequent the bullshit petty crimes, so I avoided the less egregious.

I called 911 on a motorcyclist who had crashed, unaided, into a parking meter. I got out once to chase off a duo of low-IQ gangsters stomping a white-haired woman who refused to relinquish her grip on a purse. They were apparently unarmed. I was not.

I asked if she required medical assistance, and she ran from me as if I would take up where the thugs left off.

Back in the car, nearly a block away from the greenish house, I heard a gunshot. I kicked the gas—

Then my brakes squealed as a woman-thing, legs like a mule deer, bounded in front of my headlights. She spun, her arms stretched away from her sides as if to hug the Lexus, and her insanely garish face-paint only accentuated a clown's nightmare of ferocity. I reached for the ankle holster, touched the .45, but she had already sprinted for the crowded buildings across the street. I chased after, on foot, but not far. She vanished like the horror she was.

I returned to my idling Lexus in time to find three young miscreants closing in, checking over their shoulders. The one nearest my open driver's door spotted me and flashed a mocking grin. I flashed my .45 and grinned back, and all three broke in opposing directions as if I had lobbed a grenade between them.

Finishing the circle to the next block, and the greenish house, I slowed to a stop twenty-feet from the body sprawled center street. I parked the Lexus there. Pulling the emergency flashers to block other traffic, I called 911 again as I climbed free.

"Already en route!" came the response.

A noise from the house.

Scanning, hoping for the arrival of the first PD unit, instinct prodded me toward the steps, up, and to the front door. Into the main room, I assumed it to be the proposed shopfront. Spinning to the sound of shoes, hushed voices, I halted in the path of two men. My .45 nearly fired on its own when the one man yelled, "Hey!" and swung up his revolver.

"Don't!" Recognizing the voice, "Pedersen, you ass! 'the hell!"

"I nearly got you." His gun dropped to his side.

"That might've worked both ways, Ringo. That guy in the street…?"

"Yeah, that's mine."

Sirens from all sides, the street, the house, lit up with the usual variety of white, yellow, red and blue lights flashing.

I asked if he wanted me to hide the gun I recognized.

"Is it registered?"

As I had contributed little to the evening, the ranking officer took my statement at the scene and let me move on. Pedersen gave a quick rundown on his so-called stake-out partner, and a few details to relay to our criminal consultant friend when I next bumped into him.

I circled the ward for too long. I figured, by now, my gangly spell-caster was already reading Tarot in Biloxi.

Too wound up. Over-active images of the recently terminated, like a flip-book in my mind's eye, I figured I wouldn't sleep for six months, so I drove. Then I walked. Then I drove some more.

Blood in the street I could handle, but I cursed Pedersen for lifting the lid on that freezer. There was nothing to bleach the tiny boy's image from my brain. I stopped for a coffee-to-go, then I went.

Passing my high-rise office gave me more chills, so I refused to stop. Driving under the sign for Tremé, I flashed on my little adventure with the Senator. I should have followed up on that, but I got distracted with Alya, Vagelle, and a crazed abomination named Roderick. And sure, Senator Holcroft had always been a Class-A creep, and should have been run out of town on a rail twenty years ago for his sexual creep-itude, but wasn't he just one out of thousands in this Creep City?

But that girl he drove away with was way too young, in any language. Stuff like that pisses a gal off. What pisses her off more is driving away having done nothing about it.

I needed to cruise tonight anyway, so I found myself once again rumbling out Chef Menteur Highway. I would pass that shack Holcroft was so interested in, then maybe I will continue down to the bridge. A ghostly recollection tapped in, something about Mr. Senator's second home on the far side of our big pond. And that got me thinking about Mandeville Estates, and that bloody kitchen.

I need to take up drinking.

Spotty traffic around 2 a.m., I inched onto the shoulder across from the hastily erected garages and storage sheds, whatever their use these days. With streetlights out here the stuff of science fiction, I groped beneath the driver's seat to find my police baton, stun-gun flashlight, on the off-chance I did not want to shoot whoever got up in my face tonight.

Nonchalant, I crossed the road like walking my pet alligator, but kept my other hand full of my .45.

The first space, a naked concrete slab with debris pushed to the rear by the sweep of a hurricane, most likely. I counted the standing sheds and turned between four and five. Here's where I had seen the driver park with Mr. Senator and his latest sweetheart.

Along the short gravel stretch, I maneuvered between wheel ruts and workmen's debris submerged into watery sinkholes. A loud collision of empty paint cans, and I froze to locate the culprit. Blue-white against the dark, about the size of a small dog, my light beam found an unpleasant opossum with toothy jaws wide and hissing. I kicked water to chase her off. Her teeth would have made a mess of my ankles.

A deep-throated growl rattled the aluminum walls at my back. Shed number four had a guard dog. As I turned with my light, a thin length of submerged color caught the beam. Curiosity pulled, and I stepped beyond the rear corner. I crouched above the puddle. A girl's sneaker, pink with yellow laces, turned my stomach, and my spear of regret.

The dog in number four lost sanity, rattling my already rattled nerves. Within number five, a man cursed in Spanish. Another replied, and they both slammed out a far-side door beyond my view.

I pursued, pistol at arm's length, but as I cleared the corner, an engine cranked to life. A dingy van swung onto the road, narrowly avoiding the blaring horn of an oncoming eighteen-wheeler. The semi passed between us, and I bolted for my car with little hope of catching them.

I phoned a cop friend, and described the find, though I anticipated his response.

"You found a girl's sneaker in a puddle. You thought you recognized it on a senator's underage girlfriend when you followed them out of town one day. Not this day. No evidence of a crime. Tonight, a couple of *Spaniards* ran away from you. It was dark. Should I be taking notes?"

"Never mind."

Headlights off as I could, I followed the distant red brake lights. They flashed once and swerved, but quickly corrected. He must have seen me because he cut his lights as well. Then, with the bridge approaching, he sped into a turn and I lost him completely.

"Son of a bitch!" I slowed, scanning the side roads. Nothing moved. Pulling onto a parallel side street, I scrutinized branching roads heading down to the water.

I ended at a wide, otherwise empty, gravel parking lot and stared out at the moonlit cove. Like a defeated tourist, my head lolled onto the headrest. To my left, grass and trees, a mound of earth, and Fort Pike. I nearly dozed off.

Old Fort Pike had been closed to the public for years.

In 2005, Hurricane Katrina attacked and submerged the already crumbling red-brick and mortar more completely than any attacking foreign navy might have. The waters eventually rolled back out to sea, but Louisiana officials figured they would never have the budget to rebuild. And why should they? With a historical landmark no one much remembered, that never served much purpose anyway, a fortification grown to seed, and prettier covered in green.

I strolled down to the lip of sea wall and turned my gaze to the monument wrecked against the dark shore. The habit of anyone who grew up in a place that had been abandoned for years, then returned one day on a whim, with fresh eyes. A feeling of familiarity and nostalgia, yet with uncertainty over forgotten details. A place where imagination argued with memories.

I only knew Fort Pike's story because of a jock high school linebacker I dated junior year. His only school interest had been history class, because of all the fighting-stuff. He and his "crew" used to visit the old fort with a trunk-full of beer, to screw around, get falling-down stupid, and to fight each other for no reason. At least until the cops showed up and chased them off.

Of course, I didn't tag along on those rowdy sessions, but he convinced me this was a great place to bring a date. In other words, *screw around* in a different way.

Stupid high school Patty imagined that lying on the grassy slope atop the ramparts, watching the stars and the passing ships coming in from the Gulf, might somehow be romantic. And stupid high school Patty never imagined the third-string football linebacker would profess his love by forcing himself on her. He lost a tooth that night.

Nine-months later, my ridiculously forgiving old man helped put my baby up for adoption. Senior year, I could only suspect how the second-string football linebacker managed to break both knees in a single night.

The memories never bothered me much. I used to come out here on my own, once every blue moon, simply to stargaze and dream old dreams.

Too late to pursue new suspicions, I turned away from the Rigolets Bridge. But that old fort would soon return to haunt me.

Thirty-Three

Alya

A distant car door slammed. I waited at the curb. Standt came to the window for a moment, then vanished. The porch light clicked on and the front door opened. I wished I had kept Patty's Taurus.

"Why! Who are you?" Partially shielding herself behind the door, she did not sound shaken. "I called the police."

I crossed the street. Something in me knew, whatever she had been involved in, she might want to avoid a police investigation.

"You! Korikova! How did you get this address? Throwing rocks through my windows? You are insane."

"How do you think I found you?"

"Get away! The police are on their way." She slammed the door. Locks clacked. I pictured her rigid back pressed to the other side.

"I will not run. I will wait for the police. We will both tell them about your friend. The short man I followed from the karaoke bar. Seconds passed silently as I let her figure it out. The locks again. She opened, and I said, "You did not call the police."

"Keep your distance." Her hand pushed forward, not a gun, but a ladies' pink Taser. "I have security cameras."

"I know. They are easy to see. It is why I did not run."

"What now? You want to be arrested?"

"You see I am unarmed." Lifting the Mick Jagger T-shirt above my belt line, I turned. "While we wait for your police, we can check your back door. If it okay, I will go."

She directed me through to the back of the house and flicked on the kitchen lights. Once my sight cleared, the split doorframe along the deadbolt became obvious. The door had held, but it would not have for long.

"So, what was the argument about? Did he tell you they killed your man, Colin?" I faced her, and thin bolts of electricity from the pretty pink Taser pierced Mick Jagger. Fifty-thousand volts, pretending to be fire ants, ran beneath my skin. I convulsed. My knees struck the tiles. Then my head.

Time fast-forwards for the unconscious.

How long, was my first thought after my thinker started up again—the thought repeated after the shivering fits and a short sickness. My thought became, *Where?*

All lights were out, but the marble tiles looked familiar. The kitchen, where I fell. And a clean moon lay across the room and her, Elizabeth Standt, an arm's length away. She lay on her back, head turned, staring with dead eyes. Her carotid artery had split wide. Gouts of arterial spray had decorated the cabinets and marble tiles and me. I examined my mess.

Sirens distant.

Thoughts jumbled and erratic. But I could see the black blood trail crossing Mick Jagger's mouth and down my arm to the kitchen knife in my fist.

The sirens, louder now, spurred me. I shifted.

Something hard in my other hand. A black key, old, chipped and rust crusted, its head an elaborate New Orleans-style filigree—no time to wonder on it.

Almost without thought, without a backward glance for the Administrator or her Taser, I threw my weight at the back door. It moved easily. Sprinting over the yard, parallel to the house, I pushed the key into a deep pocket. A neighbor howled. I threw myself over a four-foot fence and landed hard. Maybe I will feel it tomorrow. Crossing two more yards, I then angled for the street.

A glance back. Only one patrol car so far. *They must be inside.*

I continued my sprint to the Impala. She cranked over faithfully. More black-and-whites arrived, but I was beyond chasing for now. If they pursued, they would expect a run for the freeway.

I ran the opposite direction and Donaldsonville. Black blood down my arm. Hideous kitchen knife smeared the floor mat between my feet.

Do not get caught speeding now!

As I crossed the Sunshine Bridge, I slowed to a mousy crawl and hurled Standt's kitchen knife out the window, off the bridge, and into the Mississippi current.

Pipe Dreams. My ugly yacht-lette had remained untouched in its slip at the West End Marina. With east Pontchartrain in its first throes of pink, I swam from the Breakwater side of the marina through rainbow water not yet colored by the sunrise. Lifting free of the diesel smell, I crept hands-and-knees along the dock. I hoped to avoid security cameras. After the night raid, I felt fairly certain most neighboring yachtsmen had made the investment.

Once on deck I rolled to my back and stripped free of the bloody clothes down to my underwear. Wadding Mick Jagger and slouchy pants into a ball, tying the legs in a tight knot, I moved on my belly into the cabin and collapsed onto the dirty bench. Every bit of me spasmed.

I will never be well. Every day, every situation I threw myself into, erupted in violence. My trauma. Not an accident of fate. I asked for it. This addiction to the horror of my life. The horror was my life.

Morning colors dimmed as a fattening cloud bank touched the sun, but I knew better than to relax yet. I dug through the cupboards but found nothing useful. Beneath a bench cushion, I discovered a cavity for storing various boat utensils, rope, tackle, a single oar, and a black flag with a skull and crossbones and the words, "WHO'S JOLLY NOW, ROGER?"

I remembered the fluke anchor tied to the prow.

Crawling back outside, I untied the anchor rope. A small anchor, not very heavy but heavy enough, I hoped. I retied my borrowed, now destroyed, clothes around the anchor. Halted by a memory, I snaked my fingers into the trousers pocket and found the old key. Then, lowering the bundle over the side, I waited for it to disappear.

Afternoon dock traffic shivered me awake. Then the real shakes began. An enormous dark form shook the boat as it climbed aboard. A light tapping outside the cabin, followed by a voice I knew, Bobby J.

Vagelle

Climbing the stairs at half-past seven in the morning, the day's temperature climbed almost as quickly, or the weight of humidity reminded me of the last time I had slept. Murphy's box of journals felt weighted by emotions, especially carrying it on one arm. Shoulder muscles of the sling arm complained with the slightest pressure, but an urgency to read had me hoping against probability that I might discover anything helpful to my present-day labors.

The first-floor door flew open behind me. Hemmings would have been roused by his buzzer when I keyed the boiler room door. I hesitated.

"Is everything okay?" he said and lowered the hammer. I nodded wearily. "You have a visitor. Ms. Gunston. I figured you wouldn't mind me letting her in."

I thanked him and finished the climb.

"I helped myself to a sandwich and a beer," Patty said as I entered. She tightened in my old wingback chair, leaning her elbows on her knees, worrying the bottle in her hands. She did not look up as I set the heavy box on the black desk. I took to the desk chair and swiveled to face her.

"Thank you for everything last night," I said.

"Things gotta get done. I'm just sad that your safe house is no longer available to me. I loved that place."

"The Colonel already reached out." I crossed to the kitchen, touching her shoulder as I passed. "He's a resourceful man with many investments. Speaking of which," I wrenched the cap off a bottle, "I got a call from Bobby. Not many know that he has a few investments of his own."

"He's a smart man. I imagine that club has made a few bucks in its day."

"As well as a fifty-foot yacht."

She leaned back in the chair, followed with a couple deep swallows from the bottle. "Son of a bitch. Bobby's been holding out on us."

"He said I could tell you. I told him you could keep it to yourself."

"Like he doesn't know that, the sonofabitch."

"Well, he's found our Russian for us. He doesn't spend much time with his boat, but his was one of those broken into during that raid. I'd told him Alya and you were hiding out there at the time, so he paid a call on her this morning."

"Son of a—sorry, I already said that."

"So, tell me." Removing the leather-bound books one at a time, I set Dani's box on the floor and kicked it beneath the desk. "Did they let you in to see Pedersen?"

"He's free, as of around five o'clock. He said to fuck off with sending your lawyer down that time of the morning."

"He probably did not use those exact words."

"He'll stop by and thank you himself after his beauty sleep."

"I hope not. It wasn't Whitcomb there, was it?"

"No. I was surprised he sent an associate. The young man sounded capable enough. He'll get his court date. But why do you hope not?"

"I'd instructed Whitcomb to keep my name as far as possible from Pedersen's problems. They would only further damage his reputation within the department. When you and he spoke, him thanking me and all…"

"We were alone."

"Good. Especially as killing the captain's brother is about to escalate things. Soon, our friend's life will become a much rougher place."

"He's already under internal investigation for the Kandy killing. Oh, he says he owes you another apology. You pegged that Sergeant Barnett right. But you usually do, don't you?"

"What about my young friend?"

"I drove Jesus to the E.R. Only a sprained ankle. He may have a few nightmares later. That's the other thing you may not have heard yet."

"And you're anticipating my reaction."

"I guess somebody has to. Last night, Jesus led Frank to the back of the house, to a freezer. He'd found Danny Howse's body."

I had almost forgotten her in the room until I heard the chair. She drained the beer, walked to the kitchen and rinsed the bottle before dropping it in the trash.

"I should split," she said. "Looks like you've got a lot of reading ahead."

The black-bound books on the black desk would not move on their own. "I can't read these right now," I said, trying to will them psychically back to their box.

"You gonna be okay?"

"Who knows?"

"After I left Frank last night, I took a run by the hospital. Looked in on Roderick. He's in an isolated ward, but they told me he's stable. I'll check in on him before driving up to Alya."

I nearly answered. Too many competing frustrations interrupted me.

"I'm sorry, Nick."

"Sorry for who? Danny? Roderick? Frank? Alya?"

"That's better. That's the old Nicolaus." Her tone flipped. "I'd rather see you pissed than pathetic. Maybe if you can stay that way long enough, you can tap dance your way out of this nightmare and keep some of us out of the hospital." The door slammed.

Strapping the belly-holster, I pushed into yesterday's shirt and let it hang outside my belt. I flex-tested the shoulder. Minor improvement. I reset the sling and tightened its grip as Pedersen knocked.

"Been expecting you," I checked the bathroom mirror and decided to keep the unshaven guise for now.

"You okay?" he said as I joined him in the living room.

"Grab a beer. We need to talk." I took the wingback and waited until he settled on the settee."

"We need to talk sounds like the last words of an ex-girlfriend. Don't ask for alimony. My account's dry." He downed six of the twelve ounces. "Something I need to tell you too."

"Patty left here a couple hours ago. She made me realize more than a few things."

"Yeah, I owed you an apology. I—"

"I know. Listen, you weren't as wrong with Barnett as I was for how I handled it. I decided to avoid your anger rather than prove to you what she was."

"Well, you knew I wouldn't have believed you."

"She did not pass the smell test, as you would say. From the first day out at the Escalade, her expression said she knew of your infatuation, and she played it."

"Well, you could have used a kinder word. *Infatuation?*"

"No time to coddle. She played us with that car, when she'd given me nothing I couldn't see within the first minutes. And she missed those gangland razor cuts in the driver's seat. Driving me out to the cemetery, she did not act as police back-up, but let me walk into the ambush alone. Danny's body was left there conveniently for no one but me. Whoever laid him out had gotten word I was coming. She and you were the only ones who knew that's where I'd be."

"But you said you accepted her excuses."

"Attempting to repair our rift, I'm afraid."

"How long have we known each other? And how many times have I told you…I hate that you're always right."

"Now, to the reason I mention this at all, I want to continue our rift. Tear it wide open."

"Oookay?"

"It might not have been obvious at the time, but tell me, how did Barnett get onto your select investigation team? I assume you are too smart to appoint an investigator because you liked the way her slacks fit."

"Well, there is that. She was new to our ward, but had transferred in with recommendations."

"From whom? Your captain?"

"Among others—well, yeah. My first pick shipped out for some family emergency the week before."

"You can guess where I'm going with this."

"Barnett reporting to Beaudry, and an association with our ghouls from last night, the other Beaudry. Priest Theo got the news pretty quick about me being without a badge and gun."

"And all connected to the morgue theft of Danny Howse."

"Why the hell would they keep him in a freezer?"

"Preserving him to lay in my bed some night, no doubt. Which means they are all connected to whoever it is decided to play this fun little game with me."

"Everything is connected, you said. I don't like this game."

"So goes the cliché, knowledge is power. We know Beaudry is linked to whoever started this carnival train, and whatever gets reported to him will find its way up. We can never know who's pulling the strings unless we allow them to keep pulling."

"Fun."

"Watch for string movement. Keep it between you and me. And most importantly, let them believe they are winning."

"You want to keep our personal beef thriving and make sure they know it."

"Things will get rough for you. Beaudry will want you to suffer for last night. Take it on the chin, but don't throw yourself on your spear. I don't want you dead over this."

"I spent a winter in Canada. Sleeping in a freezer is less appealing."

"My time is better spent protecting Alya and Patty. And I need to avoid your problems, at least openly. My lawyer will help you. I've already laid it all out for him."

"I'm sure glad you have friends. Mine are dwindling fast. About your Alya…it came over the State Police wire early this morning…"

"Go ahead."

"An administrator from St. Michael's got found dead in her home. Throat cut."

"Shit." I nearly shattered the beer bottle in my grip.

"Yeah. And our sweet Russian has been identified on home video near the time of death."

"*Oh, Alya.*" My inner barometer broke, and I felt the earth swing from heartache to a bloodier impulse.

"I'll leave you to it," he said. "You're packing heat, I see. I wish you still had your sword cane instead."

"Another word of advice." Strangling the chair's arm, I fought against the onslaught of psych warfare from an unknown. *"Here's my earthquake,"* I mumbled.

"Huh? Yeah."

"Beaudry has already turned other cops against you," I said. "If you keep a distance from Barnett, she will betray herself by trying to get closer to you. Don't welcome her excuses too readily, and she will try harder. Remember, you are her job."

"I think I can take it from there, chief."

"Watch your fucking back."

"Now you sound like Patty."

THIRTY-FOUR

Alya

I almost forgot I sent my clothes to the bottom of the harbor last night. Now I woke up on the floor wrapped in a black ship's flag, "Who's Jolly Now, Roger?" Then I yelled for Bobby to wait. Pulling the long cushion from the bench, it became my shield.

"Bobby?"

"It's me, Ms. K. Everything okay in there?" His baritone whisper could never become a whisper.

"Well, I have a problem. It is a long story." *How do I say it?* "I have no clothes."

"I can wait 'til you get dressed, girl."

"Um, no. I—This is embarrassing."

"Can I get you something?"

"Not unless you have a lady's wardrobe in your pocket. I lost my clothes."

His roar shook the yacht-lette windows. I waited for it to subside.

"Now that you woke all the gulls from the Yacht Club roof…"

"Sorry, Ms. K. It caught me by surprise. You hold on. I'm sure they have something in the Clubhouse gift shop. I'll be right back." The yacht-lette shook again as he jumped to the dock, and I heard him fighting back laughter, talking to himself, as he hurried away.

He returned sooner than I expected.

"Got something here," he called. "'Tain't much, but I figured you'd prefer fast to fashionable. I'll set it outside the door."

Hugging my new favorite flag, promising to steal it and find my own flagpole, I cracked the door. Bobby threw the cabin into shadow with his mountainous back to me, so I snatched the shopping bag and retreated inside.

"They had a poor selection. I can make a Walmart run in a bit, once I know you're okay."

I thanked him and pulled a greenish, calf-length, terry cloth thing labeled "hooded beach cover-up." *Is there a woman on the planet who wears jungle camouflage to the beach?* At the bottom of the bag, he had included a modest, black, one-piece bathing suit and flip-flops.

"Oh, Bobby. Thank you, thank you. So better than I expected." I zipped the cover-up near to my neck and said, "We're good." I sat with the pirate flag across my knees.

"Now, that's fashion. You should float this rig out to the Caribbean and rob yourself a Spanish galleon."

"And maybe Hollywood will make a movie of us."

"Yo-ho." He handed me a much smaller bag. "Breakfast."

Yay.

Looming in the doorway, he might fill the corners of the cabin until I begged him to take the opposing bench. The benevolent Kolossos lowered as if expecting to demolish the seat. Wringing his paws with discomfort, eyes locked on his stretched and suffering docksiders, his gift of gab left the room while I grappled with a BLT.

"I am desperate to know how you found me," I said.

He had spoken with Nicolaus, then he revealed his secret about owning a yacht nearby.

"You remember when my club burned down. Well, with so many friends to help me rebuild, I had a drop of left-over from the insurance. It was either open a second club or—but the added headache would put me in a nursing home. Now I got the headache of night commandos breaking the door of my *Kraken*. That's the name of her."

"Did Vagelle name it for you?"

"Now you," he said. "I have to know this story about losing your clothes…unless a man is involved."

I worked at not spilling the coffee and gave him the full story. Karaoke club, Standt's home, her letting me inside. Getting zapped and waking up next to her corpse and, of course, covered in Standt's blood. As I talked his demeanor dropped from wonder to sadness.

Then, I remembered the black key. I scanned the corners until I found it lying along the base of the bench.

"I must have dropped it last night." I passed it to my giant. The face rearranged from curious to troubled.

"Where did you find this?"

"When I woke up on her kitchen floor, it was in my hand."

"I need to take this."

"Why? Does this mean something? What?"

Turning the key in his mythic fingers, he ran a gentle touch across the filigree. "Maybe."

"Bobby. Help me understand."

"Somebody is playing, maybe." Was he wondering how much to tell? "Too many characters in this city. Some play at the old religions. Stupid stuff."

"When I was young and new here, Nicolaus used to talk about the fakers. The Voodoo."

"And sometimes they don't play." He noted my expression. "Not that I believe any of this crap—pardon me, Ms. K—but those that do…"

"I need to avoid. I have heard this before."

He pushed up from the bench with difficulty and crooked a finger for me to follow up the steps and into the sunlight. I squinted at the day.

"I saw this when I got here, now I'm wondering how new this is." He pointed eye-level to the doorframe.

"I have not noticed this before." I almost touched the three curvy lines carved and revealing bright wood beneath.

Bobby turned away. He dragged his hand along the bowline, pulling away with gray-green moss between his fingers. He glanced over his shoulder once, then smeared the moss into the scratches.

"Let's get back in."

My hands trembled. He said he should leave me time to recover. He would come back with better street clothes. I begged him to stay. "Talking helps."

Then he explained some about the black key. The skeleton key, symbolic of *Papa Legba*. "Different witches have different tastes. This key is his power to lock or unlock portals to the Afterlife. Or so they like to think."

"And why did it remind you of the wavy lines?"

"I shouldn't be filling your head with all this."

"You cannot stop now. I am all suspenders." My look slightly less than happy.

"It might be *Damballah. Damballah Wedo.* But I don't recollect this connection to the other one. He is the serpent. The serpent lines stand for Creation, Wisdom, and Life."

"I am proud of you," Bobby said.

"You are proud of a crazy woman? You always say nice words, Bobby. You have done so much with your life."

"You think that much of me, that my words mean nothing? Sorry, Ms. K."

"I cannot be proud of what I have done in my life. My whole life. I have done—look, people are still dying around me."

"You have hinted about what happened to you, little Russkie. Your thirteenth birthday. Your *damage.* I don't need to hear the details. I really don't. But I know good from bad. I know what it must take for a teenager to cross continents alone, to search for peace."

"Peace?"

"But you search. How can I not be proud?"

"My Papa used to say, there is no peace—"

"—Until you finish that sandwich, I walked so far to bring you."

I offered the plastic dish to him. He just snorted. I listened to the boat music, the slap and clang of sail rigging, a hull knocking onto a dock, workers calling to workers, gulls complaining for fish.

He lowered to the floor, his elbows denting the cushion. He told me stories to distract from my stress. He told me about a friend in the Navy who had pulled him from a jungle river.

"A weightlifter?" I said. He laughed loud at that.

No, Bobby was much thinner in those days. And he told how this friend carried a harmonica in his pocket everywhere he went. He could only play one bad song. And Bobby would cover his ears and howl, all joking, for him to stop. The friend had a great stereo, a big reel-to-reel he bought at the Navy Exchange. He had recorded hours of music. All sorts. Creedence, Santana, Ray Charles.

His friend had died in that jungle, but Bobby's love for him was why, when he had the opportunity to open his own bar, he made sure he could bring in the music.

"Sometimes, I can hear that bad harmonica playing, and I say sorry to the stars for covering my ears." Then he told me things about Nicolaus I never knew, things that made them so close.

Then he told me a story about myself. About me working with my mentor. Nearly sacrificing myself for him.

"But he had done for me. Many times," I said.

"Remember, my words mean something. My stories, my life with those I am closest to, is why I exist."

With the height of the sun, I glanced at his watch, 2:10. "Have I talked so long? I am sorry."

"No worries. Do you know anything about boats?" he said.

"I know how to sleep on one."

"But not how to pilot her. I assume from the size there's not much of a head on board."

"I am grateful this still floats. Head? Oh, Navy talk. Toilet. I looked in, but I would rather wait until dark and go over the side."

He reached into a pocket, pulled a key ring, and pried free a small brass key. "At the back of the Yacht Club there's a private facility with showers. Members only, but I pay for the slip, so I got access." He handed me his key.

"I am not sure. There may be too much on and off this boat."

"It's a long wait 'til dark. I'll be here 'til you get back, in case you run into nosey neighbors. Use the beach hood. You'll look like you fit in with this rusty thing, not in a good way. But you have a touch of blood in your hair."

A long gangway with three offshoot docks, making six extended piers and many boat slips. I waited for a lull in dock traffic. With the hood pulled forward and facing away from the sun, I cleared the final row of yachts. The door with the skirted silhouette may have been closing behind someone, but I had the key.

"Anyone in here?" Once inside, I stopped at the sink and mirror. Four toilet stalls reflected behind me. No shoes beneath the doors. To my left, an alcove and the beginnings of a community shower.

I felt the back of my head and the dried blood in my hair. *Thank God for Bobby.* He had given me a pocketful of change for the shower's soap dispenser. I would use the terry cloth hooded beach cover-up as my towel, and walk back wet.

First, a toilet stop. I shot the stall bolt, hung the hooded thing on a hook. My eyes closed with the thought of Standt's blood from last night. I pulled a long breath to steady my nerves and began to untie the bathing suit strings at my neck.

Rubber-soles approached. My panic level shook. No one had entered after me. No one answered my call.

My hands came up the moment the door kicked in at me. The force stung my wrists and drove me back over the toilet seat. I pushed off the tank and saw long, thin legs in razor slashed jeans, white tube top—no feathers. She held open the door with the butterfly hand.

Recognizing that toothy grin, lightning grabbed my spine.

I did the only thing I could. I flew at her. Caught by surprise she hopped back, spun, and threw me past. My head dented the blow-drier, knocking it free of the wall.

Her time to fly now. Red talons extended, intending to rip the flesh from my back. I spun like she had, but I held the aluminum blow-drier in one hand. It broke her nose.

She screamed like a raptor in a snare. I pounded her with it until she went to her knees. She kicked and flailed from the floor, but in my mania I could not stop. This was me now. The me that sent me to that courtroom. Sent me into that hospital for the mentally ill.

"Who's Jolly Now, Roger?"

Light flooded the room. A mythological creature encircled me and dragged me into the sunlight.

"Come, little Cossack. You have had enough." Bobby's soft baritone hummed.

Thirty-Five

Pedersen

I got the call, but from a different source. I did not recognize the number right away, then I remembered.

"Rosa!" My favorite plus-sized waitress from my favorite diner.

"Frank?" she said. "Are you still watching your girl-ish figure? You've not been in for some time. Sorry to call this number. Somebody gave it to me."

"It's only been a few days, Hot Sauce."

Her laugh sent a less than comfortable vibe.

"But you never need to worry about calling me. Is there a problem? Are you okay?"

"I am still worried about you."

"I'm okay. No frettin about Frank."

"I—well, a cop came in today, for coffee. She mentioned your name."

"She?"

"A blond cutie—not that you couldn't know a blond cutie…it's just that I don't expect any police to talk to some waitress about you when you ain't here. But she says how she knows you come in here a lot, and she asked if I seen you the past couple days. Says you are in trouble with some bad people."

"I know all about it, dear. Thank you."

"But then she says how she needs to get hold of you. Something bad happened."

"I know."

"She says how she is hiding. And…"

"Rosa?"

"Well, the other thing, she got beat. Her eye all swolled up. And her cheek. She hopes she can see you. She says she hopes you will talk to her. I have her phone number."

"Okay, I'll talk to her. Thanks, Hot Sauce. And never be afraid to call me when you need anything. Anything. Okay?"

"Detective? Frank?" Her voice shaky.

"Yeah. It's me, Sarge. I'm no longer a detective."

"I need to talk to you."

"Okay, talk."

"I…"

"I'm busy, Sarge. Cleaning out my desk."

"Are you at the office?"

"Tell me what's on your mind."

"Can we meet?" She sniffed. "I'm a…I know you hate me, but…please give me ten minutes to explain."

I let her hang for a couple seconds. "You're not working today?"

"No, I—The Captain gave me a few days off. If you're in the city, I can come to you."

"I'm heading out. I have an appointment out on the Point. Algiers."

"Oh. That is a drive."

"I like to avoid your cop buddies in the city these days. If you can't wait 'til tomorrow, I can give you twenty minutes out there. I should be there in two hours."

I called for my backup P.I.

The other side of Ol' Man River, with a photographer's view of New Orleans high rises above moving waters. Algiers Point, a.k.a. The Crescent, stuck its finger back at the city thanks to the river's rude turn to the east. A part of the city, yet not part of the city, folks living here got lucky that way. I liked it because most cops there didn't know me by sight.

I told Barnett to meet me inside a leaning, torn and weathered, waterfront tavern called "Bar," or "Lunch," or any number of aliases decorating the windows and eaves. It was hard to miss.

I parked out back, "Restricted Parking," because the bartender knew my Durango by sight, and I once let him slide on a bad health violation that he promised to clean up half-a-dozen times.

"So, how long you been drivin round with that plastic bag over your window?" C.G., his nickname after retiring from the Coast Guard, carried two crates of Yuengling in from the back door.

"It's been a bit." I took the last table near the bar because I expected company. I had come early.

He set a cold one on my table. "You prob'ly know you been followed?"

"Yeah. But let's keep it to ourselves."

On his trip behind the bar, C.G. leaned toward an old barfly, unsteady on her stool. "Leave this one alone, Gladys."

"I got a cousin does real good with body work," he called to me. "Give him an hour, you can be in and out. You waiting for your date, or you want to order a sandwich before more of *their* buddies back up my galley?"

He nodded to the front door as a small squad of Marines rolled in. After checking me over, they filled a table closer to the sunlight. Obviously Marines, with their high-'n-tight haircuts, clean sneakers, and muscles beneath identical gray T-shirts with "Marines" arching across their chests. Shirts dark with sweat, they'd probably been jogging in today's hundred-degree heat. I was glad to be too old for that shit.

The room filled with noise until two of them signaled to keep the voices down. I nodded for them. One got up and crossed the room to the jukebox.

"You mind?" he said.

"You're good. Anything on there besides Zydeco?"

He winked, dropped his quarters, and Sammy Hagar yelled from the speakers, "Hello Baaaaybee!"

She wasn't right on cue, but I wondered if she had waited at the foot of the steps for an appropriate intro. She wore bug-eyed sunglasses, which remained in place until she passed the Marines' table. Their heads turned to follow, of course. She pulled the rubber band from her ponytail letting her hair drop.

"Hi, Frank." She took the chair facing away from the troops. I could see the purple and yellow swelling around the shades.

"What're you drinking?" I said.

"I don't know. Water."

C.G. had been standing close enough to hear. I did my best not to stare at her. She waited for a lull in the Hagar before talking. One of the larger Marines got up and approached.

"Afternoon, ma'am. Y'all want I should pull the plug on the box so you'se can talk?"

"You're all good, friend," she said.

"Just a business meeting," I said. "Thanks for the courtesy, Marine."

"Ma'am?" He eyed her but tipped his head to me. "He do you like that?"

"No," she said. "He's helping."

The Marine went back to his table and, before sitting, eyeballed me once more.

"Sorry." She busied herself with the water glass for a moment. "I know you must hate me."

I busied with my beer.

"It's not like you think," she said. "Last night."

"What do I think?"

"I'm not sure. You think I ran out on you? It wasn't like that."

I waited.

"Beaudry made me take the week off."

"Because of that?" I pointed to the eye.

"Partly." She looked everywhere but at me. "Also, I think maybe he's not sure if I'm partly responsible for what happened."

"And you're not."

"I screwed up. That boy being chased, and you ran for the door. Same time as I heard someone come in the back of the bakery. I ran to head him off. That's how I got this." Her black eye.

I scraped a thumbnail at the label on the bottle like I had other things on my mind.

"Honest, Frank. You know I'm a good cop. I wouldn't do that to you. By the time I got up, it was all over."

"Doesn't matter. It's done. In a week you can go back to your job. In two months I can stand trial."

"Frank…"

You can stop saying my name now. "Whichever way that turns, we won't need to bother with each other afterwards."

"When I got up, I went after you, but the front door was locked. I ran out the back and when I turned the corner, you and the boy were gone."

The front door was locked, but I had kicked the glass out. "You'll get a new partner. I'll be off the force, and happier for it."

"I can't believe that." Sincerity, then her eyes fluttered away. "You've been a cop here all your life. You can't just give that up. What will you do? Go to work for Vagelle?" There was the inquiry.

"Do you think I am so shallow? That I could grovel to him for a job after—no. All my ties to this city are cut. Like a machete cut."

"I am sorry." Her weary performance held while fastened on my expression.

"So, we should say goodbye now."

"Frank." She didn't actually pull off a full teardrop.

What an audition. Remember, you are her job. I glanced theatrically at my watch. "I gotta go." Pushed back the chair. Laid ten bucks on the bar. Told C.G. to buy one for Gladys.

I walked out the back, and almost made it to the Durango when I heard the squawk of the door behind me.

She ran at me and grabbed both of my sleeves. She had lost the sunglasses somewhere along the way.

"Please. It wasn't me."

My memories were still too raw.

"I went back early this morning. That bakery door, I checked. The bolt is self-locking. I swear to God."

The feeling of betrayal, standing in the street calling for my backup, while Priest Theo wanted to kill me. And me forced to kill him. Yeah, it was her fault.

Vagelle's words, *She did not pass the smell test.* And *you are her job.*

But we needed her too. Needed her to believe we could be okay. Friends, maybe. I donned my most benevolent face.

"I really have an appointment. Maybe we can get a beer before I shed this town."

In my side mirror, she turned for her car. I headed the opposite direction, away from the river, taking side-streets until Patty's Lexus came into view. I pulled to the curb along tree-lined streets and bright painted houses with flower boxes and white fences. I moved from my car to hers.

"How's my back-up doing? I keep forgetting how nice this ride is in here. You ever fall asleep driving?"

"I don't notice anymore," she said. "So, how *you* doing? Looked like a bit of Casablanca back there."

"She ain't no Ingrid Bergman."

Thirty-Six

Vagelle

University Medical Center, with its huge footprint on the city, existed as a tribute to its budget, with first-class modern architecture and interior designs, *décor magnifique,* that might have flown in from Vatican City. Above the Information Island floated an art project of sunlit stained glass. Walls for the entry and waiting areas displayed a tasteful variety of inlaid brass or silver artistry. No, not all hospitals were created equal.

Of course, none of this was new to me, as I had been both visitor or guest many times over the years and witness to its evolution. It merely reminded me of how much the fevered senses of the traumatized failed to appreciate where their money went. I doubted Roderick Howse, in his present condition, or any condition, would admire the effort. But he had been transferred here from Mandeville for the Level One Trauma Center.

When I arrived, despite my scruff and wrinkled attire turning the noses of hospital staff, I flashed my fake FBI credentials. "Undercover—sorry."

A nurse directed to the appropriate wing, floor, and waiting area. There I was met by a series of physicians who had not been updated on my status. Their stories all matched.

"He's out of the ICU. Vitals stabilized. Naturally, we are still monitoring closely. His injuries are life-threatening, and he's been under sedation since his arrival."

"He still has a twenty-four-hour officer on his room? I need to speak with him."

The last doctor directed me.

The policeman on the door bounced from his chair and grabbed his holster belt at my approach. Anticipating this, I held up the shield and gave him the "undercover" line. He relaxed. I had been too far away for him to read anything but the letters FBI.

"Still under sedation, I am told." I talked quickly to stave off his questions. "I was up at the crime scene in Mandeville as they carted him off. I've already questioned those in the house, and thought I'd stop by to see if the perp is responsive. Guess I wasted the trip."

"By the looks of him, sir, he's the opposite of perp. Or he's got a lot of failures in his career."

"Or maybe a lot of both." I studied the unconscious bogeyman through the door glass. The connected machinery blinked. His chest rose and fell, easy and shallow. I had no emotions left for him. He had not been "Roddy" for a long time. "How long have you been on the door…Mullins?" I read his tag.

"Swing shift, I just started. I'm looking forward to my dinner of hospital cafeteria food."

"Woof. I'll be checking in, time to time. You on tomorrow? I'll try to bring take-out. I also thought you should know, for your own sake, we picked up some side chatter. I'm sure you heard about the killing over at Veteran's? Chatter says they may have an interest in getting to our boy in there. Stay alert."

"Do you know what the hell's going on?"

My eyes were on Roderick. My mind on Alya, not his words. Not the sound of the woman's footsteps. When I turned my head, I questioned reality for a heartbeat. Berenice Tresor, *Judge* Berenice Tresor, stood beside me. I stepped back reflexively like a schoolboy caught stealing teacher's prize candy bar. The moment so odd it immediately reminded me how seldom I had seen her outside her offices or a courtroom.

She said nothing.

"Ma'am," Mullins said like he had seen her before.

One step closer to the glass. From the rear, tailored in gray bespoke suit with heels, dark hair shot with wisps of silver glinting under the hospital fluorescents. She might have been any executive posed to address a board meeting, or at a podium before a room full of foreign dignitaries, or sentencing a man to death.

"What are you doing here, Mr. Vagelle?" She did not turn.

"I believe you know the answer to that, Judge."

"Perhaps I don't. Perhaps you are keeping watch, wondering if he will awaken long enough to tell us things."

"You are an intelligent woman, Berenice."

"That's *Judge* Tresor."

"Judge Tresor, I believe you are smarter than the accusation."

Silently, she twisted her hands. The delicate gold chain attached to her watchband sparked, turning the tiny and equally delicate gold flower to catch the light. Fleur-de-lis.

An uncertain Officer Mullins shifted his stance.

Pushing a business card into Mullins's pocket, I glanced to Tresor's reflection in the glass. Expressionless.

I walked back to the visitors' waiting area and sat within sight of the nurse's station. I wanted them all to get used to seeing me in here. I also wondered if the Judge would stop for a final insult before marching off. She did not stop. In passing she said, "You do not look well. Lose the fake ID."

Checking the time, I wondered at the judge's arrival. Did she still have some attachment to Mad Madeline's son? She had implied as much back in her office, but I knew that she was not the type to maintain personal relationships. I doubted she could keep a cat.

I studied the lobby foot traffic, nurses, doctors, a janitor answering a call for cleanup. All wore face masks. My vigil might last a week. Instinct said no more than that. But for now, I needed to get to Alya.

My phone vibrated. The screen read "Bobby."

"It's about Alya?" I began jogging, "Where now? Can you stay with her? I'm leaving University. Do not let her go back to her boat."

I found the Kraken, invited myself aboard, and I tapped on the aluminum railing rather than proceeding below.

The door opened carefully, but Bobby knew I had come on deck. "I've got cameras." He tried his low voice and signaled for me to take the captain's chair. Though a quarter-century old, the Sea Ray cockpit appeared showroom new. "She's asleep. I talked her down a bit, but you should keep an eye on how she wakes up."

"Thank you, big guy, as always. How bad?" I caught a water bottle as he tossed it.

"A couple bruises. Physically, she's fine. The other one…?" He propped himself to the railing.

"Do you know what happened to that one?"

"Nope. I assume she got off under her own steam, but I was more concerned with getting Alya out of sight. We talked earlier and I figured it best not to hand her over to the cops."

"She has had an APB out on her since before last night, if this new one reports an assault, it'll be a national dragnet." I took his captain's chair.

"The law will treat her rough."

"Presumed dangerous to anyone crossing her path. It's been set up this way from the beginning."

We silenced into thought. Bobby watched incoming harbor traffic. I stared blankly at his dashboard.

"My poor Russkie," he said. "She's a tough one. I guess she comes out on top because nobody expects a sparrow to beat them half to death with a hand drier."

"Begging the question, if the person behind all these attacks has been aware of our history together—but then this story has played false since the beginning. The highway gunner had me down with my shoulder shot to hell, and he drove away without finishing me."

"Like last night, she wakes up on a kitchen floor with the woman dead, but—You think underlings might be fearful to take that final step without a direct order from the boss?"

"That's the way it's playing out. Psychopathy from the top. It's easy for a smart criminal to put someone in the ground. To the sadist behind all this, it's more satisfying to watch me suffer."

"At least for a time."

"I need you—no. Bobby, I have to insist you keep a distance from me. They know you are a friend, but I'm hoping they don't know how much you know."

"Or how close we are?"

"Maybe they'll avoid involving you. Go back to the club. I'll get Alya away from here after dark."

"Wait." He calculated some incoming thought. "The safest place I can think of may not be in this marina, but unless—"

"Can't do it, Bobby. This is escalating at warp speed. Coming at Alya, their only logical next move is to put her down."

"You didn't hear me out."

"I did. I believe they have unlimited resources and political influence. If they find out we're on the water in your boat, the Coast Guard will sink this thing without calling Ahoy."

The cabin door opened a crack with Alya's inquisitive look.

"Forget about it. This is my call." Bobby's decision, as immovable as his mass. "She's insured down to the cupholders."

"But you do need to get back to the club."

"Before I do, I'll make a call and claim my ship ain't seaworthy. Maybe damaged from that commando raid. I'll sign an order to drag her to dry dock, but you two will be drifting out with the Kraken and sunning yourselves on the Barataria. You can handle this craft."

"Nicolaus," Alya said from the hatch, "we cannot do this." She appeared unsteady on the stairs and I jumped, grabbed her arm, and walked her back down. "I am okay."

I led her to a cabin floor, better adorned than my apartment, and I sank beside her on the three-piece white leather sofa. "You are right. This can only be temporary."

"If they find us here," she said, "they will go after Bobby. Everyone close to me gets hurt."

Bobby shut the refrigerator and passed her a water bottle. She gazed with interest at his dead-blow mallet propped beside the door.

"Orange sledgehammer," she said. "That was you. But Vetty—"

"Look at me." I touched the back of her hand to see if she would flinch. "Remember our last war. And the one before."

Bobby began a soft humming.

"What?" she said.

His tune became whispered song lyrics, "I'm still standing…"

Alya's laugh turned to tears. She pressed her face into my shirt.

I had been aboard the Kraken before, so Bobby did not explain much. Being an old Navy man, and spending the entirety of his post military life in small apartments, I was shocked when he told me about this purchase. And more shocked when I first stepped aboard the fifty-footer. Despite his days amid raucous club patrons, or maybe because of them, I should have reasoned he would keep this memory of his younger years pristine and well-away from that other life. I was one of maybe five others who knew of this. Now six.

Handing me his spare keys and the access code to the shipboard computer, he showed me the locked drawer where he kept ship notes, mechanic specs, maps of the world, and emergency numbers in seven languages. As if I were following Robert Louis Stevenson to Samoa. At the back of the drawer, a loaded Colt .45 M-1911 with enough scars to have served in Guadalcanal.

Alya saw him off with a longer hug than she could be comfortable with. As he walked the planks back to parking, I asked how she was holding up.

"Some things are worth a bit of hurt," she said.

"Words I live by."

Fully fueled, food stocked to Bobby J. levels, Alya took to the passenger bench while I piloted free of the marina corral. The sun winked out behind us, and I slowed to an easy crawl.

"Are we really going all the way to Barataria Bay?"

"Not tonight. Maybe tomorrow. I want to be free of all the lake and harbor traffic, then take a large part of the day teaching you how to *navy* some for yourself. This thing is somewhat different from handling a little bass boat." I scanned the horizon and I could feel her eyes on the side of my head.

"Oh, no. You are not leaving me out on the water in this *thing* by myself. No way, bossman. I will pull in close to shore and swim back before being stranded out there."

"I will not desert you. But things happen, and I may need to leave the Kraken for an emergency, and I want to know that you can at least park her by yourself. Trust me."

"If you leave me out here for more than ten minutes, I will never trust you again."

Thirty-Seven

Patty P.I.

I can't say how long it took before I finally committed to reopening my brother's detective agency. Maybe too long.

Big brother, Mack, recruited me before graduation from LSU. Two days before. I was smart enough to have realized his plans for me had begun much earlier, likely as soon as I changed majors from Business Admin. to Finance. Up 'til then I had been a freshman jock coasting along on a basketball scholarship.

His playing private-eye had only carried him so far as his buttery tongue and pretty-boy teeth could outlast his spiraling credit card accounts. The mention of "finance" to the family schemer had been like tossing chum off my stern.

First came his offer, "Help out with the books on occasion," in exchange for spending money during the school year. As his company floundered, it became, "How 'bout once a week?" Then, I almost missed my own graduation having worked into the wee hours and oversleeping. I had slapped my alarm clock across the room and overslept.

Two days prior, I took his proposal for working full-time and handed it back with my version of a contract. I knew Gunston was moments away from locking its doors, with big brother fleeing to Brazil—his back against the wall, possibly a firing squad wall, if he could not dig his way out from under. Without insulting family, I made it clear how much hard work would be involved, what the consequences were for him should I walk away. Conversely, I would make it so he could pretend to be driving Tom Selleck's car while ignoring "the books."

He gave a shaky argument that lasted through lunch. In the end, I got sixty percent of the company without having my name on the masthead.

It took six more years for his chickens to roost.

I had suspected his casual skimming from accounts early on. Naturally, a bookkeeper would spot it. But then I nearly always found the excuses for him within the numbers. I warned him, but he would flash the teeth and chuckle. "I trust you can figure it out."

But Mack always did find ways to bring in new clients. And with my help, we began making actual money. Over time, we hired new investigators to take up the slack. I got us office space on the top floor of a five-story in the Central Business District.

Then, as we have seen so often in this world, rewarding poor behavior breeds its addiction.

Nicolaus Vagelle came into our lives.

Skimming breeds falsifying hours, begets dragging out cases long past their conclusions, begets false reporting of outcomes to keep a client on the hook for weeks, sometimes months. Until the line is willfully walked over and Mack Gunston P.I. creates crimes leading to the convictions of innocent "suspects."

Three families destroyed by bad reporting, year-long lawsuits, unaffordable fines, homes lost, personal property, wives and children…

An innocent man died in prison.

I could not handle being partly responsible, so I hired the "Consultant." And I paid him to send my own brother to Dixon Correctional on charges of Embezzlement, Fraud, Extortion… Hell, if they arrested him for selling family pets I would have believed it. He became a tenant of the state for a long time.

The company closed.

I spent a year trying to "find myself," and never quite got the hang of it. With no money after settlements, I barely avoided doing hard time myself. I ate tuna from cans and Hamburger Helper, with living conditions as comfortable as the legendary Christmas barn.

Then came the day—the call, unexpected—from the consultant who had brought us down. Believe it or not, he invited me to lunch.

It turned into a two-hour lunch, wherein he told me how good I was at my job. He had watched as I rescued Mack's blundering, persistently staggering company. Then he told me what I needed to do to become a phoenix, to resurrect from the Gunston ash heap and run with its successes.

He would be my first client. He put me on a retainer and paid much more than I would have asked. Then he sent over my next few clients. I have secretly loved him ever since.

I parked in the dreaded garage, four-stories below where I housed the Gunston Detective Agency. I hoped they had all checked out by now. Only seven of them all told, after Brown. Tonight there might be a straggler or two upstairs, if they still had cases to mine. I was confident I could handle them in small numbers.

I would not be much of a surprise to them. They would have gotten word of my surviving and were preparing their defenses, or a renewed attack. I knew their personalities well after all the years.

Hell, I had to start my digging somewhere.

I pressed the elevator button for four. I would take the stairs to five, so any lingerers would not hear the elevator ping. A trick I had once taught Alya.

Twenty minutes 'til midnight, and I spotted two of them through the glass. Mitchell and Ramone, at Ramone's cubicle. Both holdovers from the Mack Gunston years, so I let my steam build. Not too much. *Innocent until proven,* and all that. I passed my keycard over the lock and walked in like I had never left. They both sprang up.

I walked past them and to my office without a word. I closed the door, pretending I had phone calls to make, letting their crawfish simmer.

I did call Alya, then Vagelle, both still out of service. I would try again in the morning. I had stopped by Alya's yacht-lette before coming here but got nothing good out of it.

A knock on the doorjamb. I remained standing and motioned for Mitchell to enter. Ramone stayed behind.

"Hey, boss. I'd ask if you're okay, but I can see that."

I nodded.

"We'd been keeping up with all the reports, but—well, it's been a time since we heard from you. A few of us were wondering if we were jobless again." He moved closer and stuck out his hand. "Really good to have y'all back, Miss Gunston."

"Not quite sure I am back, Mitch. I've got a few things to square away before we're back in order here."

"Could you use a hand with any of it?"

"Well—" I tried not to look skeptical at him. "Naw, it's personal. I brushed past him and cleared the doorjamb and angled toward Devon Brown's desk. "I need to catch up on case files. Go through whatever Brown had on his desk. Anything the group was working on that I should know about?"

"Um…"

"What is it?"

"Not sure where to start, Patty."

"There's been an incident here since you went missing," Ramone said. "A break-in."

There. The misdirection.

"We were all back here the day after the marina killing. There's a copy of the police report in your inbox, about the break-in."

"Yeah," Mitchell said. "Wish we had more on Brown's activities leading up. Truthfully, his desk, all his drawers and files were cleared out."

"And none of you were working with him on spook shit?"

"I swear, ma'am. Whatever Brown had going, he worked it on his own."

"And his was the only desk rifled through?"

"The only desk, I think. They did throw a few file drawers to the floor."

Leaning against the desk, a more casual stance, I thought I heard movement from the breakroom.

'So…as two of my top investigators, give me your critical assessments. What have you learned since the break-in?"

"Ma'am?" Ramone said.

"Well, I'm sure you, the whole company, did a deep dive through all the accounts, active and for the past year at least. Mitch, you were the closest to him. If I recall, you were both hired by my brother around the same time, right?"

"Not sure I understand," he said. "The police took anything they thought pertinent. T'wasn't much else."

"Never mind," I turned to my office. "Thank you for all you have done in my absence."

After a short silence, Ramone said, "Should we clean out our desks, Ma'am?"

"Let's leave it for Monday. I'd rather not do this piecemeal, so might as well have a group meeting. Ramone, I count on you to make all the calls. Bring everything you've been working on, and I'll issue severance checks for anyone wanting to quit."

"This is bullshit!" Mitchell followed me in. "After all my years propping up this place." He hurled a notebook across my office. The glass on a wall certificate shattered.

I placed my foot on the chair, so I need not bend to reach the ankle holster. Their reactions were enough. Seeing my fingers near the Colt, Ramone had already backed off.

"There went your severance," I said. "Now back the fuck out of my office, while I call a locksmith to keep you out."

I had ignored one bit of business advice from that first lunch with Vagelle. His warning.

"In a company collapse, where employees were hired by a corrupt management, where for years they felt entitled to continue the money stream and high living, it is more than reasonable to assume a long-standing resentment for the usurper. "Even if you give them new jobs, you will always be the person responsible for any future hardship.""

I had felt sorry for those original Gunston employees who lost their jobs when big brother went to play for the Correctional Soccer League. Devon Brown had been close to my brother. Selling me to the biggest shark would have been easy for him, but I could never imagine murder. *How many others were there here?*

On the other side of the glass, they boarded the elevator. Colt still in hand, I rounded the corner to the break-room. Jimmy Takagi propped his hip against the snack counter.

"You gonna shoot?" he said.

"Not so long as you keep your hands on the cup. Now tell me why you're back here and not contributing to the conversation."

"I figured how it might wind up. Just staying out of the line of fire."

"You're saying you aren't a part of *the plans?*"

"You know they keep me out of all their parties. I'm here late working on a domestic and hoping to wrap up the paperwork by morning. You want, I can be gone right now."

Jimmy "Zero" to my brother, who thought it was a cute put-down for his heritage. Jimmy once said he liked the nickname, that it was his favorite fighter plane when he was a kid, and he once warned Mack that he might go all Kamikaze on his ass. At the time, I liked that. I re-holstered the Colt.

"How about pouring me a cup, and I'll get out of your hair?"

Because I liked efficiency, I stopped at Brown's desk, then Ramone's, then Mitchell's. The latter two were sharp enough not to keep incriminating laundry hanging around. At the back of a Mitchell drawer, I found a dirty and coffee-stained business card. "Lamia Anasi, Healing Arts," the fancy script printed over a line drawing resembling a Queen of Hearts playing card. It went into my pocket for the hell of it, or for the obvious non-coincidence.

Back at my desk, after reading police reports, I tore through two weeks' worth of mail, stalling, waiting for Takagi to leave. He dropped a collection of envelopes bound with a rubber band.

"Mostly bills I set aside, thinking if you'd launched a world tour or something I'd get them to someone who might give a crap."

I thanked him.

"I guess I'll take off. I can finish up in the morning. Will I be able to get in?"

"No need to change the locks tonight." I winked.

"I ain't one to give you answers," he stalled on a thought, "but your instincts are right about most people. Watch your back near Mitch."

"You ever hear of a Lamia? Or Anasi?"

He chewed his tongue for a second, shook his head. He turned for the elevator, glancing back through the door glass.

An old, discarded card. Lamia Anasi, Healing Arts. I might have flipped it into the trash, but for that Queen of Hearts. Devon's card, the night he attacked me in the bath. I guessed he would have left it on my body, had he succeeded. And that's why I left it in Vagelle's book with my warning.

Knowing Mitch, she could have been hooker, or a barfly he once bought a drink for. But Devon too?

I pulled an internet search. *Lamia*—

But search engines needed me to change to the Hawaiian name Lanai. I kept fighting them. I came across the Arabic, meaning "radiant" or "shining." An uncommon name for several minor celebrities, enough brand names, mostly clothing lines, a makeup brand, or a city in central Greece near Mount Othrys. I looked that up: *A region claiming the birthplace of Zeus and Hera and Hades*—

"Okay, my life isn't long enough to research this crap," I whispered to my empty surroundings. "This looks like a tangent for professor Vagelle."

With the office to myself, I flashed on my main reason for coming to the fifth floor. I keyed into the security cameras. My *crack investigators* had not mentioned them in all their years here, and the *why* had always been a mystery to me. Among other things, this was a security firm. It's also why I did not feel the urgency to change the locks.

The hidden cameras operated on a motion switch. Five cameras in all. Problematic in an office with movement seven days a week, sometimes all hours, which is why I scheduled a clean wipe every three months to save space on the hard drive.

A thorough screening would take longer than I cared to spend, so digging a mini external drive from the rear of a file cabinet, I plugged in, wipe it clean, and hit *download.*

As it copied, I grabbed my seldom used attaché case.

Thirty-Eight

Alya

Night, cloudless with a clear view of the quivering city lights, we anchored the Kraken well out on Lake Pontchartrain. Not so far as to be a hazard for shipping channels to the Gulf, but far enough to be clear of flight path noise from Lakefront Airport.

We spent most of our evening topside. Nicolaus said breathing or thinking proved easier out under the stars. I suspected he avoided my discomfort at being closeted together in a clamshell cabin. I was glad for a night outside without a summer storm.

He only used the shipboard computer occasionally, checking local news or Coast Guard reports. Then he would turn it over to me to study the maps, the lake shores, waterways, inlets, estuaries, and water traffic patterns. He left me web links to this model yacht specifically, Bobby's fifty-foot Sea Ray. As if I might crawl under the hood to change spark plugs.

I repeated more than once about me not spending a single heartbeat alone at sea.

Left to myself, I studied about Pontchartrain. Not for the first time. One cannot live in New Orleans for ten years without wanting to know something about it. Not surprisingly, floating this far from land can be a strong motivator for deeper research.

Me being me, I learned about the human toll this lake had claimed over the years, whether during the Civil War or Hurricane Katrina.

In 1964, an Eastern Airlines Flight 304 crashed here killing fifty-eight passengers and crew. Later that year a Trailways bus dove off the Causeway killing six more, like the lake had a quota to make. Over the years Pontchartrain had become the graveyard for more than a few private and chartered planes. In 1986, two fishermen found a woman's decomposed body. Examiners ruled it a homicide. She had died of asphyxia, a crushed trachea, but her remains had never been identified.

Nicolaus noticed my reading material and said, "How about you take a break?"

"Aaand?"

He led me to the stern and a long box filled with fishing rods, tackle boxes and other equipment.

"You are not serious. Is this more about me stranded at sea and forced to feed myself? You are a deceptive sonofabitch."

"No. I want to see you relax. It's an alien word to you, I know."

"I can relax if you park at a marina somewhere and take me to a five-star seafood restaurant. How about three-stars?" I accepted the fishing rod.

"I know you've fished a little. Patty said you enjoyed yourself at her company-chartered excursion. Do you remember how to tie a lure?"

"Stop condescending, *Papa.*" I showed him how I tied a lure. "And do not criticize my knot-making. What do I do with it when I catch it? What if I catch a bull shark?"

"Relax. I doubt we'll catch a thing at night. I just wanted you to focus elsewhere. Remember what I said about changing your line of sight?"

When the questions are as difficult to come by as answers, focus on the unrelated object. You will be surprised what your peripheral vision picks up.

I nodded for him.

He raised anchor and cranked the motor. We glided smoothly eastward, city lights drifting carelessly behind. From a drawer under the dashboard, he drew a monocular. Short, almost palm-sized, much fancier than the binoculars my Papa used. We then angled south toward distant moving lights, what he said was Pontchartrain Drive crossing to Eden Isle, and beyond that, Highway 10.

"That last point of land to the far right is South Point." He handed me the spyglass.

"Wow. It magnifies so much."

"Right of the Point is Irish Bayou Lagoon. Touch the red button on the side."

Tiny figures sprang to life in the dark. "This—!"

"—is thermal imaging. Our friend was in the Navy. Get him away from his nightclub, and he becomes a geek for new gadgetry."

"I knew he built that fancy sound system for Bobby J's, but this is—wow."

"We won't get too close. Our Sea Ray is too big for the shallows, and this lake bottom, away from the shipping lanes, can average twelve feet or less. Marshes and sand bars along the way to make for an unhappy Bobby J."

"He would forgive you."

"Only because he knows I could afford a new boat."

He fed more gas, opened it to cruising speed, and we passed beneath the bridges. He did not slow until we approached what he said to be the eastern end of Pontchartrain.

"How far do you plan on taking us tonight?"

"That's about it. I figured while we're out here I'd give you the tour. Those lights up ahead are the docks of Chef Menteur. The point, far left, that's The Rigolets Channel. Those larger ships come in from the Gulf, passing between that point and the north shore of the lake."

"An educational journey, Sinbad? You know I will never need to know all this."

"Right. You're never taking the boat alone." He drew parallel to the shore that he said was not really a shore, but more like swamp to avoid. He dropped anchor.

"You are not fishing?"

"I prefer watching you fish. Take the starboard deck chair and throw as far as you can. Breathe deep and reel in slow. Count the stars."

I spent ten minutes with the monocular to my eye, then something grabbed my line and flew with it. I almost let go of the rod.

"You need a hand?" He ran up behind me.

"Don't you dare!" I handed him the spyglass.

The spool spun. I fought to slow it. The thin rod whipped then bent like one strand of a rainbow until I thought it would break.

"He's taking it down," *Papa* Nicolaus said. "If you see the line turn under, move to the stern. Keep it clear of the prop."

"I doubt we will catch a thing at night!"

"I can be wrong too."

"And an admission! All in the same week?"

A twenty-minute battle, and he stopped offering to help when I snapped at him to back off. When I finally landed the creature onto the back swimmer's platform, I dropped to my butt.

"Redfish," Nicolaus said. "Close to thirty inches, is my guess."

"Now what?" I gulped for air. *Red* bounced.

"I don't feel much like deboning him. Do you?"

I watched the struggle, the tail slapping, the mouth working around the lure.

"Can you help get the hook out? I should reward a good opponent."

I gripped Red while Nicolaus worked the needle-nose pliers into the maw and extracted the lure with minimal injury. I lowered gallant redfish back to his lake. He came awake and swam into darker waters.

My arms hung like wet cement and my knees quaked. I made it to the deck chair but could make it no further. Without moving, Nicolaus stared at the needle-nose pliers. Then he sat at my feet. When I found the strength to lean forward, I draped my arms around his neck.

"You feel okay?" he whispered.

"My peripheral vision found something, I guess."

"I thought it might."

"Can you tell me who is—"

"No," he said. "Not yet."

He tugged lightly on my arm and, in my exhaustion, I slid from the chair to the deck beside him. He did not trap me in his arms. He took my hand in his. I laid my face on his chest and breathed in the sweat of both of us. My nerves shook me until I willed them to relax. I felt the rise and fall of his chest, the beat of his heart. Exhaustion brought me close to tears.

I had never been this emotional before my *St. Michael's Hotel.* I heard Papa scolding.

Waking, and I did not know how long I had slept. He lay there motionless, and I listened for his heart again. I almost spoke, but he released a breath.

"Shhh…"

"Your plan is to sit here all night?" I said.

"You used to be good at taking direction. Are you not comfortable?"

"I used to be nineteen."

I struggled to my feet, my legs stiff, my back and arms sore from the epic battle with Red. When my lower muscles trembled anew, he was up and lifting me in his arms. Without releasing, he tapped the light switch at the head of the stairs, the single bulb that would be our only guide.

"Your shoulder…" I said.

He carried me down and into the belly of the Sea Ray.

The incomplete glow behind us proved sufficient. We passed through the shadows to the other side where we crossed the threshold to the head. He found the shower switch. I was carried, fully clothed under the shower's rain, and my tears were obscured.

"Can you stand on your own?" he said.

I trembled again. "I would rather not." And I doubted myself, but I had no doubt of him. I pressed my wet lips to his, and neither of us could break away. My legs lowered and I stood with his help. Then we both sank against the shower wall, and to the floor. In the semi-dark, my fears tempted me in subtle waves, ebbing and returning, whispering adversaries. I refused them. I gripped the man with desperation. He sensed it, but his hands held in them a soft knowledge, a caring I had never known before him. And we would not let go.

I stirred once more during the night, disoriented. But the languid rolling water from below, and the angle of light spilling from the stairwell, brought me aware. Still and naked under a single sheet, the man beneath me breathed steadily. Sensing me awake, he remained silent but drew me closer until my mouth touched his throat. I shivered once and sleep returned.

Daylight from the starboard porthole found me alone in the sheets. I heard nothing but the soft ripples breaking against the hull. The room, empty. My body responded, and I nearly dragged the sheet with me up the stairs without thinking. A clean bathrobe at the foot of the mattress, and I snatched it. It draped me like a Kazakh yurt—Bobby's robe of course—but questions would hang as I rushed the stairs.

Nicolaus pulled away from the computer screen. At least he wore trousers.

"You're okay?" he said.

I inhaled again, and within a few steps I held him from behind. "I thought…"

"I promised."

When I finally released, he led me to the benches and rear table, a warm coffee pot, a plate with two muffins, and a large bowl of grapes, cherries, and sliced pineapple.

"Sorry," he said. "Last night you freed our breakfast fish."

"But Bobby's kitchen could sell to restaurants," I said.

"Speaking of, he texted this morning."

"Well…"

"A long list of everyone who is looking for us." His morning smile cleanly *unconcerned*.

"Anyone we did not know?"

"How long would you like to remain at sea?"

"Oh, that is an evil question, Mr. Vagelle."

A squint, as he watched the pouring coffee.

The phone buzzed. He checked the screen and passed it to me.

"Dobre utro (good morning), Patty."

"You are okay. Is he there?"

"He is. I will put you on speaker."

"Nicolaus?"

"She is safe," he said.

"I'm worried all night. Yesterday's news about St. Michael's. They have you on security cam, darlin. Then you disappeared…so I ran for your little refuge, only to find gossip there about a police response, and a grizzly dragging a woman out of the Yacht Club latrine.

"All true," I said. "The grizzly's name starts with a B and ends with J."

"Damn-it, woman! Do I need to lock you in my closet?"

"Easy, Patty," Nicolaus said.

"I know, still—"

"We can't say more right now. I'm sure you know how many are searching for her, us, and I'm *harboring* her for a while. I would have called, but any explanations need to wait for a person-to-person."

As if waiting for that moment, a large fishing trawler sounded its horn to avoid a speeding summer tourist.

"Sure, I get it." Patty said. "So, you know, our cop friend says he's handling his new life. I'm not as positive as he is."

"I am not deserting my friends. We talked about it. I have others keeping track. I'm told you had an on-Pointe meeting."

"Okay. Thanks for that. I guess I knew."

"And be careful where you show your face. Don't try to challenge your employees on your own. Step-by-step, a house divided, and all that."

She did not respond.

"One more reminder, between fist fights and shoot-outs, check in on the *Howse* when you can."

"Do you think your little codes are fooling anybody?"

"No. But without specifics their lawyers are impotent. Oh, and for your benefit as well, my friend here described the woman who attacked her in the latrine. I'm guessing it's the same one got away from your cop. Watch yourself. Without the wig she is Mrs. Clean, a dangerous Mrs. Clean."

"You mean—?"

"Slick as soap. Give us a few days to pop out of this gopher hole."

"Thank you for worrying," I said, my thoughts already adrift.

"Bye for now, my Ruskie pain in the ass."

Turning to the stern with folded arms, I ignored the new sun on the water, a cargo barge, recreation boaters, a fishing scow, and others passing toward the Gulf's expanse. The boards rocking beneath my bare feet unsettled me.

"Clean clothes in the dryer below—something's wrong." I had not heard him stand.

"Something is right?" said my doubts creeping in around me. My vision fogged over with emotions inching in.

"What did I say?"

"This. We are running away."

"We are buying time. We need breathing space. Give the authorities time to find other crimes and loosen our noose a couple notches."

"How long? You told Patty a few days. A few days buys nothing. A pleasure cruise? Sex?" The barbs flew to their own purpose. I could not control them. My phobias were back in command.

Silence momentarily inserted itself. "I understand," he said.

"You understand what? I have been running away my whole life. And now we are hiding again. You always say to me to control. I am always too impulsive. It gets me into shit."

"Doesn't it?"

"Damn you! You have no impulses? You wait. You plan your chess table. You watch everyone act so you can plan more. And still, their pieces keep moving. You can sleep while all your friends—?"

His mask fell into place.

"How could you understand…me? Your psych books tell you what I am? It has always been this way. It is what I—"

"What you hate about us?"

I wanted to say no. My broken arguments clawed to escape. But my mind kept digging through my fears to further my defenses. I never learned how to take back spoken words. Last night was gone. *Never let go* was gone.

"Hear me." His too familiar tone was meant to pacify. My waters did not want steadying at this moment. "We cannot act without understanding more. I only take the time we need to learn who they are, and we can learn nothing from a jail cell, or a hospital bed, or St. Michaels—"

The temper screaming in my ear.

"Do not do this," he whispered.

"I have done nothing. It is all done to me."

"It was not my books that told me about you." Discomfort turned his head, but he tapped his chest. "It was this. I knew you our first week together, because you are your own book. You wear your heart like a Crusader's cross."

"You think you know my life before you? Maybe our life together was my greatest lie. What were my Papa's words to you? *She is not all that you believe?*"

"Don't."

"We need to put ashore."

There was the final pivot away. His return to the cockpit. The current beneath the Kraken hull shot thru with electricity.

"To me, it was never about *sex.*" He watched the lake.

Thirty-Nine

Vagelle

Before she left me at the boat ramp, she turned back in grief. In our ten years together, I had never witnessed her emotions jackknifing for this long. She had been the life-hardened child who refused to cry. Now it socked me into silence.

"Forgive me, Nicolaus. I promise I am not running away again." She wrung her wrists. "I-I cannot hide and do nothing." As she flew off, the python coiled in my chest. Again.

Triggered again. Find her again. Never give her up, again. Deal with it, Vagelle.

As I finished securing the Kraken to Bobby's slip, my resolute fibers returned. Someone yelled "Ahoy!" and I pretended not to hear. I went below and strapped on the belly-holster and, having forgotten my physical pains, brushed away thoughts of the shoulder sling.

I trotted back to my car. Driving the neighborhood in circles out from the marina, knowing she had found her Impala, and her exit, I almost did not hear my phone ping. A text from *Patty*.

"Frank's beat up. Uni Med."

Emotions on that overfamiliar thrown pendulum, I swung with it from sadness to rage. Speed-driving through city traffic almost brought my focus back to earth. Alya had known better than I. Our world was beyond strategizing now. Beyond another wasted day. Friends lives needed to take priority. Time to deliver.

Recklessness or requiem.

Everyone had understood my inner workings. The Shrink had warned early of my force majeure. My distant past and the dead child in the trunk—*Medea's curse*—and my torment over the person who should have meant more than any Machiavellian chess game.

I raced along hospital corridors. Patty heard me coming and met me outside Pedersen's room.

"The doc says he should be okay, with time. He's seriously concussed. He had trouble breathing when the ambulance brought him in. No broken ribs, but internal swelling beneath the sternum. One cut, not life-threatening. They just took him down for an MRI to check for what they could not see. A nasty head…You okay?"

A seismic rift threatened to split my skull, so no.

"Is Alya—?" she said.

"She ran off again. I don't know where she is now."

"Fuck!" She nudged me aside as a nurse with a pharmacy cart passed between us and into Pedersen's room.

"Excuse me, nurse." I stopped her. "Has the patient already been prescribed?"

"You are?" She sounded perturbed at the interruption to her day.

"A concerned party. The injured officer is connected to a case that already resulted in one patient murdered in this hospital."

"Yes." She presented her I.D. "I understand."

"Easy." Patty touched my arm. "She was here when he came in. She's okay." My friend pulled me further into the room as the nurse departed. "You need to sit, or we can take a walk. He'll be downstairs a while."

I could not sit, so she walked with me. This time I failed to notice the beautiful design-work along the walls and around the Information Desk. Fortunately, the attendants remembered my fake FBI credentials.

"I need to check on Roderick Howse. I assume he's in his same room?"

"I'm afraid he did have post-op issues, and had to be moved one floor down." The receptionist displayed concern and located the room number.

Taking our time to the elevators, Patty told me about an encounter with Senator Holcroft in Congo Park. Maybe she was trying to distract me. She said she could not explain why she went after him, other than running with her gut after his unexpected and uncomfortable appearance with the girl.

"Maybe a discomfort born of his guilt," she said. "He could have assumed I was on the job and spying on him. He confused me with his knowledge of my now-famous bathtub scene."

"Like why would a *busy* old politician keep track of your personal problems? He does appear to spend a good deal of his time visiting our least favorite judge."

I shifted topics and told her about Alya's ladies' room attacker. I described the woman I had seen on the courthouse steps. She had known me when she signaled to GOAT that I was behind her.

"And I swear I saw that *thing* running away from your mint house," Patty said. "Pedersen said he saw her too."

"Butterfly hand," I said. "I'm about sick of butterflies lately. I'm seeing them in my sleep."

"Your Roderick—" She stopped me with a hand on my sleeve and a searching stare. "I bet he knows her."

"Because?"

"All the scars, cuts, some purposeful designs on him." She pulled a pocket notepad and pen. "That first day in here, he was all feverish. I waited outside his door while they changed wet sheets beneath him. They turned him, and between his shoulder blades—" she drew four loops, two large, two smaller, connected on a center line. "I swear they weren't that old. Raised pink scars that looked to be drawn with a razor."

"And you made the connection when I said butterflies."

"What does it look like to you?"

I opened the photos on my phone. Showed her the line of languages painted on the wall.

"Voodoo?" She smirked.

"Hoodoo, Vodún, take your pick." I scrolled to the next image. The dead butterflies along the base of the wall. "Looks to me like someone with a personal brand."

"Did you translate that?"

"Not all. It reads like a curse. With the dead butterflies, spell-casting for an enemy. Maybe targeting someone who had disrespected her."

"Or maybe summoning a demon."

"Maybe a demon like Roderick."

"This witch of Alya's, is she nuts? Or a genius who could come up with this complex hatred of you…and anyone around you? From the sounds of it, you've never met her before."

"She is not the mechanic. Her attacks lack foresight. She might be mad, but it's acting out more like a chainsaw to a power line. A psychotic who sees a target and propels herself into a frenzy.

"We have—" She handed me a soiled business card. *Lamia Anasi, Healing Arts.* "We have so little. You know how when you have nothing but a collection of unrelated crap?"

"For many months now."

"Dead kids. Bad cops. Captain Beaudry and his brother. Enough sleazy money to convince co-workers to murder me in my bathtub?"

"Follow the thought, P.I." I cornered her at the elevator doors.

"Okay," she said. "We got a Psycho flying out of your past, covered in body carvings. His dead kid in a freezer in the back room of a voodoo tourist shop…?"

"And you just found a calling card in your office. *Lamia.*"

"Your face said it when you checked the card. You don't think she sees herself in *Arabic terms of radiance.*"

We entered the elevator as doctors came out. When the doors closed, I pushed the STOP button. The card continued turning in my fingers.

"Devon's *death card,* and the queen of hearts on this one here." No longer looking at either card, she was seeing her *former friend.*

"It's just as much about the two words combined," I said. "The second one, *Anasi,* folktales originating in West Africa. The trickster, shrewd, a spirit brought to the Caribbean. Yet another gift of the African slave trade. The name, Anasi, means literally the *Spider.*"

"If it's about the two words, I'm almost afraid to ask about the other."

"You should be afraid. You were right when you made the connection to ancient Greece. As your research said, Mount Othrys is near the birthplace of the gods." My thoughts drifted ahead until she grew impatient.

"Should I restart the elevator?"

"I need to run. Please go back to Frank. You're all he has now."

"You just now figured something, didn't you?"

"I need to find a witch."

"Give me anything to hold onto, Vagelle!"

"Legend claims Lamia might have been a beautiful Libyan princess. Of course, Zeus never met a beauty he could keep at arm's length. And his wife, Hera, spent much of her time torturing these poor mortal women out of spite."

"And the important point swimming in that soup you call a brain?"

"In one legend, the Zeus-wife cursed *Lamia* with a madness to murder Zeus's newborn child. That eventually turned into *all* her children. The legend became a rot of insanity so deep it even altered her into a physically grotesque thing, a child-eating monster. Lamia became the horror, a bogey that Greek mothers told to their little ones to keep them fearfully obedient."

"And now the *Baby Eater* has business cards," Patty said. "Okay. Brings us full circle, doesn't it? The dead kids."

"And what did you used to tell me about that type?" Alya had reminded me more than once. "A true psychotic cannot refuse an impulse. Make her an impulse she cannot refuse."

Now, try to think like Alya. She would not sit. She would feel driven to hunt out her attackers. Colin was dead, as was the hospital administrator. Alya had two other options. She could easily decide to go after the judge who put her there. But no. Her priority would be the aggressor, her attacker, Ms. Peacock. *Butterflies.*

Anasi—the Spider.

Reasoning clearly now, Alya would understand the one perfect lightning rod for this witch's impulses. Herself.

"You're in early tonight." Bobby J. took up a tumbler and the bottle of Widow Jane Bourbon from the crowded shelf behind his bar.

"Not tonight." I waved him off. "Can't stay."

"I'm testing. I know why you're here. She was in earlier. She sat in your booth over there for nearly two hours. I sat with her some, but she said she wanted to be alone." He looked hurt.

"That tells me what I wanted to know," I said.

"What does it tell you? All these years, and she never treated me like that. The morning I met her hiding on that little sailer, I thought we had a good long talk. Then, after her fight in the Yacht Club head…"

"Bobby. She didn't come in for chit-chat. Or to see her friend. She's avoiding her friends."

"I tell ya, it weren't like her, the way she sat alone, no white zin, a glass of sparkling water she barely touched. Just watching the door."

"And she wasn't watching for me. She held a space here for a couple hours, then moved on."

"Then what?"

"Her next stop. She's visiting all the places she visits most. Before coming here, I stopped by my building. Hemmings said she was there for forty minutes. With the way she left me at the boat, she would not have gone there looking for me."

"She's visiting all her favorite places. What then? She's not saying good-bye, is she?"

"No. She is hoping to be seen. She's making herself a target."

His face drained of all animation, and I had never before seen this look on him.

"I need to go." I pushed back from the bar. "I need to find her before she finds what she's looking for."

"The crazy woman from the marina? Of course, she would. Our little Russkie could never go through life waiting for a next attack. She is visiting any place that nasty thing might have tracked her from before."

"She wants to draw her out as quickly as she is able, lead her to a place she has already chosen. I believe I know her strategy. My fear is the witch will see her, and be driven to strike before Alya gets to where she needs to be."

"I'm coming with. Don't say no."

"No. My friend, if this creature sees me—us—trailing her, she will vanish. We will not hear from her for a week, or a month, or until she catches Alya alone and off her guard."

"So, please tell me you can catch her before that."

"If not me, then who?"

FORTY

Alya

He was tracking me again.

He said he would not. But I picked him out of a crowd as I left the Hemmings building. He did not come forward, which added to my suspicions. And it saddened me. And it confused me.

There again, in the shadows when I left Bobby's, I could feel Vetty's presence in front of my apartment—or maybe I had alerted to something else. Baba Yaga? I did not think so, but I could not read tea leaves. Vetty's intentions were, as ever, a mystery to me. If he thought he was invisible, he was a clod. But I knew him to be the opposite. So, I assumed he wanted me to know he was there.

Why?

It had me shaking again. He should know this. If I told him it upset me, being followed, *why would he upset me on purpose?*

But now, what upset me almost as much was knowing I had wasted the entire day, wasted my *plans.* If Baba Yaga saw I had a bodyguard trailing on a leash, this plan was ended. She will have won for today. She would become a ghost to follow me at another time.

I drove slow, circling Uptown to the Garden District, St. Charles, Canal, back to Broadmore. I left the car and walked down more crowded streets, in full view beneath the lights, kicking off my internal damages as they surfaced. Ducking into the darkest shadows, I waited for him. But he did not appear. He knew I had made him.

How long would he stay gone?

Repeating my earlier trek northward, the cemeteries night when she came out of the dark at me, I took the trolley to the bus to the marina. I stopped at the seafood bar and took a table under white lights on the outside patio.

Late night, the crowd had thinned to two couples seated miles apart with remnant bowls and platters of scraps. A single waiter propped outside the front door, smoking, and waiting for the customers to fall asleep in their food. He spied me, gave a weary head shake.

I smiled my flirtiest, and ordered an alcohol-free drink. To be less obvious, if *she* remained out there somewhere, I ordered myself a last supper. An appetizer-sized bowl of crawfish and rice. He went back for a fresh cigarette, and I took my time with supper.

The witch never reappeared, but I needed to behave as if she would.

Once finished, I did not circle the docks, but used Bobby's passkey to enter the main gate. With thoughts of the black key he had taken, I strutted the docks directly to my rusty yacht-lette. If anyone marked my entry, they kept silent as I climbed aboard and into the cabin.

Earlier, I had bought two kerosene lanterns, wooden matches, and a one-litre bottle of fuel. I strung sheets around the windows, sheets thin enough to allow for light to pass. I tacked my black, *Who's Jolly*, pirate flag flat against the ceiling above the door. A homey decoration. Taking the single oar from inside the bench, I laid that across the first stair. Then I turned up the lantern lights.

What looked to be the curved edge of a porcelain bowl showed dull-white behind the bench pillow. The pillow came away easy enough. If it had been my first such human skull, and I were a more sensitive girl, I might have screamed. Instead, I leaned closer. It could have been real, with each orifice closed by a kind of tar. A thin line, cut with precision, encircled the cranium like a cap.

I reached for it. Stopped myself. Then something within me knew. Three curvy lines. *Damballah—*

I pulled it, then slammed the skull's lid back into place. I had seen what I expected. Inside, the serpent moved.

The witch knew I would come here. Whether she followed me or not, she knew my *Pipe Dreams*.

If only Vetty would stay away.

Vagelle

Her apartment was on my way. I needed to check it. Parking took longer to find than to run up to her floor, run through her rooms, and back down to my Mercedes. I admonished myself for side-tracking, but it was the next obvious place for her—*or Ms Peacock*.

The last obvious place would be our former safehouse. Roddy had not found it on his own, and by connecting killer butterfly to Danny's father, and her ability to always be at the perfect place to confront Alya, it was not a great leap to make.

But that could wait. There was a more obvious stop along my route.

Parking proved easier at the West End Marina lot, as expected, at least this late at night. While still in the driver's seat, instinct told me, *Reckless can be managed. Be smart about it.* I removed the belly holster. Shoved the Sig Sauer into my waistband, and tied my arm tight with the elastic strip. As I climbed out, scanning the outer mall, I caught sight of the man I hoped not to meet here.

A large man with a limp, with tangled black hair to his fatigue jacket lapels, crossed the bright lights of the Seafood Shack. He strode with purpose, and I picked up my pace.

My surprise nearly stopped me, as he appeared to have a key to the Yacht Club gate.

"Private Jergens!" I called to slow him. He pivoted warily, then straightened with recognition.

"I don't answer to that anymore, *Mister* Vagelle."

"You have business inside?"

"More than you. Weren't you told she needs space from you? You're still crowding her."

"That worked on me the first time. Not again."

He came toward me, his stride lengthening into a slow jog, but a jog with a hitch in it. From his carriage I knew how this meeting would proceed. He halted when my Sig Sauer located his breast bone. Ten feet away, he made his decision.

"Not quite the chivalrous knight they all say you are." He took a step. "I see the stories of you have been whitewashed some. You ready to shoot an unarmed man? A handicapped, unarmed veteran?"

"The last time I wore white was a funeral shirt." Holding my left arm tight to my side, I moved to meet him.

He lunged.

I did not shoot. I stepped to his bad side, set one foot, and kicked his knee. He hit the ground and rolled and started back up with difficulty. I continued past him, kicked again from behind. He fell again. Still resilient, he rose. And I moved, reluctant to kill him without cause. But he had size and strength on me, and he flopped and kicked from the ground, sweeping my ankle. I landed on my bad arm. Lost the Sig Sauer. He rolled onto other my arm, and I drove my heel into his hip repeatedly. He barely flinched. Trans-femoral amputation had been extensive, removing those nerve-clusters. Once I realized, I stopped his attack with a slap to the throat from my good arm.

Alya

"Sweeet-heart!" She sang from a distance as she came. Breathy as Billie Holiday, Bobby might have said. How I wish he was with me now. Him and his orange hammer. She sang it again as she drew closer, and hissed like water dripping on fire.

I loosened the edge of the door's sheet, a finger's crease. Then I backed away, more from instinct than any fear. And Nicolaus might have said, *"Looking as she does, that fear is exactly the electricity she expects to produce with this costume."* A partial shadow changing shape, swaying in and out of the haloed dock lights, stretched in a black, second-skin. A bodysuit that vanished as the light left her, leaving nothing but the ghost-blue bones, painted ribcage, spine, and all, with a glow of matching skull-paint, and that limp, gossamer cape trailing with the color of dull flame.

There she is. Ms. Butterfly. A one-creature Mardi Gras that never dies.

I moved with quiet ease to the rear of the cabin, fine-tuning my hearing, but she came silent now. No shoes on the wooden planks, no song, though I somehow knew she would not pause. *Barefeet?*

Reflecting her silence, and glad for it, I crouched at the rear of the cabin. A sleepy, musical breeze moved the rigging across the harbor, chains to masts, ropes and buckles, fore, sides and aft…and then all fell still. Like even they had been instructed to *wait*.

A metallic clang and rattle along the roof above and behind me slapped my nerves awake. Not a person. Something thrown, hoping for a response. We both waited.

Another hiss. Then a stiff, clattering rain. Stones, pebbles, gravel…but the first volley had prepared me. Her assault predictable, and my nerves unshakable, once I focused on my own fantasies. As I knew her, from the inside I knew her, from Vagelle's lessons on how this illness plays within her. *Mad as a Hatter, Alice?* Her patience would be rubbing like a hair shirt, just about now—

"Dah-lin! It's me!" *Pipe Dreams* shuddered to tell me *she* was on board. She tittered like a pretend schoolgirl. The nasty kind. The kind that believes she is the unshakable one. "I come for my mornin cuddle, *sweet-thaang!*"

There, she brought to my thoughts that other chill moment, combination of moments, the cooing of the boys as they chased me through the lightless parking garage, with the smells of damp concrete dust and rusted metal, and my fall, scraping flesh from my knees, and the ripping of my Sunday dress, and the tall, skinny one punching me, dropping his knees on me, and the short one tittering like this *thing* outside my door. My cheeks stung from the slaps. And from the laughter. Then I grew numb. That afternoon, *Trinadsat*, my thirteenth birthday, I learned what may have been the greatest lesson of my life. All pain is but a slap. And all pain goes away. In time.

Then, the next most important lesson dropped—as I found him days later, when he could not have anticipated what I had become— what he made of me—and I beat him until my fingers lost their grip, and the steel pipe fell from my hands and rang to the concrete floor. I walked free of the garage. He never would.

This bully trying to haunt me this night has no idea of my strength, Papa.

Yet careful, she hung back from the door. I went through a small list of her options.

Do not anticipate, Papa said in my ear. There is no such thing as too much planning. But all plans turn to smoke with the first punch.

"No kind words, Dah-lin? Why so quiet?"

Her options, few. Enter through the door? Wait for reinforcements? Or set fire to my pathetic little yacht-lette and wait for me to rush out? If armed, she would already be in here. Why would she come without a weapon?

More clattering gravel.

"You are quite the woman. I said that at first look, I did. I said, for all her nervous ticks, this gal won't handshake with good folk. She's jittery as a bunny in a wolfpack."

Or was her weapon inside the bowl, the skull? For all she knew, I had already died of snakebite.

"Jittery gal—yes, but she stands her ground like no scared pussy I ever seen. She don't pretend she's butch, or she'd have taken the cigarette when I offered it to her, wouldn't she? I had you goin though didn't I, *lover?*"

The witch quieted. She was thinking. She remained in place on the deck, or I would have felt her move. I knew I could wait her out. Papa had taught me hunting. Then, Nicolaus had taught me people-hunting. She strained now with the electric charge, a psychotic's compulsion, and this charge would grow without controls.

And my greatest surprise blanketed me like feather down—my own calm. I felt in control. An unexpected stillness that said I had no fear of her.

"Sing me a song, lover. A Lithuanian lullaby. Isn't that what you were when we first met? Of course, I knew you lied to me, Russian were-bitch. Long before we met, I knew all about you. You lied, and with me showing nothing but kindness on our morning bus ride."

Patience. Do not rush the rabid wolf. She will come.

"I hate people lying to me. Lying makes *the goddess* angry. So, how 'bout humming a few bars of the Russian National Anthem? I'll even let you hum it in my ear while I show you a real Cajun lovin." She cooed from the door frame, and my mind pictured *the boy* again.

Her thin silhouette moved outside the sheet-covered glass, a shadow that might have been naked, but for that skin-tight costume—one tentacle stretching to touch where Bobby had found three snake-like scratches in the wood, and rubbed moss into the wounds.

Without thinking, I reached out to the bench and felt the seductive curve of bare bone, her gift. Lifting the skull carefully to keep the cap in place, I sensed the independent tremor from within. *Softly, serpent.* I whispered. If I had a flute, I would play it.

The voice has shifted. Her Cajun accent stronger now. Drama building. About to enter.

"*Children* lie. The goddess eats children, don't you know?"

Thrown hard, a rope pulley shattered the port-side window two seconds before her howl and crash through the forward door. The black bodysuit disappeared among the shadows, but for the painted-on skeleton and her skull-white face-paint that shook me at a glance.

In her blind charge, her ankle met with the oar spanning the top stair, and she tripped hard.

As I recovered, I threw the skull and the lid fell free. She tried to catch it before she knew what it was. Then, I yanked the overhead rope, and the *Who's Jolly* flag collapsed over her.

Flying forward, I sprayed her flag-draped head with my kerosene bottle. She immediately understood that too, and roared louder. I snatched the closest lantern and hammered at the flag. And lost control of myself again. I continued to hammer. I could not stop, even when the white crossbones on the black flag caught fire.

She flailed. I waited to see which direction she would fall. When she did, I skirted the opposite way and jumped the steps for the door.

The screams painted cartoons through my mind, and I fell to the outer deck, willing to burn along with my tiny shelter in this fleeting victory. Firelight flashed and wavered behind the window sheets, then the first sheet caught fire—

Hard sounds on the deck. A man raced by me for the door. I barely saw him. When I lifted my head, he carried the creature wrapped in a smoldering blanket, and threw it at the water. He then grabbed me up— one-handed. *Nicolaus.*

I lay on the rough dock quaking. Nicky had thrown the bow lines and kicked the burning yacht-lette away from the dock and the other boats. With one painful glance at me, he spun and dove into the harbor and retrieved the witch. With one arm.

She lived.

FORTY-ONE

Vagelle

We held for what remained of the night. Alya on a hospital bed, she had been treated for smoke inhalation. Dr. Maiwand had prescribed light sleep meds.

Once the nurses left the room, I asked the doctor to go and close the door.

Leaning into the bedside, I held onto her arm. I breathed her smokey hair, felt her hand on my chest, her cheek on my neck. I whispered of her meaning in my life. Eventually her tears dried. I could not move until long after she fell asleep. An aching with each breath, and knowing how close I had come to losing her. Again.

Before leaving the room, I laid a large black button beside the pillow. A Communist Star button from a Warsaw Pact trench coat. I silently hoped Vetty's PTSD never found relief.

Patty waited at the open door to Pedersen's room. He slept as she described the doctor's report to me. His injuries, still of concern, a bit of intracranial bleeding. They could only guess on the long-term effects once swelling subsided, and he regained consciousness. The drugs helped his sleep and controlled his pain. They should be cut back over the next few days, and he would become more responsive. Moving away, we left him to Morpheus.

She followed me to Basement room B-11. We observed through the door glass as nurses and staff worked their duties around the prostrate Roderick Howse.

Attached to machines via wires and tubes feeding oxygen, saline, and blood, machines monitoring heart and lungs and brain function, his eyes never opened. His chest rose and lowered in slow, even rhythms. Occasionally, his fingers twitched.

A new policeman occupied the door today. I showed him my fraudulent FBI card.

"Mornin, officer," I whispered. "Has the surgeon been by lately? I can't stay long. I was hoping for an update."

Patty leaned into the guard, and he straightened a few inches.

"I've been on since seven, sir. I've only seen him once. Came by around eight-thirty."

"Maybe it's a good sign," Patty said. "Maybe he doesn't need constant monitoring. What ward you out of…Johns?" she read his tag aloud.

I let her distract the officer and proceeded into the room. I watched until the attendants drifted, one-by-one, to the hall. A tall male nurse approached and asked about my purpose there. I had the credentials ready.

"Do you happen to know if the head nurse on this corridor has a list of people authorized for this suspect's room? If you could, I'd like you to request one be posted, and a copy given to each police officer as they take the chair outside this door."

He glared as if I spoke Swahili.

I approached the patient's bed. His arms protruded from the short sleeves of the hospital blouse. The raised, crisscrossing scar tissue extended all the way to the hands, and again up above the collar, across his sleeping face, with one eye a lidless white. Intubation tubes taped into place only partially concealed the ravaged mouth. The artist had begun this canvas of self-mutilation in childhood.

"You are aware of yesterday's patient—" I said.

"Oh, of course. Sorry. Terrible oversight that, and I will get right on it." He departed like I had handed him a telegram from the mayor.

The living canvas had terrified the others when this shrieking Oedipus-scrap burst into our safe-house kitchen. But I had witnessed Roderick's genesis of horror, his early childhood. A young man's hatred, mostly for his own life, and his subconscious need to *feel—anything*. A realization growing with him into puberty, and beyond, and continuing across the black years to the night of attack. He would pass along something of that inner rage to me, like the roots of a poisonous and dying tree intertwining with those in closest proximity.

Patty spoke from somewhere…

As a clinician, I needed to see into the torment of young Roddy's soul. A young trauma so severe as to scar his core. The twisted id waged incessant warfare with his young developing ego.

And so, unable to move, attempting to mitigate my own turmoil with the vision of him—as I had formed him—spread beneath the sheets, I was hardly aware of my need to revisit the *why* of Roderick Howse.

Ego, as defined by Freud, the portion of the id that strives to control the baser, most primitive drives. It is the conscience, the whisper of responsibility or self-governance we all learn as we mature. But, as Roddy's core had splintered at such a young age, his ego needed to mask those inner deformities. Year after year, torment by torment, that inner hate, whether by razor, penknife, or scissors, had carved a parable of itself across his hide.

To think he had sired a son.

This was the reason, with him standing on my doorstep pleading for my help, I had no other recourse. I needed to find Danny for him.

Now, Danny was dead, and I loomed over him, and I relived that distant experience of young Roddy, re-imagining the night, the exact moment I performed the unthinkable act that forever destroyed this child. I realized my fingers touched the scars of his arm when I felt a tear tap my hand. I do not recall backing into the corner and lowering into the visitor's chair.

When I looked up, Patty stood at the door with a reflection of grief.

End Part One

Please turn the page for a sneak preview of the next

Nicolaus Vagelle & Alya Korikova

Thriller

by G.J. Bingham

A STUDY IN VENGEANCE

The Trilogy - BOOK II

HADES' TOUCH

A Cerberus Awakening

Alya

Though I had a key to the building, I broke the lock on the alley door to the boiler room. Having not been down here for more than a year, I counted on Hemmings's lethargy to leave a place neglected, especially the boiler room. He only visited here in emergencies. My assumption proved right. No security cameras inside or out, and the workman's ladder, canted against the blocks beside the light switch, had not been moved.

Leaving the door ajar, I lowered the ladder to where it might have accidently fallen, obstructing a burglar's entry. I hid in a corner behind the building's air conditioning.

I did not wait long. This would have been one of those emergencies.

Hemmings burst in with a curse and a hammer in his fist, throwing light switches as he came on them. With his head on a pivot like a trained Spetsnaz guard, his eyes strained at the shadows.

Ta-daa! The door with the fallen ladder blocking. His shoulders relaxed some, but he came to inspect the door and lifted the ladder to its previous stance.

Leaning his head out, like a gopher to the daylight, he showed his hammer bravely to the outside world, then ducked quickly back in. He inspected the door frame, and discovered the snapped lock, and swore again.

Several long breaths of indecision later, he replaced the ladder to reblock the door, and hurried from the room. As I suspected, he would go for his toolbox and return to make a quick fix of the door until he could call a real repairman.

I followed after giving him a good head start.

He turned into his apartment. I turned the other direction and up the stairs as quickly and silently as possible.

Dr. Maiwand's second-floor door opened below, and I dropped flat to the third-floor landing. He immediately spotted Hemming's open door and went for it, calling for the landlord.

The rest was easy. I unlocked, then locked Vagelle's door behind me.

Was it wrong of me to flee the hospital?

The memory of last night's violence, and my burning yacht-lette, *Pipe Dreams*. Trying to kill the mad Baba Yaga.

Then too many hands on me, medical teams, emergency room nurses. Too much crowding. My anxieties. Haphephobia—a high-pitched wailing alarm in my head ending in an abrupt silence, with the touch of one other. Only Nicolaus.

Holding my hand, touching my cheek, then lying beside me so I might hear his breath until I fell asleep. But I woke alone, and afraid the authorities would corner me in that room, and carry me away. I needed escape.

I had found his note with the location of my Impala. I drove too fast. I drove far. When I found what I was looking for, I returned to the city calmer than when I left. I carried it still. His walking stick.

Not certain what to search for here in his rooms, there might be something he would know that I did not. I needed a crumb of information. A tiny arrow to point the way forward for myself. Just a scrap of knowledge. Maybe the scrap would lead me to another scrap. A slice of conversation. A name I had forgotten that might strike a chord in my clouded memory.

As with the last time I closed myself in here looking for answers, I lost the moment amid icy emotions. This apartment—my shared apartment with *the man*—flooded my senses. The smells. The angle of light at four in the afternoon. Furniture rigidly unchanged. Books. The Thomas Moran painting above the fireplace mantle—sunlight on the canyon waterfall surrounded by darkening cloud shadows. What time of day was there in the painting? The walking stick turned in my hands.

This had been home to me, either living or working here, for my entire adult life. All of this had been my *comfort*. If I sat to take it in, I would be lost to Morpheus' arms.

I began pacing to break the trance. The niche beside the fireplace held only a memory, so I moved there. I held the memory in my fingers. The walking stick with the silver wolf's head, the other end with the hidden blade, with new scratches along the shaft I had not seen before. I touched it with reverence. Then I propped the relic in its standing niche.

My black L-desk by the window where the child-me started my work for the Consultant all those years ago. An old cardboard box had been kicked beneath the desk. Atop the desk, a crooked stack of six black leather-bound books, textured leather without print. Books to write in.

As I sunk in, I glanced a loose slip of white paper in the open box with a single name, handwritten in ball point.

"Daniella."

I had been stuck to the floorboards inside the door wondering and hoping for any clue, a scrap, a name—and now…

"Who the hell is Daniella?"

Those first few years were golden. He was old for his age, and after me playing the hard-ass elder partner during the early months, I soon realized he wasn't buying my act. I started out calling him "Bootcamp," because Rookie sounded too cliché. I went through a half-dozen nicknames for him. Then he became "D.O.," Detective Overachiever. Of course, he saw through it all, like from a distance. Like I was the transparent man, and he was indulging me.

I closed the first book believing the story had begun elsewhere, so, in turn, I flipped the cover for each volume.

"Jake Murphy, Lt. NOPD — 2005/2006"

To Be Cont'd in

BOOK II

Afterword

*

The book you now hold is a work of fiction—how's that for a bold statement? Yet due to the nature of this tale, characters, and related illnesses, I feel some, dear reader, may need a bit of explanation as to who I am—or more accurately, who I am not. While my *fictional* detective, for purposes of these stories, is labeled a "criminal psychologist," I claim no such authority.

Do not take medical advice from me.

All I can lay claim to, beyond Psych 101 class—half a century ago—is a long and eventful life, and an interest in studying what makes humans tick, particularly those humans whose behavioral ticks deviate somewhere beyond the borders of *compos mentis;* beyond the well-trodden territory most of us try to occupy (most of the time); and with an understanding of adverse consequences, should we negatively impact…anything.

I promise this is not a treatise on whatever *real* madness roams our television screens on any given day. The real world is scary enough, and much less entertaining than what bounces around inside my skull. And my primary objective, for most of my life, is to entertain. To offer a brief respite to the everyday—or why else should a writer expect anyone to read their fiction?

"So, you say your husband stopped for a few drinks after work then drove his minivan through the neighbor's living room window? Here's my fun novel about traffic accidents."

Perhaps I should get back to the point of this Afterword. Just a bit of caution to anyone believing they should read the ramblings of this "pretend criminal psychologist," and think this is, in any way, a prescription for whatever may be ailing them this week.

But I know you're smarter than that, he said, as large manufacturing companies print warnings on a packet of drinking straws: *"Do not force straws up your nose."*

So, around the age of fourteen, Mom gave me her collection of Sherlock Holmes…and here we are.

Beginning this journey with an interest in murder, or crime in general, having personal experience with "bad stuff, and the people who perform such," I understood early that for any story to carry the gravitas of even fictional crimes, that those crimes would always leave (fictional) victims in their wake. And for the criminals to succeed with their "bad stuff," they must be endowed with a psychological bent lacking sympathy…and here we are.

Even fictional detectives need to breathe.

It's about "creating humans," or as close as any writer gets. I could no more commit murder on paper with an old lady detective joyfully pedaling her Schwinn through a rose garden day after day, humming a jaunty tune, than I could play bocce ball with my cat. Evil is real. Evil people don't care. Recipients of evil bear the scars, as do those who try to help them. If I am honest with my reader, that kind of darkness is a disease and it infects everyone it touches.

(We'll call that Bingham's Analysis.) My personal philosophy: if angels do exist, they must be sad.

Herein resides my study of darkness, the illnesses, from the trauma related to the genetically deformed prefrontal cortex. From the casual narcissist to the psychopath and everything in-between. Once upon a time, I lived in a barracks with the full assortment. I had witnessed some of it. Avoided as much of it as I could. Pardon my lapsing into the following confusion (for legal purposes):

For the critics, and for ease of reader understanding, I am fully aware of the ever-changing clinical terms of modern psychology. No language changes so fast as that which can be argued by modern university grads on a daily basis. In years past, we had watched as "shell shock" became "combat stress reaction" became "Post-Traumatic Stress Disorder." New words, same painful illness. On an unrelated front, some language changes occur thanks to evolving science, some to accommodate societal acceptance; "Psychopath" or "sociopath," while they are separate in cause and effect, are no longer acceptable clinical diagnoses; the words have been morphed into the all-encompassing, and happier sounding, "antisocial personality disorder (ASPD)" (which requires redefining in order to treat the patient—but that's not my job either). For my "fictional purposes, and ease of reading, I have decided to stick with much of the "common language." That which most common readers understand.

To those who read my first book of the series, "Hades' Kiss," you will recall my co-protagonist, **Alya Korikova,** came into the story suffering from childhood trauma. A painful aversion to human touch—labeled "haphephobia." It is a real thing.

As I studied, I learned that such a condition might be the result of repeated childhood suffering. "Complex-PTSD." It is created in a young mind by a feeling of being trapped, with no possible rescue, and the perceived knowledge that emotional injury is everlasting. (Nearly impossible to explain in simple terms.)

To my curious and sympathetic mind, this would be the most horrifying emotional state for anyone living with and among crime stories. The more I studied, the more saddened I became, and I understood the devastation to the lives of these children, a devastation without a cure. A lifelong inner battle that is fought one circumstance at a time, one trigger at a time. Daily lives "managed" by the sufferer, and those who try to help. I try, in the writing, to relieve my Alya's pain as much as I deem practical, while staying true to the character. (No writer wants his reader to suffer overlong, trust me).

Conversely, and with story in mind, the only logical partner strong enough, and knowledgeable enough, to be of any help to dear Alya, any hope for her to *overcome*, was a psychologist who would understand her illness. Hence, **Nicolaus Vagelle,** my detective, was born.

Thoughtfully submitted.

—GJB

ABOUT THE AUTHOR

G. J. BINGHAM

An award-winning writer and artist, with more than forty years in publishing. Born in Chicago, he served four years as a Law Enforcement Specialist in the USAF. From there he began his career in the Arts. Comic books, graphic novels, short fiction, multimedia, theme park attractions, film, television, and now novels.

Winner of The Jack Kirby Comics Industry Award, "Best Graphic Album 1984" for his translation of the epic poem Beowulf. Co-winner of the Golden Apple Award, nominated for the Harvey Award and Will Eisner Comic Industry Award, "Best Graphic Novel 1987" for "Batman: Son of the Demon." Moving his talents to Hollywood, he contributed to film for thirty years, and won the 1998-1999 Primetime Emmy Award for "Background Designer." His Western Art has won awards and hung in some of the most prestigious galleries in the country.

"Hades' Kiss"

Kindle Best Indie Books: "Best Beach Read" Summer 2024

American Fiction Book Awards 2024

Finalists in Mystery/Suspense & Thriller/Crime

18th Annual National Indie Excellence Awards

Finalist in Crime/Fiction

To learn more about Nicolaus and Alya,

be sure to pick up their debut novel-in-stories, Hades' Kiss.

And if you've enjoyed reading Hades' Heart,

keep an eye out for…

Part 2 of

A Study in Vengeance

Hades' Touch

Learn more at www.GJBinghamwriter.com